Grannifer's Legacy

by

Trish Vickers

Dedication

This book is dedicated with endless love and thanks to my children,
Simon, Tristan and Heidi.

Enormous love and gratitude is also given
to everyone who helped Grannifer's Legacy come to life, including:
Trevor Chambers: my dear friend and story reader
Carole Head: my wonderful friend and manuscript transcriber
Ivan Hampson: my gardening friend and supplier
of endless gardening tips

Kerry and Abby from Dorset Police HQ:
for helping to recover my lost work

and Simon, Tracey and Izzy at Magic Oxygen:
for breathing life into my words.

Foreword: Trevor Chambers

This is a remarkable book, written by a remarkable woman.

To understand just how extraordinary both she and the book are, I'd like to ask you to try an experiment. Take a pen and a few sheets of paper and begin writing a short essay about anything you like. Not difficult you may think, but in this experiment you have to write it all *blindfolded*.

From the first word to the very last, you aren't allowed to look at what you're writing, or re-read what you've just written. That rule also stands if you stop writing, then you revisit the piece several days or maybe even weeks later. I'm sure you'd be able to appreciate just how difficult and frustrating a task it would be, so now try to imagine writing an entire novel of several hundred pages in the same way and devoting years of your life to completing it.

It might sound impossible but it's precisely what Trish Vickers has done with Grannifer's Legacy, in what will be her first, and only novel.

Trish Vickers has been completely blind for over 11 years. She lost her sight to diabetes and this book was written during that period.

Only a few people have read this book, but all of them agree, the book *'is so Trish'*. It has a gentle style, warmth and affection. The absence of mean spirited or spiteful characters (including dogs and pigs) is everything that Trish embodies in real life:

"Come on, tell your aunt Cassie all about it. Oh, that's me by the way, Cassie Meadows."

"Jennifer Cade – hello. You don't want to hear about my problems..."

"Look, I know I talk a lot, but I'm a good listener too. Tell you what, I was just on my way to the tea shop – my mum owns it – let's go there, get a cuppa and dry you off. Then if you want to talk..."

That is *so* Trish and despite the multitude of problems she's encountered in her life, she always prefers to talk about yours.

I got to know Trish about 6 years ago when, as a driver for a local blind club, I collected her and took her to the club's regular bi-monthly meetings. We soon became good friends.

Trish didn't know how to read braille and she didn't have use of a computer. She wrote simply with a pen on paper, using a system of elastic bands on a clipboard to keep the lines separated on the pages. I was aware that she was writing this book and she would often discuss it with me, but the work seemed endless. Then, one day, disaster struck... or so it seemed.

Her son, Simon, visited once a week to read her work back to her and her friend Carole used to take Trish's manuscript, typing it up for her as she went along.

Trish was particularly looking forward to one such visit from Simon following a flash of inspiration which prompted her to write 26 pages in a marathon session of writing. When Simon arrived, he had the onerous task of telling his mother that the pages were blank: her pen had run out of ink and she obviously knew nothing about it.

She feared the work would be lost forever and that she'd have to try to recount the story and rewrite it. However, word got around and rather incredibly, Dorset police officers got to hear of the problem. They kindly agreed to try and help and they gave up lunch hours and breaks, using forensic technology and studying the indents that had been made by her pen. It took 5 months, but they eventually deciphered the text and gradually recovered her lost work.

Trish has always been incredibly grateful for their help.

"I could remember the gist of what I had written but there was no way I could have written exactly the same way again," she said. "I am so grateful. It was really nice of them and I want to thank them for helping me out."

Trish completed Grannifer's Legacy, but life was about to throw her another challenge she wouldn't be able to overcome; terminal breast cancer. She is now sadly at her end of days, but enjoying listening to the whir of excitement going on around her as the book is being turned into a published novel.

Why should you read this book?

Firstly, it is an entertaining, gentle story written by an author with superb powers of description. Secondly - and perhaps even more importantly – it is an astonishing achievement in its own right, completed in the face of great adversity, with tenacity, patience, dedication and great focus of memory, produced under circumstances more challenging and strenuous and than many of us could imagine.

I am honoured to have been asked to write this foreword. All Trish's friends agreed it was necessary for someone other than Trish to write it. She is so self-effacing that if she had written it, it is unlikely she would have described the extraordinary difficulties under which she completed the manuscript and she might not even have mentioned her blindness at all. If that happened, her inspirational journey and the unique background to this novel, would never have been uncovered.

I hope my foreword adds something more to your enjoyment of reading Trish's book.

Chapter 1

Still half asleep, Jennifer lay in her bed desperately trying to make sense of the turbulent muddle of thoughts that continuously spiralled around her head. Surely this must be the remnants of a terrible dream? She drew back the covers and, now fully awake, realisation hit home that this was in fact reality and her ideal life of just a few months ago had changed almost beyond belief.

There had been no indication that the interior design company she'd worked for since leaving university would suddenly fold, making all its staff redundant, and to add insult to injury, her boyfriend of nearly three years suddenly decided he 'needed to find himself' and left.

"Thank you very much Mr Clark Mackenzie; did all our plans for the future mean nothing to you?" she cried out loud as if he were in the room with her. "Oh, Mac, did it really mean so little to you?" She drew a sob-ridden breath and, as she took on board the most recent and totally awful upheavals in her life, tears fell from her eyes.

"Oh, Grannifer," she whispered, hardly able to speak. "Why did you have to leave me? Darling Grannifer, I miss you so much."

She cupped her hands over her face, gulping several times, trying desperately to contain her misery. How could this wonderful, strong and yet so tender lady, so full of love, so full of life, be no more? Thoughts of Jennifer's great grandmother overwhelmed her and she sobbed uncontrollably.

After what seemed like an eternity, Jennifer calmed and, taking a few breaths, she went to the kitchenette and turned on the kettle. While it heated, she wiped her face with cold water, then prepared some toast.

Taking this and her coffee to the table, she pulled back the curtains and opened the window.

It was a pleasure to see that the newly started day was in complete contrast to how she was feeling and, although still early, the sun was bright and already quite warm. She broke some of the toast in to small pieces and put them on the outside sill. Before long a collection of birds were selecting their preferred morsels and sharing her breakfast, just inches away. They seemed almost oblivious of their observer, now sitting, mug in hand with the hint of a smile playing on her mouth.

"What was it you used to say, Grannifer? 'Sunshine shoos the blues away...' Come on then darling, let's go for a walk and do some shooing." She tried to keep the moment of being a bit more cheerful going; not easy, but she'd give it her best.

Opening the wardrobe, she sorted through the few clothes she had brought with her. Not sure what to wear, she stopped and looked with glazed eyes at the new dress. She'd bought it to go and visit her beloved Grannifer, but the planned vacation didn't happen. Just weeks before she was due to go, her treasured great grandmother passed away in her sleep.

Jennifer sighed, bit her lip, and took the dress from its hanger. "Well, I bought it to visit you darling, so if we are going for this walk together, it seems the right thing to wear."

It also seemed appropriate to put on the beautiful shrug top that Grannifer had given her for her birthday, and was colour perfect for the pretty sun dress mixture of delicate blue green and yellow flowers on a soft pink background.

Brushing her dark blonde hair, then sipping the rest of her second coffee, Jennifer stepped into the sunlight and looked around her for a moment, taking in the still quite empty little village which had been her hideaway sanctuary for the last week or so.

Unfamiliar with the area, Jennifer had no idea which direction to take, so just strolled along, admiring the sights of this pretty little village. It was a simple place, but she felt comfortable with the surroundings. Enjoying the neat, but not over-manicured gardens, she wished she could identify the flowers by name. She pondered that if she was ever lucky enough to have a garden of her own, she'd need help to make it look as pretty as these.

"What did we used to call that Grannifer? Oh yes, colourful little jewels in an earthly treasure chest!" She smiled at the memory. The tranquillity of her surroundings was in stark contrast to the hurly burly of London, which is just what Jennifer had wanted as the refuge away from the turmoil that her life had turned into. "Yes, lack of chaos and peace... mm... This is more than just peaceful, it's empty; where is everyone, anyone?" She queried her solitude.

Further down the lane she got an answer as a distant church bell chimed. "Oh my word, only six o'clock! I thought it was at least mid morning; what on earth time did I get up?" Surprised at the warmth of the sun so early, she decided it was just the sort of weather to make a day of it, and coming across a noticeboard, studied it for inspiration of what to do. Nothing much in the village. She read the posters and information flyers. Oh, now then, this one's a possibility:

Honey Bee Farm

Come and enjoy the beautiful areas of fruit trees,

heathers, bee hives and our Farm Shop.

"That's it, Grannifer; our destination for today's outing. You always said it was good to have something to aim for! There's even a map." Following the directions on the noticeboard, Jennifer enjoyed the gentle stroll, which took her away from the village and into the surrounding countryside, along winding lanes, edged with hedgerows and wild flowers. Eventually she arrived at a large five bar gate at the side of which was a beautifully hand-painted sign.

"Welcome to Honey Bee Farm"

It looked inviting and nicely laid out. She entered and wandered along the gravel drive. A neat signpost indicated the areas to discover the various delights of this pleasant little farm, and it was easy to drift away from the hassles of life whilst there. Jennifer found the sights and fragrances most relaxing.

"I need to come here again," she mused. She opened the door and entered the shop. "Morning," a friendly voice called out.

"Oh good morning." For some reason the sound of a human took her by surprise; she realised she hadn't had an actual conversation for about three days.

"Is it OK if I look around?"

"Yes of course; let me know if you need any help."

She looked around at the items displayed. Then realisation hit her that such a lot of these were familiar to her from childhood and the many holidays she had spent with Grannifer and Grandpa. Everything in the well-stocked store cupboard - home made jams and chutneys, each topped with little gingham covers; somewhat old fashioned, but cute – she recognised. She enjoyed making these and popping them on jars. "Giving the finished product its hat," as Grannifer used to say. There

11

was a whole section devoted to the bees. Not just honey, but candles, polish, sweets and other munchies, whole honeycomb... Oh there was just so much.

An air of melancholy washed over her with the bitter-sweet memories of the past. That's all she had now, just memories. She sighed deeply fighting back tears. After a moment of recovering her self-control, her eyes settled on something which gave her a boost of inspiration – flapjacks! Grannifer had shown her how to do hundreds of things over the years, but the one thing she excelled in was flapjacks. Grandpa had said they were just as good as his wife's. She remembered the day he'd first said it and smiled. Mentally running through her larder for required ingredients, she called to the assistant "Do you have any oats?"

"Oh yes my dear; just to your left and up a shelf."

She found them easily and took the bag to the counter.

"Everything in the shop is produced on the farm, you say? Very impressive. I'll come again." She said her goodbyes and departed, happy with anticipation.

As she left the farm and walked back along the country lane, there was almost a spring in her step. She'd received a compliment from the shop lady about her new dress, and she had a project (OK, so far it was only flapjacks, but for her, it was a big step forward). The sun was warm and for the first time in weeks she felt positive and... yes, almost happy.

While she walked she recalled the many wonderful holidays she'd spent with her great grandparents – more than twenty years' worth. There never was a time she hadn't wanted to go those many miles up country and spend a couple of weeks or more with these two wonderful people. As a child she was taken by her parents, but as an adult she still enjoyed the bubble of excited anticipation as she travelled ever closer. Grannifer had helped her through the sadness when Grampa passed away. She'd seemed so strong and positive. Jennifer admired her so much for that.

Before she realised it, an hour had passed.

"Mm, must be halfway home I reckon." She laughed a little for speaking out loud.

It was not long after that that despondency overwhelmed her again. From absolutely nowhere, the skies blackened and torrential rain fell. Within moments she was saturated, absolutely soaked to the skin and looking like the proverbial 'drowned rat'.

Desperately she tried to cover the paper bag containing the oats with her shrug. Her thoughts that things couldn't possibly get any worse were proved wrong when her foot misjudged a large stone, slipping off it in the wet. The pressure of the incident broke the strap of her sandal and to add the final insult, she had indeed got an injury too: one twisted ankle which was hopefully no more than a strain.

It was hard to differentiate between the rain and her tears which streamed across her cheeks. Painfully she hobbled on; what else could she do? Each step was racked with pain. She was oblivious to the vehicle that had pulled alongside her.

"Hi, want a lift? Hello – would you like a lift?"

The female driver called again then, noticing the obvious distress of the bedraggled pedestrian, she jumped out of the car and offered help. Thankfully, Jennifer allowed herself to be ushered into the most welcome dryness of the old, but quite beautiful car. Having seen her in, the driver got behind the wheel and started to chat.

"Wow, where did this lot come from? One minute it's glorious sunshine then this deluge! I'd almost decided to roll the top down on the old girl – lucky I was in a rush this morning, or we'd be…" She stopped mid-sentence as she glanced at Jennifer and noticed the tears streaming from her eyes. "Oh, are you OK?"

Jennifer sniffed and wiped her cheeks with the back of her hand. "No, not really."

Pulling the old car into a small lay-by, the girl turned off the engine.

"Come on, tell your aunt Cassie all about it. Oh, that's me by the way, Cassie Meadows."

"Jennifer Cade – hello. You don't want to hear about my problems…"

"Look, I know I talk a lot, but I'm a good listener too. Tell you what, I was just on my way to the tea shop – my mum owns it – let's go there, get a cuppa and dry you off. Then if you want to talk… Gosh I thought I recognised you. You've been in a couple of times haven't you? Always sit by the window. Good to put a name to the face. Oh dear, there I go again – you'll have to tell me to shut up; everybody does!!" She started the car and drove on.

Sitting in the comfortable tea rooms, Jennifer poured her heart out to the friendly Cassie "… and to top it all, the rain has made this all wet, so when I open it, it'll probably be porridge… so much for flapjacks!" There was a pause in the conversation and they both laughed.

"Where are you staying?"

"I've rented a little flat near Market Square. Just a short let, while I sort my head out. I'll be heading back to London soon. Shame, I rather like it here. I'll miss it." She looked wistfully out at the glistening world outside.

"Do you have to?"

"Sorry, have to what?"

"Go back? You've said it's all gone pear shaped in your old life – why not make a completely new start... here?"

Jennifer thought for a moment. "No, I couldn't... could I?"

"Why not? This place could do with some new characters around. I reckon it would be a good thing all round!" Cassie smiled "Think about it."

Cassie's mother approached the table with another pot of tea. "How's your ankle feeling, dear?"

"Oh, a lot better since you strapped it up for me. Thank you, Mrs Meadows."

"Please, call me Helen; everyone does!"

"OK, thank you Helen."

They poured more tea and chatted for quite some time. "My goodness, look at the time. Your dad will be home soon and I haven't even started dinner yet!" Helen said her goodbyes and left.

"Your mum's nice," said Jennifer.

"Yeah, I think so, but thanks for saying so."

The girls continued to chat as if they'd known each other for years instead of hours. "Got any plans for tomorrow?" enquired Cassie. "We could make a picnic and I'll show you a lovely spot which explains how the village got its name."

"Sounds interesting – let's hope the weather doesn't repeat today's."

"I think it will be OK, but I'll bring a brolly... just in case!" They laughed.

***

Next day, Cassie drove her old Citroen through Market Square, which was once again bathed in beautiful warm sunshine, and pulled up outside Jennifer's flat. She beeped her hooter.

Looking through the window, Jennifer smiled as she saw the funky green and yellow car which contained her new friend. The two girls acknowledged each other with a wave.

Picking up a large straw bag, Jennifer left the flat and went down to join her friend. As she approached the car, Cassie smiled. "Hiya, how are you feeling today?"

"Pretty good thanks, and you?"

"Yeah, I'm fine; how's your ankle?"

"Not bad actually; your Mum would make a good nurse." She gave a soft giggle and got into the passenger seat. "Your car looks even lovelier in good weather. What made you choose a jazzy little motor like this?"

"Actually, it was more a case of the old girl choosing me. I've always called the 2CVs deck chairs on wheels…" she laughed, "but I spotted this one and HAD to have her. Have you noticed the number plate?" Jennifer shook her head. "Have a look when we get out and you'll see what I mean."

They drove for a few miles chatting as they went. "Won't be long now and I'll show you some really nice scenery."

"Oh good. I've brought my camera so I can show Mum and Dad where I've been hiding."

Cassie pulled into a small car park which was surrounded by trees and Jennifer went to the rear of the car and studied the number plate. "C A S 5 1 E… oh, now I see what you mean; it reads like your name! That's really good."

Walking across the car park to the far corner, Jennifer noticed an ornate iron gate. As they opened it there was a strangely appropriate squeak that suited it perfectly. "Ooh, it's like going into a secret garden."

"It's better than that," replied Cassie. "You wait."

With a slightly different note to its squeak, the gate was closed to and they walked along a short hedge-lined alleyway. The far end opened onto a riverside walk and one of the prettiest vistas that Jennifer had seen. "Oh this is wonderful – hang on, I must take a picture!"

"Don't use all your film up; there's more to see."

Jennifer restricted herself to just the one shot. It seemed that every few minutes there was another something that was worthy of being caught by the camera: beautiful plants and trees, water birds galore, occasional crafts of every size and shape floating up or down stream, and the views on the far shore were wonderful.

"I'm sure I'll be able to use some of this when I've got my new place…" She seemed to drift off mentally for a moment. "Actually do you mind if we sit for a mo? My ankle is feeling a bit achy."

"Don't mind at all; actually do you fancy having some of the picnic bits?" Sitting on the bank, they dangled their toes in the refreshing cool water.

"Makes you feel like a kid again, sitting eating sandwiches and splashing your feet about. Ah to be young again."

"Coo, hark at grandma – you're hardly ancient!" Jennifer laughed as she agreed with her companion.

"This cold water seems to be helping my ankle you know. Do you fancy a flapjack? I managed to salvage most of the oats. Here, one of Grannifer's special recipes."

"Mm, yes please... I've been meaning to ask you. I know this lady was your lovely great grandmother, but why Grannifer?"

Jennifer gave a little laugh. "It was actually a mistake on my part as a little girl. You see, she and Grampa had three boys – they'd have liked to have had a daughter too, but it didn't happen. Each of the sons had a son, so still no females. Then lo and behold, I came along! Great granny was over the moon with a girl in the family at last. I was named after her and we developed a really strong bond."

Cassie was interested, but still quizzical. "But why Grannifer?"

"I'm coming to that! To avoid confusion I called my mum and dad's parents Nanny and Grandad, and THEIR parents were Granny and Grampa, but in this case I got confused with hearing people call her Jennifer whilst I called her granny. The two kind of merged together and I started calling her... the two names together... GRANNIFER, and it stuck!"

"Now I see; well it's pretty unique."

Jennifer smiled. "She was pretty unique. Friend, teacher, everything; all rolled into one amazing package. You'd have loved her."

"Yeah, I reckon."

"This is really nice here, but what has it to do with giving Miraford its name?"

"Ah, that bit is still to be revealed," said Cassie with a twinkle in her eye. "Let's get this lot packed up and we'll move on."

Continuing their riverside walk the girls chatted freely, discussing anything and everything, from food and fashion, to music and even past boyfriends. They found that they had a lot in common, but where their opinions disagreed they enjoyed lively debates. It was fun and, enjoying each other's company, time passed quickly. Cassie stopped walking and addressed her friend directly. "We're almost there and I've got a suggestion which I think you'll appreciate when we arrive."

Jennifer was curious. "You want me to walk for five minutes with my eyes shut?"

"Don't worry, I'll hold your arm – trust me," she giggled.

Slowly Jennifer replied. "OK, let's go for it; I suppose you know what you're doing." Curiosity was tempting Jennifer to peek but she resisted temptation. "Oh this is weird; are we nearly there?"

"Almost. Not far now. We're just about to stop, but keep your eyes shut until I say – all right?"

"OK."

"Oh, and you might want your camera ready." Jennifer waited with anticipation. She felt in her bag for the camera. "Ready... open and enjoy!"

Obeying the instruction, Jennifer stood and gazed at the sight in silent awe, then "Oh my goodness! Cassie, this is amazing!"

Before them was the most beautiful scene Jennifer had ever experienced in her life. For as far as the eye could see was just a vision of fields, hills and trees, but magically tinged with colours from the beginnings of the setting sun. The sky itself was a mystical blend of delicate blues, mauves, pinks and creamy yellow. Stunning as this was, the whole picture was reflected in the serene water of the river. "I've never seen anything so beautiful. It's stunning."

"Mm, I knew you'd like it. Apparently many years ago when the first people started to settle here, the river was smaller and this bit here was a ford whereby they could get to the other side. Nobody seems to know why it has this incredible ability to reflect SO accurately, but it does, and that's why it was called Mirror Ford. Over the years it changed from Mirror Ford to Miraford. Did you take that photo?"

"Oh crikey! I almost forgot."

"It's always nice here, but around sunset is the best time." They stayed for a while, sometimes talking, but often in quiet contemplation. As they walked back to the car Jennifer was not very chatty. "You all right? You've gone quiet."

"Yeah, I'm fine. I was just thinking."

"Go on then; penny for your thoughts?"

She took a deep breath then, exhaling gently, a confused expression came across Jennifer's face. "I was just trying to work out if... you see it might be OK but... I mean, what if? And of course, organising it would be... oh, I don't know!"

"What are you babbling on about? You're not making any sense."

"Precisely. I mean, does it make sense or is it the craziest thing?"

"What ARE you going on about... oh my God, you're going to move here!"

"THINKING about it... oh Cassie, I don't know. What if it isn't the right decision?"

"You could move back."

"Yeah, I suppose. Let's get a pen and paper and a glass of wine and sort out some of the details."

"I think this might take longer than a glass of wine..."

***

Entering the tea rooms, Jennifer looked at the counter. "Morning Helen."

"Oh hello dear. Cuppa?"

"Mm, coffee please." She took her usual seat by the window. Helen approached the table and placed two pretty china mugs on the place mats.

"I can spare a few minutes to join you, so come on, fill me in. How are things going?"

"To be honest Helen, I can't believe it; my feet have hardly touched the ground! I've arranged more time on the flat while I look for my own place. Mum and Dad are dealing with trying to sell my old apartment and my cousin and his wife want to buy the furniture so that's really useful. I've got four properties to view and as soon as I can I've got to go and see my solicitor. I think that's it for now!"

"Whew, I'm tired just listening to you!" she smiled. "You know if there's anything we can do to help."

"Yes I know; thank you."

They finished their drinks. "Is Cassie around? I wondered if she wanted to look at places with me."

"She's at the studio just now but she'll be back soon." Her friend was a keen artist and sculptress and could often be found at her small studio, covered in paint and plaster. Jennifer had promised to commission something once she'd sorted somewhere permanent to live.

Cassie arrived.

***

It was a few hours later when the girls walked back into the tea rooms.

Helen looked at them with a smile on her face. "How'd it go? Any good?" Their despondent faces gave her the answer. "Oh, I'm sorry love. Never mind; something will turn up. What was wrong with these ones?"

"Well if you like modern square boxes, I suppose they were OK. The gardens were so neat a weed wouldn't even dare look in them, let alone try and grow. Honestly Helen, they weren't at all what I am looking for. They just were not me; I want more ramshackle with character. A project to get my teeth into, I suppose."

They hadn't noticed that an elderly gentleman sitting at one of the tables had been eavesdropping on their conversation. "Er, excuse me," he called to the chatting ladies. "Sorry if you think I'm rude but I couldn't help overhearing. Do I take it you are looking for a property, my dear?"

"Yes, I am," replied Jennifer. "Why, do you know of somewhere?"

She walked to his table where he gestured for her to sit down. "Possibly, but you did say you wanted a project, yes?"

"Ooh, yes, tell me more!"

Curiosity had got the better of Cassie who joined her friend and the

18

gentleman. "This sounds like it could be interesting. Anyone want tea while we find out?" She indicated to her mum.

"My name is Jim, by the way."

"How do you do? I'm Jennifer and this is Cassie."

"The place I'm thinking of was in a bit of a bad way when I last saw it and that was a good many years ago, so goodness knows what it's like now!" He sipped his tea. "When I were a lad, young Fred Perkins was one of my best pals. All us kids from the village would congregate at Freddie's to play. Oh it was great; so much space to run around and we could go anywhere on the farm as long as we didn't interfere with crops or machinery. It was like paradise."

"Er Jim," Jennifer interrupted him, "Sorry to butt in. I know I wanted a project… but a farm? I didn't really mean anything that big."

"Oh no lass, most of it's sold on now. Let me explain." He drained his cup. The girls looked at each other a little anxiously. He continued with his story.

"When Freddie was in his twenties he emigrated to Canada. Now, old man Perkins, he carried on with the farm for, I suppose, fifteen or twenty years, but then he was took ill. Nothing too drastic, but it took its toll and he couldn't really do the work he had been – well he was getting on a bit an' all that. Anyway, he sold most of the land, just keeping the house and enough garden to keep him out of mischief."

He chuckled. Jim looked as if he was in bit of a daydream for a moment. "I liked the old boy – reminded me of my dad… anyway he stayed on his own there for several years, then out of the blue decided to visit his lad in Canada. The visit became permanent, until he went to meet his maker. Ooh, must be… er… seventeen years now."

Jennifer looked quizzically at the friendly storyteller. "So Jim, who's been in the house since?"

"That's the point… no one; poor ole place is just sitting there waiting."

"Waiting, waiting for what?"

"To be a home again."

Jennifer looked across the table at Cassie with a quizzical expression. Her friend answered the silent question, raising her eyebrows and shrugging her shoulders. "Wouldn't hurt to take a peek." Then she smiled looking back at Jim.

Jennifer asked who she should contact. "I've got Fred's address somewhere – leave it with me."

"I forgot to ask- what did the farm turn into?"

"Ah, Mr Perkins sold it to Pinkerton's Cider. They use it as one of their orchards. Yes, just hundreds of apple trees… looks a treat in spring when the blossom's out."

Jennifer was trying to stop herself getting too enthusiastic: this was sounding better and better by the minute. Something had to go badly wrong. She didn't trust that her luck could have changed so dramatically. The trio chatted for a while longer then said their goodbyes.

That evening, alone in her flat, Jennifer took stock of the day. "Oh Grannifer, I wonder what I might be getting us into."

***

It was a few days later, and Jennifer was sitting in the bar of the Miraford Arms waiting for Cassie to join her after work. It was a surprisingly chilly evening, but the landlord had lit a welcoming log fire, and as she waited, Jennifer stared into the hypnotic flames.

"Hiya, sorry I'm late – it took longer to empty the kiln than I'd planned."

"Oh hello; actually, I hadn't noticed the time. I was watching the darts match earlier; Jim was playing. He's not at all bad you know. Got our team the winning shot."

At that moment the man himself approached their table. "Evening girls."

"Oh hello Jim, I was just telling Cassie about the match. You're a dark horse. You didn't tell us you were a darts expert!"

"Ooh, I wouldn't say expert, but I've thrown a few over the years," he chuckled. "I'm glad I've seen you; I found old Freddie's address. Not only that, but I found out his phone number."

"Oh well done Jim; thank you. So all we have to do now is contact your friend and…"

Jim interrupted Jennifer. "Already done lass. I called him last night. Had a right good chat we did; well we had lots of years to catch up on!" He started to relay some of the conversation he and Freddie had had. The girls tried to look interested. Realising he had wandered well away from the reason for calling Freddie, Jim stopped. "Hark at me going on. I asked him what plans the family had for the old house and he said they'd be only too happy to get rid of it! Reckon they'd rather have the cash. Well, not much use to them when they're so far away, eh?"

"So we can have a look at it then?"

"Any time you want to."

"Oh wow! Are you busy tomorrow?"

"That's fine with me, but be prepared. The old place hasn't been lived in for a long time; it will likely be in a bit of a state."

The sounds within the quaint 18th century pub faded momentarily as

Jennifer's mind drifted. The chat and laughter, clinking of glasses, even the crackle of the blazing fire all melted into a gentle hum. She took on board the gleaming horse brasses which adorned the rough stone walls and low beamed ceilings. Solid oak furniture with comfortable padded seats were variously covered with leather and tapestry. Old lanterns were hung, all giving soft gentle light. The atmosphere was warm and friendly, and she blessed the day she discovered this previously unknown village. It seemed to her that this feeling of comfort and relaxation was not just from her pleasant surroundings, but more so from the welcome she had received since she arrived in Miraford.

Jim had replenished their drinks and he and the girls exchanged stories of events in their lives, most of which caused a lot of laughter. Jim entertained Jennifer and Cassie with his tales of mischief as a boy, right through to his job as a carpenter. The three chatted away happily throughout the evening, the difference in their ages hardly apparent until at one point Jim spoke of his grandson who he'd only known for the first six years of the boy's life. Jim and his wife Mary had a daughter who had given birth to the lad when she was only seventeen. Not feeling that she wanted to settle down and be 'just a mum', she'd left to explore new things. She took the youngster with her but that was the last Jim and Mary saw of them. Yes, they received the odd letter or card, but nothing more.

"Oh, how sad," said Cassie.

"So you don't even know where they are now?" asked Jennifer.

Jim shook his head. "No, 'fraid not; I'm not even sure if they've still got our surname. All I do know is he was named Timothy James… the James bit was after me!" he smiled proudly. "Anyway, enough of this. Who wants another drink?"

"My turn," insisted Jennifer. "You've bought the last two rounds."

"OK Jenny lass, if you like." Jennifer stiffened and held her breath. "Are you all right?" he queried.

"Oh yes, I'm fine. It's just that nobody has called me Jenny since Grannifer."

"That's a shame; it suits you." He gave her a weak apologising smile. "I'm sorry, I'll not do it again if it upsets you."

Taking a deep strengthening breath she smiled back. "Actually, no – it was a weird moment, but nice to hear it again. You can call me Jenny whenever you like!"

He thanked her. "Now, where was I?" Looking like her old self, Jennifer picked up her purse. "Getting in another round I think!" She walked to the bar.

Cassie spoke to Jim. "I think that was a big hurdle she just climbed over."

"Yes, I reckon lass, but as long as we can help her climb over, well, that's what friends do, eh?" She agreed.

Jennifer returned with a tray of drinks. "Only just made that. Did you know it's almost closing time?"

After a while, as the pub started to empty, Jennifer picked up her drink. Making an attention seeking cough she spoke. "While we still have a little liquid left, I would like to propose a toast." The two looked at her expectantly, holding their drinks ready. With a silly 'put-on' voice she began – "Unaccustomed I am at making speeches…" They made pretend mocking jeers. "No, seriously, I just wanted to say thank you. This has been a lovely evening, but since I first arrived here you've made me welcome and you've helped drag me back into 'happy land'."

Cassie gave her a playful nudge. "Ah, you soppy old thing."

"No, honestly, I'm really grateful – so please raise your glasses to 'friendship'." In unison they repeated her toast and clinked their glasses. As they were finishing the drinks, a bell rang out. "Time ladies and gentleman, please."

Jennifer took one last look at the now just glowing embers of the fire. She felt content and more than a little happy.

Chapter 2

Next morning, Jennifer was pottering restlessly around her small flat. She smoothed covers, wiped surfaces and plumped cushions for the umpteenth time. She looked at the clock again. "Still two hours to go. Grannifer, this is crazy. I wasn't like this before I viewed the other places. What's the matter with me?"

Deciding to force herself to eat something, she prepared a small breakfast. Taking up her usual seat she placed the tiny morsels of bread on the outer sill. This had become a routine and her feathered companions calmed her somewhat. "I wonder what this place will be like, and will I like it enough to buy it? I know it'll need a bit of work doing it up, but I'm up for a little challenge occasionally. We'll tidy the garden and soon make it look nice."

She smiled as she spoke her thoughts out loud. "Yes, if it looks like it has potential… mm, I've got an almost good feeling about this."

Her thoughts were interrupted as she noticed Cassie pull up outside with Jim beside her. Jennifer grabbed her bag and left the flat excitedly. She joined her friends in the car and after greeting each other, they made their way towards the outskirts of the village.

Jim gave directions. "If you take the next right then follow the lane to the end, you'll see the orchard ahead of us."

Jennifer felt bubbles of excitement and anticipation deep inside her. She thought she would burst. "Oh please, let me like it," she thought over and over.

"Apple trees ahead," shouted Cassie excitedly. Parking the car alongside a large stone wall, they got out.

"Where is it Jim?"

"Just along here my dear. There, see that gate?" Walking towards this entrance, the girls were oblivious of what lay behind it, the large stone wall still keeping secret the property on its other side. As they stood at the dilapidated gate, only just attached to one of its hinges, they were speechless. Almost at the same time, the girls broke the silence.

"Oh my God!"

"Crikey!"

Jim joined in. "Er, um, well you did say you wanted a project. Something to get your teeth into."

"Teeth, yes. I'll need at least a machete to get through that lot. It's a blooming jungle!"

"I thought we were coming to view a house – where is it?"

"I think I can just make out the roof and chimney over there. Can you see beyond that rather delightful forty foot bramble only just holding its own against the ivy?"

Jennifer noticed Jim's disappointed expression at her sarcastic remarks. Giving him a sympathetic smile, she slipped her arm around his waist. "I'm sorry; it's just bit more of a 'project' than I'd imagined."

Cassie joined them. Standing on the other side of Jim, she completed the trio's mutual comforting cuddle. They stared at the tangled mass of vegetation. "So how do we excavate this lot? I'm OK with trudging through the grass and ivy, but those brambles look absolutely lethal."

They all pondered the problem. Jim smiled. "I've just remembered: I've got my secateurs in my pocket."

Jennifer laughed. "Secateurs? Oh Jim, you are priceless. Nice offer but this lot would take an eternity!"

He agreed. "s'pose you're right, but now we're here let's try and pick a path through. I'll go in front and you two follow behind."

"I'm game if you are," said Jennifer.

"Yeah, go for it!"

Proceeding with his mission, Jim stomped and crushed the long grass and weeds underfoot. He bashed the higher things with a sturdy piece of wood and on the odd occasion used his secateurs. "I knew they'd come in handy," he thought to himself and smiled. As he went along, he utilised sticks and anything he could find to stake up and hold back the more stubborn bramble. He was making good headway.

Although probably two and a half times their age, Jim's strength and agility impressed the girls. Using hushed voices they commented to each other "He may have a few years under his belt, but he doesn't act like a pensioner."

"No, he's obviously very fit."

"I may be old, but I ain't deaf yet."

Biting their lips they both felt embarrassed. "Sorry Jim, but we were complimenting you!"

He laughed. "Shouldn't be long now; I've come across concrete." Jennifer and Cassie cheered. It had been hard work, but after an hour or so they were through the jungle and standing in front of the house. Jim faced them. "There you are Jenny; your new home if you like it."

"Do you know something, I think I do!"

"Better check the inside first mate, before you commit yourself."

"Why are you rummaging under the window sill Jim?"

"Apparently this is where the old boy used to keep the keys. Ah... yes, this feels like it. There, you do the honours lass."

He gave it to Jennifer. Jennifer clasped the key tightly in her hand. "Oh my!" Sensing the enormous difference to her life which could lie beyond the door, she drew her clenched fingers to her lips. She whispered, "Darling Grannifer, help me make the right decision." She turned to her waiting friends and smiled. "Come on, let's see what it's like."

They walked together to the large front door. It had a very weathered look about it, but was surprisingly solid and opened with comparative ease. Inside was a roomy entrance hall. Several feet in front of them was a wide flight of stairs. To the right of these was a short passage which led to a door. They all entered the room and looked around.

"Oh my God; there's one of those really old range cooker things... I wonder if it still works?"

"No reason why it shouldn't; just needs a good clean."

"Yes, not to mention the rest of the place. There must be a ton of dirt in here. It'll take a month of Sundays to clean this lot." Cassie had a slightly despondent expression as she spoke.

Jennifer was still investigating with her head half in a cupboard. "Well I think you'd be a bit grubby if you hadn't washed for about thirty years!" She reappeared and the other two burst out laughing. "What? What?"

"You've got a really dirty face and a big dusty cobweb in your hair!"

"Oh well, never mind; I was planning a bath next week anyway!"

They all laughed. "Come on. I want to see more!"

With a smile on his face, Jim nodded towards the door leading to the hall through which Jennifer had just disappeared. "I think she likes it! Come on lass, let's go and find her."

***

Cassie was first to find Jennifer in the living room. "Look at some of the furniture Cassie – I wonder if it comes with the house? And have you seen the floors? And the walls – they're as solid as rocks. Some of the windows need attention but… what?"

Cassie was staring at her with a bemused expression. "Do I take it you have a great liking for this place?"

"Liking? Cassie – I love it!!"

Realising she had been babbling somewhat, Jennifer looked sheepishly at her friend. "Sorry, I'll calm down and try to act like a grown up." She giggled. "Talking of grown ups… where's Jim?"

"Checking the stairs to make sure they're safe."

"Oh, he's such a darling! I would have just gone running up there and possibly put my foot straight through."

"Precisely why he's checking them"

They then went into the hall and called him. "Upstairs, come and have a look."

There were seven steps to begin with and then a right turn up another three. A final right turn led to four more steps. This then became a landing which flanked the front wall – two bedrooms were above the living room with a third over the kitchen. This was also where the bathroom was situated. They then found Jim and he looked up from where he was examining the floorboards. "So what do you think, lass?"

"It's more than I could have wished for. Thank you so much for telling me about it."

"You're welcome love. I think some of the wood needs seeing to but I can help you with that."

"Oh, of course, you're a carpenter. Wonderful! Thanks."

"I've done a quick check of a few bits Jenny, but you need to get experts in – if you want to buy it that is."

"Yes, you're right Jim. How about we meet back at the pub later? I'll bring a note pad and we'll make a 'to do' list."

Replacing the key, they set off back to the village. After dropping Jim at his cottage the girls went to the tearooms.

"Hi Mum."

"Hello Helen."

"Hello girls. Good grief – look at the state of you! Been down a coal mine have you?"

"Not quite, but we really need a cuppa and Jennifer can't wait to tell you her news."

Helen listened with interest. "You'll need help with certain bits if you buy it love. You know – plumbers, electricians and the like."

"Yes, Jim said the same. We're having a brainstorming session tonight at the pub. Why don't you and Don join us?"

"Mm, that would be nice – it's not often I get to go out with my hubby these days. He has a lot of contacts too, so I'll ask him."

Soaking in the bath, Jennifer enjoyed retracing the layout of the house. "I hope you like it as much as I do, Grannifer. I know it'll take a lot of work, but I've got a really good feeling about this. With all the stuff you've taught me over the years, I reckon I'll do okay." Sliding further under the bubbly water, she grinned to herself.

The muted sounds from within the Miraford Arms increased in volume as Jennifer and the Meadows family opened the door. They greeted friends and acquaintances as they walked through the pub and selected a table, settling in to the comfy chairs around it. Don joined Helen and the girls with their drinks. "Look who I found at the bar!"

It was Jim. The men sat down. "Did you manage to unblock the drains, Jenny?"

"I'm sorry?" She looked at him quizzically.

"Well, you look a lot cleaner now than you did earlier!"

She smiled and gave him a pretend punch on the arm. "Cheeky!!"

They chatted happily for a while and Jennifer took her pen and notepad out of her bag. "Come on then guys, get your thinking caps on – I need a list of everything I have to do to get the house up and running."

Cassie looked at her friend. "Well, first of all you have to actually buy it!"

"Yeah, that might be a good starting point!"

Jim said that he would contact Freddie and sort out some details now that Jennifer actually wanted it. Suggestions flew thick and fast with Jennifer scribbling down ideas.

"Do you think I really need a survey? After all, it's been standing there for a hundred years or whatever."

"You really should," advised Don. "Just in case, and anyway, it will put your mind at rest."

Jennifer nodded. "Okay, you're right, I know. Running through the other items – so, check electrics, plumbing, water and phone. Anything else? I can't help feeling there's something I've forgotten."

Cassie grinned. "How about a herd of goats?"

"Oh my God, yeah; the garden! Perhaps I'd better see if the army could lend me a hand!" They all chuckled.

"Is it really that bad?" asked Helen.

"Honestly, just believe us – it's worse!"

Don looked thoughtful. "I wonder if I could persuade the team to help out?" Don was a keen footballer with the local club.

"Dad, that's brilliant. We could make it into a party!"

"Yeah, a garden party! Oh Don, if you could persuade them that would be terrific. Tell you what, I'll provide stuff for a BBQ – with drinks too of course."

"Sounds good. I'll ask them on Saturday."

"Wow, this is really happening isn't it? Thank you all so much."

The following days were bit of a blur as Jennifer arranged and organised the things on her list. A week or two later she invited Cassie to her flat for dinner.

"Mm, yummy casserole mate!"

"Thanks, it's one of Grannifer's recipes. Actually there's something to do with her that my solicitor wants to see me about. I'm going to London on Thursday to see him about it."

"Perhaps she left something for you in her will?"

"No, that was all sorted out before I came to Miraford. I've got no idea what it's to do with. I've got to sign stuff to do with the apartment too. Mum said I've got a buyer. Good eh?"

"Oh yes, I'm really pleased for you. Mystery about Grannifer though – have you really no ideas?"

Jennifer shook her head, "No, won't know 'til I get there."

Throughout the evening the two friends chatted and listened to music. All too soon it was time for Cassie to leave.

"Thanks for a lovely evening; it's been great. See you tomorrow."

As Jennifer walked to Cassie's studio the following day, she enjoyed the now familiar sights and people of the village. It felt that she had been there for much longer than just the four and a half weeks. Such a lot had happened, with so much more to come!

"Hi Cassie!"

"Oh, hiya! I'll be with you in a minute." She did a bit more to the sculpture she was working on, and then joined Jennifer.

"I've made us coffee."

"Ooh, well done. I get really thirsty when I'm working here."

"I can imagine! I love your studio; there's always something interesting to see."

Cassie smiled. Taking a sip of her drink, she nodded towards a table. "There's the designs I told you about – have a look and see if anything takes your fancy."

Jennifer started flicking through the pages. "Oh, I like them all. You are clever!"

"Thank you. Tell you what, why don't you take it with you on

28

Thursday; it'll give you something to do on the train."

***

She got to the station and on the train returning to London, Jennifer watched the passing countryside through the glass. Before long, she realised that her concentration was more on her reflection as she focussed more on her own features. She saw a face which had confusion written all over it. What on earth could Grannifer have waiting for her at the end of the journey?

Pulling herself back to reality, she popped a sweet in her mouth and started browsing through Cassie's folder. She was glad of the distraction, and before long the train arrived at her station. Stepping on to the platform, she beamed at the sight of her mother waiting for her.

"Mum!" she shouted, breaking into a run. She was soon being held tightly and she reciprocated the enthusiastic cuddle.

"Oh darling, so good to see you. How are you? You're looking well."

"I've got so much to tell you."

"All in good time darling; Dad's waiting in the car. Let's see if we can prise lunch out of him and then you can tell us all your news."

Her parents listened to their excited daughter as she recalled everything that had happened in Miraford.

"Well, I must say, the place obviously agrees with you! It's good to see the sparkle back in your eyes."

It was almost three o'clock when Jennifer approached the imposing looking door, beside which on the wall was a shining brass plate - 'Lawrence and Dunn Solicitors'. She took a deep breath as she entered.

"Good afternoon," the smart, friendly receptionist greeted her.

"Er, good afternoon. I have an appointment with Mr Lawrence – Jennifer Cade."

"Ah yes, he's expecting you. I'll let him know you're here."

An inner door opened and a suited man in his mid-fifties shook Jennifer's hand. "Hello, won't you come through?" They sat either side of the large desk. "Would you like tea – coffee?"

"Er, no thanks."

"Don't look so worried my dear; I have something to pass on to you." Her expression was still one of concern. "Look, I'm due afternoon coffee, why don't you join me?"

She relaxed slightly with his cheeky persona, "Oh all right then, thank you." As she sipped the drink, she listened intently.

"I received instruction from your great grandmother, Mrs Jennifer Amelia Cade, that on the occasion of her death, I was to contact her friend and neighbour, Mrs May Duncan. Four months after her date of

29

passing I complied with her instructions, which is why I have now contacted yourself." He sat back in his chair and picked up his coffee, a pleased look on his face for having got the explanation out.

"I don't understand; what has all that got to do with me?"

"Ah well, your grand – sorry great grandmother – left something in the care of Mrs Duncan which she wanted you to have after a bit of time after her passing."

"So, what is it?"

"Three items actually: a parcel, a Post Office book and a letter." He opened a drawer in the desk. He took them out and handed them to Jennifer.

Her hands shook. "Th... th... thank you." As her eyes rested on the envelope, Grannifer's handwriting was there: 'For Jenny.'

"Mr Lawrence, would you mind, er, can I open them here please?"

"Of course, my dear." He handed her a letter opener.

Nervously she took the folded sheet of paper from the envelope. There was a gentle waft of Grannifer's delicate perfume. Jennifer bit her lip as she read:

Dearest Jenny,

That you are reading this means that we have already said our goodbyes. But remember my darling, that I will never really leave you; our love so strong will keep us together always. I hope my gift will be of assistance at times when I can no longer be there.

Darling Jenny, I also want to thank you for not just being the most beautiful and loving great granddaughter I could have wished for, but also for being a very precious and most treasured friend. So much love always my Jenny. Take care and be happy. Remember I am only a whisper away.

Kisses always, from your Grannifer.

Jennifer drew the sheet of paper to her mouth and kissed the words tenderly. Handing her a tissue, Mr Lawrence said "She was a lovely lady."

"Yes, always will be." She gave a sad smile.

"Do you want to...?" He indicated towards the parcel and Post Office book.

"Oh, er, yes of course." She carefully placed the letter to one side. "Oh my word; this is a savings book in my name started in the week I was born. Oh Grannifer, you are naughty... thank you."

"Mm, now for the mystery parcel. I wonder what it is." Untying the ribbon, she folded back the paper wrapping. "It's a book! Oh and look, can you see, Grannifer has decorated the cover herself; she was always good with that sort of thing."

As she leafed through the pages a broad smile lit up her face. "Ooh you clever lady. Look Mr Lawrence, all the things Grannifer has shown me over the years. Tips, recipes, decorating… everything. She's recorded it all like a wonderful reference book. She knew I wouldn't remember it all. Oh you brilliant wonderful darling! What a legacy! Isn't she fabulous Mr Lawrence?"

He smiled in agreement and with Jennifer now feeling much happier, they bade each other goodbye.

Jennifer spent her overnight stay with her parents; they were always good company.

As they drove to the station the following morning, she rested her hand on their shoulders. "It's been lovely to see you both, but I can't wait to get back to get started with the house! Can't wait for you to see it; you will come soon, won't you?"

After the farewell hugs and kisses, Jennifer's parents waved as her train departed. On their own journey home they agreed that it was good to have their bubbly, confident and very happy daughter back again. The recent months of trauma had been painful for them to witness, but now that was past and she was starting to live again.

Leaving the station, Jennifer popped into the studio before going to the flat. "Hello Cassie, are you there?"

"Uh-huh, out the back." She emerged from a room. "Hiya, how did it go?"

"Oh marvellous, and there's your folder by the way. There's quite a few I'm tempted with. Are you busy this evening? I've loads to tell you."

Later in the pub "So you see, in less than twenty-four hours! It was a real roller coaster of emotions, but Mr Lawrence was such a sweetie, and Mum and Dad were brilliant. It was great to see them, but I just couldn't wait to get back to here."

"Crikey, and they reckon I can talk! I'll say lass, I've been stood here for ten minutes and you've hardly drawn breath!"

Jennifer looked over her shoulder to see the friendly figure holding a pint. "Hello Jim. I was just telling Cassie about London."

"So I heard lass. Sounds like you had a successful trip." He pulled up a chair and joined them. "Actually Jennifer, I've got a bit more track for your roller coaster."

She gave a questioning look. "Oh yes, what's that then?"

"Old Freddie reckons you can start doing stuff on the house whenever you like!"

31

"But we haven't done the contracts or anything."

"He's not bothered. Said if it all goes pear shaped, he will reimburse you for any outlay, but he said you can start as and when. Always was easy going was Freddy."

With a look of disbelief on her face, she slumped back in her chair. "Pinch me someone; I must be dreaming."

Later, as she lay in her bed, a wave of contentment washed over her. Her mind recalled all that had happened. So much in such a short time. She yawned and snuggled under the bedclothes. Smiling as her eyelids closed, she drifted into a beautiful relaxed sleep.

***

Enjoying the usual breakfast routine, Jennifer chatted out loud to her feathered companions. "This is all really exciting, but I'm glad I'm going to have to put my 'sensible head' on". She gave a little chuckle. "Yes, I definitely need to get well and truly organised!" She sipped her coffee. "Come on girl, now where to start? Mm… notebook. Always good to have a list to work from."

Having another drink, she studied the items from the 'brainstorming' meeting. She crossed out with satisfaction the things that had already been dealt with and made various notes against others. Turning the page she wrote on the top 'things to buy', then underlined it. There followed quite a profusion of cleaning implements – broom, dustpan and brush, cloths – the list went on.

"Now Grannifer, you've always told me soda crystals will cut through greasy things and I'll need white vinegar to clean windows with scrunched up newspaper to buff to a shine. Hope it doesn't end up smelling like a fish and chip shop!"

She listed bits she could remember off the top of her head but thought it would be a good idea to check Grannifer's book for more ideas. The following pages had their own headings and after an hour or two she complimented herself on what she had done so far. Noticing the outer sill was free of crumbs she smiled wryly. "Cor, what a load of greedy guts you are – I gave you double rations today!"

Closing the notebook, Jennifer placed it and the pens in her bag. Sitting further back in the chair she stretched. "Ooh, time for a walk I think; give the old bones a bit of exercise."

As she approached 'Meadows Tea Rooms', she noticed the inside lights went off. Soon after, Helen came out and locked the door. "Hello, hello, what's all this? Are you skiving?"

Helen jumped when she heard the serious voice behind her. Turning around she smiled. "Oh hello Jennifer. I wondered who that was."

"This is unusual for you; how come you're closed up? Everything all right?"

"Yes fine thanks; I just need to go to into Lamton quickly. I'll be back in a couple of hours. Did you need something, dear?"

"No, not really. I just came for a walk and thought I'd come to you for a chat. No matter – I'll see you later."

Helen noticed the slight disappointment in Jennifer. "Why don't you come with me? We can have a natter on the bus." Jennifer smiled and nodded.

"Yes, why not? I'd like that and I haven't been to town properly since I arrived here." Sitting on the bus she showed Helen the various lists.

"This one here - 'sort Contents', with the bits you don't want and you'll not be selling – there's a nice charity shop in town. I'm sure they'd like to take some stuff off your hands."

"Brilliant. I'll have a word with them while you do your bits. Thanks Helen."

As Jennifer left the charity shop she saw Helen coming down the street. "That was good timing! How did you get on?"

"Really good. They were really happy with the thought of new stock, and even have a van that will pick it up if I can't get it into them myself. I've got a phone number to call when I've sorted things out. Honestly Helen, I can't believe how well everything is going."

"I've got more good news for you – oh here's the bus!"

As they travelled back to Miraford, Helen explained that Don had already contacted team members who were only too happy to help. "He's arranging a suitable day with them at practice today."

"How wonderful; I'd better start getting the beers in and sort that barbecue!"

Cassie was in the tea rooms when they got back. She looked even more cheerful than usual. "Hiya; you look happy. Won the lottery or something?"

Grinning like a Cheshire cat, she replied "Better than that!" She poured coffees. "Here, have this and I will tell you."

They sat down. "Well don't keep me in suspense."

"I heard from Paul this morning; he hopes to be back by the end of the month! Isn't that wonderful?"

"Oh yes mate; I'm so pleased for you. I can't wait to meet him."

Paul was Cassie's boyfriend. His work took him abroad and the contract he'd been working on had meant he was away for almost six months. "I'll have to ask him to introduce you to some of his mates."

"Oh no, I don't think so. That toe-rag Mac has put me off boyfriends for the foreseeable future. Relationships are OK for other people, but I'll pass for the time being."

She took a gulp of her drink. "Oh I almost forgot…" She told Cassie about the charity shop.

"Excellent. We'd better get back to the house ASAP and start sorting eh?"

***

Over the next few days the girls busied themselves collecting boxes of various sizes. When Cassie was working at the studio, Jennifer made arrangements with plumbers, electricians and other trades people to get utilities up and running in the house. Soon they were sufficiently set up to at least make a start with the sorting.

"… tell you what mate, it's a good job neither of us are scared of spiders. This place looks like you've decked it out for a Halloween party! All you need are a few ghosties and the odd witch's broom and we're away."

"I know what you mean, but if there are any spirit people here I'm not bothered; it all feels just so… well… friendly."

They carried on chatting as they sorted. "Old Mr Perkins left a lot of his clothes didn't he? And rather good quality. I reckon the charity people will make good use of them."

"Yeah, and these rugs and things. You sure you don't want these bits of furniture?"

"No, I'll keep the older things. I'm going to have a go at restoring them. Grannifer has a few tips in her book! I'll get rid of the more modern stuff."

"Modern? There's nothing under forty plus years old!" They laughed. "Well you know what I mean."

They finished the first of the bedrooms. "Fancy a drink and a little break before we do the next room?"

"Good idea."

"It will be much easier to clean without so much in here."

"You'd better be careful it doesn't float away… there's so much dirt in here that's probably weighed it down to the ground!"

"Ha ha, very funny – actually the survey says it's solid as a rock. I'm so chuffed with it all. And all thanks to Jim. I'd like to get him something as a thank you. Any ideas?"

"Not off the top of my head. If you asked him he'd probably say 'Just buy me a pint lass!'"

"Ain't that the truth? No, I want to do something special."

34

"He really is one of those really genuine extra specially nice people."

"Shall we crack on then? If we do a bit more then we'll make a move home. I don't feel like cooking though. What's the food like in the pub?"

"Oh you're in for a treat: best pub grub in the village!"

Jennifer thought for a minute. "Hang on, it's the ONLY pub in the village!" Cassie smiled.

***

Later that evening as the girls finished their meal, Jennifer licked her lips and wiped her mouth with a serviette. "Mm, you were right – that was delicious. We must do this again! Oh look, there's your Mum and Dad."

Cassie waved to them across the bar. "Hello love, hello Jennifer. How are you?"

They returned the greeting by patting their stomachs. "We're fine. A bit full up!"

"Ah, sounds like you've just had a Miraford Mixed Grill – just the ticket if you're really hungry. Got room for a drink?"

"Yes please."

Don went to fetch them whilst Helen took a seat. They were busy chatting when Don returned. Placing the tray on the table, he said "I saw Jim at the bar. He's coming over in a minute."

"So that is who the extra pint is for. I did wonder: thought for a minute you'd forgotten how to count Dad!"

Soon Jim had joined them. "Oh this is lovely. We've got the brainstorming team together again." Jennifer smiled happily.

"I've sorted things with the football lads. You OK if we come at the weekend? About two o'clock Saturday after practice we thought."

"Really? Oh Don, you're an angel. Thank you. I'll get the BBQ stuff sorted; ooh this is so exciting!" Everyone laughed as Jennifer, with her fingers clenched, clapped her wrists together.

"Fine. I know these guys. It'll be fun." Cassie smiled reassuringly at her friend.

Comforted by her words, Jennifer nodded. "Yeah, you're right. Tell you what this reminds me of – a stall I helped Grannifer with at a fête. All we need is a string of bunting!"

***

Before she knew it, it was the weekend. Cassie, Jennifer and Jim had set up the BBQ. Just then a van pulled up. "Yippee, they're here,"

Stepping out from the dilapidated gate, the trio laughed as the football team poured out of their mini bus, joking around with each other as they collected an assortment of tools and equipment from the back of the vehicle. Amid the revelry, Cassie joined her father. Kissing him, she spoke briefly. Don blew a whistle. Getting the men's attention he spoke. "As promised, there will be a BBQ and beers later on." Everyone cheered. He held his hand aloft. "But before that, a lunch has also been provided."

The men did an appreciative, but half comical "Woohoo!"

"Come on then chaps, tools at the ready. By the left, quick march!" With gardening implements of varying shapes and sizes held to their shoulders, and each man sporting a broad grin, they marched into the bedraggled overgrown garden. Jennifer, Cassie and Jim laughed at the strange army and joined on the tail end, mimicking the troop.

In the partially cleaned kitchen the girls had laid out a selection of sandwiches and a large plate piled high with flapjacks. Mugs of tea and coffee were passed around and everyone tucked in, eagerly munching the unexpected but very welcome lunch. The humorous banter continued and the lively buzz of conversation was akin to a party. After a while Don calmed them down and suggested that some sort of strategy should be worked out as to the best plan of action for tackling 'that there jungle.' Ideas flew left right and centre, but in a short while everyone had a rough idea what they were doing. Suitably refreshed they all ventured outside.

The boisterous banter continued as everyone set about attacking the prolifically overgrown vegetation. As they cut, slashed and yanked away, there were shouts of "Have at you" and "Take that you varmint", with the occasional cry of "Ah – he got me" when a particularly vicious thorn made contact. It seemed for all the world that they were playing at being warriors fighting through this jungly enemy, like overgrown schoolboys. In reality they were a very organised and dedicated team of wonderful people helping a friend in need. Jennifer was amazed at the speed with which they made a substantial impact.

"This is incredible" she remarked to Cassie as they dragged more of the larger brambles to what had been designated as the bonfire pile. "I could never have done this myself in a month of Sundays."

After a couple of hours the girls disappeared into the house returning soon after with trays filled with mugs of tea and coffee. "Break-time," they announced. Putting tools to one side the men willingly took their drinks. Amongst the usual shears, strimmers, scythes, long handled loppers etc., Jim noticed something which one of the men was using which had taken his interest. "Don't see many of them around these days lad, not round here anyway."

"No, it's good isn't it? My uncle gave it to me; he called it a staff

36

hook. Apparently it's mainly from the West Country. I'd not heard of 'em before but it does the job, eh?"

The subject of their conversation was a heavy curved blade on a good quality strong handle. "I've had it for a few years but never had a chance to use it 'til now. Good way of christening it!" The two men chuckled. Having drained their mugs and rested a while, everyone started work again.

With the evening came relaxation for the group of intrepid gardeners. A couple of settees had been brought outside and Jim was positioned in front of the living room window having appointed himself cook-in-charge. Although now resting in comparison to the busy work of the day, there were still jovial conversations and animated interaction and there was a definite party atmosphere going on. Walking with drinks in hand, the girls reached the gate. Looking back at the scene they had temporarily left, they chatted. "Look at Jim; he's really enjoying himself. What IS it with men and barbecues?"

"Beats me! I love the chef's hat he made – he's so up for a laugh isn't he?" They chuckled. "Tell you what Cassie, I've only just realised how big the place really is."

"Yeah, I know what you mean. Have you thought what you will have in the garden when it's all clear?

"Got a few ideas but I don't know how much land there is at the back yet. I'd quite like a pond I think – I like water somewhere near to look at."

As they talked, Don joined them. "Message from the chef – your dinner is ready. Er, before we join the others... we've been talking, the lads and me, and – well, they wondered if you would like us to come back again and clear the rest of it with you? They'd quite like to see the end result, you know?"

Jennifer was dumbfounded. "Oh Don, really?" Amid a smile she bit her lip. Her eyes glistened. Passing her glass to Cassie, she threw her arms around Don's neck. "Thank you."

"Our pleasure love. Come on now – let's get a burger before they turn to charcoal!" Arm in arm they walked back to the party. All too soon it was time to clear things away and everyone went home.

It was a very tired but extremely happy lady that snuggled into her bed that night. "Oh Grannifer, aren't some people just the most wonderful friends?"

***

Over the next few weeks the footballers returned as often as they could, usually as a team, but occasionally just two or three together if they had time to spare. It seemed they had got hooked on conquering the jungle and were determined to see the end result as soon as they could.

To Cassie's delight, Paul had returned and had soon joined in with everyone else in the mission to clear the area. Bonfire piles were scattered around, waiting to be dried out enough to burn. As the work progressed and further away from the house, Jennifer was ever more astounded at the size her newly acquired property was turning into.

As the girls heaved yet another heap of brambles on a pile, Jennifer stretched, then with her hands backward above her hips, she rubbed her back with her fingers. She looked around at the perimeters. "I really like that old stone wall; it makes a beautiful border."

"Yeah, it's really nice. Mind you, I don't envy whoever built it – must have taken forever!"

At this point, Paul joined them. Slipping his arm around Cassie's waist, he whispered "No time to stand around chatting now."

"Oi cheeky, we've been working! Actually we were just admiring the wall."

"You can admire the bottom of it soon – about another twenty feet and we'll be there I reckon."

"Oh, that's wonderful! Let's have a cuppa to celebrate!"

"Honestly, you and your coffee!"

"Yes, I know, but it's a good way of making the guys take a break. See, there's method in my madness!" She smiled knowingly.

As they drank they chatted about some of the discoveries which had been made. "I rather like the bike I found. Mind you, I think it will be OK with a bit of TLC."

"I think you'd need some tyres."

"Yeah, and a saddle might be useful!"

"Ah well, now you're just being fussy." They laughed. "There's an old milk churn – oh, and a couple of cart wheels. Well, the metal bits seem OK. Know anyone who's good with wood?" Everyone looked at Jim. He in turn looked behind him. Turning back he smiled. "I could give it a go I reckon; I'll add it to the list."

He chuckled, but Cassie noticed a slight look of worry on Jennifer's face. Taking her friend to one side she asked "What's up mate?"

"Jim – I know he offers but... do you think he's taking on too many of these jobs to help me? I don't want him to overdo it."

"I'm sure he's fine, but we'll keep an eye on him eh?" Jennifer gave a slightly reassured smile.

Rejoining the men, the girls found them still verbally categorising the things which had been found. "We brought most of it over here for you to sort through Jennifer, but there's a stone structure over there." He pointed. "We're not sure but looks like it might be the remains of a pot or summat."

"Oh, I do hope so. Wasn't I saying the other day? I'd love some watery thing."

Jim had a knowing smile on his face. Two small outbuildings had been uncovered. Jennifer likened them to little crofters' cottages. "I think they're so cute."

"I'm really liking that sundial," Cassie joined in. Although the bottom wall was getting ever nearer, Jennifer said she thought enough had been done for today. "Who's up for a pint? My treat!"

Nods and smiles abounded. Before long they were reunited in the Miraford Arms with Jennifer picking up the bill. "You sure about paying for all this, mate?"

"Oh gosh yes. I'm so grateful to everyone; you've all worked so hard. I can hardly believe the transformation. I'm glad I've taken snapshots throughout. I'm going to do a special album, kind of before, after and ongoing! It'll be great to look back on over the years."

"So you're thinking of sticking around then?"

"Mm, er, yeah, I reckon I might." They laughed. As the girls and Paul chatted, Cassie looked at her boyfriend, with a questioning look. She raised her eyebrows.

"Well, - who won?"

Paul sported an over emphasised sad expression. "You might have warned me – this bloke has got an unfair advantage!"

"What do you mean?"

"He's too good!"

Everyone laughed. "Oh yes, I suppose we should have mentioned it!"

"So lass, are you pleased with the way things are going in the house?"

"Ooh am I? And to think, it's all thanks to you Jim. Is there anything I can get you as a proper thank you?"

"Don't be daft Jenny lass; you've already bought me a pint – that's enough!"

Cassie smiled. "I told you that's what he would say!"

"Yeah, well I don't think that's enough, but I'll think of something. The other thing Jim… I'm worried you're taking on too much. I don't want you overdoing things on my behalf."

"Don't you fret lass. I'm fine. If anything, you two lasses have perked me up. I've been thinking about all those years I've missed with my grandson and you girls being about his age... well, it's kinda nice. Doing stuff for you that I might have done with him. Know what I mean?"

Jennifer nodded and gave his hand a squeeze. Jim coughed. "Anyway, who's for a refill?" He gave his eyes a wipe.

Chapter 3

Sharing her breakfast as always the following morning, Jennifer spoke aloud to her bird friends. "Well my little darlings, I'll be moving on soon but I won't be far away. I hope you find our new windowsill."

She pondered for a moment. It would be quite a massive change to her life in so many ways. This little flat, originally just a space to hide away, had been her home and she'd grown to love it. No more would she overlook the market square with the characters of the village busily going about their daily routines. She reassured herself that all of these things would still be here and easily accessed should she feel the need to experience them. But there again, she would have plenty to keep her busy at the house.

It had been a daunting job to clean thirty years of dirt and dust, but that had been accomplished and the unwanted items got rid of. Now it was time to decorate and put her own stamp on it. All her years of interior design would now have new meaning. This time it was not just as a job, but the creation of her own home.

***

During the next few days Jennifer enjoyed shopping for the first of many things her new home would need. Although she wanted to keep the kitchen fairly traditional and in keeping with the farmhouse style, she did allow herself a few modern conveniences: a fridge freezer, microwave, cooker and a washing machine. She also bought a bed and a stereo. Other than these, she just concentrated on store cupboard items. She also picked up a number of colour charts from a DIY store. "Might as well start getting my head into decorating mode!"

Before she knew it, the weekend had arrived. "My last night here with you, little flat. Thank you for being my sanctuary when I needed one."

***

As the birds pecked at their breakfast next morning, Jennifer got her camera. "Even if I can't take you in person, at least I'll have your photo." She took a few shots. "There we go my little companions, bye bye for now."

Collecting the last of her possessions and making sure everything was clean and tidy, she left. As she locked the door for the last time an element of sadness caught her. "Come on you soppy thing; we're on to a new bit of life!!" She wiped her eyes and put a determined smile on her lips. As she walked to the roadside, Cassie's familiar yellow and green car drove up.

"Hiya Jennifer. All set? Exciting isn't it?"

As the girls turned into the lane they saw the minibus just pulling up ahead of them. Cassie parked her car as the footballers tumbled out of their vehicle in their usual exuberant manner. "Hello Jim, you taken up footie now as well as darts?"

"Oh hello Jenny; no not these days although I used to play a bit in my younger days. No, the lads just gave me a lift."

"Hi everyone."

The men acknowledged Jennifer and Cassie. Don approached the girls. "Reckon we'll get this finished today!"

Jim joined them rattling a box of matches. "And I'm going to start getting these bonfires out of the way. I've bought a hosepipe."

Jennifer looked quizzical. "Are you going to wash them away then Jim?".

With a tone which indicated 'don't be stupid' he rolled his eyes and replied "No, this is for safety. We don't want to burn the place down before you've even moved in do we?"

Jennifer laughed. "I know. I was being facetious!"

He chuckled. "Come on then, let's get started!"

It was about an hour or so later that a cheer went up from the bottom of the garden. Jennifer ran to join the men. "What's happened, what's all the cheering for? Oh my word… you've finished! Oh guys, well done!"

"And look what we found in the corner." They moved apart from each other to reveal a gate. As she looked with interest as to what might lie behind her garden wall, Jennifer squealed with delight. "A river. I've got a river at the bottom of my garden!"

Running back to the bonfire attendant. "Jim, guess what?"

He had a huge smile on his face. "You've found it then?"

"You knew, didn't you?"

"Well it were there when we were lads, so I reckoned it might still be!"

As they were all relaxing later Jennifer giggled. "And to think I was hoping for a pond!"

With the front garden fires fully extinguished, everyone was now tending a thirst at the rear of the house. "We'll have to all get together in November and have a proper bonfire night party. I can do sausages and jacket potatoes." Jennifer seemed excited at the thought of the idea.

"So you don't think you'll have a posh garden by then?"

"Er, I don't think so Cassie. I doubt I'll have even got it dug over by then, let alone planted up."

Hearing their conversation, Don joined in. "Couldn't help overhearing. Our goalie, Melvyn thinks he might have a solution. Hang on." Don looked around the group locating his team mate; he called him across. "Hi Mel, can we borrow you for a moment mate?"

Mel joined Don and the girls. "I was telling Jennifer about your idea."

"How do you get on with pigs?"

"Jennifer looked surprised. "Er well, apart from my last boyfriend, I've never really had much to do with them. Why?"

"Well if you don't mind having some here for a couple of months, they'll sort this lot out for you. They'll eat right down including the roots which should stop your brambles coming back! Bit like piggy rotavators! What do you think?"

"I'm interested, but I wouldn't know the first thing about looking after them and where would I get pigs from anyway?"

"I can help you with both of those. When I'm not playing football, I'm a pig farmer," he smiled.

"It sounds good to me, but I don't know about looking after dozens of porkers."

"Cor no love; three or four would do the job. We need to organise a few things first, but if you're interested…"

She thought for a moment, "Well, it does sound less back breaking to have piggy gardeners. If you think I can cope… I'm game."

"We have to get you a smallholder's licence that will cover you in the future, if you want to have goats, sheep, or whatever. There'll be other paperwork to say they're living here, but I'll deal with that. Oh, and we need to sort those gates. They will escape given half the chance."

"I'll sort the gates out for you Jenny." Jim had joined the group.

"I'll help you Jim." Paul added.

"Ah, thank you lad," Mel continued. "They need a shelter and a bit of mud to wallow in."

Jennifer was getting into this now. "Well there's those little outhouses and, er, um, ooh ah – that old pond. We could make that their mud bath!"

"Sounds good to me. I'll lend you a water trough. Apart from water, just feed them veggie scraps and pig nuts; that'll do 'em. Oh, and they quite like lots of milk."

"So looks like we're on then."

"Yeah."

"Ooh yes, I'm looking forward to it."

Saying goodbye to her friends that evening, Jennifer was for the first time alone in the house. Alone yes, but she did not feel lonely. Ringing in her ears was the laughter of these treasured new people in her life, and of course, Grannifer was only a whisper away. Taking one last look around the garden which seemed so much bigger without anyone else in it, she went indoors. Putting on some music she made a drink and enjoyed the memories of the day. Leaving her little flat seemed an awfully long time ago.

***

She woke early the next morning and looking from an upstairs window was transfixed by the gentle mist hanging magically on the cool damp morning. Quiet and still, she smiled at its mysterious beauty. Putting her dressing gown around her, she went downstairs. Flicking the kettle on, she opened the back door. The air was sweet with just a hint of the damp ashes from the bonfire. "I wonder if the birds here will enjoy sharing breakfast like my old friends in Market Square?"

Having eaten breakfast, Jennifer pottered around her house through the morning, occasionally stopping to add another 'need to get' in her notebook. Eventually she went to the garden to get rid of more bonfire ashes.

She repeated this for a couple of days. Pleased with her efforts, she stood at the bottom wall looking back to the house. She hummed a tune to herself – something distracted her. Stopping her singing, she listened intently. Yes, there it was again – a kind of whimper. What could it be? Following the sound, she found herself by the small outhouses. She peered cautiously between them. Crouching slowly so as not to frighten it, Jennifer spoke gently to the bedraggled dog which was licking its front paw.

"Hello sweetheart; where have you come from?" Still wearing her gardening gloves, she tenderly stroked the poor creature's head. "Please don't bite me and I'll try and help you."

It was apparent very quickly that this was a very friendly dog but far too weak to give much of a fight even if it wanted to. Carefully she picked it up. "Come on darling, let's take you in and see what's hurting you."

Placing it on the large kitchen table, Jennifer noticed a tag on its collar. "Soaki, mm, that's an unusual name. Oh well, there there Soaki, good dog, let's see that paw. Good dog."

She kept reassuring the animal as she gently examined for injury. "Oh my word, look at that. You poor thing – that's a big old thorn stuck in there. Hold on and I'll take it out." As if it knew it was being helped, the dog let Jennifer remove it and then licked her hand as if in gratitude. "Oh you're welcome. Well I'm no vet, but I think we need some antiseptic on there and then I reckon you need some food and drink."

Not having anything more appropriate, she scrambled a couple of eggs and after they'd cooked she placed them near the water bowl on the floor. "Oh, you like eggs then Soaki?" The dog wagged its tail. "Mm coffee I think, then I need to think about finding your owner."

On the reverse of Soaki's tag was more writing – Kingfisher Houseboat. "Ah, now this seems as though you might live not too far away. "If we're going walkies, I think we'll put a little bandage on that sore paw. I'll finish my coffee, then we'll make a move."

As she chatted, the dog looked at her intently as though understanding every word. This made Jennifer laugh. "Oh you are a sweetie pie aren't you?"

After Jennifer made a makeshift lead from a long scarf, the pair headed along the tow path. Soaki seemed to know the way and after about twenty minutes, an attractive oldish houseboat came into view. Yes, this was the one, with a beautifully hand painted sign next to the gangplank.

Standing by the vessel, Jennifer called out "Hello, er, ahoy, anyone there?"

A good looking man in his mid thirties popped his head out of a door. "Hi, someone calling?"

"Er, yes – I think I've found your dog."

He quickly bounded on to the riverbank. "So Soaki, you're back! Where've you been girl? I was so worried." Cuddling the dog who was licking his face and wagging her tail madly, it was obvious there was a great love between them. Eventually the young man acknowledged Jennifer. "Oh, I'm sorry; I thought I'd lost her forever. She disappeared days ago. I looked everywhere and couldn't find her. Thank you so much for bringing her back. Er, would you like to come aboard? I'll make us a cuppa and you can tell me where you found her."

There was something familiar about him, but Jennifer thought he maybe just had one of those faces. Inside the cabin, the man made tea, whilst Jennifer told how she'd found Soaki. "Sounds like a hawthorn; they're pretty big. Y'know, I can't thank you enough for what you've done."

"That's okay. I'm pleased to have helped. Unusual name you've given her!"

He smiled. "That came from when I found her. Classic thing of unwanted litter – someone dumped the poor little mites in the river. I found 'em and she was still alive. The only one mind; five of 'em didn't make it. I buried the others and nursed her back. Called her Soaki 'cause she was soaking wet!"

"How can people do such terrible things?"

"Dunno, beats me. By the way, I'm TJ."

"How do you do, I'm Jennifer."

They smiled as they shook hands. As they chatted, little things that TJ said got the cogs in her mind turning. "You've said your mum had family from around here – do you mind me asking? Does TJ stand for Timothy James?"

"How the hell could you have guessed that?" He looked at her in disbelief.

"I'm not 100%, but I think I know your grandad!"

"You are joking?"

"No, from what you've been saying, I think it's a strong possibility."

He sat back in his chair. "Whoa!" TJ sat silent for a while, collecting his thoughts. "So will you take me to meet him?"

"Er, yes of course, but we need to do this carefully."

He questioned her reply "How do you mean?"

"Well, although I'm sure that you will be the best surprise ever, we don't want you to to be such a sudden shock that might freak the old darling out! I care about him too much for that."

Thoughtfully, he responded "Yes, I see what you mean."

Jennifer smiled reassuringly. "Leave it to me and I'll sort it. By the way, what's your surname?"

"Barton – TJ Barton."

She smiled. "Right Mr Barton; I'll see what I can do."

"Would you like another drink?"

She smiled as she stood up. "No thanks; it's getting on. I need to make a move."

TJ and Soaki walked Jennifer back along the tow-path. As they chatted, the walk seemed shorter. At the gate he thanked her again for helping Soaki. "And one more thing – would you mind if I called you Jenny? It suits you so much better!"

She laughed out load. "Do you know, Jim said those very words to me." She entered the garden. "I'll let you know how I get on. Goodnight."

Inside, she checked the time. Ten past eight. "Oh well, no time like the present." She got washed and changed, then walked into the village.

The pub had its usual friendly glow and buzz of conversation. Entering the door, she spotted Jim. Joining him at the bar, she tapped his shoulder. "Hello Jim."

He looked around. "Oh, hello Jenny. How you doing? Haven't seen you for a couple of days."

"I'm fine thanks – I finished my bonfires."

Sitting at a table she asked "Do you know Jim, all these months I've known you, and I've got no idea what your surname is..."

"Barton, lass."

She smiled. "Oh right." She eased their conversation into talking about their families. "I miss Grannifer so much. If you could get someone back in your life, who would it be?"

"Oh, I think my Mary."

"Yes, I'm sure. I didn't necessarily mean someone who'd passed away."

He looked pensive. "I do wonder about our Timothy – how he is, what sort of young man he's growing into – you know."

She squeezed his hand comfortingly. "Have you tried looking for him?"

Shaking his head he replied "I wouldn't know where to start, lass."

"How about if I helped you. Would you want to meet up again?"

He gave a suppressed laugh. "I doubt it's possible, but if it were, I can't think of anything I'd like more. But..." His words trailed away.

Jennifer bit her lip. "Jim... I think... er I think I..."

"What is it, love?"

Oh well, she thought. I've come this far, so taking a deep breath... "Jim, I think I've found him."

He looked at her stunned. "What did you say? I think I heard you."

She told him and explained the day's events to him. "Tell you what Jim, I've had an idea. How about I cook a nice meal tomorrow? You and TJ can come round and do some mega catching up while you munch?"

47

"I couldn't put you to all that trouble lass."

"Trouble? Are you kidding, after all you've done for me? It would be my pleasure." She sipped her drink looking over her glass into his glistening eyes. "So, that's settled then. I'll see TJ during the day and ask him round. Does six o'clock suit you?"

"That would be perfect. Thank you Jenny."

She smiled lovingly. "Fancy a refill?"

He nodded emotionally as the enormity of the evening really started to register. "Here you are Grandad; look I even splashed out and got some crisps!"

It was nearly five thirty the following day. Jim had left his cottage and was heading towards the outskirts of the village. TJ walked along by the river towards Jennifer's garden gate, Soaki leading the way enthusiastically.

Jennifer checked that dinner was all organised and the table was properly laid out. She looked at the clock for the umpteenth time. "Quarter to six. Have I forgotten anything, Grannifer? Oh, I do hope this goes okay!" She sighed and checked the meal again.

Jim looked at his watch as he turned into the lane. "Ten to. Nearly there!" His pace quickened slightly.

TJ stood by the gate, looking at his watch. "Five to six," He exhaled then walked to the river's edge. He picked up a stone and threw it into the water. He watched the ripples for a moment then went back to the gate.

Jim had arrived at the front gate waiting anxiously for the allocated hour.

Jennifer paced around the kitchen. "Nearly six." She perched on a chair.

Almost simultaneously there was a knock at both the front and back doors. "Oh, they're here." She opened the kitchen door and smiled at TJ. "Come in." She ran through the kitchen whilst still talking. "I've just got to answer the front door."

Smiling at Jim, she beckoned him in. "He's here, darling."

The two men stood at each end of the large room. "Hello Grandad."

"Oh hello, Timothy."

Tears welled up in their eyes. Striding eagerly towards each other, they threw their arms around one another and hugged tightly. Jennifer went back into the hallway and sat on the stairs to give them a moment of privacy. Soaki joined her as if instinctively knowing that the kitchen was not her place just now. Jennifer stroked her head gently. Soaki wagged her tail appreciatively.

Several minutes passed, then TJ appeared. "Ah, there you both are. Care to join us?"

Soaki ran to her master. Jennifer rose from the staircase and followed them back into the kitchen. "Anyone like a drink before dinner?"

They sat around the table chatting. The conversation flowed easily and Jim was heartened that TJ remembered the few yet very precious years of his childhood which they had shared. "Do you remember the water fight we had and Nana chased us round the garden 'cos we made her washing all wet again?"

"Yes, and to make matters worse, she didn't duck low enough under the line and ended up with a pair of my pants on her head!"

They all laughed heartily, even Jennifer, who was really enjoying their stories, but more so the fact the men connected so well. Jennifer stood up. "Right, let's eat. You both said you liked chicken so what I've coo…"She didn't finish the sentence, but stared in amazement at the two men who had both tucked their thumbs into their armpits and started clucking. "Buek… Buek… Buek… Beuk…"

"Timothy, you remembered!"

"Of course Grandad – you can't have chicken without pretending to be one!" They had joined together with the last sentence.

As they laughed, Jim managed to splutter an explanation. "Sorry Jenny; it's just something we always did. It used to make Mary laugh!"

Jennifer raised her eyebrows and smiled. "I'm not surprised; you look ridiculous!"

They all laughed again. The conversation was fluid throughout the evening as they divulged the experiences they'd had in the many lost years apart from each other. "So you never married? Kids?"

TJ shook his head. "No to both, I'm afraid. Almost thought about getting wed at one point but it didn't happen. She wasn't ready to commit."

"Yeah, I was almost there myself."

"Sorry Jenny; didn't mean to speak a bad memory."

"Oh no, that's okay – after all, he was one of the reasons I came here. So I s'pose I ought to thank him really!" She gave a resigned smile. "Oh for goodness sake – I forgot pudding. Anyone want? It's only apple pie and ice cream."

"Mm, yummy. Is it home made pie?"

Looking exaggeratedly indignant, she pretended to be insulted. "Of course it's home-made – how dare you!"

"Ooh, sorry! In that case, yes please!"

Chuckling at their role play she went to the freezer. As the men scraped their bowls she felt satisfied that yet another of Grannifer's recipes had hit the spot.

Eventually it was time for Jim and TJ to leave. As they said their goodbyes, Jennifer slipped Soaki one last treat accompanied with a secret wink. Everyone hugged and they went home. Locking the doors, Jennifer gave a tired but contented yawn. Looking at the pans and dishes she sighed "I'll sort you lot out in the morning." She turned off the light and went to bed.

***

Having sorted the kitchen out in the morning and pottered about generally, she settled down with a mug of coffee. It was just after midday. About to take a sip, she was surprised to hear a knock at the front door. As she opened it, she was amazed to see an enormous bouquet of flowers with legs underneath. A hand appeared at the side of the display. "Delivery for Miss Jenny Cade."

"Oh my goodness – er, thank you!" She took the flowers and went indoors. As she read the attached card she bit her lip and her eyes welled up. "Thank you our dearest Jenny, not only for our wonderful meal, but for bringing us together again. With love, Jim and TJ."

With the beautiful surprise gift laid before her on the table, Jennifer drank the coffee she had made before the knock at the door. Reading again the words inside the card she smiled.

"Oh, but what can I put them into? I only have a couple of vases and they are only any good for a bunch of daffs or perhaps a few roses, but this lot..." Running through her mind for ideas she suddenly hit on a possibility. "I wonder..."

Moving some of the bits around it, she cleared a space and looked enquiringly at the churn which had been discovered in the garden. "I wonder..."

Taking it to the back door she ran inside and buried her head in a cupboard, pushing and poking things about. She emerged triumphant with a wire brush in her hand. "This should do the trick." To her delight, it did actually clean up quite nicely. "Oh crikey, I didn't check it for holes. I didn't notice any – oh please be OK." She crossed her fingers. Filling it with water she stood back staring at the paper she had stood the churn on. "Please stay dry..."

After ten minutes, relief took away her concerned expression. "Oh good". She smiled broadly. Emptying the water back into buckets, she managed to carry the churn indoors. Placing it beside the staircase she poured the water back in and arranged the bouquet. It was perfect. Did she really need to keep going from the kitchen to the living room? And was it really necessary to keep remembering things she'd forgotten upstairs? Probably not, but each time she passed her flowers she felt a glow of happiness. The heady fragrance wafted in the air and filled the large hall with the beautiful scent. "One more thing to do."

She picked up her camera and took the photos. "For the album!"

That evening as Jennifer entered the Miraford Arms, she was pleased to see both Jim and TJ at the bar. Approaching them she pointed. "You are both very naughty boys!" Standing between them she slipped an arm around each. "Thank you so much – they are beautiful."

"Glad you like 'em lass – not that we could ever thank you enough for what you've done, but we thought you might like some flowers to keep you going 'till you grow your own!"

They sat at a table chatting. "We've had a right full day; Timothy has shown me his boat and we've done some fishing – he came back to my place for some dinner, then we came here and he beat me at darts."

"Sorry, did you say he beat you at darts?"

"He did that! Brilliant game – hopefully he'll join the team." Jim looked proudly at his grandson.

"So you two have got things in common then?"

"I reckon it must be our genes... I even like woodwork – just like Grandad."

Jennifer was at the bar getting more drinks when the door opened. She beckoned excitedly to Cassie and Paul. "Hello Jennifer. What are you jumping about for?"

"You'll never guess. Hang on." She bought two more drinks. "Come over here."

Jim stood up. "Hello Cassie, Paul. Please may I introduce you to Timothy – my grandson." He beamed.

"Call me TJ." They all shook hands. As they took their seats, Cassie sat open mouthed.

"But how? When? I thought... Oh my God Jim, I'm so pleased for you."

With shared explanations from each, Jim, Jennifer and TJ told of the reunion. "AND he can play darts!"

Play acting, Paul groaned, placing his forehead on the table. "Oh no, not another one!"

Everyone laughed. As the conversations continued Cassie smiled at her friend. "Well done mate; this is brilliant!"

As the evening progressed, talk inevitably turned to Jennifer's house. Everyone had taken not only to the friendly new addition to their village, but also to the project of renovating her property which had lain deserted for so long. "Timothy, Paul and I thought we'd make a start on your gates soon Jenny. How does Wednesday suit you?"

"Oh yes, that would be fine. Can I help too?"

"Me too?" Both girls were eager to do as much as possible in every aspect of the renovation.

"Course you can; the more the merrier!"

The following day the girls went into Lamton. "It feels like ages since we've had a girlie time together, doesn't it?"

"Yeah, I know what you mean – all these men around all of a sudden. Not that I'm complaining!" They giggled and then laughed even more as they recognised the schoolgirl attitude they had adopted. "Come on, let's get some lunch and I'll tell you some of the ideas that I've got for the bedroom."

As they ate, they continued to chat. "Ooh, I've just remembered – when we've done the shops I want to show you somewhere on the way home." Cassie smiled at her friend. "I'm not going to tell you what, but I think you'll like it!"

"Give me a clue."

"Nope, it's a secret!"

"Oh you're a meanie."

"Well, it might give you something to do."

"Yeah right, like I haven't got enough to do already!"

No matter how much she probed, Cassie wouldn't give any more clues. On their return journey Cassie took a detour and eventually pulled into a large parking area. Jennifer read a sign – 'THOMPSON'S RECLAMATIONS'. They walked around the yard which was nicely arranged, but absolutely crammed to the hilt with anything and everything. "Gosh, this is amazing! Oh look - garden furniture!"

She ran excitedly to the area. After spending an hour looking around, Cassie rolled her eyes. Jennifer was just giving the details for delivery. "I didn't think you'd actually buy anything today."

"Well, you know me - see it, like it, get it!"

"So what have you ended up with, Miss Can't-Resist-A-Bargain?"

"Well, there's that table and benches for the garden, a bird table, that lovely log basket and some bits to go with the range cooker. Fifty five quid in all – what a deal! And they can deliver. Wa-hey!" She clapped her hands. "Come on, let's go before I spot something else."

It was early evening by the time they got back. They walked to the front door loaded up with shopping. "I can't wait to see those flowers."

"Before you see them, close your eyes as you go in and just take a big sniff."

Cassie did as she'd been instructed. "Oh wow, that is wonderful."

She opened her eyes. "Crikey mate, that's the biggest display I've ever seen."

"I know; imagine what I thought when they were delivered!" After dumping the many bags, they made coffee. "Whew, it's not 'til you stop that you realise how tiring spending money can be. But it's fun, ain't it?"

It was just after nine on Wednesday morning. Jennifer crouched by the front door to pick up some post. She jumped from a loud knock on the door. "That can't be the guys already – I thought they were coming at lunchtime."

Half looking at the doormat, the envelopes in her hand, she opened the door. "Oh, good morning."

"Morning Miss... er... Miss Cade?"

"Yes, that's me, can I help you?"

"Delivery Miss – Thompson's Reclamations."

"Oh, wow, I thought you were coming next week. Er, yes. Can you get them round the back please? Would you like a coffee?"

"That's very kind Miss." He walked back to his van.

By the time Jennifer had made the drinks, the men had arranged the bits outside the kitchen and were sitting on the benches. "Sugar?"

"Two please."

"Not for me love. I'm sweet enough already!"

Jennifer joined them.

"Been here long?"

"No, just moved in – I'm still setting it up."

"If you need anything particular, give us a call. We'll let you know if we can get it." He handed her a card.

"Thanks; that would be useful."

They chatted for a while as they drank. "Well, this won't do. Come on Bert – work to do. Thanks for the coffees Miss."

"You're welcome."

They left and Jennifer admired her new additions. It was a nice morning so she made breakfast and ate it outside, to her delight. The first visitors to the bird table came quickly and did not seem perturbed by their observer. She smiled, and bade them welcome.

"Ooh, my letters!" She made another cup of coffee and returned to the garden with her mail. As she sorted the post into order, she looked across at her feathered friends. "I must get a bird book so I can identify them. Oh lovely, a letter from Mum. Hello, what is this?"

She opened the mystery envelope first. "Way hay – I'm officially a smallholder! I must let Mel know. Right, now for Mum's."

She always enjoyed her mother's letters full of news about the family and updating her on things that her parents had been doing. "Oh brilliant; they're able to come and stay for a long weekend in two weeks' time. Nice one."

She finished reading and then went indoors. "Mmm, just after eleven. Coo, where has the time gone? The guys will be here soon."

Tidying up, she put her new cooker accessories on the top of the range. "I must get you sorted out and learn how to use you."

She laughed at herself for talking to a kitchen appliance. All too soon it was half past twelve. There was a knock at the door. "Hiya! Come in, I'll put the kettle on."

Cassie looked knowingly at the men - "I told you that would be the first thing she would say."

"Timothy not here yet?"

"Not yet. I'll go and see if he's coming."

Jennifer went to the tow-path. She waved at TJ walking towards her, his dog eagerly ahead. "Hello Soaki. How are you?"

She rubbed Soaki's back vigorously and the dog wagged her tail with delight. "Hiya TJ – kettle's on!"

"That's what I like to hear. How are you?"

They continued chatting as they walked to the house. Before long they were in the front garden, sorting and organising the various bits for the gates. "It was good of Don to bring the big pieces of wood round for us."

"Yeah, he's a good Dad. I've carted a lot of stuff in my old girl, but I don't think she'd have managed that lot." Cassie looked fondly towards her distant 2CV.

Jim explained the type of gates they were going to be 'constructing'. "We'll do them both as 'kissing gates', then the pigs won't be able to escape."

"I really need to think of a more appropriate name other than just being known as the Old Farmhouse. I need you all to get your thinking caps on, please!"

Jim stretched. "Well, I always think better with a mug of tea in my hand!"

"Good idea Jim. I'll put the kettle on. Oh, and by the way, I've made some …"

In unison, everyone shouted "Flapjacks… Hurrah!" They ran to the door and pretended to fight past each other to gain entry, laughing as they went.

Having had a break for about half an hour, Jim slapped his hands on his knees. "Come on you slackers, there's another gate to build!"

"Oh you slave-driver. We've only had two cups…"

"Na, stop moaning. Come on, troops in line by the left."

They quickly stood one behind the other - "Quick march!" They marched down the garden, giggling like children. Reaching the bottom wall, Paul looked at them in despair. "Er, guys – I think we've forgotten something!"

"What?"

He raised his eyebrows. "We've left the wood and tools in the front garden!" They groaned and went back to fetch the bits.

"With this being more straightforward and smaller, we should be finished fairly soon Jenny, then you'll be all set for your piggy friends."

"That's wonderful – thanks so much guys."

Having experienced the first gate, the team had the second one finished in no time. "Now who's for dinner? I've made a massive hotpot – so I hope you're hungry."

They looked at her with pretend sad expressions. "Oh Jennifer, I'm not really a fan of hotpot."

"Thanks for the offer Jenny love, but I couldn't eat a thing."

"Na, you're all right mate; I ate lots at lunchtime."

She looked at one to another. "Oh, I thought…" It was then she noticed TJ trying to stifle a smile. "You rotten lot! I thought I was gonna be eating hotpot for a week!"

They all laughed. "You kidding? We're ravenous!"

"Hope you like it. Should be okay; it's one of Grannifer's recipes."

As she dished up, they sniffed the air like the Bisto kids in the old advert. "Well, it definitely smells good!"

With every plate all but licked clean, Jim spoke for all of her guests. "Jenny love, that was delicious – you are a very good cook."

She smiled appreciatively. "Thank you very much; I'm glad you all enjoyed it, but I can't really take the credit. I just followed the instructions in Grannifer's ledger!"

Cassie joined in. "I think you are underselling yourself, but your Grannifer does sound like an amazing lady. I'd have liked to have met her."

Jennifer looked wistful. "Yes, she was wonderful, but if you look through her book, you'll feel like you know her." She smiled at her memories, "Anyway, who'd like a drink?"

They cleared the table and continued chatting through the evening. Soaki rested her head on TJ's lap having also been treated to a bowl of the hotpot. She had sat patiently with her tail wagging as her dinner cooled before she was allowed to eat.

Next morning, Jennifer 'phoned Mel to let him know that she was ready for her curly-tailed friends to take up residence. "Monday? Yes that will be fine, and will you pop in on Sunday to see I've got everything sorted? Brilliant, see you then. byeee!" She hung up the receiver and smiled. "Tee tee – I'm going to have some piggies!"

Feeling a little like a child awaiting Christmas, she decided to distract herself with a walk in to the village. It gave her a feeling of comfort that the cottages and gardens and the people that she met on her journey were all very familiar to her. She felt at home. As she walked into Meadows Tea Rooms, Helen beamed. "Hello stranger! Long time no see. How are you my dear?"

"Hello Helen. I'm fine thanks. How are you?"

"Yes, I'm good. I hear you're all ready for your pigs to come."

Jennifer nodded. "They're coming on Monday. Actually, I was going to ask a favour. It would seem they like milk even if it's going a bit like yoghurt!" She wrinkled her nose. "Anyway, I wondered if I could buy any you have over, rather than you throwing it."

"Of course love. I don't usually have much, but you're welcome to any I can't use. Want a cuppa while you are here?"

"Mmm, please."

They continued chatting. Before long, Cassie joined them. "Hiya Jennifer. How's things?"

"I'm trying diversion tactics to ease my excitement. Thought I might go back to Honey Bee Farm – fancy coming?"

"Yes, I'd like to. Oh, but I'm meeting Paul at four – do you mind if we drive there?"

Jennifer smiled. "No, of course not. Actually if we're going in the old girl, do you mind if I grab a couple of bits from the shops before we go?"

Cassie agreed and they arranged that she would get her car and meet Jennifer in the Market Square with her purchases.

When they joined up again, Cassie was surprised to see her friend with a baby bath and a container of baby oil. She climbed into the 2CV. Cassie looked at her with a quizzical expression. "Jennifer? Is there something you want to tell me?"

"Mm? No, like what?"

Cassie nodded towards the bath and then at her friend's stomach. "Are you...?"

"What? Oh God no – gerroff, no way!" No, these are for the pigs!"

"The pigs?"

"Yeah, I thought the bath would be good for their fruit and veggies, and the oil in case it got too hot... did you know they can get sunburnt?"

"Cor mate, are you sure you don't want teddies and blankets to tuck them in at bedtime? They won't want to go back to Mel by the time you've finished with 'em!" They laughed at the image of snuggling them into little beds and Jennifer singing them a lullaby.

Before long they were approaching Honey Bee Farm. "Do you know, the amount of times I've driven past here and I've never actually been in!"

"Oh, you're in for a treat. It's lovely."

The wandered around the outside areas and, as Jennifer had done all those months ago, ended up in the shop. "I can see why you like it. It's nice isn't it?"

Jennifer nodded. "Ah – this is what I wanted – pure beeswax! I'm gonna start renovating some of that old furniture – Grannifer's way!"

They collected a few other bits which were too tempting not to buy, then set off to the village.

"Cheers for the lift home. I might see you all later. byeee." She waved as Cassie drove away with a 'beep beep' from the attractive fun car which Jennifer thought suited its owner so well.

Putting the bath with all her shopping in it on the table, she made a drink and went down the garden. Going through her new gate, she went to the river's edge and sat on the grassy bank. She sighed with pleasure at her surroundings. Sipping her drink, she then broke pieces of bread and threw them to some ducks who had joined her. "Don't squabble – there's enough for all of you!"

From the bubbly excitement she experienced that morning, Jennifer was now calm and relaxed. She decided to make the most of the few hours she had until she joined her friends at the pub. She fancied a jacket potato for dinner, but remembered Grannifer's words and didn't waste the oven space, so she also made a rice pudding and a casserole. "Oh yes, and if I put a metal skewer through the potato, it cooks from the middle too. Thanks Grannifer; that'll make it ready sooner."

She looked forward to eventually using the range, but for the time being the old electric cooker was doing the job well enough.

"Right, now for my attempt at a bit of restoration!"

Collecting together some sandpaper and a dustpan and brush she went upstairs. "Easier to do it up here than bring it downstairs." Jennifer decided to begin her first attempt at renovation with one of the smaller pieces of furniture. "I think you'll do." She selected a smallish chest of drawers.

She took the top drawer out and rested it on its back, likewise with middle one, but as she reached for the bottom one she noticed something at the back of the nearly empty unit. "Hello, what's this?"

She reached in and took hold of a bundle of papers. Sitting cross legged on the floor, she examined the pieces. "Oh, it's a marriage certificate, and a photo too. This must be the wedding!"

There were other odd bits and pieces, a couple more pictures and envelopes which had Mr Perkins' name on. She put them all together neatly and checked there was nothing else. As she started to rub with the sandpaper, she wondered what should be done with her find. She decided to ask Jim – perhaps he could contact Freddie and see if he wanted them. Yes, that would be the best thing.

Lost in her thoughts, it was not long before she had finished sanding the first drawer front. Using the brush, she swept the dust away. "Mmm, not bad."

Eager to see what might be an indication of the finished article, she carried the drawer downstairs. She placed it on the table and found some soft cloth. "Better check the oven before I get stuck in with this."

Soon she was applying the beeswax and rubbing it into the wood. "How am I doing Grannifer? I'm following the grain like you have told me." Smiling, she completed the first application. "Right, coffee, then I'll give it another coat."

Pleased with her efforts, she put everything to one side, had her meal and then got ready to meet her friends.

Chapter 4

Jim was intrigued to hear about Jennifer's discovery and said he would contact Freddie. "Should know by Saturday. I'll let you know then."

"I'm coming in for the market. If you'll be here about lunchtime, I'll pop in. I need to get some fruit and veg for the pigs."

"Oh yes, they're arriving on Monday aren't they? Er, don't they just eat scraps?"

Cassie joined in. "Oh no Jim – not our Jennifer's pigs, nothing but the best for them! Did their bunk beds and teddies arrive yet?" She looked at Jennifer and they both laughed, remembering their conversation earlier.

"Anyway, why shouldn't they have a few treats? They're gonna earn it sorting my garden out!"

Everyone agreed. "Well, I wouldn't fancy digging that amount of land, that's for sure lass!"

As Jennifer woke on Saturday morning, she stretched and propped herself on one elbow. She'd placed her bed in such a way that she could look through the window and see the river without actually getting out. She liked this view down the garden with the rustic old stone wall which flanked the borders. She imagined it in the future when it would hopefully be filled with colour and fragrances. And of course, just beyond the bottom wall were the willow trees dotted along the river bank. She had always been very fond of willows. Their elegant branches swayed with even the gentlest breeze, as a butterfly might flit through the air. With the lowest leaves playing with the surface of the water, they were so serene, so cathartic and calming.

"Mmm, quite lovely. To think this wonderful house has enjoyed overlooking this willow bank all these years... that's it! I've got a name! Oh my darling new home, I'm going to call you Willow Bank House!" With a gleeful smile she went downstairs.

The birds joined her as always for breakfast and the sun shone brightly in the pale blue sky. There were just a few fluffy white clouds, but she enjoyed watching them slowly change shape as they floated by.

***

Later that morning she set off towards the village taking a sturdy shoulder bag with her. Peering through the window of the Miraford Arms she was pleased to see Jim and TJ. She bought drinks and joined them at their table.

"Oh cheers lass. We were just about to get a refill. You are obviously a mind reader!" Jim chuckled.

"We're waiting for Angela to come. Do you want me to order you anything?"

She shook her head slightly. "No thanks Jim, I've already organised a sandwich. I had breakfast earlier so I didn't want much, err... why are you laughing?"

"You haven't had an Arms sandwich before then?"

She replied slowly "No – why?"

He looked innocent and gave a slight shrug of his shoulders. "Oh, er, nothing."

The barmaid arrived at the table. "There you go Jim, two ploughmans. Yours is just coming."

"Thanks Angela. Looks lovely."

She reappeared with another plate. Jennifer stared open mouthed. "Err, thank you."

"Enjoy your meals." Angela smiled and returned to the bar.

"I thought I just ordered a prawn sarnie – whew!"

She studied the food before her. There were six triangular cut quarters of sandwich filled to bursting with prawns. Alternating brown and white bread, these were surrounded with colourful salad of every description and two large pieces of lemon wedges. There was also a large portion of crisps – just for good measure!

Jim gave a little laugh. "Do you want some help lass?"

"I just don't know where to start!"

Jim pointed at one of the end sandwiches. "That looks as good as anywhere, and I know that Angela has boxes so you can take home whatever you can't eat now."

"Oh, clever lady. What a relief – I can't stand waste. Actually I'll probably be grateful for an easy snack later. I've got to dig up some soil to make the pigs' mud bath!" She started on the sandwich Jim had indicated. "Mmm, yum. This is scrummy."

TJ finished his mouthful. "I'm heading back to the boat in a couple of hours. Do you want help with your digging?"

"Ooh, that would be really nice, if you're sure you don't mind."

He smiled. "Wouldn't have offered if I did!"

"In that case, thanks very much."

As Angela gave the box to Jennifer, she rolled her eyes. "I know, I always put too much on the plates, but I like to give my customers value for money and I'd rather they had too much than not enough!"

"Well, you certainly do both. Thanks a lot. It was lovely; see you again soon."

She said her goodbyes to Soaki and the guys and walked to Market Square. She was well acquainted with the vendors and chatted happily to them as she went from one stall to another. She liked this small, but popular market and had enjoyed observing it from her flat window each Saturday. The sights and sounds had often entertained her. As she wandered, she was drawn to the toy stall. "Mmm? I wonder. Oh why not?"

As she continued, she bumped into Cassie. "Why have you got a bright pink football? Oh, don't tell me – plaything for your piggies!"

Jennifer smiled sheepishly. "I thought they might like it. Anyway, if they don't I'm sure Soaki will."

As they walked on, they chatted and laughed, stopping every so often to buy things. Eventually they reached the fruit and veg stall. "This is what I really came for."

"Hang on mate, I know you want to treat them, but strawberries and asparagus? Are you not going a little too far?"

Jennifer gave her friend a playful smack. "You nutter; they're for me!" They laughed.

By the time they'd finished buying things, Cassie said there was no way Jennifer could carry it all home, so she would give her a lift in the car. As they drove along, they spotted TJ and Soaki. Beep beep. They pulled alongside. "Do you want a lift?"

"Oh cheers; that would be nice."

As they sat in the rear seats, the dog nuzzled at one of the bags. "Soaki, no – leave it!"

Jennifer responded. "She can probably smell the treats I bought for her. When we get home girl – nearly there."

They sat in the garden with their drinks discussing the best way to get prickle-free dirt for the mud bath. Soaki munched happily on one of her dog chews.

"Oh, I forgot to tell you – I'm calling this place Willow Bank House – do you like it?"

They both nodded. "Yeah, I like that. You need a nameplate."

TJ joined in. "Do you remember my Kingfisher sign?"

"Oh yes, it's lovely."

"Well, I did that myself, so if you want, I could do one for here."

Jennifer thanked him. "Well I s'pose we'd better get stuck in with this digging."

"Well it won't do it itself!"

"Mmm, we wish!"

Choosing the bonfire pile nearest to the old pond, they shovelled ashes into a wheelbarrow which TJ took to the bottom corner of the garden. "Oh good, we were right: the fire burnt right down to the soil. Looks quite nice too."

"That explains why everyone has such lovely gardens around here!"

Once they were rid of the ashes, they filled the pond with the freshly dug earth. "If I get the hose Jenny, do you fancy putting the kettle on again?"

"Cor, you sounded just like Jim then! No mistaking you're his grandson!" She chuckled as she went indoors.

***

As Jennifer lay in her bed that night, she looked through the window at the star studded night sky – her thoughts drifted, and once again she felt blessed and so very fortunate to have such wonderful friends. Most of the sparkling gems were a mystery to her, but she did recognize the constellation of Orion. She watched for a while, then turned on her side, pulling the covers around her shoulders. She smiled happily. "Night night Grannifer darling, I love you." Closing her eyes, she drifted into a contentedly deep and very peaceful sleep.

***

Jennifer woke with the morning sun shining brightly through her window. Its warmth kissed her cheeks. She lay for a while enjoying the comfort and listening to the birds singing. "Mmm, this is all very nice but I'd better get up – things to do."

She went downstairs and made her usual coffee. She broke a slice of bread into small pieces for her bird friends and sipped her drink while she watched them. It was a routine she looked forward to each morning. It was still quite early, but she had plans.

Loading the wheelbarrow with the ashes from the other bonfire piles, she proceeded to fill the hole they had dug the previous day. She worked hard for a couple of hours. Pleased with her achievement, she treated herself to a lazy bubble filled bath and then a larger than usual breakfast. "Must be all that work – I'm not usually this hungry in the mornings!" She laughed. "Extras for you too eh!" The birds tucked in again.

Singing along to the radio as she washed up, she was interrupted by a knock at the door. "Hello love."

"Hello Mel. Come in – I'm ready for your inspection. I think I've sorted everything"

They went through to the kitchen. "Coffee?"

He nodded. "Yes please. So you're looking forward to having the pigs then?"

"Oh yes, I've really got into the idea." She gave him his mug and they went to the garden benches.

As they chatted, she pointed to the mud bath. "Hope they like it!"

"Looks fine to me, and the gates seem good too – you've worked hard."

"Thanks, but it was very much a joint effort."

Mel gave his approval to the outbuilding as the 'sty' and laughed at the pink football. "I don't know how long it will last though. They'll probably burst it quite quickly. Well, Jennifer, this looks like a right nice pig holiday park! I'll get the bits out of my truck."

Jennifer and Mel brought in the water trough and also a bale of straw for the pig bedding. "If you keep this in the smaller of the outhouses it will be easy to get to, and with its door still pretty well intact, it'll stay dry."

He showed her how much they needed in their 'bedroom', as Jennifer was calling the temporary sty. "I'll keep the pig-nuts in the kitchen with their fruit and veg."

Mel smiled. "Probably a good idea, or they might try helping themselves!"

They had another cuppa and made final arrangements for the delivery of her piggy guests the following day. "I'll see you tomorrow then."

"Yep, I'm looking forward to it! byeee!" Closing the door, she gave a satisfied sigh.

Unsure as to what to do with the rest of the day, she decided to go and sit by 'her' bit of river and work out a plan of action. The gentle flow of the water had a mesmerising effect which helped her to organise her thoughts without any effort. Before long she was back indoors. She set about preparing things for a meal later on and taking a drink with her, she went upstairs to finish sanding and waxing the chest of drawers.

"Nearly done Grannifer! What do you think darling? Not bad for a first effort eh?"

Having completed her first restoration project, she thought it would be a good idea to start on something else. "Might as well keep the momentum going while I'm in the mood – ah, I know!"

She went downstairs to collect some other decorating bits. "I'll get that old paper off the walls first."

As she reached the bottom stair she was interrupted by the phone ringing. "Hello? Oh hi Cassie … No I'm not really busy. Just about to start doing the bedroom. Thought it would be nice for Mum and Dad when they come. Why? … Ooh, I haven't had Chinese for ages! Tell you what, bring it here and as a treat, I'll let you help me strip the paper! But only if you're good!" She laughed with her friend at the cheeky comment. "Okay love. See you in an hour … byre!"

In the kitchen she spoke out loud to the vegetables she had started to prepare. "Well my dears, you'll have to wait 'til another day – good job I hadn't started cooking you already!" Clearing things away she prepared the table and awaited Cassie's arrival.

Feeling in a slightly mischievous mood, Jennifer found some old magazines. Selecting some of the more colourful pages she pulled them out and made Chinese lanterns which she remembered from her childhood. Hanging them wherever possible, she then cut two large circles from the pages. She then cut each from the outside to the middle. Overlapping the edges by an inch or two, she stapled them creating a low cone shape. Placing one on her head, she giggled - "Voilà, two coolie hats!" She quickly applied make up to give her eyes an oriental look. Then she waited.

***

It was only a few minutes before there was a knock at the door. She quickly donned her 'hat' and opened the door. Putting her hands together she bowed respectfully and, and in her best, but frankly not very good Chinese accent, welcomed her friend. "Most honoulable lady, welcome. Please to enter ma humble abode. You velly welcome!" She bowed again.

Joining in with her friend's play acting, Cassie bowed respectfully in return. "Haa, thank you velly much most honoulable friend!"

They shuffled daintily into the kitchen then, turning to face one another, burst out laughing.

"Where do you conjure up these crazy ideas, and so quickly? I only spoke to you an hour ago!"

"Oh, I don't know… I'm just in a daft mood. Oh, I made you a hat too."

Cassie placed it on her head. "Mmm, perfect fit!"

They dished up the meal and settled at the table to eat, chatting away as they did so.

Finishing their meal they collected together the things required to strip the wallpaper. Heading up the staircase, Cassie couldn't help enquiring "Jennifer, I thought we were just getting paper off the walls!"

"Yeah, we are."

"So why have you got a squeezy mop and bucket?"

"To soak the paper. It should help it to come off more easily. You'll see!"

In the bedroom Jennifer wetted the sponges of the mop and applied it over the walls. "See? It's a lot easier and safer than standing on something and stretching!"

Cassie smiled. "Don't tell me – one of your Grannifer's ideas?"

"How'd you guess? And it's quicker too!"

They waited for a short while, then started pulling the paper off. "Give you a race – your wall against mine!"

"Okay, loser does the washing up!"

"You're on – and the winner makes coffee!"

"Hey, that's not fair; you've already started!" They chuckled.

It was about an hour later. Cassie cheered "Finished my wall! Nar, nar – I won!" She helped Jennifer get the last bits from her wall. "Come on mate, break time."

In the kitchen, they agreed "Shouldn't take too long to finish off. We've made good headway. Thanks ever so for helping Cassie."

Her friend smiled. "That's okay; I enjoyed it."

***

Happy with the knowledge that the first room was prepared and ready, Jennifer lay in bed that night thinking about how she would decorate it. As she filtered the various ideas and what she would need to buy, she pictured the finished room in her mind's eye. Before long she had drifted off to sleep.

With the warmth of the morning sun once again acting like a wake up call, she smiled happily. "Oh good, a lovely sunny day to welcome my piggies."

She went downstairs and, with coffee and toast in hand, proceeded to tell the birds about the pigs.

Jennifer busied herself throughout the morning, checking and re-checking that everything was ready for her new residents. "Oh, this is crazy. I've sorted their bedroom, the mud bath, the food bath is ready, the gate is shut and the water trough is filled." She drummed her fingers on the table. "Oh Grannifer, I'm so excited, I can't wait for them to arrive."

With a couple of hours still to go before Mel was due, she decided to distract herself from clock watching and made an actual list of things needed for the bedroom. The walls were in good condition, so she would paint them and give some added interest with stencils. Grannifer had details of stencilling in her book. Jennifer's experience in interior design would deal with the furnishing requirements. She made a sketch of her ideas and was pleased with the potential design for the finished article.

"Just got to do it all for real now. Only thirty five minutes to go. Mmm… I know what to do to chill me out." She made a coffee and took it to her spot on the riverbank.

With about five minutes to go before Mel was due to arrive, Jennifer went excitedly to the front gate to welcome her guests. Clutching a bowl filled with quartered apples, she peered down the lane. "Oh good, here they come!" She waved happily. "Hi Mel, how ya doing?"

"Hello Jennifer. We're okay, you?"

"Oh yes, I'm fine, but I feel fit to burst with anticipation, I do hope they like me."

Mel chuckled as he got out of his truck. "I'm sure they'll love you. Right, let's get these little ladies into their new home!"

They got the pigs into the garden where Jennifer kept them distracted with apples whilst Mel secured the gate. They walked around the outside of the house to the back part of the garden. The pigs seemed to be enjoying investigating their new residence.

"Aren't they lovely Mel? They're so cute. Do they have names?"

Mel shook his head. "We haven't given them any, but you can if you want to. Might be a good idea not to get too attached to 'em though."

"Yeah, I know, but you know what I'm like!" She gave a slightly apologetic smile. "What breed are they?"

"They're a mix of Tamworth and Gloucester Old Spot."

"Mmm, don't think I'll get any names from those… but we'll see. I'll watch them for a day or two and see if anything appropriate comes to mind."

Mel sat at the garden table on one of the benches while Jennifer made drinks. He called in to the kitchen. "They seem happy to be here. They're having a good nosey around!"

Jennifer joined him. As they chatted, Mel ran through a few details about feeding her new friends. "So you know how to call them, yes?"

"Yes, I rattle the bucket and call 'pigs, pigs, pigs' in a high pitched voice."

"Yep, that should do it. And you got the bath for their vegetables, but they are inquisitive creatures so they'd probably enjoy looking for it on the ground. Plus it'll get them munching away the roots and stuff. After all, that is why you've got 'em isn't it?"

"Oh yes. Do you know, I'd almost forgotten that!"

They laughed. "Well, if you're okay with everything, I'll get on home. Give me a ring if you need anything."

They said their goodbyes and Jennifer returned to the bench. On her own now, she felt a bit anxious. "Please Grannifer, help me to look after them well."

Taking a deep breath, she watched each pig to see if it had any distinguishing marks or attitudes which might distinguish one from the other. She was surprised to notice that, far from looking identical, she quite quickly worked out who was who. "Oh, this is fun – now you need some names. Let me see… now ladies, you're all quite orangey but 'you' missie are a bit more pink, so obviously, you'll be Pinky, and that one has a sticky up ear and a very curly tail, so you can be Perky. Not very original I know, but easy to remember and they suit you! Now what about you other two?"

One of the pigs was nuzzling at the ground near Jennifer's feet and she found herself scratching the back of its neck almost like petting a dog. This amused Jennifer and the little pig seemed to be enjoying the attention. With the closeness and comparative stillness of the animal, Jennifer was able to study its markings more intricately. "Oh look – the spots on your back look just like a flower, and here on top of your leg. Oh how sweet. Mmm let's see – ooh I know, Grannifer's favourite – Primrose! Yes, that'll be your name. Now then, three down, one to go."

She studied the remaining pig. Nothing sprang to mind. "Oh well, something will come to me – no rush."

Deciding that it would soon be time for their afternoon feed, Jennifer went indoors to prepare the fruit and veg. Singing along to the radio, she cut up the food into pieces. Suddenly she was aware of something beside her. Looking to her right she saw one of the pigs with its front trotters on the bench and its snout trying to reach the food on the table. "Hey you little pickle, what do you think you're doing? You shouldn't be in here. Come on – out!"

She ushered it back in to the garden and shut the door. "Well! I reckon she'll be one to keep an eye on, and I think she's just got her name, cheeky little madam. So we've got Pinky, Perky, Primrose and Pickle!"

She finished preparing the food then when outside. "Well, here goes."

Rattling the nuts in a basket and using a high pitched voice she called out "Here piggy pig pig pigs, here pig pig pig pigs!"

To her amazement and delight all four came running towards her. As she scattered handfuls of pig-nuts followed by fruit and vegetables, she chuckled heartily. "Wa-hey – it worked! Oh, this is wonderful. Ooh, camera – got to get a shot of this!" She watched them for a while and then went back in to the kitchen.

"Must make sure I shut the door properly." She checked it was secure and began preparing her own dinner.

Later that evening, Jennifer returned to the garden to make sure the pigs knew where their new 'bedroom' was. She had no need to worry. As she peered into the temporary sty, she saw all four of them snuggled in amongst the straw. She smiled and in a hushed voice she whispered "Night night my darlings. Sleep well."

It had been an eventful day and Jennifer was satisfied with how things had gone but felt extremely tired. She tidied the kitchen and made herself a night-time drink, then made her way up to bed. It was not long before she fell into a deep and very contented sleep.

***

Next day, her breakfast routine took somewhat longer than her usual bits for herself and crumbs for her bird friends, but seeing the pigs already rummaging around the garden was, she thought, a nice way to start the day. Rattling the bucket, she repeated the previous days call "Here piggy pig pig pigs." They came scurrying to her.

"Hello Pickle – trust you to be the first! Ah, good morning Perky, hello Pinky and good day to you too Primrose."

As she scattered the food she thought how appropriate Primrose's name was. She seemed to have a daintier gait than the others. "Yes, you really suit your name!"

As she watched them, and the birds, Jennifer wondered if she should get other more permanent animals in her life. "I do so enjoy them. Mmm, this will need to be thought out properly."

Her train of thought was interrupted by the phone ringing. "Hello. Oh hi Mel… yes everything's fine…" She chatted to him for a while then returned to her coffee. "Well my little ladies, I've checked that you'll be okay to be on your own, so I'm going in to Lamton tomorrow. Oh crikey, there's the phone again!" She didn't mind the second interruption – it was Cassie. Jennifer confirmed that she was in for the rest of the day and looked forward to her friend coming round. Although it was only a few days since she'd seen her, it felt like a long time – so much had happened.

Hearing the familiar sound of the 2CV engine followed by its friendly 'beep beep', Jennifer opened the front door and greeted her chum. "Hiya, kettle's on."

"Oh great, I'm gasping."

They went through to the kitchen. "Go out and meet the ladies – I'll be there in a mo with the coffees."

Cassie went outside. "Oh, Jennifer, they're lovely." She sat at the table. Jennifer joined her. "Coo, I need this. I've been in the studio since early and I'm as dry as a bone. Had this statue I needed to finish, then Mum wanted me to call in to the Tea Room and the old girl needed petrol, and Paul asked if I'd give him a lift to the station. He had to go to his parents for something or other and... Oh sorry mate, I'm babbling aren't I?"

Jennifer laughed. "Just a bit. Drink your coffee and I'll introduce you to the girls."

Cassie enjoyed hearing how her friend had spent the previous day installing her piggy gardeners and thought their names suited them. They continued chatting and discovered that they both intended to go to town the following day. "Great, so I'll pick you up at ten, we'll have some lunch when we get back and then we can start painting."

Later, as Jennifer prepared the pig food, Cassie went to her car. She returned with two large cartons of milk. "Mum gave me these for the girls – to be honest I think she deliberately ordered too much so she could give it to them!"

"Oh that's lovely. Please give her a hug from us, and a big thank you."

They went into the garden and Cassie was given the honour of calling them for their dinner. She giggled with delight as Pinky, Perky, Primrose and Pickle all ran towards them. "This is such fun – aren't they just so cute?"

"Yeah, I'm loving them. I just hope the novelty doesn't wear off!"

The following morning Jennifer woke early. While the pigs ate breakfast, she checked the water trough and mud bath, then cleaned out their sty/bedroom. She got ready for her trip out and while she had her breakfast, spoke to her girls. "Now, listen ladies, you've got to be good while I'm not here – no getting up to mischief!" She looked specifically at Pickle. Smiling, she went indoors.

Cassie arrived and they got on their way. "I'm really nervous about being away from the house. I s'pose this is like the first time a parent leaves their child for the first time. I hope they'll be okay."

Cassie reassured her friend. "They'll be fine. It may be the first time you have left them, but Mel didn't sit and babysit 'em did he?"

"Yes, I'm sure you're right. Anyway, why did you have to go into town?"

"It's Mum's birthday next week and I want to get her something nice."

"Oh, me too. Helen's been so kind to me. Are you planning a party?"

"Well, Dad and I were thinking of a special meal, but I reckon a party would be better."

"You can have it at my place if you like – she wouldn't know anything about it then!"

"Brilliant – I'll double check with Dad."

As they walked along Lamton High Street, the girls discussed possible gifts for Helen. "Does she like jewellery?"

"Oh yes. But I think Dad's got an idea along those lines. He mentioned maybe getting an eternity ring."

"Ooh, how lovely, and so romantic!"

"Yeah – he can be an old softie like that." Cassie smiled thoughtfully.

"I could still get earrings or a necklace, I s'pose."

They stopped by a jeweller's window. "Ah, now they're nice." Jennifer pointed out some sapphire and crystal earrings."

"Yes, they're lovely and sapphire's her birthstone too!"

"Come on, let's go in and have a closer look.

"Good morning ladies." The smart young assistant welcomed them. "How may I help you?"

They told him about the earrings which he brought to the counter for closer inspection.

"They are very pretty Cassie. What do you reckon?"

The young man interrupted, "Would you be interested in seeing the full set?"

"Er, yes please."

Cassie turned to her friend and whispered "This sounds like it could be getting expensive; not that mum's not worth it, but..."

"There you are madam – our Moonlight Collection, only just in. I don't expect it will be here for long – it's quite stunning isn't it?"

"Mmm, yes. Do you think you could put it to one side for half an hour while I think about it please?"

He agreed and the girls left.

"I really like them but… Oh Jennifer, I don't know that I can afford it all!"

"Would your mum like it?"

"Like it? She'd love it!"

"Well, how about I buy one bit and you and Paul give her the rest? Yeah?"

"Oh mate, are you sure?"

"Yes of course, and that solves my problem of what to get for her. Come on, let's get them before we change our minds."

They returned to the shop and bought the sparkling set of earrings, bracelet and necklace.

"Wow, I thought I'd be hunting for hours, and lo and behold – first shop we looked in and bingo!"

They laughed as they walked towards the large department store. "Hopefully I'll have the same luck in here."

As they reached the floor with the furniture, the girls headed towards the area set aside as bedrooms. They were immediately approached by a middle-aged man. "Good morning. May I help you?"

"Er not at the moment thank you. I'd like to look around first."

Jennifer looked at Cassie. "I wish at least they'd let you get up to the first bed before they pounce!"

"Yeah, I know he's doing his job but it's nice if you have at least a minute first."

They wandered around pushing their hands down on various mattresses.

"You got a better idea of how they feel if you lie down on them." The girls looked behind them to where the voice had come from. An older lady smiled at them.

"I didn't know if we were allowed to."

"Of course my dear – how would you know if it was right for you otherwise?" She went to walk away.

"Actually – could you help me please?" Jennifer liked the fact that this lady was not pressure selling.

Miriam turned out to be the most helpful assistant, and after listening to Jennifer, showed her several beds. "Actually my dear, I don't know if you'd be interested, but we have an ex display model which is almost half price, and it is still almost perfect."

"When you say, almost perfect… what's wrong with it?"

"There's a tiny scuff at the base of the head and it is minus its casters." She looked around her, then in a hushed voice, "They actually

71

sell these casters in the hardware department downstairs."

Jennifer returned the smile she'd been given by Miriam. "What do you think, Cassie?"

"Worth a look mate."

They were delighted with the divan and Jennifer followed Miriam to her desk where they sorted the order and arranged delivery. "Thank you Miriam. You've been most helpful."

They said their goodbyes and went to the next floor down. "Right, now for the paint and brushes."

Cassie pushed the trolley while Jennifer selected the bits from the shelves, checking her list from time to time.

"You're very organized, mate."

"Grannifer's training. She always swore by a list. If I didn't do it this way, I'd be all over the place."

They made their way to the check out. "I'll pay for this lot, then I think it's time for a cuppa. What do you reckon?"

Cassie nodded."Don't have to ask me twice!"

Enjoying their drinks, they also shared a Danish pastry. "I know we're having lunch when we get back, but this looked too scrummy to leave on the counter." They laughed as they tucked in.

"Could we pop into the reclamation yard on the way home?"

"Yes, of course. Anything special?"

"Mmm, possibly. I think I remember an old metal headboard thing when we went before. If it's still there… well, we'll see."

Cassie looked at her watch. "We've got… forty three minutes left on the parking. Do you need much more?"

"No, just about done. I've just got to grab those casters, then quickly into the art department for some card, then that's it." She gave a satisfied smile and they left the café. Laden with armfuls of shopping they happily put everything into the car. "Whew, that was heavier than I thought it would be! Did we get here in time?"

"Yep… and two and a half minutes to spare."

They climbed aboard and made their way to the reclamation yard.

"Hi girls – back again!"

"Hello, yes, I'm hoping you've still got something I saw last time." She remembered seeing the metal bed head. "Oh good – look it's over there. Er, excuse me. Can I have a closer look at that please?"

The assistant came over and moved things out of the way.

"Thank you. How much is it?"

"That's fifty for the whole lot."

Jennifer gulped – "Sorry, did you say 'fifty' for one rusty bed head?"

72

"No love. That's for the whole lot. It's a surround frame. Head and base with side frames.

"Oh, I see." She looked disappointed. "You wouldn't just sell me that bit would you?"

"Sorry love, but I can't really split it."

"I did really only want the head bit. I don't suppose you'd take... er thirty?" She gave him her best 'pretty please' look.

He considered it. "Tell you what – make it thirty five and we'll call it a deal."

Jennifer smiled broadly and gave him a hug. "Oh thank you." She went to the office to pay. "You have my address already, yes?"

"Oh yes Miss Cade. The guys remember you. They don't often get drinks offered, so you are one of their favourite deliveries."

They laughed. "Well, I've nearly always got the kettle on."

Cassie nodded. "She's not joking."

As the girls left, Jennifer called back. "Oh, be careful when they come, to shut the gate please."

"You acquired a dog then?"

"No, four pigs!"

His look of disbelief as he silently mouthed "Pigs", made the girls giggle.

As they drove home Cassie sighed. "I don't know how you do it – fifty down to thirty five!"

"Well, Grannifer always said there's no point getting older if you don't get crafty with it."

"Well, I dread to think what you'll be like when you actually hit old age!"

"Ooh yes. I probably won't be allowed out!" They laughed.

As they pulled up at the end of the lane, Jennifer looked eagerly towards the house. "I can't see any of the girls – I do hope they're all right."

"Let's grab the shopping, then we can get in and put your mind at rest. I think you should have got chickens instead!"

Jennifer looked quizzical. "Huh?"

"Well, you're doing a good impression of a 'mother hen'!"

"Oh, funneee!"

They unloaded the car and went into the house. Jennifer went straight through to the back door. "One, two, three... oh four! Well at least they're all here. I'll check for signs of mischief later!"

They made lunch and sat in the garden to eat. "We did really well today – we've got everything we planned."

73

"Yeah, even Mum's pressie and a rusty old bed frame!"

"Oh look, the birds are looking for crumbs – they seem to know I'll feed them if I'm out here and munching!" Jennifer put some bits on the bird table.

The two friends enjoyed watching them pecking away and the pigs too still amused them. "Right then 'missus', this is all very nice, but it's not getting your room decorated!"

"Ooh, you're such a slave driver!" They laughed and went indoors.

As Jennifer started to pick up the decorating bits, Cassie tutted "Oh darn – I forgot to call Dad about the party." She moved back to the door. "I'll phone him from the garden – I get a better signal outside."

"Why don't you use my landline?"

Cassie came back and went towards the hallway. "Cheers love... hey this is a weird vacuum cleaner."

Jennifer joined her friend. "Eh? Oh, that's not a cleaner – I hired it the other day. It's a sander. I've been doing the floor boards. I'm going to stain them with varnish... hopefully it will look quite nice."

Cassie looked impressed. Jennifer started to take things upstairs while Cassie chatted to Don. "So what do you think Dad, do you reckon Mum would like a party? No, not a problem, it was her suggestion. Okey dokey. I'll tell Jennifer. She'll be really pleased. Right, see you later, love you, byeee."

She helped to take more things upstairs. "Er mate, we've just had lunch so why have you got half an onion in a saucer on the windowsill?"

"Another of Grannifer's tips... it somehow soaks up the paint fumes. Clever huh?"

"Mmm, bet it makes dinner tasty!"

"Oh gosh no. You don't eat it afterwards!"

They put on some old clothes and started to paint. "Cor, that wind has got up. Look at the trees blowing about."

"Yeah, well at least we're in here."

Cassie started to relay various songs with any reference to wind. Jennifer stopped painting. "What the hell is that racket?"

"Charming! I thought I had quite a good voice. I was in the school choir!"

"Not you're singing silly – listen!"

They both moved towards the door hearing loud crashes from downstairs. Suddenly serious - "Oh God Jen, I think you've got burglars!"

She went to go onto the landing but Jennifer pulled her back. "If we're going to tackle whoever that is, we'd better arm ourselves... just in case." Cassie nodded. They grabbed the nearest 'weapons' they could lay their hands on and crept nervously down the stairs. They reached the kitchen door. "They sound like they're in here. Ready?"

Jennifer took a deep scared breath and put her hand on the handle. With a worried expression, she looked towards Cassie. In a hushed voice, she counted - "One... two... three... now!"

They burst into the kitchen shouting loudly to frighten the intruders. Their imaginations had run riot on the journey down the stairs, but far from the gang of cut-throat robbers they were expecting, there was no one in the room. However, there was a sea of carnage. Cupboard doors were open and the contents of flour, rice and cereal packets were strewn over the floor. The vegetable rack was over turned and its food was everywhere.

"Oh Jennifer, what a mess! But at least the burglars have gone."

They heard a noise under the table and peered cautiously. "Pickle! You bad girl!"

Pickle looked up briefly then continued to munch on the apple she had selected from her rampage. The girls looked at each other. "I knew she was going to be trouble!"

"How did she get in though? Oh crikey – I bet I didn't shut the door tight when I was going to call Dad. Sorry mate!"

"Can't be helped – I s'pose the wind blew it open and Pickle just took advantage."

"At least it wasn't some vicious intruder."

"Fat lot of good we'd have been."

They looked at each other's 'weapons' still in hand. "So, were you going to paint them to death?"

"Well these brushes were the first things I found."

"Well, what about you with your lamb's wool roller. I suppose you were going to tickle them into submission!"

They started laughing. "Well, I think while we're here, we might as well have a coffee."

"Good idea. You put the kettle on and I'll get Pickle out. You really did give her the right name!"

As the girls had their drinks, Jennifer pondered. "I think I'm going to try and make a 'piggy cake'. It seems a shame to waste all that food. If I put enough liquid in for the rice and eggs to set it... what do you think?"

"Ugh, it's been on the floor!"

Jennifer nodded towards the pigs who were chomping at roots. "Somehow I don't think they'll mind a little bit of dust from my kitchen when they must eat soil by the kilo every day! Anyway, I washed it this morning. Cheeky!"

"Sorry, I didn't mean to offend!"

"I'll check with Mel just to be sure."

They found it surprisingly easy to sweep the floor clean. "Lucky it was all dry stuff. Imagine if she'd tipped a bottle of oil or something too!"

"Ooh don't – I'd be clearing it for weeks!"

A bucket of hot soapy water and another blitz with the mop soon had it spick and span again. Making doubly sure that the door was shut, they returned to their decorating. As they painted, they discussed what things they needed for Helen's party. "I'll make a birthday cake if you like."

Cassie looked dubiously at her friend. "Promise me you won't get it muddled with the pigs' one." She smiled cheekily.

"I'll try not to."

"Don't forget your speciality…"

"Of course, and I'll make it extra special – fruit soaked in brandy first!"

"Ooh yummy – bags I be taste tester!"

Getting their 'sensible' heads on, the two friends continued to discuss various ideas for the party whilst carrying on with the decorating.

"I like these paint pads Jennifer; they're really good for covering walls quickly. Is this another of Grannifer's ideas?"

"Actually, no not this time. A friend introduced me to them at my old job."

"Oh well, just one of the few things your lovely lady didn't teach you!"

"Yeah, Grannifer's tips were more old fashioned ways of doing things." She had a wistful expression. "I do like the traditional ways when I can use them, but some modern ideas can often be better. I have got a brilliant way to fill in the gaps in the floorboards though. A Grannifer special."

Cassie stopped painting. "Oh yes, and what does that involve? Sounds like a job for Jim's woodwork skills!"

Jennifer smiled, "No, nothing so energetic. For the bigger gaps you use string dipped in wax – that helps it to be waterproof as well as filling the gap, and for smaller cracks and holes you make a mixture of sawdust and glue. Hey presto – one floor ready for staining and a top coat of varnish. Good eh?"

"Excellent, but start in the corner furthest away from the door!" They laughed at the idea of getting stuck in a corner. "I know it sounds funny, but I have heard of people doing it!"

They continued and were soon finished with the main covering on the walls.

"I like the colour you've chosen."

"Yeah, me too. I'm glad you like it. I thought the pale mauve would suit male or female guests, and I'm going with rich deep purple accessories. With the bedstead and a curtain pole in black wrought iron effect, I thought it should look quite nice."

"Sounds good to me – I can't wait to see it finished."

Jennifer glanced at her watch. "Oh crikey, it's nearly ten to five – I should have fed the pigs at four!"

"Ooh, you naughty lady – if you're not careful, your gardeners will be going on strike!"

They went to the kitchen. "It won't take long with both of us preparing it."

"Not that Pickle is bothered about it being late – she's already had a mid-meal snack!"

"Yeah, honestly I can't believe what a cheeky little madam she is."

Jennifer called the pigs and Cassie made a drink. "They've already made a good start on the stubble haven't they?"

"Yes, I just need to scatter their food further down the garden each day, but yes, they're doing a good job."

They stopped chatting as they heard a voice calling from the bottom gate.

"Knock knock, is it OK to come in?"

"Hello TJ. Yes, come and join us."

"I've got Soaki with me. Is that OK? With the piggies, yeah?"

"Yes, she'll be fine. I checked already with Mel. They are all fine because of his dogs."

TJ and Soaki came up the garden, the dog investigating the pigs with curiosity. "I bet she's thinking what a strange canine each of these is."

TJ and the girls were amused by her reaction. "She's good with them though, isn't she?"

"Here you are Jenny, the main reason for our visit."

He handed her a parcel. With a questioning look she took it from him. "Oh, thank you... what is it?"

"Open it and see."

Untying the string and unwrapping the paper, she gasped in amazement at the gift. "Oh TJ, my name plate. It's beautiful. Cassie, look at this!"

"Wow mate, that's really lovely. You should do these and sell them.

That's nicer than any I've seen in the shops."

Jennifer interrupted. "Talking of which, how much do I owe you?"

"Cor no, I don't want anything. Have it as a house warming pressie." He smiled.

In disbelief she got up and gave him a hug. "Oh, thank you so much."

She gazed down again at the varnished piece of wood. Its ornately painted words 'Willow Bank House' were surrounded with dainty flowers and a riverside scene at the bottom, with willow trees framing the outer edges. "It's so delicately painted. Are you a professional artist?

He chuckled. "No, I just enjoy it as a hobby."

"Well, I'm very impressed" Cassie added to the accolade.

"It's actually willow wood – I found a broken off branch so I used it for the plaque." He patted Soaki who was now sitting by his side. "So how are you getting on with the pigs?"

Jennifer and Cassie both gave expressions which were smiles, but with a slightly dubious hint to them. "Well, mostly OK, but we have a bit of a mischief maker in the group." They proceeded to tell TJ about Pickle's exploits.

As the evening wore on, it started to get rather chilly. "That wind is getting up again. Shall we go indoors?"

Cassie and TJ agreed and the three friends went inside, closely followed by Soaki. They continued their ideas about the surprise party for Helen. "I'll let Dad know what we've thought of and see if he's OK with everything. Then we can start inviting people."

Jennifer gave an excited shrug of her shoulders. "I'm really looking forward to it – I love parties!"

The next few days seemed to fly by as Jennifer busied herself with the decorating. She used a sharp craft knife to cut shapes in the card and stencilled shapes of leaves and flowers randomly over the walls using subtle shades of deep purple, green and bronze. She was pleased with the effect, especially when she added tiny highlights of white and gold which were only really noticeable when a light caught them. She particularly enjoyed the early morning glints from the sunshine. With the room totally empty of any furniture, it was with delight and amazement to her just how quickly she accomplished her first room in her new home.

"There Grannifer, nearly all done – just the bed and curtain rails to sort, then it's in with the furnishings and I'm ready for Mum and Dad's visit! What do you think, my darling?"

She smiled as she imagined the encouraging words that Grannifer always gave her.

***

All too soon it was Saturday again and Jennifer looked forward to her weekly visit to the market. She'd arranged to meet Cassie outside her old flat and after the early morning routine sorting everything for the pigs and the birds, she collected her bags and picked up her list of 'things to get'. Attached to this she had stapled a sheet of paper with splodges of paint on. This was her colour swatch of those she'd used in the guest room.

"Another of your practical ideas to save the guesswork getting it all wrong, eh darling?" Her little comments out loud helped to keep Grannifer close to her and, although her loss was still incredibly painful, these occasional chats gave her comfort.

As she walked into the village, the sounds of the market were audible before it came into view. A little buzz of excitement made Jennifer quicken her pace slightly. Seeing Cassie ahead she gave a wave. "Been waiting long?"

Cassie shook her head. "No, only a few minutes. We've both timed it well."

They chatted in their usual non-stop manner as they walked along. As they strolled around the market, the girls enjoyed their weekly catch-up with the stall holders. As they approached the fabric stall, Jennifer beamed as the lady running it held up a bale of material. "I think this is the colour you were asking for. Is it right?"

Jennifer took the colour swatch from her bag. "It looks about it. Let's see how it compares."

They put the paint samples alongside the bale. "Oh, it's perfect. Thank you so much"

Smiling, the woman asked how much Jennifer required.

"Well rather a lot actually. How much would you want for the whole lot?"

"Well I suppose I could do you a special price for such a large quantity. How about fifty pounds?"

Jennifer did a quick mental calculation. "Yes, that sounds fine. Thank you. I'll need more stuff in the future. Are you always here?"

"Most weeks, but not during the winter."

They completed their transaction. "Right, I'll make sure I buy everything I need before you go into hibernation then!"

They laughed and said their goodbyes. As they continued from one stall to another, Cassie stopped.

"Hey, look at that one there!" She pointed to a vendor with a whole stand full of party trinkets. "I've never seen him here before. Come on Jennifer; I think he'll be useful for next Friday's do for Mum."

They went excitedly to the new stall. They collected together a mass of things: everything from table decorations and wall hangings to balloons and party poppers.

"This is wonderful, and just at the right time too."

The salesman put everything into bags and the girls moved on to the fruit and veg stall. "When we've done here, do you fancy getting some lunch at the Arms?"

Jennifer nodded. "Oh yes, that would be lovely. Feels like ages since I've been in there."

Very much aware of Miraford Arms plentiful portions, Cassie and Jennifer decided to share a lunch between them. As Angela brought the well-laden platter to the table, they showed her the items they had bought for the party. They were shocked when she snatched the bags from them and took them towards the bar. As she reached the counter, she said in a louder than usual voice "Hello Helen. Hi Don. Long time no see." She looked across to the girls table and mouthed "Phew" and exaggeratedly wiped her brow.

Cassie, in response mouthed, "Thank you."

Seeing her parents round the corner, she called out "Mum, Dad, hiya. Want to join us?"

Smiling, Helen pulled up a chair. Don came soon after with a tray of drinks. "Got anything good at the market?"

Jennifer showed her the fabric. "Just this really, and stuff from the greengrocer's stall. What about you? Did you get a chance to look around?"

Helen shook her head. "Not enough time. Don insisted on bringing me out for a pre-birthday lunch, but then I'm back to the tea rooms."

Jennifer looked interested. "Oh, your birthday. When's that Helen?"

"Not 'til Friday... but this is the only day we've got a break at the same time."

"Well, happy birthday for Friday."

Helen smiled. "Thank you dear."

Noticing that Jennifer and Cassie had finished their lunch and were starting to say their goodbyes to Helen and Don, Angela called across to them waving a large plastic bag tied at the top. "Don't forget your bits for the pigs!" she winked.

"Oh yes, thank you Angela." Jennifer collected the bag, saying in a hushed voice "Thanks again. That was quick thinking on your part."

"You're welcome. Can't spoil the surprise, can we?"

The girls giggled as they got outside. "Cor, that was close – good old Angela eh?"

Chapter 5

Arriving back at Willow Bank House, Jennifer rushed upstairs with her bail of fabric. "I've got to see what it looks like against the walls… Oh Cassie, it's perfect."

Now standing in the bedroom doorway, "Mmm, it looks beautiful, I can't wait to see it finished."

"Well, hopefully it will be done by next weekend… Mum and Dad should be here by then."

"Will they be here in time for the party? It would be great if they could join us."

Jennifer bit her lip. "Oh crumbs, I forgot it was all happening at the same time! Gosh, it's going to be one heck of a busy week."

With this realization hitting home, Jennifer suggested getting the birthday cake made. "I've already got the fruit soaking so it won't take long to get the rest done."

"Why are you soaking the fruit? And in what?"

Jennifer smiled at her friend. "Soaking the dried fruit makes it really nice and juicy. I'll let your nose tell you what liquid I've used when we get downstairs."

In the kitchen, a lidded container was placed on the table. "Open it and take a sniff!"

Cassie did as instructed. "Cor mate – am I supposed to drive home after that? Smells like a brewery!"

Jennifer laughed. "If the end result is only half as good as Grannifer's, it should be really good. I'm using her recipe." She started getting the other ingredients out. "Oh bother, it's time for me to feed the girls!"

Cassie interrupted. "I'll do that if you want to carry on with the cake."

"Oh cheers, that would be a big help."

They went about their tasks and before long Cassie returned to the kitchen. She rolled up her sleeves and washed her hands. "Right, second in command reporting for duty, sah!" She mockingly saluted. "What can I do to help?"

"OK, you asked for it... take a turn in beating this!"

Jennifer passed over a bowl containing some soft dark brown sugar and some butter. "That's got to be beaten until it's almost white!"

"You what? It's brown; how do you get it to go white?"

"Just keep beating; you'll see! It's hard work but... trust me, it does get paler and paler."

They took it in turns and Cassie was amazed at the result.

"Now, we add beaten eggs, a little at a time, then the flour and fruit. We fold the flour carefully with a metal spoon so we don't knock the air out."

Cassie smiled. "That sounded as if it was the way your Grannifer explained it to you, yes?"

Jennifer with moist eyes nodded and took a deep breath to compose herself. "Now then, I've got the cake tin lined and the oven on, so we put the mixture in – and then put the kettle on. While I do the coffees you can lick the bowl as a reward for being a good little helper!"

They laughed as Cassie dropped her hands and pretended to be a little girl. "Ooh, fank you Mummy!"

Jennifer checked the time. "Five o'clock I reckon. With the oven on for a few hours I ought to make use of it... I'm going to give the pigs' cake a go!"

Cassie looked bemused. "''It won't be as intense as Mum's birthday cake, will it?"

"Cor no, I'm just going to mix everything together and hope for the best! I've got to cook the rice first though, I think."

"Isn't it all muddled together? Don't say we've got to pick out every single grain."

Jennifer smiled. "No, not at all. I had a brainwave the other day – look." She showed her friend three containers. "I used a sieve to get the flour out, then I used a colander which let the rice through but not the bigger bits of cereal. Hey presto, separated ingredients!"

"That's genius! Well done mate."

Cassie started cooking the rice while Jennifer beat some eggs. She

83

then added the flour. When the rice had cooked, the girls stirred it into the mixture. Finally, they put in the cereal and chopped up vegetables. After piling it into a large roasting tin, they put it in the oven.

"Oh well, they'll either eat it or they won't. I'll find out tomorrow eh?"

They tidied the kitchen and then sat chatting about the surprise party for Helen.

"How long did you say this cake has to cook?"

Cassie looked with disbelief at Jennifer's answer. "Several hours? You are joking!"

"Well, it could easily be that long. I've got this on a slightly higher heat so probably five should do it."

"Wow, that's a lot of cooking!"

Jennifer checked the time. "Actually, it's had a couple of hours already. Time to put its paper lid on so it doesn't get too brown." She removed it from the oven and put layers of greaseproof paper on top. After returning it to the heat, she took out the roasting tin. "Well, the piggy cake looks done!"

Cassie looked on. "Mmm, yummy... I hope they appreciate all the effort!"

"Well, it's got two chances – either they'll eat it or they won't. I'll let you know in the morning." She smiled and shrugged her shoulders.

As the evening progressed, the girls realized they hadn't actually had any dinner. "To be honest, I don't think I can face any more cooking."

Cassie agreed. "Tell you what, how about I jump in the old girl and get something from the chippy?"

A broad smile adorned Jennifer's face. "Oh yes, that would be lovely. I'll get things ready here, butter some bread, and get the plates warmed."

Cassie looked at her with a mock serious expression. "I'll only be a few minutes... I don't want to get back and find you dressed up like a fisherman!"

Jennifer looked quizzical. "Oh, you're thinking of the Chinese meal – no, you're all right... I'm too tired tonight!"

Before long, Cassie returned. As she stepped into the hallway, she closed her eyes and took an ecstatic sniff. "Oh mate... if the cake tastes half as good as it smells, it's gonna be amazing!"

Jennifer tried to look humble and grateful at the compliment, but found herself agreeing heartily. "Yes I must say, I reckon you could be right. Good old Grannifer hasn't let us down."

They dished up the dinner and tucked in. "Oh, this takes me back to being a kid. We often had our choice from the chip shop as a Friday night treat."

Jennifer nodded. "Yeah, us too. I reckon loads of people did. I tell you what I enjoyed even more… being by the seaside and sitting on the beach and eating out of the paper."

"Oh yes, I haven't done that for ages. How about we do that soon? We'll get this weekend out of the way, then think about a day trip."

Jennifer grinned. "Gosh I'd like that… can we go somewhere with a pier? I love piers!"

Cassie smiled. "Yeah of course… wherever you like."

As was the usual thing for the two friends, they chatted non-stop and before they had time to notice, it was nearly eleven o'clock. "Good grief, look at the clock. I reckon we should check the cake. I think it should be ready now."

Jennifer carefully lifted the tin from the oven.

"Well, it looks great," Cassie commented with a satisfied smile. "But how do you know if it's cooked in the middle?"

Jennifer had one of her 'well according to Grannifer' expressions. "There are a couple of ways. Firstly you listen to it to see if it's singing."

Cassie looked dubious. Jennifer explained. "It's a kind of hissing noise, but the other way is to stick a hot skewer or thin knife in – if it comes out clean… then it's done!"

They both put their heads near the hot tin. Cassie started to giggle. "I think it's forgotten the words of the song!"

"Shush – how can I hear if you keep laughing?"

As her words trailed away, Jennifer started laughing too. "Oh well, looks like it's hot skewer time!"

The girls played make-believe as if they were performing a surgical operation. Broad smiles danced on their faces. "We have success!"

"Brilliant, and you let it cool in the tin you say?"

"Uh-huh, so I'll do that in the morning, then it's all systems go to get it marzipan-ed and iced. I hope Helen likes simple; I'm not very good at the decorating thing!"

Cassie reassured Jennifer. "Don't worry, we'll tackle it together."

"Phew, thank goodness for that!"

"Well I'd better make a move home, I've got a sculpture to get on with in the morning."

They said their goodbyes and after waving farewell, Jennifer locked up and went to bed. It didn't take long for her to fall asleep

***

As she woke the following morning, Jennifer lay enjoying the aroma of the previous night's baking which still wafted through the house. The morning sunlight created spectrums of colour that danced on the walls.

She went down to the kitchen and started to prepare the breakfast. With a dubious expression, Jennifer took the tin with the 'piggy cake' in and cut four pieces. "Well, here goes, let's see what they reckon."

Back in the garden she gave her usual call and the pigs ran towards her. "Hello Pickle – trust you to get here first!" She gave the cake to the most mischievous of her girls. It disappeared in a trice.

"Well, you obviously like it – good job too since it was you that caused it! Here you are Perky." The second portion was devoured with similar gusto. Primrose and Pinky gave similar accolade to the gastronomic creation, which pleased Jennifer no end.

"Mmm, perhaps I'll give the recipe to Mel?" She chuckled as she scattered the rest of the food around. While the pigs ate, Jennifer did the rest of the jobs piggy-connected: topping up their water trough, cleaning out the sty etc.

Later, having sorted out her own breakfast, she put crumbs of the piggy cake on to the bird table. Before long this was also being tucked in to by her feathered friends. "Looks like it's a hit with the birds as well," she mused. "Perhaps I ought to patent it… first of all, get a pig to run riot in your kitchen, then sweep up the chaos and cook it." She laughed at the idea.

As she unwrapped Helen's birthday cake, she removed it from the tin and gave a satisfied smile. "I think we might just have a success here as well, Grannifer – thank you for the recipe darling."

Taking the marzipan and apricot jam out of the cupboard, she set about covering the cake. As she rolled it, she was grateful again for Grannifer's tip of adding a little corn flour to the icing sugar dusting. This really did help to prevent the paste sticking.

Before long, with a coffee in one hand, she dialled Cassie's number. "Hi mate – thought I'd give you a progress report. I've done your mum's cake and the pigs loved theirs." They chatted for a while and arranged to meet up later.

Mindful of the busy week which lay ahead of her, Jennifer decided to put her 'let's get organized hat on', so putting the kettle on for coffee, she got her pen and notepad. Taking these and her mug into the garden, she placed them on the table and sat on the bench. Settling in to 'think' mode, she was unaware of the companion beside her. Before long she felt a nudge at her elbow. Looking down she saw one of her girls staring up at her. "Oh hello Primrose. What are you after? Ah, I know!"

She started to tickle and scratch the pig's ears. "You're a funny one aren't you? I swear you almost smile when I do this!"

She picked up her pen. "Right young lady, you go and do some gardening... I've got lists to write!"

Almost as if she understood the comments, Primrose trotted off and joined her friends further down the garden. Jennifer chuckled to herself. As she sipped her drink, she made headings at the tops of a few pages, underlining each one with satisfaction. "Well, at least that's a start... now all I need is the detail."

She began with the obvious things to do. Under the 'party' page she wrote: decorate cake, make flapjacks, lights for garden, blow up balloons, buy food and drink... the list got longer and longer. Then of course, there was the bedroom. She wrote 'Telephone Thomson's re bed surround.' She hoped this would arrive in the morning so she didn't have to make the call and could set to work painting it up. Next came 'Make curtains and bedspread.'

Before long her pages were almost full. "Oh my, I knew I was going to be busy, but I don't know if I'll get all this ready in time." With her elbows resting on the table, Jennifer covered her face with her hands. Momentarily a huge wave of despondency engulfed her, but before she allowed it to take hold, she turned her thoughts to her beloved Grannifer. The wise words and encouragement that had been ever present throughout her life filled her mind as though the wonderful lady herself was sitting there with her.

"Come on my Jenny, that's not like you... do as much as you can and what doesn't get done, doesn't get done. The world won't stop spinning because a list didn't get completed!" Jennifer smiled. "OK Grannifer, I know you're right. So let's get started!"

Now with a positive attitude, she went indoors and made a start. She got her sewing machine and needle box. Before long she was measuring, cutting and stitching. "Mmm, I think this bedroom is gonna look... rather... nice!" She giggled excitedly as she scooped the finished drapes and ran up the staircase.

Hanging them at the window, she stepped back to look. "Yeah, not bad... though I say it myself."

Returning to the kitchen, she smiled broadly as she crossed out the first thing on her list. Now feeling a lot more positive than she had, Jennifer managed to get through a few more of the things on her list, evermore encouraged as she put a satisfying line through each to eliminate it. Making herself a late lunch, she prepared her 'gardeners' afternoon meal.

"Here piggies, come on girls," she called as she rattled the container of pig nuts. It never failed to amuse her the way they all hurried towards her, each with their individual style. Primrose – ever dainty in her gait, and Pickle with a cheeky, almost brazen attitude. Pinky and Perky, like their piggy namesakes were often together, and would occasionally almost seem to be sharing the same bits of food. Not at all the typical 'greedy pig' image.

Whilst the girls were still munching, Jennifer took her own mug and plate indoors then set about freshening the sty bedding, water trough and mud bath.

As she answered the door that evening, Jennifer was pleased to see that Paul, TJ and Soaki had come around with Cassie. She smiled broadly. "Hi guys! Come in." They greeted her and entered the house.

As they all made themselves comfortable in the living room, Jennifer was curious. "What's with the musical bits?" She scanned the assortment of instruments they had bought with them. Cassie smiled. "We were chatting and had an idea of an extra surprise for Mum."

Jennifer looked quizzical. "Tell me more!"

"Well, you know Mum was born in Scarborough, then the family moved nearer here soon after…"

"Yes, you told me, but…"

Cassie continued. "Well Scarborough Fair has always been one of her favourite songs, so we thought we would sing it for her at the party!"

"Oh that sounds like a lovely idea, so who can play what?"

TJ picked up the guitar. "Well I can strum an OK tune on this."

Then taking a mouth organ from his pocket, Paul added "And I'm not bad with this – used to practise while I was abroad… and it didn't take up much room in my luggage!" he laughed.

"And you know I like singing" added Cassie. "And we've all heard you joining in with the radio!"

Jennifer looked slightly embarrassed. "Oh, I didn't know anyone was listening!" She diverted the conversation away from herself. "So who plays the tambourine?"

At this, Cassie and the men giggled. "Well, we cannot possibly leave out the fifth member of our group."

Jennifer furrowed her brow. "Sorry… fifth member? Who else do you mean?"

Cassie held the tambourine whilst TJ stroked Soaki. As she wagged her tail it hit the instrument rhythmically. "How are you at patting a dog while singing?"

Jennifer laughed. "Oh I reckon I could manage that all right. What a brilliant way to add percussion – I love it!"

They continued chatting for a while, then Jennifer dramatically slapped her hand to her head. "Oh my goodness, what sort of hostess am I? I've not even offered you a drink yet!"

She left the room and went to the kitchen. Cassie joined her, and curious to know what the girls were doing, Soaki followed. "Don't worry little drummer – I haven't forgotten you." She giggled as she placed a bowl of water on the floor.

"So you like the idea of a song for Mum then?"

"Oh yes, definitely... but I'm a bit worried about whether I'll get all the other things ready in time."

Cassie noticed the concern which had overcome her friend. "Hang on mate, you're not doing this on your own. We have four pairs of hands here." Soaki barked. "And a willing canine!"

"Oh I know. It's not just the party things: I've got all the stuff to do before Mum and Dad get here and..."

Cassie interrupted. "Yeah, so? I can help you with those too."

Jennifer hugged her friend. "Oh thank you; you've no idea what a relief that is."

They heard music. "O-oh, sounds like the guys have started without us!"

Returning to the living room, the girls gave out the drinks and settled themselves down. Jennifer looked around at her friends. "OK, so where do we start?"

Cassie checked. "Does everyone know the words? I'm assuming we all know the tune!" There were a few dubious expressions. "I anticipated this so..." She felt in her bag. "Ta-da! I've copied out the lyrics – read and learn my friends!"

"Ooh – fank you Miss!" Jennifer shifted and pretended to wipe her nose on her sleeve like a school child. Everyone smiled. They enjoyed her impromptu play acting.

"We need to find a key we're all comfortable with. How about this for starters?" TJ strummed a chord and they each picked up the note and held it for a few seconds.

As the room fell silent Jennifer smiled. "Oh wow, that was lovely. Look out Glastonbury – here we come!" Everyone laughed.

"Jennifer, we know you've got an imagination that's a bit wacky, but I think putting us at a music festival on the strength of one note is a bit far-fetched... even for you!"

TJ brought the girls back down to earth. "Well I don't know about Glastonbury; if we don't start practising we won't even be ready for 'Partybury'!"

"Yeah, you're right – how about we sing a whole verse and see what we think."

The evening continued with each of them suggesting things they might try and before long they had worked out a good rendition of the song, including harmonies. Pleased with their musical accomplishments they decided to take a break.

"Coffee anyone?"

"Shall I make it Jenny?" TJ offered. "I could do with stretching my legs."

"Oh yes if you like, thanks."

While TJ went to the kitchen, Jennifer and Cassie chatted about other things to do with the party. They didn't notice Paul writing on a scrap of paper. When TJ rejoined them Paul showed him his scribbles. "What do you think?"

TJ nodded. "Yeah, I like it. Let's see what the girls reckon."

"Reckon what?" Cassie had overheard the end of the conversation.

"Paul has had an idea for the rest of the song."

"Yeah, an extra verse especially for your Mum."

Cassie took the paper over to Jennifer. As they read it they both smiled. "Oh yes, that will make a perfect ending."

Jennifer agreed. "Let's drink our coffees, then we'll give it a trial run."

Finishing his drink first, TJ picked up his guitar and started playing. As he finished, his audience applauded. "That was lovely TJ. What was it? I didn't recognize it."

He smiled. "Ah well, there's a good reason you didn't Jenny – on account of the fact that I made it up!"

Everyone was amazed. Cassie spoke for them all. "Is there no end to this man's talents? Brilliant artist and he can write an amazing tune!"

Paul added "And he makes a good cuppa!" They all laughed.

***

As she snuggled into her bed, Jennifer recalled the pleasure of the evening spent with her friends. Cassie's comforting words had taken away the worries she had felt and the ideas that had been bounced between them all for the party made her really look forward, rather than dreading it as she had done earlier. Pulling the bed covers around her shoulders, she recalled their singing and the beautiful tune that TJ had played on his guitar. She smiled and drifted off to sleep

***

The following morning she was pleased to see the familiar faces of the Johnstone's delivery men at her door. "Good morning Miss Cade. We've got your bed frame."

"Oh hello, that's great. Would you like a coffee? I'm just about to put the kettle on."

"That's very kind of you. We'll just get the things off the van."

As they walked away from the house, Jennifer called after them. "They're probably still out the back, but can you make sure the pigs don't escape?"

The men looked at each other. "Did she say pigs?"

"Oh yes, the boss did mention something about them… I thought he was joking."

As they joined Jennifer they chatted and were impressed that she could identify each of the girls, and by the use of them to do the 'gardening'. "What are they like as lawn mowers? Mine's in need of a trim!" They chuckled.

As she surveyed the delivery, Jennifer pursed her lips. "Oh Grannifer, I knew this would be a bit of a project, but I don't remember it being as grotty as this. Well, I suppose the worse it looks now, the better it will seem when it's tarted up eh? So, where to start… ah ha, before and after photos." She ran indoors to get her camera.

With the initial pictures taken, she then proceeded to clean each piece of the bed frame with her wired brush. She was amazed at the amount of rust and dirt which came off. "Well, that'll make it lighter to carry upstairs," she joked to herself.

Sweeping up the debris, she then set about getting ready to paint. By using the black metal paint, she hoped it would look like the nice wrought iron which she imagined it was when made. "Ah well, here goes!"

Totally engrossed in what she was doing, Jennifer was unaware of the figure behind her. "Hello Picasso!"

She spun round. It was TJ. "Oh, you made me jump!" How long have you been there?"

"Just a couple of minutes – but I've been knocking on your back door for a while. It was Soaki who heard you singing first so we came round to find you."

Slightly embarrassed she stood up. "So what do I owe the honour of this unexpected visit? Don't tell me you fancied a cuppa and didn't want to drink alone!"

They laughed. "Well no, but if you're putting the kettle on, I wouldn't say no."

As they made coffee, TJ explained that he'd arranged with Cassie last night that he'd come round. "She was worried about you thinking you'd have to do the party bits on your own, so I've come to start getting bits organized!"

"What, already?"

"Well yes. I can start putting lights up and sorting the music… if you want me to."

She smiled. "Actually that would be a big help. I'll get the boxes of fairy lights and – oh, what do you need to fix them in place?"

"Probably OK with tape if that's all right with you."

"Yeah, I've got masking tape so it shouldn't leave a mark when we take them down."

"Don't tell me… another of Grannifer's tips?"

"You catch on quick, Mr Barton!"

They finished their drinks and settled into their projects, TJ arranging the lights and Jennifer back with her painting. Time went quickly and before she knew it, Jennifer realized it was feeding time for the girls again. As she tidied the paint and brushes, TJ appeared at the door. "How goes it Jenny?"

"Just finished. What do you think?"

He examined her handiwork. "Mmm, not bad, but you've missed a bit."

Jennifer was dumbfounded. "Oh no… where?"

He smiled a broad cheeky grin. "Only joking! No, it looks good. Come and see what you think of my efforts."

They entered into the hallway. "Oh, this is lovely. I like the way you've criss-crossed on the ceiling. And you've even done the stair rail!"

"Aaand…" He led her to the living room. "Ta dah!"

Looking around, she was filled with wonder. "TJ, this is perfect – I'd no idea we bought so many lights. Helen will love it."

"So Jenny lass, I take it you're pleased with the result?"

"Coo you sounded just like Jim then!" They laughed.

"Oh crikey, I'm supposed to be doing the girls' afternoon grub. They'll go on strike if I don't get a wriggle on!"

While Jennifer prepared the fruit and veg, TJ made coffee. "You must get through hundreds of jars of this stuff."

She nodded. "Yeah, and I can show you the evidence – I wash and store the empties. Thought I'd have a go at making jam and chutney… now I'm a country girl. Hang on, I've just had an idea!"

TJ shook his head and raised his eyebrows. "Oh no. I recognize that look – what are you planning now?"

"Let me sort the girls out and I'll tell you… don't worry, it's a good-un!"

She finished preparing the pigs' dinner, but before she took it out to them she noticed that Soaki had nearly emptied her water bowl. "Oh darling, let's fill that up for you."

As she placed the bowl back on the floor, Jennifer kissed the friendly dog on her head. "Oh you have been such a good girl while we've been busy... would you like a treat?"

As if she understood the words, Soaki wagged her tail enthusiastically. Jennifer smiled and picked out a large dog biscuit from the supply which she kept for when Soaki came to visit. Picking up the pigs' food she went to the garden accompanied by TJ who brought the mugs of coffee. Jennifer gave her usual call to rally the girls. "Here piggies!" She rattled the bucket.

TJ smiled his broad smile. "I love the way they all come running when you do that!"

"Yeah, they're cute aren't they? Hang on though; there are only three of them. Oh no, where's Pickle?"

She called again and ran towards the far side of the garden. She was just about to round the corner of the house when TJ called her. He was investigating the opposite side of the property. "Jenny – Jen. It's OK – she's here."

Jennifer ran to join them. She blew an almost silent whistle with relief. "I've never noticed any of them go towards the front of the house before – that gave me bit of a scare. Thought I'd lost her!"

"No need to worry. She's fine. Look, she's munching away with the others."

With a resigned nod, Jennifer sat on the bench and at last managed to start drinking her coffee. The two friends chatted whilst watching the antics of their four legged companions. "Looks like your fugitive found some soot somewhere on her expedition – she's got black splodges all over her."

Jennifer looked across to the pig with more intensity. "Oh no – no! Pickle, you haven't!"

TJ looked with surprise at Jennifer's outburst. "What?"

"There isn't any soot... I think that's paint. She found my bed frame!"

"Oh – oh! Sounds as if Picasso and friend might need to get the brushes out again!"

"Well, er yes... but what is Mel going to say when I tell him one of his animals has decorated herself with metallic paint?"

They did the best they could to see just where Pickle had managed to adorn herself. As she dialled Mel's number, Jennifer took a deep breath. "Hello Mel? It's Jennifer... Yeah I'm fine thanks but I've got bit of a problem..." She explained what had happened.

As she returned to TJ, he looked at her with a questioning expression. "Well? Was he angry?"

Jennifer shook her head. "No, once I'd established that the paint wasn't near her eyes and mouth, he actually thought it was quite funny! He reckons she'll rub it off herself in the mud bath and stuff. It was good that she only brushed against it – might have been a different story if she'd found a puddle of the stuff."

TJ stood up. "Come on, let's go and see what damage she's done to your art work."

"Oh crikey, yes."

They went to the front of the house and examined the frame. "Actually, it's no too bad: a retouch here and there will make it OK again. I'll fetch the paint and brushes."

"Tell you what... if you do that, I'll find something to make a barricade around it 'til it's dry. Don't want a repeat occurrence do we?"

"Oh that would be good – thanks."

Packing away the bits again, Jennifer, TJ and Soaki went indoors. "Do you realize, with all this palaver we haven't had anything to eat? Are you hungry?"

TJ rubbed his tummy. "Well now you mention it, I am a bit peckish."

Jennifer studied the contents of her fridge. "I've got most things – got any preference?"

TJ pondered for a moment. "Have you got eggs? I make a pretty mean omelette!"

"Oh, if you want to. I was going to make something but if you want to be chef, I'm OK with that. I'll lay the table and get something for Soaki."

They each got on with their jobs and before long were enjoying their meals. "Mmm, this is really nice. Where did you learn to cook so well?"

"Oh here and there – Mum encouraged me and I worked for a while in a small restaurant – picked up a few tips there. And living on your own – well I'm not keen on ready meals, and eating out gets a bit pricey if you do it too often. Anyway, you didn't tell me your idea."

"Sorry... idea?" She looked quizzically at him. "Oh yes, I'd forgotten about that. When we sing Helen her song, we haven't got any lighting down there so I thought we could make Tilley lamps and hang them around. Grannifer and I used to paint jars and put little candles in – they look ever so pretty."

"So you've got the jars, I've got plenty of paints, all we need is the candles!"

94

"And I've got loads of string to tie round and make the handles!"

"We've got Cassie and Paul round tomorrow, so if we all get stuck in it shouldn't take too long to do."

Jennifer smiled. "I think this is going to look really lovely."

TJ looked affectionately at his companion, enjoying her infectious childlike enthusiasm.

They chatted on into the evening until it was time for TJ and Soaki to leave. "I promised Grandad a game of darts – want to join us?"

"Oh I'd like to but I've still got things to do here… but send my love to Jim." He said he would. "And thanks again for all your help today."

"You're very welcome."

They hugged briefly, then Jennifer gave Soaki her usual kiss on the head. "Bye bye little lady."

Having seen them to the gate, Jennifer went back to the kitchen and tidied away the few bits of washing up. "Well Grannifer, that was an eventful day. Quite busy, but nice!"

***

The following morning Jennifer went with a slight feeling of trepidation to investigate the bed frame. She lightly touched various areas with her fingertip checking each time for signs of black marks. With puffed cheeks, she gave a relieved breath of air. "Yippee, success!"

She moved the sections into the hallway. "Mmm, they are heavier than I thought. Better wait for some help to get 'em up the stairs." After she'd done a few small jobs, she dismantled TJ's barricade.

She had just finished her lunch when there was a knock at the door. "Wonder who that can be?"

"Hello, Miss Cade?"

"Yes."

"We've got your bed."

"Oh right, are you able to take it upstairs for me please? I was just about to have a cuppa. I can make extra for you both while you're doing the honours with the bed."

The men seemed a little taken aback by her rapid burst of conversation. "Er, we don't usually, but um, yes all right then. Thank you."

"Great – tea or coffee? Oh, it's the first room on the left on the landing."

Chatting that evening with Cassie, Jennifer relayed the bed delivery experience. "Honestly mate, I don't know what came over me. I suddenly went into babble mode and completely bamboozled those poor men. Before they had time to draw breath, I'd persuaded them to take the divan and mattress upstairs… and all on the strength of a cuppa when they'd finished!"

Cassie laughed. "And I thought I was the one with the motor mouth!"

"Er, talking of a persuasive tongue, do you reckon I could talk Paul and TJ into taking that frame up for me? I'd have done it myself but it weighs a ton."

At that moment the guys entered the kitchen. "Aha, speak of the Devil. We were just discussing if you two were strong enough to transport Jennifer's bed frame upstairs. She thinks yes, but I'm not so sure…"

Paul raised his eyebrows at his girlfriend. "Oh, is that right? Come on TJ, we'll show 'em!"

TJ tutted knowingly. "Where do you want it put?"

Jennifer giggled. "First room on the left, please." She nudged Cassie playfully.

"You are naughty!"

Back downstairs Paul and TJ took on the persona of overacting strong men, strutting round the kitchen flexing their muscles and pretending to crack their knuckles. "Any other little jobs you ladies need us tough guys to do?"

Jennifer entered into the fantasy world. Placing the backs of her fingers under her chin she fluttered he lashes. "Oh sirs… you are so clever. What would we do without such big strong men around?"

Cassie rolled her eyes. "Honestly, what are you lot like?" They all laughed.

"Tell you what, if we don't get stuck in and get these jars painted, we won't have them ready for Friday."

"Ooh Paul, you're such a slave driver!"

"Yeah, but he's right. Come on gang, let's get decorating!"

Amid the friendly banter and laughter, the painting of Tilley lamps was well under way. They compared and complimented each other's designs, and before long had each decorated several jars. Surveying the collection when they were finished, Cassie bit her lip. With glistening eyes she looked at her companions. "Thank you guys; Mum's gonna be really made up with all this – they are beautiful."

Jennifer hugged her friend comfortingly. "It's our pleasure, and it's been fun. And if anyone is worth making the effort for it's Helen!"

The boys joined in with the accolade. "Hear hear!"

Cassie smiled. "Time for a break me thinks. Let's get a drink organized and we can retire to the living room and relax."

"Uh uh. Refreshments yes, but I think we ought to go through the song a bit more. We've only got a few days and we want it to be right, don't we?"

Jennifer feigned exhaustion. "Oh but Mister Barton, we is ever so tired!"

"Gercha! I'll give you tired…"

She squealed playfully as TJ chased her through the hallway and into the other room.

Later, as Jennifer said goodnight to her guests, she and Cassie confirmed their arrangements for the following day. "So I'll finish a few bits at the studio, and with luck I'll get to you for about half eleven."

"OK, and I'll have the things ready to decorate the cake." She sighed heavily. "And that should be the last of the major bits to organize."

"Yep, just twiddly little bits after that!"

Jennifer nodded as she crossed her fingers. They hugged. "Night night then. See you tomorrow."

As she closed the door, a tired but very contented smile played on her lips. "Getting there Grannifer, we're getting there!" She locked up and made her way to bed.

Chapter 6

The early morning sunlight filled her room and Jennifer laid on her bed enjoying the sound of the birds singing. She watched the crystal's rainbow colours reflected around the walls and smiled at their gentle beauty. She turned to look at the clock. "Twenty to seven. Mmm, I s'pose I ought to get up." She stretched and slipped her legs from under the covers.

Downstairs she began the routine she was now very familiar with – kettle on, prepare the girls' breakfast, breadcrumbs for her feathered friends, make a cuppa, go out to the garden and call the pigs. She had all this down to a fine art and within minutes of entering the kitchen, she was sitting with her own breakfast and drink watching the pigs and birds also tucking into their own munchies.

After she'd cleaned the sty and dealt with the water trough and mud bath, she prepared the kitchen table ready to ice the birthday cake. All the jars from the previous evening had been carefully moved to the back of the counter out of harm's way. She studied them with pleasant recollection of the fun time with her friends whilst they were being painted. Picking up one she held it aloft. "Mmm, I wonder? Grannifer, I think I've just had one of those 'light bulb' moments... or should I say 'T-light' moments?" She giggled to herself as she replaced it. "Now then, let's get this cake under way."

As she rolled out the fondant icing, Grannifer filled her thoughts. "Jenny love – this stuff is such a blessing. You've no idea what a palaver it was to make royal icing. You spent ages trying to get the surface level. Those holes and bumps seemed determined to make their mark – almost like they were playing a game of 'who can annoy the cook most'!" The memory consumed Jennifer. She sighed. "Oh Grannifer." She wiped her eyes with the back of her hand.

With the cake covering finished, Jennifer tidied away the things not needed for the actual decorating. "You always taught me to clear away as I went, didn't you darling?"

She pottered around the house for a while. "Reckon I ought to check my 'to do' lists." Getting her notepad and pen, she settled on the settee. "Oh, looking good. Not much left."

There was a knock at the door. "Hiya mate, you're early! Come on in."

"Whew, I hope you've got a coffee on the go!"

"Er, yeah – just give me a mo." Jennifer looked at her friend with concern. "What's up Cassie – you seem rattled about something?"

"It's my mum. She's told Dad that she wants to go away for the weekend... a long weekend... like from Friday to Monday!"

"But... oh she can't. We've got to stop her! Oh Cassie, what can we do?"

They sat at the table, each of them feeling shell-shocked. Jennifer took a deep breath. She stood up and made their drinks. "Come with me. Bring your mug."

"Where are we going?"

"To the river. This is gonna need some serious thinking time!"

As they walked down the garden they each collected stones. "How many do you think we'll need?"

"Ooh, it's a big think – I reckon about ten each."

Sitting on the grassy bank, the girls took it in turns to throw the stones in the water. They watched the ripples. "What did Don say?"

"Oh, you know Dad – he bluffed it for a while, said he'd talk about it later, made some excuse that he was late and left as quick as he could."

Several stones later - "What's your mum's favourite food?"

"Eh? Why?"

"I think I've got an idea."

"OK. Well, to answer your question, she's rather fond of Italian."

Jennifer turned to face her friend. "Would your dad join in with a bit of a fib? Just an itsy-bitsy little white lie. Nothing too awful?"

"Probably... what have you got in mind?"

Jennifer explained.

"You know, it might just work. Let's call Dad."

She took her phone from her bag. "...so you're OK with this then? Brilliant, just make sure you're not at home then Mum will have to take the supposed call from the restaurant... Yeah I know it's really

99

expensive... That's why she'll change her mind... Yeah, I'll pass that on... See you later... Love you too, byeee!" Cassie finished the call with her father.

"Well that's stage one of the assignment to salvage the party... oh and Dad said good luck!"

"Great, and look... we've still got three stones left!"

They both laughed. "Not 'quite' as big a problem as we thought!"

"So now stage two: we've got to get Helen back home for a little while..."

"I've got an idea for that... you just let me know when you want her to be there."

Taking their mugs, the girls went back to the house. "Fancy a little glass of wine? Dutch courage and all that."

"OK, just a small one." Cassie took her phone. "Shall I call her then?"

"No time like the present... go on then."

As she dialled the number, Cassie exhaled. "...Hi mum, can you do me a huge favour? I'm with Jennifer. We were thinking of going to the shops and I can't find my purse. I might have left it at yours the other day. Would you be a darling and pop and have a look for me please?" She bit her lips cautiously. "You can go at three? Oh thanks a million. See you later. Love you, byeee."

She turned towards Jennifer with a satisfied smile, then raised her eyebrows and gave a nod. "Stage two accomplished. Come three o'clock and it's over to you!" She picked up her wine.

They clicked their glasses. "Cheers. Here's to a successful outcome!"

They waited for the allotted time. "Right, she should be there by now. Ready?"

Jennifer looked worried. "Er I think so. Crikey, I feel like it's opening night at a West End show – oh Cassie, what if I muck it up?"

"Don't be daft, you're good at accents. You'll be fine. Oh, and don't forget to withhold your number!"

"Oh yes – good thinking."

Helen was just checking under cushions for the purse when the phone rang. She tutted. "Oh who's that in the middle of the day?"

She stopped searching and picked up the receiver. "Hello?"

"Ah, bon journo. I'm a speak a weeth Missy Meadows yes?"

"Er, yes."

"Ah, bueno – thees ees just a thee con-a-formaysion a for a Friday at Casa Melchiorre. You a please tell a your a papa yes? Remember no word to your-a mama… beeeing surprise-a yes? We make it a nice a fora her. Thank you. Arriva datch!"

Jennifer replaced the handset and turned to face Cassie. "Well? What do you reckon?"

"Wow mate, I didn't know you spoke Italian!"

Jennifer raised her eyebrows. "I don't, but hopefully nor does Helen. If we took her by surprise enough we might have got away with it!"

Cassie's mobile rang. "It's Mum." She answered "Hi Mum, any luck with the purse? You've what? Casa Melchiorre… wow, who's a lucky girl then! Oh yes, I see what you mean. What are you going to do? Will you tell Dad or could you wing it and act surprised on Friday?" She did the thumbs up sign for Jennifer. "Oh, and you wanted to go away… Yes of course. Perhaps next weekend instead!"

By now she was beaming and trying desperately not to laugh. "OK Mum, I'll see you later darling. Yes I love you too – byeee." She ended the call and the two friends hugged, laughing as they did so.

They made an impromptu song and danced around. "We saved the party – da da di da da!"

After a while they calmed down somewhat. Jennifer tried to take control. "This is all very well and good but if we don't get started, we won't have this cake décor…" She stopped mid-sentence. "What are you eating?"

Cassie looked guilty and answered with a mouthful of food - "Fepjek!"

"What?"

Cassie chewed then swallowed. "Flapjack!"

Jennifer pretended to be annoyed. "Oi, they're for the party… what are they like? Any good?"

Finishing another mouthful "Not half – I reckon they're your best yet."

Jennifer smiled. "S'pose I'd better try one just to make sure you're not fibbing, but then we must really do this cake."

Cassie saluted. "Yes Ma'am!"

"Being serious for a minute, have you got any ideas how we can do this?"

Cassie fetched her bag. "Well, it just so happens that I have had a thought or two. I made this at the studio. Thought we could stand it on top."

Jennifer unwrapped the small tissue-covered object. "Wow mate, it's a miniature version of the tea rooms. Gosh, you're so clever."

Cassie looked pleased. "Oh I'm really pleased you like it. I think if we just do some pretty piping on the rest that should be enough. Perhaps some nice ribbon around the edge. What do you think?"

Jennifer agreed heartily and before long the cake was finished. "Excellent. That's another step nearer being ready!"

They tidied up. "Oh crikey, it's time for the girls' dinner already. The day just whizzes by. I don't know where the time goes!"

"Come on, I'll help, then we'll sit and relax for a while."

As they sat chatting, Jennifer told Cassie about the idea she'd had earlier for the jars. "So if we glue glitter to the underside, I thought it might catch the light and sparkle. What do you think?"

"Yes, I like that. Should look really nice. I've got PVA glue, but we'll need to buy the glitter. Shall we go into town in the morning? There's a terrific art shop I know."

"Right, so we'll do that and be back by lunchtime – then we can get glittering!"

"Actually if we have time, I'd like to see if I can find a nice party outfit."

Jennifer looked a little shocked. "Gosh, I'd forgotten all about what to wear. I'd better join you on the party gear trek. Oh how awful – we've got to increase our wardrobes!" They laughed.

***

As the girls trundled along in Cassie's funky little car they chatted happily. "I can't believe the party is tomorrow – when we started arranging it, it felt like so far away then all of a sudden ..."

"Cor yeah, I know what you mean. Can you think of anything we might have forgotten?"

Jennifer thought hard. "No, I'm sure we've got it all covered. The guys are coming round in the afternoon to blow up balloons and help out generally." She giggled. "Even Jim reckons he can blow up more than Paul and TJ put together! And my mum and dad will chip in too."

"Oh gosh yes, I'd forgotten they'd be here by then – I can't wait to meet them in the flesh. I feel like I know them already!" She pulled into a parking space.

"So, where to first?"

Cassie indicated with the nod of her head. "The Art Shop's just over there, so if we get the glitter now at least we know that's dealt with." Jennifer agreed.

Before long they were in their third dress shop. "What do you think of this one?" Cassie asked.

Jennifer wrinkled her nose. "I'm not keen. I think it's the colour." As she studied her friend, something caught her eye over Cassie's shoulder

102

towards the back of the shop. "Stay there; I think I've spotted just the thing."

She returned with a beautiful emerald dress. "I imagined this next to your hair."

Cassie held it against herself, her deep auburn curls cascading over her shoulders. She turned to look in a mirror. "Oh wow – if it fits, I'm having it!"

Minutes later she was paying the assistant.

"Your Paul won't know what's hit him when he sees you – that looks gorgeous!"

"Oh thank you – now what about you?"

"I think I like the one in the first shop best – let's have another look."

As she tried it on, Cassie smiled and nodded enthusiastically. "Definitely. I really like that. Come on then missus – get your purse out before you change your mind."

Jennifer took the deep lavender, almost peacock blue dress to the counter. Handing her the change, the assistant smiled. "I saw it on you when you showed your friend – it looked really lovely."

"Oh, thank you very much."

They left the store. "Time for a cuppa methinks!"

"Oh yes; good idea."

As they drove back to Miraford, Jennifer had an idea. "Before we go home, can we squeeze in a quick visit to Honey Bee Farm?"

"Yeah of course. What do you need?"

"Some plants for Helen – I'll tell you more when we get there."

Cassie was curious but knew her friend well and whatever she had in mind would be worth waiting for. When they arrived Jennifer asked Cassie to find some miniature roses. "Get your mum's favourite colours – two or three. I'll meet you in the shop." She disappeared leaving Cassie behind.

When she returned, she placed her plants on the counter. Cassie read the labels. "Rosemary, parsley, thyme and sage."

Jennifer rearranged the pots. "Now read them!"

"Parsley, sage, rosemary and thyme – oh her song! How clever; she'll love it!"

"I picked up this basket too. They should all fit in."

"That looks nice, dear – is it for a present?"

Jennifer smiled at the now familiar lady who was serving them. "Yes, for a very special lady. It's her birthday."

Cassie beamed at the kind words about her mum.

Arriving back at Willow Bank House, the girls gathered up their shopping and went indoors. "I'll check the girls are OK, then we'll have some lunch."

As they enjoyed their food, they chatted about the morning. "Considering we were only out for a few hours, I think we did really well."

Jennifer agreed. "Yeah, let's hope that continues when we sparkle up the jars!"

The venture was successful and by two fifteen they were admiring their handiwork. "Just got to wait 'til they dry then we can tie on the handles, then they're all done and dusted."

Cassie did a 'thumbs up' and smiled broadly. "I reckon this is going to be the best party ever!"

***

Throughout the afternoon the two friends pottered about doing things for the following evening. They folded serviettes and placed them alternately between plates; cut string in lengths ready to tie on the Tilley lamps as handles; baked small cakes and pastries; hung decorations and displayed the plants in the basket, finishing it off with a pretty ribbon bow.

"It's nice of Angela to lend us the glasses – I've got quite a few, but not enough for a gathering this big! Are you sure no one has let it slip to your mum?"

Cassie smiled. "Absolutely not. They want it to be as much of a surprise for her as we do."

"Oh gosh, I hope it all goes to plan – I'm starting to feel a bit nervous."

"Don't worry mate; it'll be fine."

"Tell you what, how about we go to the Arms later – loads of party people will be there and we can put our minds at rest that everyone knows what they're doing."

Jennifer nodded. "Yes, I'd like that – I feel like I haven't been there for ages. It'll be a nice break."

As they ordered drinks at the bar, Jim spotted them and came over. "Hello strangers; long time no see. Where have you been hiding?"

Jennifer smiled broadly. "Hello Jim." She gave him a hug and kissed his cheek.

They found a table and sat down. They chatted about the party. "Oh yes, I knew there was something I was gonna ask you." Jim took a sip of his pint. He wiped his mouth and resumed talking. "I was playing darts with me mate Barry earlier – you know Barry?"

The girls nodded.

"Yes, the old devil beat me five games to my four – I think he's been practising on the quiet."

Jennifer and Cassie looked at each other. "So what did you want to ask Jim?"

"Mmm? Oh yes, he said he's got a marquee and do you want it for the party? Seems like you've got a lot of people expected and…"

The girls beamed. "Jim, that would be wonderful. How do we tell him 'yes'?"

"Easy, he's over there!" Jim beckoned to Barry across the crowded pub and he came across and joined them.

They arranged that he would come to the house at lunchtime. "It's not huge, but should help with a bit of overflow space."

Cassie grinned. "This is getting better and better!"

"Glad to help m'dear."

It seemed that at least half of the Miraford Arms patrons were going to be at the party and there was a general buzz of excitement about it.

After a couple of very enjoyable hours, Jennifer returned home. She made a milky drink and went to the living room. Having put on some soft music, she settled on the settee. Cradling her mug, she enjoyed the calm relaxing atmosphere. "Well Grannifer, big day tomorrow; not just the party bit, but Mum and Dad are coming in the morning – I do hope they like it here as much as I do." She smiled. "Oh, it'll be lovely to see them."

It wasn't long before she took herself off to bed and soon drifted into a deep and very contented sleep.

***

Next morning, as she fed the pigs their breakfast, Jennifer heard the familiar sound of her parents' car horn - 'beep be beep'. She ran eagerly to the front of the house and hugged her mother enthusiastically. "Why's Dad still in the car?"

"Checking the mileage!"

Her father emerged. "Hello pet. A hundred and twenty seven exactly!"

They hugged. "Good journey?"

"Yes – but I'm dying for a cuppa."

"I'll get the kettle on then I'll show you around."

They carried luggage in with them, Jennifer chatting rapidly as they did so. "Slow down darling – we've got plenty of time to catch up. Let's get that tea and then you can give us a tour."

Jennifer kissed them. "Sorry – I'm just so happy to see you both."

When they were sitting in the garden with their drinks, Jennifer pointed out which of the pigs was which and told her parents the itinerary for the day. With a wry smile her father shook his head. "You don't do things by half, do you girl?"

She shrugged her shoulders. "It's not just me Dad; all my friends have been in on it too! They'll be here soon. You'll love them."

"I'm sure we will. So – if we've got this busy day ahead, you'd better show us around before they all turn up, eh?"

It was just before midday when there was a knock at the door. "Hiya Barry."

"Hello love – one marquee as promised, plus a few weedy fellas to help put it up." He chuckled as his companions jeered and grumbled in mocking tones.

"You're a fine one to talk! Cor, hark at Mr Universe. Like to see you do it on your own – never mind the insults, let's get it built then we can have a cuppa!"

At this remark everyone cheered. Jennifer laughed at their antics. At that moment, Cassie's car pulled up. All of a sudden there were people everywhere.

Cassie came in, followed by Jim and Paul. Amid the ensuing chaotic flurry, Jennifer managed to proudly introduce her parents to her friends.

"We're pleased to meet you all at last. It's good to put faces to the names. We feel as though we know you all already! I'm Jonathan by the way – but call me Jon."

"And I'm Sally; pleased to meet you."

They all chatted for a while, then Barry interrupted. "Where do you want this set up, Jennifer?"

She followed him to the garden. "I think around here would be good," she indicated. "What do you think?"

He nodded. "Yes love; I reckon that will be fine."

Everyone settled into their various jobs and before long things were taking shape. Sally and the girls were in the kitchen. "Oh look, there's a dog just come in!"

"Ah hello Soaki! Mum, this is Soaki and that means somewhere out there will be TJ."

Sally made friends with the affectionate canine whilst Jennifer put down a bowl of water for her. As they chatted, they set up a tray of mugs ready for the promised tea and coffee.

"So the food you've planned for the party is all sorted – yes?"

Cassie and Jennifer nodded.

"It sounds like a nice selection, but I thought your mum was expecting Italian?"

"Well yes, but that's not real."

Sally raised her eyebrows. "I know that, but you've included some Chinese and Indian with your English buffet – don't you think a bit of antipasti would be a good thing to include?"

"Oh Sally, yes of course; I'll get some bits from the village."

"Hold your horses young lady; what if Helen sees you? I'll get Jon and we'll go. Just give us some directions – yes?"

Cassie sighed. "You're not just a pretty face are you?!"

Sally laughed. "I have me moments dear!"

Amused by her mother's tongue-in-cheek comment, Jennifer smiled as she made her way to the kitchen door.

"I'll see if they are ready for their cuppas yet." She returned soon after. "Five teas, four coffees and whatever you're having."

Cassie looked surprised. "Have they finished already?"

Jennifer nodded. "Uh huh – and it's looking good!"

They put the trays on the bench. "Come on guys."

As the workers collected their mugs, Jon approached his wife. "Come on lad, I'll introduce you to my better half. Sal, you haven't met this one yet."

They shook hands. "How do you do Mrs Cade – I'm TJ."

She smiled. "Lovely to meet you and please – call me Sally."

He responded with one of his beaming smiles. "Thank you Sally – I see where Jenny gets her good looks from now."

Sally looked a little bashful. Later as she chatted with her daughter - "He's very charming…"

"Mm? Oh TJ, yes, he's a real sweetie – and very talented too. Did you notice my house nameplate? He made that."

Sally gave a knowing look.

"What? Oh no! We're just mates Mum – honest."

"Okay, if you say so!"

Jennifer rolled her eyes and tutted. "You go and get Dad and I'll check my cupboards for anything vaguely Italian."

Sally called to Jon who was enjoying an impromptu game of football. Collecting his keys he muttered playfully "Cor, I dunno – hundred and twenty seven miles and I've got to go shopping!"

Sally pushed him towards the door. "Come on Mr Grumpy – we won't take long."

As they left, Cassie laughed. "Oh Jennifer, I love your mum and dad – they're such fun."

"Yeah, I know. We're dead lucky in the parent department, aren't we?"

In and around Willow Bank House was a hive of activity, with everyone pitching in to get ready for the party that evening. Helen was a very popular lady around the village and everyone wanted her birthday surprise to be as perfect as it could be.

Sally and Jon returned. Placing various bags on the kitchen table they sat down. "What a lovely village; everybody is so friendly. I see why you decided to settle here, darling."

Jennifer smiled at her mother. "I knew you'd like it, and yes, it was just what I needed to help me get sorted."

Sally started to unpack the bags. "Your dad and I got things that we remembered we liked when we were on holiday in Italy – hope that's okay!"

"Yeah, fine, so what have we got?"

"We picked up ready-made pizzas and these lovely biscuits which you dip in this wine – that's Cantucci and Vin Santo. And I couldn't resist this tiramisu." She licked her lips. "Yum yum – anyway with the rest we'll create some nice nibbles. There's pancetta, olives, pistachios, mozzarella and tomatoes – they make a nice salad. Pascuttio and Pasetto wine – I think with the pasta salad you've done, that should give Helen a little hint of the restaurant she was expecting!"

Cassie went over to Sally and gave her a hug. "Thank you so much – we thought we'd covered everything, but this is like the icing on the cake."

Sally hugged her back. "You're very welcome. Talking of cakes, I take it you've arranged a birthday cake."

"Of course – Jennifer guided me and we made one."

Jennifer noticed the dubious expression on her mum's face. "What's that look for?"

"Well er darling, apart from coffee and toast you're not renowned for your culinary expertise."

"And flapjacks!"

"Oh yes… and flapjacks, but…"

Cassie interrupted the banter between mother and daughter. "We had expert advice… from Grannifer. It's one of her recipes!"

Sally pretended to wipe her brow with the back of her hand. "Whew, that's all right then!" They all laughed.

At that point TJ came in. "We're ready for the Tilley lamps."

"They're in those boxes – I'll help carry them down."

"Ooh – me too. I've been looking forward to this bit!"

They picked up a box each and walked down the garden. Sally was curious and followed with interest. On the river bank was a long tow rope. Paul, Jon and Jim were waiting and they all helped to tie the lamps securely at intervals to the rope.

"We'll hoist it up between the two trees when it starts to get dark, then give Don the nod and he can bring Helen down for her musical treat."

The four friends chatted excitedly with each other. They managed to keep the actual details of their surprise song secret from everyone.

"We can use bales of straw to sit on; the girls won't mind lending their future bedding for one night!"

Talking about the pigs reminded Jennifer of the time. "Whoops – I'd better feed them their dinner or they won't get settled in bed before everyone gets here."

It took about an hour and a half for the last bits to be done for the evening celebrations. Leftover lamps were hung along the left wall of the garden to illuminate the now well trodden trail from the back door to the riverside gate. The pigs had been fed and their sty made ready for the night and the buffet and drinks arranged. People started to go home to get spruced up and into their party attire. Cassie gave hugs and kisses as she thanked everyone.

"Right, now to go home and get dressed up and ready for our supposed 'mystery' evening that Dad has told Mum he's taking us to. It's really weird – we all know the surprise, but Mum's still pretending she doesn't know when she does, but she hasn't got the foggiest idea that her secret isn't the real one!! I told her that we're popping in here 'en route' just to meet your parents. Ooh, I can't wait to see her face!" She crossed her fingers. "Here's hoping it all goes to plan."

Jennifer crossed her fingers too and nodded. "Should do mate – everyone's worked their socks off to get this far. Anyway, we'll find out in a couple of hours."

They said goodbye and the mania of the day subsided. "Here you are pet. I've made us a cup of tea before we get ourselves dressed up."

"Oh thanks Dad; that's just what I need."

As the house started to fill with guests, the now familiar buzz of excited anticipation increased. Jennifer got a call on her phone from Cassie. "Okay everyone – they've just left. They'll be here in about five minutes. Remember keep out of sight and shush!" She placed a finger to her lips.

She slipped a chunky cardigan on to cover her pretty dress while she opened the door and made sure the hall was in darkness. A little glow from the living room would be the only illumination until Helen was in the house.

The knock at the door instigated a few giggles and mutterings of 'they're here'. Jennifer whispered as loudly as she dared "Shush – she'll hear you!"

Opening the door, she greeted them. "Hi everyone – happy birthday Helen – come in. Mum and Dad are in the living room – come through and I'll introduce you."

Allowing Helen to go first, Jennifer walked close behind and as they approached the partially open door, she reverted back to her Italian persona. "I a hope-a you don't-a mind-a – but-a thees Casa Melchiorre – she need-a to be another time yes? We theenk-a you deserve a beet more a celee-barasion!"

With this, Helen turned. "That was you on the phone – oh my..." She was lost for words.

The door opened and lights turned on. Suddenly before her was a room filled with her friends and relatives. Smiles abounded as everyone cheered. Music was turned on and the party was under way. Jennifer introduced Sally and Jon, and Don promised the birthday girl that he would indeed take her to Casa Melchiorre very soon. He embraced her. "Happy Birthday, darling."

With the party in full swing and the moon taking its place in the ever darkening sky, the Tilley lamps were lit and made secure in their places.

Cassie stood beside Helen in the kitchen selecting things to eat. "This is a wonderful spread darling – who did it?"

"We all pitched in, but it was Sally who made sure we included the Antipasti!"

Helen smiled. "I must remember to thank her – she and Jon are very nice aren't they?"

"You having a good time then Mum? Not too disappointed about the lack of posh restaurant?"

"Oh gosh no – this has been my best birthday ever – what a wonderful gift!"

"Oh, this is just your party – your pressies are still to come. Hold on there a mo."

Cassie left briefly and returned with Jennifer. They gave Helen the prettily wrapped little boxes. "Hope you like them."

The girls watched in anticipation as Helen opened up the jewellery boxes. "Oh..." Helen drew in her breath. "Oh, these are exquisite. Thank you. Thank you so much."

They all kissed. "We've got something else. You'll have that later!" They looked at each other and giggled.

"So, how's this food. Any good?"

Various people around the table commented that it was all very nice. Jim pretended to slur his words - "Idza goood shebang mid jrivin – aiv ad do er yer flepjecks – hic!"

Sally adopted a matronly tone – "Yes, Jennifer Rae – just how much alcohol did you put in them?"

Cassie queried her friend's middle name. "Ray? That's a boy's name."

"It's RAE. Grannifer's suggestion 'cos she said when I was born it was like a ray of sunshine. Soppy I know, but I like it."

Across the room Paul was subtly trying to get the girls' attention. When they noticed they went to the back door.

"TJ and Soaki are waiting by the river – you two ready?"

The girls grinned and nodded. Cassie found her Dad in the marquee. "Dad – give us five minutes then bring Mum down – okay?"

He did the thumbs up and smiled. Word spread around the guests about the impending mini concert and slowly everyone wandered towards the back of the garden. Don held Helen's arm and escorted her. "The kids have got a surprise for you."

"What, another one?"

The straw bale seats had been covered with pretty throws. Cassie and Jennifer sat slightly off centre with Soaki in front, her head by Jennifer's knees. Paul stood beside them and TJ on the right side stood with one foot on the seating. Behind them the trees on the far bank reflected on the gently flowing river, as did the soft moonlight and the candlelight from the suspended lanterns. With the scene set, all that was needed was the guest of honour. Leading his wife through the gate, Don showed Helen to her seat facing the quintet. She sat, bemused as to what was happening. The other guests gathered nearby.

As they picked up their instruments, Cassie spoke. "Hopefully you'll enjoy this Mum – make sure you listen to the last verse – you won't have heard it before!"

Jennifer stroked Soaki's head which made her wag her tail. This tapped gently against the tambourine which Cassie held. Paul and TJ played a short intro on the harmonica and guitar. They sang the words to Helen's favourite - 'Scarborough Fair'.

As she watched and listened Helen's eyes glistened and she held her fingers to her mouth. They sang the normal verses then came the special ending …

"Helen, though you are Scarborough born;
We're so glad that you didn't stay,
'Cos you light up our lives,

Like a bright sunny morn,
And with lots of love,
We just want to say…"

TJ strummed in a different key and everyone joined in with a resounding rendition of 'Happy Birthday'. At the end everyone clapped and cheered.

Helen was beside herself with joy and hugged and kissed the four friends with gusto. "Oh, that was wonderful – thank you so much!" And then crouching down to Soaki, "And you were the best tambourine player I've ever seen!"

As everyone made their way back to the house, Cassie and Jennifer linked an arm each with Helen. "Come on Mrs Meadows… you've got some candles to blow out and a cake to cut."

"And – one last thing to carry home. A little reminder of your song."

Helen rolled her eyes. "As if I could ever forget that!"

Back indoors the girls gave Helen the basket of roses and herbs. "Thank you my darling; this is all too wonderful for words."

Sally then led Helen to the cake, now adorned with lit birthday candles.

"We have two very clever daughters; this is all their own work!"

"Make a wish as you blow them out Mum."

"I don't really need to… I think all my wishes have come true already in this one fabulous night. Thank you everyone!"

She blew out the candles and everyone cheered again. Jim took her arm, "Come on birthday girl; I've been waiting all night for a dance."

He whisked her away to the living room. Others followed suit and the revelry continued.

Hours flew by and feeling in need of a break from the noise and bustle of so many people, Jennifer went back to the riverbank. She sat, this time facing the water and relaxed as she watched the hypnotic flow. She liked the moon's reflection which was fragmented by the river's movements.

"Ah, there you are!" She turned to see TJ. "You all right?" He walked over and sat beside her.

"Yeah, I'm fine – just fancied chilling out for a little while."

"I know what you mean – it's been bit of a hectic day."

"Cor, you can say that again, but it's gone well hasn't it?" They continued chatting.

After a while TJ noticed her shivering. He slipped off his jacket and put it around her shoulders. Turning her head to thank him, they were very closely face to face. He kissed her lips.

"Oh – sorry…"

She smiled. "That's all right."

He smiled back. "Truth is, I've wanted to do that for a long time."

Looking into his eyes she smiled again then rested her head on his shoulder. He put his arm around her and they enjoyed watching the river again, but now even more happy… and together.

They sat snuggled together for a while enjoying the tranquillity of the river bank. The lantern and candles had finished, but the moonlight caught the glitter on the jars, so too the ripples of flowing water. Jennifer turned her head from TJ's shoulder and faced him.

"S'pose we ought to go and join the others – they'll be sending out a search party!"

He turned towards her and kissed her forehead. He smiled and nodded. Standing up, he took her hands. "Hallow me to hescort you, me lady!"

As she rose she gave a little courtesy. "Oh thank you sir – so kaynd of you!"

They giggled at their play acting and went back to the house. Party night turned into morning – and as the early hours of Saturday crept in, the revelry began to calm.

By about three o'clock most of the guests had said their goodbyes and made their way home. Those who were left helped to tidy up a bit but Jennifer said not to worry too much. "I'll blitz the place properly when I get back from the market."

Jon looked with astonishment at his daughter. "Er, market? When is that?"

"In the morning – I usually get there for about ten; got to get the girls' fruit and veg!"

Jon responded with an exhausted exhalation of breath.

Jennifer laughed. "Don't worry Dad – you don't have to come – I'll wake you up with a cup of tea when I get home!"

Sally appeared with a tray. "Talking of cuppas – nightcaps before we get to bed."

As Jennifer said goodbye to TJ and Soaki at the bottom gate, he took her in his arms again and kissed her. "Night night Jenny; see you later!"

They smiled and he and Soaki walked along the tow path back to their houseboat. Jennifer watched them for a moment, their figures silhouetted in the early morning light. It was an extremely happy and contented Jennifer that snuggled into her bed.

Chapter 7

She slept for just three – maybe four hours, but it was the sweetest sleep. As the warm morning sunlight bathed her room, she woke refreshed and still smiling. "Oh Grannifer – I hope that wasn't just the most beautiful dream…"

She went downstairs and was surprised to see Sally already there. "Mum, I thought you'd be having a lie in."

They kissed. "No, the sun woke me and I thought I'd come with you to the market."

"It's a good alarm clock, isn't it? And so much quieter!" They laughed. "I'm glad you want to come with me."

Sally made tea while Jennifer fed the pigs. Before long they were walking through the pretty village towards Market Square. Jennifer pointed out the flat she had before Willow Bank House. As they continued around the market, Jennifer introduced Sally to her stall holder friends. Laden with various bits and bobs they eventually got to the greengrocery stand.

"Hello Jennifer. Come for your usual?" Alf the stall holder had always been interested in how the pigs were doing. "How are your little ladies doing?"

"Hi Alf – they're not so little now – must be your lovely fruit and veg making them get all big and strong! This is my mum by the way."

They all said their hellos and chatted for a while. Jennifer bought the things she would need for the week and they made their way back home. As they got about a third of the way, a horn beeped and a truck pulled alongside them. It was Barry.

"Hello – want a lift? I'm just going to get the marquee."

They clambered aboard. "Cor, that was good timing. Thanks Barry. The walk is very pleasant but the girls' grub is starting to feel very heavy."

Before long they were home and ready for a cuppa. "I'll go and wake your dad."

"No need Mum – I can see him in the garden."

Sally changed direction and went to the back door. "Hello darling; you're up already then! I thought you were going to have a lie in."

He gave her a kiss. "I did for a while but thought I'd make a start with clearing some of the party stuff."

Jennifer joined them with a tray of mugs. "Morning Dad; sleep well?"

"I'll say. Like the proverbial log. Thanks pet."

They all had their drinks and then helped dismantle and pack away the marquee. Halfway through the proceedings TJ, Jim and Soaki arrived. The men helped with the dismantling while Soaki played with the pigs. She was particularly fond of Pickle. Jennifer did wonder if the most inquisitive of her four wards sometimes thought she was a dog. She was often to be found playing with the football and ran around the garden with Soaki when she came around.

Everyone allocated themselves a job to do. TJ said that since he had put the lights up in the hallway and living room, he would deal with them. "Can you help Jenny, so I don't drop them as I get them down?"

They dealt with one strip of lights at a time so as not to tangle them. To pack them away, each set was wound loosely around stiff card. Jennifer held the lights whilst TJ wound. As he approached her he smiled and when he reached her he kissed her. "I reckon we got the best job… there's another dozen or so sets to wind up!"

"Oh, goody gumdrops! Let's do the next lot!" They laughed.

It was early afternoon by the time everything was done. Sally suggested late lunch/early tea which was readily welcomed by all and sundry. With a few nibbles left over from the party and some freshly made sandwiches, the mini-feast took on the feeling of a workers' outing picnic. There was a lot of chat about the previous night and how successful it had been.

As her home returned to as near normal as possible, Jennifer sat with her parents, TJ and Soaki, and they chatted in the comfortable living room.

"It was fun arranging the party, but I must admit I'm glad it's done with. Might be able to put my feet up occasionally now!"

115

TJ smiled at his newly acquired girlfriend. "How about we start that relaxation as of this evening. It seems that even Sally has been stuck in the kitchen since you arrived." He looked at Jennifer's mum and smiled.

"Oh, I don't mind ... all hands to the pump and all that!"

"Well, I think you deserve NOT to work on your break away, so how about you all come along to my place this evening and I'll do dinner?"

"Ooh, I'm up for that – how do you fancy dining on the high seas Dad?"

He looked a teeny bit anxious. "I'm not actually a very good sailor."

TJ laughed. "Don't worry Jon; Kingfisher is as solid as a rock. You'll hardly know you're afloat!"

Sally beamed. "Well, I think it sounds lovely. Do you want us to do anything to help?"

TJ tutted playfully and raised his eyebrows. "No... thanks for asking, but the idea is for you just to take it easy and enjoy."

Sally pretended she'd been told off. "Sorry, force of habit!" They all laughed, enjoying the moment.

That evening, as they walked along the tow path, Jennifer linked arms with her parents. "This is lovely – I'm so glad you've come. Ah, there we go. Can you see the boat?"

"Gosh, it's bigger than I imagined. Isn't it beautiful?!"

Jon agreed with his wife but looked with trepidation at the gangplank. "You're sure it's safe?"

Jennifer laughed. "Course it is – come on silly. Just follow me!"

She led the way. "Helloo! Permission to come aboard?"

TJ opened the door and greeted them. "Come on in and get settled. Dinner will be about fifteen minutes."

They went in and sat in the cosy lounge. TJ poured drinks and joined them.

"This is lovely TJ. How long have you had it?"

He looked thoughtful. "Er, I got her about nine years ago but it took me a good eight months before she was habitable – bit of a mess when I bought her but it was kind of love at first sight – and I like a challenge!"

"Bit like our dilly daughter – you two are well matched I reckon."

TJ looked at Jon. "I think so!"

They continued chatting... 'DING'.

"Ah ha, dinner is ready! I thought you'd be fed up with Italian but you said you liked spaghetti bolognese – so these ees what I a make-a for you!"

As they enjoyed the meal, they were impressed that it was all his own work. "No – not a packet or jar in sight – cooked from fresh ingredients!"

"Well I'll pinch your recipe if you don't mind – this is quite scrumptious."

"With pleasure, dear lady. I'll swap you for one of your favourites – yes?"

Sally agreed and Jon joined in. "Make it her Fruity Ginger Loaf – it's the best."

"Oh, thank you darling."

She kissed her husband for his compliment. Jennifer smiled at her affectionate parents.

When the meal was all finished, Soaki played her bit as hostess by allowing each of their guests an allotted amount of one-to-one contact. Ear tickling and head stroking were very relaxing for humans, so she made sure that Sally, Jon and Jennifer each had a turn. Although she saw this as part of her duties, it was not exactly a chore. In fact, she repeated the attending-to-her-visitors a few times. Well after all, it was her job!

It was also part of her remit to make sure that everyone got home safely, so of course she and TJ had to escort them back to the tow path. Everybody obviously thought she had been an excellent hostess because they each gave her kisses and cuddles before saying goodnight and going into the house.

Over the following few days Jennifer enjoyed showing her parents around Miraford and the surrounding areas. Sally and Jon were very impressed with the variety of shops to be found in Lamton. Not just the usual big stores found nationwide, but a good many independent shops: family-run concerns which, although situated in this large town, retained a friendly familiarity more akin to a smaller village.

She of course had to share her 'Aladdin's Cave' – the reclamation yard – and her first discovery, which started the spark of the new life which she was so happy living.

"While we're here pet, why don't you pick out some bits for your garden?"

"Lovely thought Dad, but if I plant anything, chances are the girls will eat it!"

"I'm ahead of you there… if we get some trees then we can put cages around them."

Jennifer smiled at him, "You are so clever… in that case, yes please; a tree would be lovely."

The Cade family caused a few bemused looks from passers-by on their return journey from Honey Bee Farm. Jon and Sally's car looked more like a greenhouse on wheels!

It took several trips in and out of the garden to unload the profusion of plants and other paraphernalia which they had bought.

"Oh gosh, just look at this lot... did we actually leave anything at the farm for anyone else to buy?"

Sally laughed at her daughter. "Well you do have a lot of garden to fill darling, and we wanted to give you a moving in present, so..."

"I love it all. Thanks Mum, and each time you visit, you can see how they're growing."

They hugged. "Where's Dad gone?"

They wandered around calling for him. Before long he was discovered pacing around the garden.

"I reckon if you put the apple here, the plum here and the cherry about here..." He marked the ground with his heel. "...then, maybe repeat over there ..." He pointed.

Jennifer and Sally stood with their arms folded and a wry smile on their lips. "You've never been this enthusiastic about our garden, darling."

He shrugged. "I know... but this has got so much potential – it's um, well it's like a blank canvas isn't it?"

"Got it in one Dad – glad you like it." She gave him a grateful hug as she had her mum.

It was mid afternoon. Jennifer was busy sorting out the pigs while Sally and Jon were making a snack and drinks.

"The cuppas are ready – how's the cheese on toast doing?"

Jon looked under the grill. "I'll tell you when – it's almost there. Call Jennifer in and then we can tuck in."

Jon went to the back door. "Come on pet – grub up!"

She came in and washed her hands. "Ooh, I'm looking forward to this. How did we manage to miss lunch?"

Jon rolled his eyes. "Well, if you remember we were busy emptying Honey Bee Farm of quite a lot of their stock!"

"Oh yeah." They laughed.

Sally pondered. "It was a lovely place... and the shop. For some reason it reminded me of Grannifer..."

Jennifer smiled. "It did the same to me the first time I went there."

As they finished eating there was a knock on the back door. It was Jim, TJ and Soaki.

"Hello; this is a nice surprise. Come in."

"You're too late for Mum's cheese on toast but we were going to refill the mugs... want a cuppa?"

They accepted the offer and joined the family at the large table.

Jennifer put the kettle on again and filled Soaki's bowl.

Jim caught sight of a headline. "Can I look at your paper for a minute, please?"

"Yes of course Jim."

Jon passed the local newspaper. As he read the article, Jim tutted. "Well I'm blessed; oh what a shame. After all these years too." He puffed out his cheeks.

"What's up, Grandad?"

"What is it, Jim?"

With a sad expression he pointed where he'd been reading. "Old Joshua's boatyard – closing down."

"Where's that Jim? I don't think I know it."

"Mm? Oh, down at the Jingles."

They looked at him quizzically. "The Jingles? Where the heck is that?"

Jim chuckled. "That's what us kids called it. You might have noticed 'Chandlers Lane' – near the top of the village. Leads down to the river and that's where Joshua's place is."

"Oh yes, I've been past it. But why The Jingles?"

"Well, that's the noise sailing boats make when they're all rigged up. Not that that was the sound you got from Joshua's boatyard... more bang bang and sawing." He laughed again. "Yeah, we kids loved it. Old man Josh used to let us go and look around – as long as we kept to a safe distance while they worked, and he sometimes gave us a sixpence if we helped polish up wood and brass. Yeah – happy days!"

"So what stuff is there, Grandad?"

"Oh – anything and everything to do with boats."

TJ looked interested. "If he's closing down, he might have some interesting bits for sale. I'd like to have a look."

Jennifer nodded. "Mm – me too; sounds fascinating."

By this time everyone was getting the urge to go on the excursion. "Well, we have another day here – how about we wander round there tomorrow?"

Jennifer suddenly looked disappointed. "Oh yes, I'd forgotten you have to go home on Thursday – you sure you can't stay any longer?"

"Na – sorry pet, but we'll come again soon – promise!"

Jennifer gave a weak smile and nodded. TJ gave her a cuddle. "Come on – cheer up. We've got all that gardening to do – got to make it look posh in time for Sally and Jon's next trip here, eh?"

Sally smiled at him and mouthed "Thank You" in acknowledgement of his comforting words to their daughter.

Jim chipped in. "Well if it's your last day for this visit, we'd better make it a good-un! When we've done Joshua's place, how about we descend on the Arms and have a meal? Er... how are you at darts Jon?"

Jennifer rolled her eyes. "What's up Jim – running out of victims?"

Jim looked playfully incredulous – "Jenny lass – what a terrible thing to say!"

Jennifer smiled at Jim and then to her father. "What do you reckon Dad; you up for the challenge?"

Jon drew his breath through his teeth. "Well, I'll give it a go – I've thrown a few arrows down at our local, but..."

Sally joined in. "Don't worry darling; it's only a friendly. I'm sure Jim will be gentle with you!"

TJ had noticed the expressions within the Cade family. "Er, I'm not sure Grandad but I think there's bit of a wind up going on here."

Jennifer laughed. Jim looked across the table. "Do I take it you do more than chuck a few darts in your local?"

"Well I do captain our team, so I suppose the answer to that is er... yes!"

Jim rubbed his hands together. "Hee hee – this is gonna be a good-un!"

Jennifer tutted and rolled her eyes. "Oh dear; clash of the Titans. This will be worth watching!"

Everyone laughed. TJ stood up. "This is all very well and good, but we're wasting good planting time – who's up for a bit of digging? Come on Jenny; tell me where you want what."

They went into the garden, with Jim, Sally, Jon and Soaki close behind them.

Plants were placed and re-positioned several times before the correct positions were decided with a great deal of laughter as they pretended to play 'tree chess'. "Red cherry to green apple four!"

"Ooh – green plum to red apple two!"

"Oh no, that's checkmate!"

Before long, holes were dug and the trees were staked and planted. "Oh my – this is starting to look like a proper garden."

TJ took her hand. "We're not done yet Jen – where do you want these roses?"

They picked up various pots and read the labels. "This one's a rambler so perhaps by the wall?" She pointed.

"OK m'lady – there it shall be."

Everyone joined in. Suddenly Jennifer stopped. "Hang on a minute – Grannifer said something about roses – I'm just going to check her book."

She returned soon after carrying a bowl containing banana skins. "I knew there was something – we put these in the hole before putting the rose in. Stashed full of potassium apparently and really good for roses!"

TJ looked impressed. "Well done Grannifer – let's just hope they don't slip over in the night."

Jennifer gave him a gentle tap. "Oh, you are daft!"

He smiled at her. "Yeah I know – but I get it right sometimes."

With this he wrapped his arms around her and kissed her. She responded likewise. They were interrupted by the sound of hammering and went across to help Jon and Jim who were starting to put the protective fencing around the trees.

"There you go lass – hopefully this'll keep your piggies out."

Sally emerged from the kitchen with a tray. "Come on guys – break time!"

Everyone took a mug. "You're a mind-reader, Sally."

As they drank, Jon nodded to the profusion of plants in trays on the top of the outbuilding. "So what about that lot, pet?"

"I'm going to get some baskets and hang them up – if I do them high enough even Pickle won't be able to reach them!"

She looked affectionately at the pig who still had the remains of black paint on her back.

Finishing their drinks, Jennifer and TJ set about sorting the sty ready for the girls to settle for the night. They made sure that each of the newly planted fruit trees and roses were well watered and then tidied away the tools. The cool of the evening had taken Sally, Jon and Jim indoors, so with the gardening jobs dealt with and the pigs comfy in their beds, the couple joined the others.

They spent a pleasant evening chatting, when the conversation took on memories of years back and different board games they used to play. "Well, I've got Monopoly if anyone fancies a game."

Before long they were eagerly throwing dice and deciding what and when to buy. There were groans if they had to pay out or 'Go to Jail', and a huge laugh when Jim won a beauty contest. He pouted his lips and patted the back of his head.

"Oh well deserved Jim; you're loverly!!"

They all had a lot of fun, and in between turns Jennifer and Sally prepared a simple meal. The hours sped by and it seemed all too soon that TJ, Soaki and Jim had to go home. Arrangements were confirmed for the following day and hugs given when they all said goodnight.

***

Jennifer woke early next morning. She lay in her bed for a while enjoying the memories of the past few days spent with her parents. "Oh well Grannifer – if this is their last day before they have to go home, we need to make the most of it."

She got up and slipped her dressing gown on. Tiptoeing quietly past her parents' room so as not to disturb them, she went downstairs. In the kitchen she surveyed the Monopoly game still on the table. Smiling at the recollection of the previous evening she put the kettle on to make coffee. As it heated, she put away items from the draining board then packed the game neatly in its box. She wiped surfaces and was pleasantly surprised at how quickly she made everything clean and tidy.

"Mm, that didn't take long."

Taking her mug, she went through the hallway to the living room. There was little to do, as once the cushions were plumped and the rug straightened, this too was tidy.

"Could probably do with a vacuum but that's noisy."

As she drank her coffee she suddenly remembered a recent purchase from a charity shop. Putting her mug by the sink, she squeezed to the back of the broom cupboard. As she manoeuvred herself past various piles and handles with an array of mop heads, bristles and long feather dusters, she at last found the carpet sweeper she had been looking for.

As she lifted it up, the base caught in a mop bucket handle – this in turn knocked a broom, then a domino effect of dustpans and brushes, tins of polish from the shelf, piles of neatly folded yellow dusters and a spare dishcloth flew about as if bewitched. Although Jennifer grabbed at things in a desperate attempt to catch them, and no matter how much she said "Shh", the objects with a mind of their own cascaded from the cupboard and careered into the kitchen.

The noise, although short-lived, was deafening. With a resigned tut, Jennifer extracted herself from the chaos. "So much for trying to be quiet – I'd have been less noisy with a dozen vacuum cleaners!"

Disappointed that her plans for a bit of silent housework had been scuppered, Jennifer turned her back on the mess and sat at the table with her hands under her chin and sighed miserably.

She didn't hear the back door open. "Morning pet; you're up then! What's this – having a sort out?"

She spun round to see Jon and Sally coming in from the garden.

"Huh? What the... where? Oh!"

"Morning darling... coo, you've been having fun."

Jennifer stared open-mouthed. "I thought you were still in bed!"

As Sally put the kettle on, she spoke to her husband. "I asked you to leave a note, Jon."

"I did! I slipped it under your bedroom door – honest!" Jennifer shook her head. "I didn't see anything."

She went upstairs to look. Jon followed. "Nothing here Dad."

"Er yes, there it is…"

He bent down and pulled at a corner of paper which was under the carpet. He handed it to her sheepishly.

'Dear Jennifer, we're going for an early walk by the river – might even feed some ducks! Back soon. Love Mum and Dad. Xxx'

She laughed as she read the note. Back in the kitchen she relayed the events of her morning. They all laughed.

"I'd have loved to see you shushing everything as you tried to stop it falling!"

"It was crazy – one of those slow motion moments. I could see it all going on and could do nothing to stop it." She shrugged her shoulders. "So much for trying to have everything tidy – the place looks like a bomb's hit it."

Sally hugged her daughter. Jon smiled and started an imitation. "What would Jim say… 'Ee never mind Jenny lass… we'll soon get it sorted'."

Jennifer laughed. "That's very good Dad – you've got him off to a T!"

As Jon helped Jennifer to pick up and replace the renegade pile of escapees, Sally started to prepare breakfast.

"That's a lot for three of us Mum – did your walk give you an appetite?"

Sally smiled. "Well yes it did, but we met TJ so he and Soaki are joining us. They should be here soon."

"Ooh lovely. I'll lay an extra place."

With her mum in charge of the human's meal, Jennifer set about preparing the pigs' fruit and veg. She had this down to a fine art and with scoops of pig nuts put into what she called her 'rattle bucket', it was only a few minutes and she was into the garden calling the girls. The scattering of their food, as Mel suggested, moved progressively down the garden. Her 'gardeners' were doing a good job and Jennifer was now at least three quarters of the distance between the house and the bottom wall.

Being completely involved with her familiar routine of bucket rattling and high pitched "here piggy, pig, pigs" call, she was totally unaware of the figure at the gate.

TJ stood with his elbow on the post, his chin resting in his hand. He smiled as he watched her interacting with the girls as they came running to her. He let Soaki through and then came into the garden himself.

"Hiya Jenny. You all right?" He kissed her.

"Oh hello. Yeah I'm fine – you?"

He nodded. Jennifer greeted Soaki and they all went up to the house.

"Ah, good timing, I'm just going to dish up!"

As they chatted whilst they ate, Jennifer relayed the experiences of her morning. TJ gave a somewhat stifled chuckle. "Oh, classic – er I mean, poor you!"

Changing his expression to one of empathised sympathy, he tried to hold the look but couldn't. His laugh was infectious and in less than a few seconds they were all laughing.

With breakfast over and the table cleaned they got ready and went to meet up with Jim. Pulling up outside his cottage, Jon beeped his car horn. Within moments Jim appeared at his door. He gave a cheery wave as he walked along his path to the gate.

As they drove along, Jim called out directions for Jon.

They pulled up at the boatyard and Jim smiled. "It's just how I remember it – the old place hasn't changed a bit."

Jennifer held TJ's hand and they walked towards the long wooden building. "Isn't it lovely – so full of character."

Soaki was enjoying investigating this new area and was soon making friends with a rather elderly labrador who had come over to greet the visitors. An old gentleman came towards them. "Hello there. Can I help you?"

Jim stepped forward. "Morning Josh – how are you?"

Joshua gave a quizzical look and, squinting his eyes, he scrutinised Jim's features. "Well I'm blessed – it's young Jimmy!" They shook hands vigorously. "How are you?"

"I'm fine, but what's all this in the paper – surely it's not true; you can't close this down!"

"Case of having to Jimmy – come inside and I'll tell you over a cup of tea."

They all followed him inside. As they did so, Jennifer's eyes darted around, her face full of wonder as she took on board her surroundings. They all followed Josh up to his office which had more than a passing resemblance to a captain's cabin. He motioned for them to sit down.

Sally made herself comfortable in a large leather chair. "What a lovely room Joshua. It's like we've been transported onto an olde worlde ship."

He smiled. "Glad you like it my dear. It took a lot of years to find all the bits and bobs – but I enjoyed searching!"

He handed mugs of tea around. "So Josh – why have you decided to close down after all these years?"

Joshua gave a resigned look. "You've answered your own question Jimmy… all these years. I'm getting too old. I'm ninety next month and I haven't got the wind in me sails like I used to. Time to batten down the hatches and take a rest."

Jennifer looked amazed. "You wear your age well if I might say so."

"Thank you lass – it's kind of you to say so."

So what exactly are your plans for this place?" TJ was curious. "If you are selling things off I'd be interested in buying some; I've got a houseboat further down the river."

"Aye lad, you'll probably get your wish. It'll probably take me a few months to clear me last orders, then I'll start putting the place to bed. Doubt I'll find anyone to keep it as it is, so…" He looked wistful.

They continued chatting for a while and eventually made their way back to the car. They waved as Jon drove back up the lane. "What a nice chap."

"Yes, really lovely. I almost burst out laughing when – no offence Jim – but when he called you 'young Jimmy'!"

They all giggled. "Well, he's known me since I was a nipper. It's what he's always called me. But I know what you mean: it was strange to hear after all these years!" He chuckled along with everyone else.

"So where are we off to now?" Jon queried as they reached the top of Chandlers Lane.

"Well I told Cassie we'd meet up with them at the Arms at about half past two. What's the time now?"

Sally checked her watch. "It's a quarter to, darling."

"Cheers Mum. Well I guess it's off to the pub then, yes?" They all agreed.

"So Jon, you still up for this darts match then?"

"Absolutely Jim – I'm looking forward to beating you… er, playing you!"

"Ho ho – fighting talk there young man!"

Jennifer laughed at their mock teasing. "Well I've seen you both play – and I wouldn't like to say who is the better player. This is gonna be a game worth watching!"

They piled into the Miraford Arms laughing and joking. Jennifer and Sally organised their table whilst the men went to the bar to get their drinks.

"Angela love – can we reserve the dartboard for a while? This young whipper-snapper thinks he can beat me!"

"Sure thing Jim – I'll rope it off if needs be. This sounds like it will be worth a look!"

They took the drinks to the table. "What are you laughing at?"

Jon told his wife about Angela's quip. "If we're not careful Jim, they'll be taking bets on us."

"Wouldn't put it past 'em Jon!"

It wasn't long before Cassie and Paul joined them. Jennifer and Cassie were quickly into their usual interactive conversation, each telling the other what they'd been doing since they were last together. Cassie laughed as her friend described her broom cupboard experience.

Paul meanwhile was hearing about the ensuing darts match. Amid the buzz of what seemed like a dozen conversations at once, Jon called across the table. "Jim, I don't know if we're eating first or playing – but the oche is free."

"No time like the present lad – 'part from anything else you wouldn't move very far after one of Angela's meals!"

"That's true Jim. I ordered a sandwich once and couldn't finish it."

Sally raised her eyebrows. "Er, I'd better rethink my choice then. I was nearly decided on the Miraford Arms Special!"

Jennifer and Cassie shook their heads. "Not unless you're really, really hungry."

Everyone laughed as the locals all nodded in agreement.

"OK then Jim – that settles it – darts first."

The two men took their drinks and walked towards the dartboard. Everyone did likewise and found the best place to watch. Word had spread throughout the pub and in no time a huge crowd had gathered to watch the spectacle.

"What do you think Jim – 501, end on a double, best of three?"

Jim pursed his lips as he nodded. "But how about we make it best of five?"

"Fine by me."

TJ offered to do the scoring, and Paul took a coin from his pocket. "Shall we toss for who goes first or is it nearest the bull?"

Choosing the coin, Paul spun it in the air. Jim called tails. "Sorry Jim, it's heads. Jon to go first."

They both had a few practice throws, then the first game started. The crowd fell silent.

TJ chalked the scores and called the totals. He took exceptional pleasure if three treble twenties were thrown and as if it was a professional match, he shouted dramatically "One hundred and eighty!"

The now totally engrossed audience ooh'd and aah'd and cheered at the appropriate times. Tension ran high.

The two men were well suited opponents and by the final game had won two each. As the patrons of the Miraford Arms fell silent, scarcely daring to breath, Jennifer held Sally's hand. Jon threw his first three darts. Then Jim took his shot keeping up with fairly even scores, the game nearing its conclusion.

Jon needed ninety eight and Jim a straight one hundred. Jon threw his first dart – treble sixteen. Paul mouthed to Cassie "Bulls eye to finish."

The second dart flew through the air. It hit the wire and stuck in the twenty five. The crowd gasped and he threw again into the five.

Jim took his place on the oche. He took a deep breath. He quietly reassured himself, "Treble twenty – double top."

He threw. He tutted as again the dart stuck in on the wrong side of the wire.

"Treble one." He composed himself. His second dart found its target – "Treble nineteen."

He puffed his cheeks, took aim and threw. Finding its mark the dart stuck securely into the double twenty!

The crowd erupted into massive cheers and Jon and Jim shook hands then hugged.

"Well done, Jim – thanks for a great match."

With a beaming smile Jim responded. "No lad – thank you – you almost had me there!"

"We'll have a return match next time we're here, yes?"

"Oh you bet lad. I'll look forward to that." He chuckled.

Sally nudged her daughter's elbow. "Tell you what darling, if we don't eat soon I reckon I'll be sticking with my choice of a Miraford Special. Am I the only one who's hungry?"

Jennifer smiled. "No Mum – you're not on your own. I've got a rumbly-tum too!" She looked at the clock above the bar. "Coo – no wonder we're hungry; it's gone half past four. Oh crikey – the girls!"

"What's up pet?" Jon had heard her cry out.

"I forgot the time and I should be sorting the pigs – and we haven't even ordered our meal yet and by the time we get home it will be…"

He put his finger to his lips. "Calm down – we can order our food – I'll drive you to the house, we'll find the girls and be back in time for our dinner!"

"But haven't you been drinking?"

Jon laughed. "Only a shandy and soft drink love – come on, what are you getting from the menu?"

Leaving Sally to place their order, they left the pub.

"Back in a bit," Jennifer called to the others, leaving her mum to explain the swift disappearance of her family.

Less than half an hour later they walked back through the doors of the Arms. "That was blooming quick. You found the secret to time travel?"

"Not quite Jim but it's amazing what you can do when you're hungry and there's one of Angela's meals waiting for you."

Not realising that the subject of her accolade was standing behind her, she turned round as Angela spoke.

"Ooh, thanks very much Jen … the cheque is in the post!" They both smiled broadly.

With all the meals now on the table, the gathering of friends tucked in. Even Soaki was provided for.

Having eaten, they continued to enjoy the rest of the evening in the delightful old pub. Don and Helen had joined them after work.

As the bell rang and 'time' was called, it was a bitter-sweet atmosphere that engulfed everyone. They had enjoyed a lovely visit to Miraford, but Jon and Sally had to go home in the morning.

"Don't worry though guys – we'll be back again as soon as possible."

With their last hugs and kisses everyone said their 'goodbyes' and made their way home.

The following morning Jon packed the car whilst Sally and Jennifer made a drink before they left.

"I'll miss you Mum. It's been lovely to have you and Dad here."

"Likewise darling, but we'll come again soon. We've had a really nice time, and your friends are super. It has put our minds at rest to know you have such good people around you."

They hugged. "I knew you'd like them – and they do you too!"

Her dad came in. "Is this a private cuddle or can anyone join in?"

He joined them. "Ah yes – really nice crowd. I'll have to get some practice in before our next visit – can't have Jim beating me again!"

They laughed. "Yeah, he's a good player all right. I knew it would be a good match."

There was a knock at the door. It was TJ and Soaki. "Oh good, I haven't missed you. Here's that recipe I promised you Sally."

She smiled as she took the sheet of paper. "Thank you TJ. I'll send my Ginger Loaf on when we get home."

"Or you could bring it next time you visit!" He smiled

encouragingly.

Sally nodded. They took their drinks and sat in the garden.

All too soon it was time to leave. Hugs and kisses abounded and noticing Jennifer's tear-filled eyes, TJ wiped her cheeks. He turned to Sally. "Don't worry, I'll look after her."

Sally smiled back. "Yes, I know you will."

They waved and watched the car until it was out of sight.

"Come on Jenny; things to do."

She looked at him with curiosity. "What things?"

"I had a thought for the garden – I've drawn a picture. Come on, see what you think."

She followed him indoors then led her through to the garden and sat her at the table. "I'll be back out in a moment – then I want you to tell me what you see while you've been sitting here!"

He went back inside. Totally perplexed, Jennifer looked around.

TJ returned with two coffees. "Well?"

"Er, just the usual really. There's Soaki playing with Pickle, Pinky and Perky nuzzling around and Primrose here having her ears tickled. The trees we planted and the stone walls – what else do you want me to say?"

He took her hand and led her diagonally to the bottom of the garden. "When you showed me Grannifer's book, I noticed one of the comments she'd written – 'There's always more than one point of view'. Now, I know this isn't really what she meant – but look now, and tell me what you see."

Jennifer studied the view. "Well there's still the animals but now I see the house, the two outhouses, even down the garden to the front wall. Oh you are clever, so, if I get another table and benches…"

He shook his head. "Not quite what I had in mind."

They returned to the table and whilst drinking their coffee, TJ produced another sheet of paper. She looked with awe at the beautifully illustrated drawing which had been titled 'Jenny's Summer House'."

"Oh TJ, this is gorgeous, but…"

He put a finger to her lips. "I've had a word with Grandad, and if you like it, we'll build it for you. Old Joshua had some lovely wood there so we can buy it from him, and you can decorate it however you like – that's if you do like… do you? Like it I mean?"

He'd started to sound a little unsure. She smiled broadly and hugged him tightly. "I don't like it… I LOVE it!!"

Holding her in his arms TJ chuckled. "Do I take it you're OK with it then?"

"Oh yes, it's beautiful. It reminds me of a Swiss chalet. Do you really think you could build it?"

"Yeah, I reckon. With Grandad on board we'll sort it."

She kissed his cheek. "I'm so lucky. Thank you."

"You are most welcome ma'am!"

He returned a kiss. "S'pose we'd better let Grandad know, then we can organise the things we need."

With a broad smile, Jennifer scrunched her shoulders. "Oh, this is so exciting. Just wait 'til I tell Mum."

***

It was mid afternoon when the phone rang. Jennifer picked up the receiver. "Hello. Oh hi Mum, you're home then – Good journey? Oh good – Hey, you'll never guess. TJ drew me a picture; we've got to dig out the footings then put down some hardcore, then lay cement and then they can build it! It's going to be beautiful, a different view and everything! Mm? Oh didn't I say? The guys, Jim and TJ – they're going to build me a summer house! Isn't it wonderful?"

She listened for a while. "I don't think I was babbling was I? Oh sorry." She laughed.

Calming down, she had a proper chat with Sally. They talked for nearly half an hour. "OK then Mum; I'll call you next week. Love you, byeee!"

She replaced the handset and joined TJ. He'd been playing football with Soaki. "She makes a good goalie. You know, I reckon if ever Mel can't play in Don's team she could take his place!"

Jennifer laughed as he kicked the ball high and his faithful canine jumped up and caught it. Then she returned it to her master for another go.

"Even that weirdo pig of yours has been chasing it around!"

Jennifer pretended to look indignant. "I beg your pardon – I know Pickle is an unusual pig, but she's not a weirdo."

"Let's face it though Jen, she sometimes tries to do the same thing as Soaki – I think she thinks she's a dog."

"I can't disagree there, but I love her all the more for her quirky ways."

She joined in with the game until interrupted by the phone ringing again.

"Ooh – aren't you the popular one today!"

She returned soon after. "That was Cassie. She and Paul will be round soon."

"Oh jolly good – I'll get Paul to help start digging the footings."

130

Jennifer playfully tapped his arm. "Cor. You're rotten you are – he's been at work all day. At least let him get in the door!"

He feigned looking disgruntled and 'told off'. "Oh all right then; I'll let him get through the door!"

As they joked, they heard Cassie's car pull up. "I'll let them know we're in the garden."

Jennifer ran around the side of the house. TJ called out – "It's OK; I'll get the front door!"

He disappeared into the kitchen. Almost at the same time they greeted their friends. "Hi guys. Come in."

"Er, why don't you come this way? We've been playing football."

"Nah, you don't want to walk all the way around there – cut through the house. It's, er, quicker!"

"But if you come this way, I can show you the roses we planted near the wall."

Cassie and Paul looked bemused by the strange, almost argumentative banter between the couple. Cassie whispered in Paul's ear "There's something going on here but for the life of me I can't work out what." Then louder, "I'll tell you what; I'll go round with Jen – you go with TJ."

Jennifer almost squealed. "No, no you mustn't!"

TJ grinned "Yes you can; great decision."

Jennifer resignedly threw her hands in the air. "Ah well, at least I tried. Don't blame me!"

Their guests looked mystified. Paul went indoors. TJ put his hand on his friend's shoulder. "Paul mate – got a little proposition to put your way."

By the time they had walked through the kitchen and out of the back door, Paul was examining his stomach and biceps. With a furrowed brow he looked at the girls. "Would you say I'm getting flabby?"

"Now, I didn't say flabby." TJ had a cheeky grin.

"Then what on earth are you on about? Honestly, this bloke here has been saying I need some exercise, some sort of workout. And something about leggings? I draw the line at leggings."

"Oh, did I say leggings... I meant footings – we need to dig some."

Eventually they explained everything and they all laughed. "So that is what all that palaver was about when we arrived. Honestly you two are are... pretty weird."

"That makes three of us then; it's what TJ called Pickle!"

They continued chatting happily. "So have you got all the cement and stuff to put in this hole I'm told I've got to dig?"

He mimicked a sad face and sniffed. Collectively the others sympathised. "Ah, poor Paul."

They pretended to play violins. "Actually, I've got no idea exactly what and how much of the what we need to get. Er, did that make sense? I know what I mean but…"

"It's OK Jenny – we understood."

TJ smiled at her. "Anyway, until a few hours ago I didn't even know I'd be needing cement and stuff."

"Shall I pick some up in the old girl?"

Paul shook his head. "Probably not the best idea, love – not if you value your suspension. Anyway, should be possible to get it delivered."

"Good thinking young man!" Jennifer turned to TJ. "So, Mr Builder – what exactly do I need to get?"

"Give us a tick, and I'll work it out."

"While you do that, I'll make us a cuppa."

Leaving the men to their calculations, the girls went into the kitchen. While the kettle boiled, they found the phone number of a local builder's merchant.

Within an hour things had been arranged, and the area for their latest project marked out, the digging already started.

***

At the end of the day Jennifer sat on the edge of her bed and took stock. "Whew Grannifer; was it really only this morning that Mum and Dad went home? It's been so full of things happening, I can't believe it's still the same day."

She yawned. Turning off the bedside lamp, she turned her sleepy gaze towards the window. She smiled at the black star-studded sky. Still smiling, she lay back and snuggled beneath the covers.

Chapter 8

The following morning, now refreshed after a good night's sleep, she busied herself with her usual routine of sorting the pigs and enjoying watching the birds as she ate her own breakfast. Things seemed calmer and almost back to normal. As she pottered about singing along with the radio, there was a knock at the door.

"Morning – Miss Cade? McKinley Builders."

"Oh yes, hello."

As the two delivery men unloaded her order, Jennifer looked on in amazement at the apparent ease with which they seemed to deal with the heavy containers. When she verbalised her admiration they smiled. "Oh it's just what you get used to, and knowing how to lift 'em."

Before long they had put everything in the garden and went on their way.

"Gosh, that was quick. I didn't even have time to offer them a cuppa."

As she returned to her jobs around the house she was surprised to hear Cassie calling her. "Cooee, Jennifer, you there mate?"

Joining her friend, her smile turned to a concerned expression. "Hi Cassie, what's up love? You all right? You look... um sort of sad. What's the matter?"

Cassie started to cry and they hugged. "Oh darlin', what is it? I've never seen you upset like this before."

Cassie sobbed. Still being cuddled by her friend, she calmed down enough to speak.

"My... studio... I'm going to... lose... my stu... dio." She sniffed and tears ran down her cheeks.

"Why? I thought you had a like sort of never ending rental arrangement on the place."

Sniffing again, Cassie responded. "I did, but the owner's got problems and he's got to sell the property."

"Can you afford...?"

Her words tailed off as Cassie closed her eyes and dolefully shook her head.

"No way; I couldn't afford it."

Jennifer sighed and gave an extra squeeze to her hug. "How long before you've got to get out?"

With a shrug of her shoulders she replied "Oh, possibly a few months – he's not sure. Could be more, but that's not the point. There's nowhere else I can move to. It took me ages to find this one and... Oh Jennifer... I love it there!" Her bottom lip quivered.

Jennifer had made mugs of coffee. "We'll start looking for somewhere... even better than what you've got now."

"But..."

"No buts, there's two of us looking this time! And Grannifer always said two heads are better than one!" She smiled. "Don't worry. Something will turn up."

Taking a deep breath, Cassie forced a smile in return. Jennifer racked her brains to come up with an idea that would cheer her friend up.

"Oh, by the way, did you see my temporary garden feature – just until I have the creation you'll be making?"

Cassie looked surprised. "No, where is it?"

"Down by the side of the house – come along; I'll show you."

They walked together, Cassie still curious. Jenny proffered her hand with a flurry of over-enthusiastic revelation. "Ta da! I call it 'Sound Support System'. What do you think?"

Cassie burst out laughing. "Oh you daft bat! It's a concrete mixer!"

Jennifer laughed too as she hugged her friend. "I know, but I had to do something to cheer you up! I just hope Jim and TJ know how to work the thing."

"We'll soon find out – look, they've just come through the gate."

They all greeted each other and then the men investigated the morning's delivery. With their usual gusto, the group all got stuck in to the job at hand. Even Soaki did her bit by barking encouragingly. With support boards around the perimeter they filled in the layer of hardcore.

"Right, I think before we do the mixer we have a cuppa and some lunch."

"The lady of the house has spoken. All those in favour, raise your hands!"

All four stuck their hands into the air and they made a collective exodus to the kitchen. They each helped to prepare drinks and sandwiches.

"And if you're all good children and finish all your sarnies – I've got an extra treat!"

As Cassie, Jim and TJ looked expectantly at each other, with one voice they all cheered – "Hurray – flapjacks!"

Jim drained his mug then placed it quiet deliberately on the table. He rubbed his hands together and looked at the others. "Right, come on then you guys; there's work as needs to be done!"

He stood up and went to the door. Jennifer smiled and followed close behind him. "Oh my, this is exciting. I've never made concrete before!"

Cassie looked at TJ. "She's easily pleased! Come on mate – let's go help before she does something weird or crazy."

"Or both, knowing Jenny!"

They joined Jim and Jennifer who looked fit to burst. "So what do we do first?"

TJ held her shoulders. "Calm down darling... it really isn't that exciting." He kissed her cheek and smiled. "We have to put four measures of sand to one of cement. Then add water 'til it's the right consistency."

"Ooh, just like making a cake!"

"Um, yeah, kind of."

With the gloopy mixture poured into the area, they all helped to spread it around as evenly as possible. Then, holding a big board, Jim and TJ worked across the surface until it was completely flat.

"Gosh, that looks really professional. Well done guys. So is that it now?"

"Not quite Jen. We need to wash this mixer out or McKinley will have your guts for garters!"

As they cleaned the mixer and all the other tools the temptation to splash each other was too much and before long a full-on water fight was in progress. Squeals of laughter were abundant as various containers from the kitchen were filled with water and the contents hurled at each other.

As they sat dripping wet and out of breath, TJ grinned. "Whew – almost as good as that one when I was a kid, Grandad!"

"Aye lad – almost!"

TJ noticed a wistful look on Jim's face. He knew that the memory had brought his grandma Mary into Jim's head.

"Tell you what Grandad – how about we go to the boat and get some dry clothes on? I don't think anything of Jenny's will fit us!"

Jim nodded. "Good idea Timothy. Anyway, I don't think drag suits me."

They chuckled. TJ told Jennifer of their plans. "Be back ASAP."

"Okay, see you in a while."

While the men were gone, Jennifer and Cassie raided the wardrobe and got themselves changed.

It was about half past five when Jennifer realised yet again that she was late preparing the things for the pigs. "Oh crikey – the girls! I'm such a bad mother!"

Cassie giggled. "Oh I'm sure they don't mind staying up late!"

They prepared the food together. They'd just finished when Jim and TJ returned.

"Hiya guys. Cassie and I were just talking about dinner; do you fancy a takeaway? We could ask Paul to pick up something on his way here."

They nodded in agreement. After a brief discussion they decided on Chinese, and Cassie phoned Paul.

It was nearly eight o'clock when Cassie answered the door. "Hiya darling – that didn't take you long." She kissed him.

"Well, you all sounded hungry so I walked as quickly as I could. Actually, I cadged a lift with Barry part of the way!" He returned the kiss then stood back and studied his girlfriend. "New dress, babe? I don't think I've seen that one before."

Cassie laughed. "Well you might have seen it… just not on me. It's Jennifer's!" She proceeded to tell him about the water fight.

Everyone cheered as Paul entered the kitchen laden with bags of fragrant Chinese food.

"Cor, you're a welcome sight mate – we're famished. Did Cassie tell you all the stuff we've been doing?"

"Yeah, some of it – I must come and see this work of art foundation."

Jennifer joined in the conversation. "Don't be too long or the food will get cold… but it is worth a look. Smooth as the proverbial baby's bottom!"

"Well, it's not quite that smooth – but we're pleased with the result."

Paul looked impressed. "Well – I'd better give it a neutral opinion – since you all had a hand in doing the work."

"Are you implying we might be biased because we slaved over a hot

136

cement mixer for days on end?"

"Oh no – but I'll give you my marks out of ten for flatness and creativity!"

He strode purposefully through the back door. Everyone joked and chatted as they waited for the impromptu judge to return.

He reappeared at the door.

"Well?"

He smiled. "I know you'd over-egged the flatness bit, but ten out of ten for the creative touch!"

They looked mystified. "No, come on; what do you really think?"

Now it was Paul who looked confused. "Honest guys, there's a random design all over it. Go and look for yourselves; it's still quite light out. Oh, by the way Jennifer – did you know the pigs are still up? They having a girls' night out?" He smiled at his own joke.

"Oh crikey. I bet I know… oh they haven't!"

Jennifer rushed out, closely followed by TJ, Cassie, Jim and Paul. Staring at the indentations, realisation hit home.

"One of the little darlings has been investigating!" Jennifer rolled her eyes. "And I bet I know which one… Pickle!!"

She checked each of the girls' trotters as she ushered them into the sty for the night. As usual Pickle was the last one in – always still rummaging around the garden.

"Oh Pickle – it was you. Look at your trotters. You silly girl – there's concrete between your toes!"

TJ bought a bucket of water. "I take it foot bathing is required?"

Jennifer sighed deeply. "Absolutely! Thanks darling."

They worked together and soon had Pickle sorted.

"Now then Missy, into bed and no more mischief!" Jennifer patted Pickle's rump affectionately. "I know she's always up to something or other… but she makes me smile."

TJ took her hand. "Come on you old softie – dinner's getting cold!"

"Oh no! I forgot about the food!"

Returning to the kitchen, Cassie smiled. "All done? I put the grub on low in the oven. Shall we eat now?"

Jennifer gave her a cuddle. "Thank you."

As they tucked in to their meal, Jennifer apologised for the damage to their hard work.

"Actually – I thought it was quite artistic."

"Trust you TJ, but we have to do it all again."

Jim spoke. "Don't worry Jenny lass. It'll be rock hard by tomorrow, then we can patch it up."

She smiled at him. "Oh, if you're sure." Relieved, she finished eating.

The following morning, before she started her regular routine of feeding the pigs, birds and herself, Jennifer went to examine Pickle's additional decorations. "Mm, well, it's different, but it can't stay... still there's no reason why it can't be recorded."

Having returned to the house, she was back moments later with her camera. She took a few shots. "Well, at least one of those should be OK."

She carried on getting all the breakfast done and then got ready for her weekly excursion to the market.

Cassie was waiting for her. "Morning Jennifer – you all right?"

"Hiya. Yeah I'm fine. You?"

Cassie smiled. "Yes, though sorry about yesterday. I'm more positive today. Thank you for being there."

They hugged. "That's what friends are for."

They did their usual wander, enjoying the chats with their stall holder friends.

As usual Jennifer spent a long time at the fabric stall. "I've got to do the other bedrooms. Mine can wait for a bit but the other spare room needs doing, ready for any time I have more than a couple to stay."

Cassie smiled. "And apart from that... you just love interior designing!"

Jennifer rolled her eyes. "You're not wrong – I'm seriously thinking of starting up my own business."

"Why not. You know your trade."

"Yeah well... I haven't decided properly yet," she tutted. "That'll be two of us looking for somewhere to work from."

"Make that three..."

They stared at the girl on the stall.

"Sorry, I didn't mean to eavesdrop."

They said it didn't matter and asked what she meant. Laura explained that she wouldn't have her pitch for much longer.

"Oh how sad. Give us your number and if we hear of anything we'll give you a ring."

Bidding Laura goodbye the two friends continued around the market. "Oh look, that's what I need." Jennifer started selecting hanging baskets.

"Do you have brackets to hang them from, please?"

"Of course my dear; how many do you need?"

"Erm, seven please."

"Cor, you've got some planting ahead of you."

She nodded and smiled as she paid him. "My mum and dad bought me loads as a house warming present."

Taking some of the baskets to help carry them, Cassie, with a twinkle in her eyes joked with her friend. "You sure you've got enough?"

"Well I know you will think I'm mad but… I'm not sure that I have. And anyway, he didn't have what I was hoping to get."

"What's that?"

"I'd really like a couple of those hay rack things."

Cassie looked sympathetically. "Tell you what: before we go home we'll pop round to Johnstone's. They might have some."

"Cheers mate – that would be lovely." As they neared the veg stall the man who always served them waved.

"Come on – fill me in. How are you girls doing?"

He was always intrigued by Jennifer's updates on the pigs. He roared with laughter when they told him about yesterday's events.

As they walked to the car they looked at each other bemused. "I didn't think it was that funny."

"No, nor me. I bet he's a riot when Christmas crackers are pulled!" They laughed.

With the car already quite full, Cassie playfully warned her friend. "Hay racks – don't go looking at anything else!"

Jennifer pushed her bottom lip forward and lowered her head, but soon broke into a smile. "Ha! Ha! Success – look, just what I wanted."

"Er Jen – you said you wanted two."

"I know – this is just an extra one for… er um – for luck."

She gave a broad grin. Cassie shook her head. Before they reached the car Jennifer diverted and cried out excitedly. "Oh my goodness – look at that!"

Cassie rolled her eyes. "Oh no – what's she found now?"

She joined her friend. "What on earth is it?"

"It's an old turnstile – isn't it wonderful?"

"Yes Jennifer, it's very nice, but you don't need one!"

"As if I'm going to buy it – I'm not daft you know!"

"I just think if you had half an idea how to use it – you would."

"Yeah yeah! As if I'm going to find a use for a turnstile."

Back at Willow Bank they unpacked the shopping. "Have you got everything you need to do the baskets?"

Jennifer nodded. "Uh huh – I'm using another of Grannifer's tips."

Cassie raised her eyebrows. "What gem has she come up with this time?"

"Old woollies for the liner – she used to save old jumpers for the job but I bought a woollen blanket from the charity shop."

Cassie was impressed. "Oh yes, 'cos wool holds water – clever."

"And – if you have an old saucer to pop in before you add the compost that helps retain even more."

They carried on chatting whilst putting things away and preparing lunch. "S'pose after we've eaten we'd better get stuck in and repair the Pickle's handiwork."

"Don't you mean 'trotters-work'?"

They giggled. As they discussed the various antics of the pigs, Cassie looked thoughtful. "I suppose we'll have to put our trip to the seaside on hold while you still have them. Can't leave them on their own for a whole day."

Jennifer smiled and tapped the side of her nose with a finger. "I'm ahead of you there mate – I've already asked TJ if he'll piggy-sit for me. He's fine with it – so, all we have to do is decide when and where."

"Brilliant! To be honest I don't care where, as long as it's soon. I just feel like a proper day out."

Eventually they set about making up some more of the concrete mixture. "Lucky we didn't use all of the sand and cement."

"Cor, absolutely. I've got flour and water so we could have mixed up some papier mâché but I don't think it would be as good."

They laughed. "So what was it? Four measures of sand to one of cement?"

"Yes, that was it. How about I stir, and you add the water?"

Cassie nodded. "Certainly dear… with any luck we'll have this patched up and good as new by the time the guys get here."

"Yes, and I think we'll put up a barricade, just in case."

Jennifer looked accusingly at Pickle who had wandered over to see what was going on. As Jennifer spooned the prepared concrete into the trotter-shaped holes, Cassie smoothed it level.

"There, that's the last one."

"Good job too – we haven't got any mixture left."

"Whew, that was lucky. Right. Barricades, coffee and then we'll put up the baskets."

They cleaned the bucket and tools as they had yesterday, but more sensibly this time. As they dealt with the plants, another of Grannifer's tips came in useful. "Yeah, whenever I did this with her and Grandpa we always rested the basket on a plant pot or a bowl – stopped it rolling around. Hopefully next year I'll be able to use my own home-made compost instead of buying it."

"You've decided to stick around then?"

Jennifer shrugged her shoulders and wrinkled her nose. "Well... I think I might as well – what do you think?"

"Mm...OK then, if you insist!" The two friends chuckled.

"This a private happy place or can anyone join in?" It was TJ.

"Oh hello love." Jennifer returned the kiss he had planted on her cheek. "What, no Soaki?"

"Oh yes, she's following with Grandad – I've come on ahead to make sure the kettle's on."

"Hey cheeky – well you know where it is!" They pulled faces at each other and then smiled. He disappeared into the house.

"Hello girls – has he made that brew yet?

"Hiya Jim – just doing it! How are you?"

"Fit as a fiddle, thank you lass – you?"

"Oh, we're fine"

"Those are looking nice – where you putting 'em?"

Jennifer pointed. "I've got to put the brackets up first."

"I'll give you a hand after we've sorted that concrete out."

With smug expressions the girls folded their arms. "We've already done it!"

"Ooh, aren't you the efficient ones!" He looked impressed.

"Well, we'll down this cuppa and get these 'ere baskets up." At that moment TJ appeared with a tray of mugs.

All too soon the afternoon had slipped away. Jennifer took the pigs their food and scattered it even further down the garden.

"You are a good team of workers my darlings. Won't be much longer and you'll have munched your way through all the roots and weeds. Well done girls!"

She stood for a moment and looked towards the house. The perimeter walls were now adorned with occasional splashes of colour. She smiled as she enjoyed the new editions. TJ joined her and slipped his arm around her waist. "Happy?"

She nodded, "Yes, very."

He looked into her bright blue eyes and a gentle breeze caught her blonde hair. Carefully he moved her hair off her face and kissed her lips. They embraced for a moment. "I've been sent down to let you know that Grandad has made us all a drink. I er... I s'pose we ought to... "He gazed at her. "Oh Jenny – you are so beautiful."

He kissed her again. It was a magical moment but unfortunately interrupted by a call from the kitchen door. "Come on you love birds – you've got the rest of your lives to canoodle; these drinks are growing icicles!"

They laughed. "Oh honestly, what's he like?"

They returned to the house and joined Cassie, Jim and Soaki in the living room. "Good cuppa Jim!"

"Aye lass – years of practice!" He beamed and gave a knowing nod.

They continued to chat and relax for a while. "I can't be too long before I go. I said I'd meet Paul in the 'Arms' at eight. Anyone fancy coming along? I can fit us all in the old girl."

"I'd like to. I know we were only there a couple of days ago but it feels like ages!"

Jim and TJ agreed and even Soaki appeared to have been listening. She got up from her adopted rug and stretched herself and after a shake, sat in front of TJ with an expectant expression.

"It's all right you old boozer – you can come too." They all laughed at her antics.

"She pretends to be asleep – but she hangs on every word doesn't she?"

TJ agreed as he lovingly stroked her head.

"Right, I'm going to make sure the girls are snuggled safely in their beds, then I'm ready when you are." Jennifer gathered the empty mugs and put them in the sink as she went through the kitchen.

They all climbed into Cassie's car and were very soon enjoying their friendly local. Cassie found Paul about to be served at the bar. "Hiya darling. What do you fancy? Your timing is impeccable – I was just getting drinks in."

She kissed him, then looked quizzical. "Ordering drinks… who are you with?"

"Oh, I found this couple loitering about and asked if they'd like to join me and my gorgeous girlfriend."

He nodded in the direction of their usual table. Cassie followed his indication through the clusters of Miraford Arms patrons and spotted two familiar figures.

"Ah, it's Mum and Dad." She made her way to them. Giving hugs, she pulled up a chair. "So how did he persuade you to join us? You don't often manage to get out of an evening."

"Well, he told us how upset you've been about your studio. We didn't realise. Why didn't you say something to us darling?"

She gave a heavy sigh. "I didn't want you worrying – you've got enough to deal with."

Helen took her hand. "But my love, we're your parents – that's our job – sharing your kids' concerns comes with the territory. Good, bad or indifferent, we're here for you."

Cassie sniffed. "I know – thank you and I'm sorry."

Helen wiped a tear from her daughter's cheek. "Anyway, the idea was that we all get together to cheer you up – so no more sad faces. Yes?"

Cassie smiled and nodded.

"Hey, make room. I found this trio of trouble-makers at the bar – oh, sorry Soaki – perhaps that should be a quartet."

He placed the tray of drinks on the table, sat next to Cassie and gave everyone their glasses. "Before you all guzzle your drinks, I'd like to say something."

They all looked at Paul in anticipation. "You all know I always refer to this lady as my 'gorgeous girlfriend'. Well I've been thinking for a while now. I don't want to call her that any more."

He turned to face Cassie who by now bore a serious and somewhat confused expression. Paul put a finger gently to her lips and stood and faced her. "I'd prefer to call you my 'fabulous fiancée'." He knelt on one knee and took her hand. "Cassie darling, will you marry me?"

She bit her lip and tears filled her pretty green eyes. Stiffening a laugh she threw her arms around him. "Of course I will."

They kissed and everyone clapped and cheered. Paul stood up and acknowledged Don and Helen who had come round the table to join them. "Er sorry Don… I should have asked you first."

Don smiled. "That's really nice of you son… but I'm already married."

Everyone laughed. By now the whole pub knew of the proposal and a rousing chorus of 'For they are jolly good fellows' filled the air. Angela arrived with champagne and glasses. "Compliments of the house – congratulations!"

Smiles and good wishes were abundant throughout the evening. When the initial excitement had died down somewhat, Jennifer and Cassie managed to get a few moments together. They hugged tightly. "Oh Cassie – I'm so happy for you. What a lovely surprise. You kept that quiet!"

"Good reason for that mate – I didn't know anything about it. I was as amazed as you!"

They giggled and hugged again. "He's told me he has bought a ring but left it at the jeweller's so we can pick it up together, and if I don't like it then I can choose a different one. We're going on Monday. Oh Jennifer – isn't he just the most wonderful boyfr…, er, fiancé ever?"

They laughed again at her correction. "So are your feet going to be on the ground enough to walk around the seaside on Tuesday?"

"Oh gosh, yes I think I need it more than ever to calm down and sort my head out. These last few days have been such a roller coaster – I'm not sure if I'm coming or going!"

They joined everyone else. "Come on you two – there's a backlog of drinks here. Everyone's been buying them for us!"

Cassie looked at Paul. "Darling, I do believe you're a touch tiddly."

He gave her a sly grin. "Yes I know, but it's not every day you get engaged!"

By the end of the evening everyone was decidedly merry. Cassie cuddled Angela as she said goodnight. Still half draped on the friendly landlady, she slurred "I've left thee owld gerll houtside. I'll bick herr up – erm tom-tomorrow!" She grinned, pleased with herself for getting the sentence out – well almost.

Angela smiled. "Good idea Cassie – night night darling."

Outside everyone said their goodbyes and went in their various directions home.

***

The following morning with, surprisingly, not even a hint of hangover, Cassie and Paul arrived outside the Miraford Arms and climbed into the bright little 2CV. Cassie started up the engine and, with her familiar bright smile now returned to her face and with her auburn curls cascading around and over her shoulders, she looked the picture of happiness.

"Before you start driving…"

She turned to Paul. "Yes darling?"

He leant across and kissed her. "I love you."

She smiled. "I know, and I love you too!"

They drove out of the village. Every so often people waved as they passed or gave a thumbs up sign. They giggled at the reactions. "I think we can take it that people are happy for us."

"Yeah, I reckon, but I didn't think the 'Arms' was big enough to hold the entire village. Were there really so many in there last night?"

"I don't think so, but you know the Miraford grape vine – you only have to sneeze at the top of the village and within a minute someone at the bottom will say 'Bless You'!"

He rolled his eyes. "Oh yes, I'd forgotten."

As they arrived in Lamton, Cassie found a space. She parked the car and full of excitement walked hand in hand along the High Street. "That's the shop." Paul pointed.

"That's where we bought Mum's birthday present – Paul are you sure? It's rather expensive."

He raised his eyebrows and pulled an exasperated expression. "Will you stop it. You're worth whatever it costs – and more. Okay?"

She smiled lovingly. "Okay."

As they entered the jeweller's the assistant greeted them, "A good morning again sir, and this is your young lady. Good morning Miss – I take it congratulations are in order?"

They thanked him and Cassie tucked her head cosily into Paul's shoulder. "We've come to see if I made a good choice with the ring."

"Certainly sir. I'll fetch it."

Cassie was unaware of the nods and winks exchanged between the two men. When he returned to the counter he placed a pad and small tray in front of Cassie with one ring right in the middle of it. Cassie stared in disbelief. It was a large cluster of pearls with the tiniest of garnets in between. There was a centre stone of onyx, all in a silver setting. She stared, not knowing what to say. So not her style and not anything like any sort of engagement ring she had ever seen before.

Trying his hardest to be serious – "Well darling, what do you think?"

"Er well, I um!"

"Perhaps sir's alternative choice may be more to the young lady's liking?"

He removed the ugly ring and replaced it with a box.

"See what you think of this one, Cassie."

She picked up the box and gently opened the lid. A beautiful, dainty ring with a centre emerald, surrounded by diamonds with a platinum setting and shoulders merging into the twenty four carat band. It glistened like nothing else she could recall before. "Oh Paul, it's beautiful."

"Better try it on then." He took it from the box and placed it on her finger. "How does that feel?"

She smiled broadly. "It's perfect; it could have been made for me."

"Er well… it was actually. I'm only glad I got it right!" They kissed.

The assistant, grinning behind interlocked fingers spoke. "Your, er fiancé insisted you would be all right with our little joke Miss. I do hope you were not too upset."

Cassie leant across the counter and pecked him on the cheek. "You're forgiven."

They all laughed. "Come on fiancé – let's get a celebration coffee and maybe even a cake to go with it!" They said goodbye and left the shop.

Cassie pulled up outside Meadows Tea Rooms. "Back in a mo

darling – I promised I'd show Mum!" She disappeared leaving Paul open mouthed in the car. Before he knew it she was back in the driver's seat. "She loved it; now off to Jennifer's."

Paul sat staring at the whirlwind beside him. He shook his head wistfully. Why was he surprised? – this was partly why he had fallen in love with the chaotic bundle of energy that was soon to be his wife. They stopped at the end of the lane outside Willow Bank. Jennifer came running out. "Oh let me see." She drew a big breath. "Oh Cassie... that is gorgeous."

By now TJ and Soaki had joined them. "Mm, not bad." Jennifer slapped TJ's arm. "Only joking – it's really lovely; it goes with your eyes."

Paul looked smug. "At least someone has noticed."

"Never mind mate – perhaps it takes a fella to notice the comparison – the girls just go all soppy over jewellery."

The girls gave Paul scorn-filled looks, but were soon chatting and giggling as usual. "Come in mate – I'll get us all a drink. What do you fancy?"

The guys went into the house and joined the girls. Cassie asked "Has he told you what he did in the jeweller's?"

Jennifer changed the direction of her stare. "Honestly Paul – that was a bit naughty! How did you get that fella to go along with you? He's rather – well sort of stuffed shirt and a bit posh."

TJ looked bewildered. "What are you on about? What happened?"

They told him and as the tale unfolded they all ended up laughing. "Cor – that'll be a new one being told at the next jewellers' convention – or whatever they have."

The day progressed and when it was time to see to the pigs, Jennifer tried to be terribly organised and efficient. "TJ, what I usually do is prepare their fresh fruit and veg like this – then put the pig nuts into the rattle bucket – then I..."

He stopped her talking by planting a big kiss on her lips. "Jenny – darling – I've watched you doing this for long enough to know your routine... just enjoy your day at the seaside and don't worry. The girls and I will be fine."

She smiled coyly. "I know; I'm just an old worrier!"

146

Chapter 9

Tuesday morning came, and both Jennifer and Cassie had woken early. The familiar 'beep beep' sounded as Cassie pulled up by the front gate.

"Yippee – she's here." Jennifer ran to open the door. She grabbed her bag and kissed TJ and Soaki goodbye.

"Have a great time – we'll see you tonight."

She beamed as she ran to the car, waving. She climbed into the 2CV. "Hiya mate – gosh, I don't know why, but I feel like a kid going on my first day trip without parents."

"I know what you mean – I'm dead excited too!"

They giggled. "Oh I just know this is going to be a really special day!" They drove to the train station. They bought their tickets and got on the platform. The train arrived within a minute. "Gosh, that was good timing – let's find seats by the window."

They climbed aboard and before they'd even reached the first stop, Jennifer struck her 'cheeky schoolgirl persona' – "Are we nearly there yet Mum?"

Cassie rolled her eyes, then with a stern look "No we're not! And if you don't behave I won't buy you that ice cream that you wanted!" She gave a complacent smirk, folded her arms and sat back in her seat.

Jennifer pushed her bottom lip up and looked suitably told off. A couple sitting on the opposite side of the carriage looked at each other with subdued wonder. Their worries were soon laid to rest as the girls burst out laughing. Before long they were all chatting. "We thought you were serious to start with – what a relief!"

As the miles sped by Cassie was curious. "What are you writing in your notebook Jen?"

"I'm pinching ideas for Willow Bank. If I see a garden I like, I'm jotting it down as a possible for mine."

"Ah clever – got anything interesting yet?"

"Mm, a couple a maybes."

As the journey continued, the two friends chatted away as always about anything and everything. Main topics of conversation were obviously the engagement, Helen's party, the darts match and general things whilst Jennifer's parents were there. "My mum recognised something between TJ and me even before I did."

"Mm, yes. Sally's a very canny lady! I hope she and Jon will visit again soon."

Jennifer smiled and nodded. "Oh, don't worry – they'll be back again as soon as possible; they loved it here."

As well as the 'fun' subjects, they had an occasional serious moment discussing what they might do about finding new premises for themselves regarding work. "I hope Laura finds something too. She's nice."

"Yes – we'll have to keep our eyes open for her too. Here – fancy a sweet?"

"Yes please – what I really fancy is a nice coffee!"

"Well we'll find somewhere when we get there – won't be long now. Two more stations then we'll be at our seaside!" They both cheered.

All too soon the train stopped. An announcement called out over the tannoy - "Weston-Super-Mare – this is Weston-Super-Mare." They collected their bags and stepped down onto the platform.

They made their way excitedly into the street. As they took in the sights and sounds, they laughed with sheer pleasure. "Oh Jen, we've actually got our day trip!" She took a big sniff. "You just know that you're by the coast – smell that air, and listen – seagulls!"

Jennifer shook her head. "Uh uh – no such thing!"

Cassie looked in amazement. "What are you talking about? Can't you hear them?"

"Of course I can but they're not seagulls. They are gulls, but called things like 'black headed gull' and 'herring gull' – loads of different species, but not seagulls."

"Okay Miss Clever Clogs, but that's the first time I've ever heard that. How did you know?"

Jennifer gave a shrug and with raised eyebrows, "Just one of the things I was told by…"

Cassie joined in - "Grannifer!"

"She popped a lot of information into your head over the years, didn't she?"

"Yep! Oh look, a café!"

They went into the cosy café and found a table. Cassie picked up a menu. "Do you just want coffee, or something to munch as well?"

Jennifer thought for a moment. "I wouldn't mind something – but not masses. I want to leave room for our beach treat."

"Ah yes, fish and chips while we stare at the sea."

"So, how about... we get a round of sandwiches and a cake and share them?"

"Yep, sounds good to me, then we can head off and find the wet stuff!"

They ordered their food and drinks. "Ah, this is what I needed." Jennifer licked her lips as she sipped her cappuccino.

They relaxed in the café discussing things they might like to do throughout the day. When they'd finished their snack, they left and carried on walking down the street. "Are you feeling suitably sustained for a while?"

"Mm, yes thanks – it was nice. Not as good as your mum's cake, but nice enough!"

"Cor if it was, we'd still be there eating it for an hour or more!!"

They laughed at the thought. "And no room for fish and chips later!"

"I wonder how far it is to the beach."

"About ten minutes from the station; I asked the ticket collector."

"Oh goody gum drops. That means we'll be there soon."

They turned a slight corner. "Ye hey, look – wet stuff!"

Their pace quickened as their excitement notched up a gear. "Hang on mate; let's just go into 'grown up mode' while we cross this road – it's quite big!"

Jennifer looked playfully at her companion. "Okay Mummy – do I need to hold your hand?"

Cassie rolled her eyes. "Oh, gerroff! You should be on the stage – you slip into other characters so easily! Come on, it's clear."

On the far pavement they stood and properly took in the vista. They stood for a couple of minutes taking in the sights and sounds around them. There were various groups of families and children playing in the sand. Some were building castles, others making gullies towards the water in the hope that they could cause the waves to flood in and make rivers. Two youngsters were doing their best to bury their father from the waist down – he casually read his newspaper pretending not to know that his lower limbs were disappearing. Further along the beach there was a queue of excited kiddies waiting for their turn of a ride on the placid well-behaved donkeys.

In the opposite direction there was a pier which stood proud and bright in the sunshine, stretching slowly into the sea. Crystal sea glinted as the waves broke against the strong pylons which held it firm and steady. At the far end, way above the water was a profusion of rides, brightly coloured, in contrast to the predominantly white painted structure on which they were situated.

Jennifer had been taking photos. "Here, turn around and smile!" They stood closely together grinning cheesily. Jennifer held the camera at arm's length and clicked the button. "At least that'll prove we were here!"

They laughed. "Probably end up as one of those awful ones that we're too embarrassed to show anyone."

"Yeah, more than likely."

They began to stroll along the promenade. "If you fancy a paddle, do it while the tide's in, or you might have a long walk later – apparently when it's right out you can't even see it from here."

"Who told you that? It wasn't Paul or TJ winding you up?"

"Uh uh – that fella at the station – apparently Weston-Super-Mare is famous for it."

Cassie looked impressed. "Anything special you want to do… apart from the chips later on?"

Jennifer nodded. "I really would enjoy a wander on the pier – possibly while it still has wet stuff lapping around its legs."

"Okay – let's go have a peek at the pier."

They walked a little quicker, chatting and laughing as they went. As they neared the entrance, Cassie nodded in the direction of shops on the other side of the road. "Look what I've spotted!"

"Right you are mate. After the pier experience, we'll grab some and come back to the beach and munch."

They did a 'thumbs up' to each other and turned in to the stone entrance. Soon they were walking traditional wooden boards. They stopped every so often to either lean against the railings or to sit on one of the benches. As they walked further along, the girls were intrigued to find a selection of shops. "Ooh, let's have a peek."

Cassie smiled at her friend's enthusiasm. "Jen, they're just shops – you have seen shops before!"

"I know, but… they are shops on a pier!"

Cassie shook her head and tutted as she laughed. "Come on then –

you won't be happy 'til you've bought something."

They looked around and chatted about the items on display. "I'm going to be very good and only buy if I really need it."

"Yeah yeah – I've heard that before!"

Admittedly, Jennifer was very restrained – in the first couple of establishments. Things changed though when she found a large collection of scarves. "Oh Cassie – look! Oh I know just how I can use some of these."

Soon both of them were holding the soft colourful pieces of fabric. Some were square in varying sizes, others long and some triangular. "So what outfits do you want to accessorise?"

"Oh, I wasn't thinking of wearing them. I've got ideas for décor."

"Of course you have – silly me. Who on earth would expect Jenny Cade to wear a scarf?"

Jennifer gave Cassie one of her raised eyebrow looks which encompassed a twinkle in her eye and a tell-tale smile. It was one of her famous expressions which said "Just watch me!"

By the time she'd finished, Jennifer had accumulated a dozen scarves, plus she'd also found some bits of jewellery at the counter. Cassie had treated herself to one chiffon scarf and was waiting outside the door. Jennifer joined her. "Come on, I've just discovered they do ice creams a little bit further on – I'll treat us. Want one?"

Cassie smiled and nodded. "Mm – yes please."

As they approached the ice cream vendor Jennifer clapped her hands. "Oh, jolly good – it's soft whipped stuff! I'm going to have a ninety nine – what would you like mate?"

"Ooh, same as you please – do they have a sauce as well as the flake?"

"Coo – you want everything. Shall I see if they do nuts as well?"

Cassie laughed at the mock sarcasm. "Of course. I'll have the works!"

She found a nearby seat and waited for Jennifer to join her. She looked at the view beyond the pier's railing and got quite lost in her thoughts. The noises of her surroundings drifted into the background and her mind wandered. She was suddenly brought back by the sound of an affected cough. "Ahem! One super deluxe extra special ninety nine for madam."

Cassie turned to see Jennifer holding two of the most enormous ice creams she had ever seen. "Oh my giddy aunt – crikey Jen, I was only joking, when I said I'd have the works!"

Jennifer shrugged. "Oh well, you're only young once – and this is our special day out and… well, I think I got a bit carried away with the choice of toppings, so – I got a bit of everything!"

Cassie laughed. "What am I going to do with you?"

They sat and tucked in to their frozen treats. "Good job you got spoons and serviettes. This is probably what we would get if Angela did ices at the 'Arms'."

Jennifer, with her mouth full and cream all over her lips, mumbled her agreement and nodded.

It was quite some time before they had consumed sufficient to feel confident enough to walk along and eat the remainder. When they eventually finished they smiled cheekily at each other. "That was very indulgent!"

"Yeah, I think it's what you'd call naughty but nice!"

"Oh, absolutely!"

As they continued to enjoy their new surroundings, the two friends entertained themselves as they watched the other people on the pier. They tried guessing what their occupations might be. "I reckon he works in the city."

"Why?"

"Well normally all suited and booted, not a hair out of place – so, on holiday, time to relax. Silly T-shirt, oversized shorts, sandals… but still with socks." They giggled. "Oh and that lady must run a sweet shop – she just so looks the part!"

Occasionally they caught snippets of conversations as people passed by. Two which overlapped had the girls laughing out loud. "Well Elsie, I'd bought everything I needed for the stew …", "… and when we got home he opened the bag and a little kitten popped its head out with a bow tied to its collar."

Jennifer mused "I wonder what they had for dinner and if the food had morphed into a cat?"

After a while of 'people watching', they strolled further along the pier eventually reaching the amusements. After an hour or so of slot machines and games, they made their way to the rides. After a few goes they decided to wander back to the promenade. "Oh my word – that was fun – I haven't enjoyed that sort of thing for ages!"

"Yeah, I know what you mean – we must do this again – perhaps bring the guys too."

As they reached the road, the smell of the chip shop wafted across. "Are you hungry enough?"

"Oh yes – the ice cream was ages ago. Hee hee, I'm looking forward to this."

"This is what I've been looking forward to."

"Yes I know – you've told me so often I nearly gagged you with one of those scarves you got."

Jennifer pulled a face. "Sorry, didn't realise I'd gone on! Oh, I forgot – I bought something else at the same time. I'll show you when we've eaten these."

"This is really scrummy – well worth waiting for."

Conversation flowed easily as always and as usual the subjects were many and varied. Staring out at the waves and the pier in front of them, Jennifer commented how lovely it would be to work in one of the shops on it.

"Imagine that as your job… you wouldn't take much persuading to get up for work would you? Oh, talking about coincidences, you know we saw that turnstile on Saturday? When I was getting the ninety nines the chap serving me said there used to be turnstiles to get in years ago."

"What? To the ice cream shop?"

"No-o-o, to get to the pier, silly."

They smiled at the thought of Cassie's misunderstanding. "And it wouldn't be very easy getting back through with your hands full of cornets and lollies."

"Oh you do have the daftest imagination!"

They put their empty wrappings in a carrier bag. After wiping her fingers, Jennifer rummaged in her shoulder bag. "I got you this – I hope you like it." She passed a candy striped paper bag to her friend.

"Oh Jen – thank you, but why?"

"Well if you need a reason, call it an engagement pressie – but I just saw it and thought it was your sort of thing so…" Cassie smiled. "Well, open it then!"

Tentatively she undid the folded bag and took out the item neatly folded in tissue paper. She studied the dainty bracelet in her hand. The collection of natural stone beads was threaded on to an elastic wrist band. "Oh mate, this is beautiful – all my favourite colours too! Thank you."

"Something to remember the day by."

"As if I need anything – this is one of those stick in the head forever days!"

"I wonder what the fellas are doing."

"Well, Paul's got the day off, so he and TJ are probably chilling out at the Arms or kicking a ball around your garden."

"As long as mine is looking after my girls, I don't care how else they spend the day."

"Talking of the Miraford Arms, do you fancy finding a nearby hostelry and having a little drinkie-poo to round off our lunch?"

"Spiffing idea, m'lady!"

They gathered their belongings and set off. Carrying their bags, they strolled along the beach enjoying the feeling of the sand beneath their feet. After a while, they stepped up to continue along the promenade. It was nice to experience the different sights and sounds and wandering into the shops filled with typical seaside paraphernalia. They bought some odds and ends to take back home, mainly what Jennifer called 'daft little trinkets to give as pressies'. She was particularly pleased though when she found a selection of hats.

"Oh look – I've got to get this for TJ." It was a captain's hat. "He can wear it when he's on board Kingfisher!"

Cassie was also happy with her discovery of a shop selling jigsaws. "Believe it or not, he loves them. Yep, give my Paul a really complicated one and he's as happy as a sand boy."

She smiled at the front picture showing an old-fashioned ship with sails and lots of rigging. "Perfect – that should keep him entertained for a while."

With several bags between them they wandered on, eventually finding a bar. As they sat with their drinks, Jennifer wrote out a postcard. "Do you want to add a line or two? It's for Mum and Dad."

Cassie smiled and nodded, "Yes please." They had a second drink, then continued their walk.

It was starting to get a slight chill in the air as the sun went down and the evening sky turned from its bright blue to a rich navy hue. Jennifer snapped away with her camera capturing the last of the sunset as the sun finally sank in the west. She then focused on the pier which now took on a magical look as the coloured lights upon it detailed the outline of its majestic structure.

"I love the change of seasides when it gets dark. Suddenly it turns into fairyland!" She scrunched her shoulders and smiled contentedly.

Cassie agreed and linked her friend's arm. "Come on soppy; there's still things to do before we go home!"

They continued to enjoy the evening as they had the whole day, but eventually it was time to make their way back to the station. As they walked along the platform, Jennifer felt a tap on her shoulder. "Did you get your ice cream?"

She turned to see the couple from the morning. They all chatted whilst waiting for the train, Cassie going into great detail about the over-the-top ices. They all laughed and exchanged stories of how they spent their day. On the homeward journey, Jennifer waxed lyrical about the pier.

"You really enjoyed that bit of the day, didn't you?" Cassie was almost serious in her tone.

Jennifer sighed. "Mm – yes I did – I've always liked them ever since I was little." She thought for a while and then smiled. "Imagine if we could put that pier on our river at Miraford."

Cassie rolled her eyes. "Well, if you did, it wouldn't be a pier any more – it would reach to the other bank and be more like a bridge!"

"Er yes, I see your point. Oh well, we'll just have to come back here again, eh?"

They pretended to be disappointed. "Oh, what a shame."

Although the trip out had been wonderful from the moment they had woken up, it had also been very tiring for both the girls and inevitably, with the melodic sound of the train, they found themselves dozing. Jennifer watched the passing scenes through the carriage window for a while. No longer were the gardens visible that she had observed with such interest earlier. Now the houses they belonged to were silhouettes with warm glows at the windows. Street light illuminated towns and villages, and the moon occasionally cast reflections on the lakes and rivers. These images pleased her, but before long her eyes closed and, like her companion, she drifted off to sleep.

The train jolted slightly as it pulled into a station. Jennifer woke and rubbed her eyes. She gave a little yawn and gently rubbed her cheeks to revive herself. With her chin now resting on her left hand she peered through the glass to find a name plate. Leaning across she touched her friend's arm. "Cassie," she called softly, "Cassie mate, time to wake up."

Cassie stirred. "Mm?"

Jennifer smiled at the dozy response. "Wakey wakey darling; we're nearly home."

Cassie stretched and blinked. "Oh, how long was I asleep?"

"Dunno love – I went off too, but we've only got one more station then the next one's ours."

They began organising themselves, collecting bags together and making sure they had everything.

Now fully awake and back to their normal chatty selves, they made their way back to Cassie's beloved car. They climbed in and made their way back to the village. "Weston-Super-Mare was lovely, but it's nice to be home eh?"

Cassie nodded. "Sure is; there's no place like it!"

Hearing the familiar sound of the 2CV pull up outside Willow Bank,

TJ came out to meet them. Soaki was close behind him wagging her tail excitedly.

"Hiya darling, hello Cassie. No need to ask if you've had a good day: look at those smiles!" He hugged Jennifer. "Come on – Paul's got the kettle on. I assume you're ready for a cuppa?"

They all went indoors. Paul and Cassie kissed and he cuddled her. "Ooh ouch!"

"What's up love?"

"Cor, my arms are really sore."

They examined her arms and shoulders. "You've caught the sun. Didn't you put any cream on?"

Cassie looked guilty. "I forgot, and I didn't think it was that hot."

TJ joined in. "The sea breezes and the salt in the air... it's misleading. Jenny, have you got any lotion to put on this lobster?"

Cassie tapped his arm. "Rotter!! It's not my fault. It's my red hair and pale skin – I always burn easily."

Jennifer looked at her friend sympathetically. "Gosh, that is sore – I hadn't noticed before. Not to worry; Grannifer to the rescue!"

They all watched with curiosity as she went to a plant on the window sill. She broke off a couple of leaves. "There you are – break the leaves and squeeze out the gooey stuff. It's aloe vera – great for burns!" She gave a satisfied smile. "Now then; where is this coffee?"

With Cassie feeling much more comfortable, they took their drinks into the living room. The girls hardly drew breath as they babbled happily, telling their partners all about their day.

"Sounds like you had a great time – bet they forgot all about us stuck here, Paul!"

Paul nodded. "Yes mate – not even a second thought."

"Not true!"

Jennifer jumped up and disappeared from the room. She reappeared seconds later with the bags of 'pressies'. The girls huddled together in the corner of the room facing the wall. As they rummaged through the bags they giggled with each other. "No, that's for my mum and dad, and this is for Jim."

"Ah, here's those…"

"Shh!"

"Oh yeah, sorry." They laughed again.

Paul and TJ looked on with curious wonder. "What on earth are they doing over there?"

Paul shrugged and shook his head. "Dunno mate – your guess is as good as mine."

By now Soaki had joined them and was busy sniffing at the bags. She paid particular attention to one and nudged it hard with her nose. It made a loud squeak and she took a step backwards, excitedly wagging her tail. "Oh yes, very clever – so you've found yours!"

Having done their sorting, Jennifer and Cassie rejoined their partners and started to hand out their gifts. Soaki sat expectantly, her tail beating on the carpet. "Oh you sweetheart. You've been so patient – let's give you yours first!"

"Yeah, we want our pressies!"

Joining in the façade, the girls told them off. Paul and TJ looked upset. "We're sorry!"

"Really?"

They nodded. "OK then; you can have yours next!"

The men clapped their hands happily. Out of the first bag, Jennifer took out the squeaky object. It was a comical octopus with a bright pink body, big boggly eyes and turquoise tentacles. She threw it in the air for Soaki to catch. Another loud squeak rang out. "She likes that!"

"I've got something else but I'll give her that later."

The rest of the gifts were given. "We've got you a key ring each. They are torches as well!"

Paul had a speed boat, and TJ a light house. "Oh, they're really cute. Thanks girls."

"That's not all. We got you a stick of rock each. And these are your proper pressies."

Cassie gave her remaining gift. "Oh wow, thank you darling; I shall enjoy doing this." He kissed his fiancée, then showed TJ the jigsaw.

He nodded approvingly. "Nice one."

"And this is for you, darling." Jennifer gave her remaining gift to TJ.

"Thank you." He opened the bag and pulled out the hat and placed it on his head. "Cheers Jenny; it's smashing. Does it suit me?"

"Very nice – makes you look most distinguished!"

He smiled broadly and hugged his lady. "Thank you darling. I love it."

She smiled happily. "OK Soaki, your last pressie!"

Jennifer produced a large dog biscuit which was shaped like a shark. "Where on earth did you find that?"

"There was this shop just stuffed with daft novelty things – we spent nearly an hour in there. It was such fun!"

"We thought it would be nice if you came with us next time."

"So, you're planning a return visit?"

Jennifer wrinkled her nose as she smiled. "Yeah – it was fun."

Cassie joined in. "Be careful, she's besotted with the pier... wanted to bring it back to Miraford!"

Jennifer rolled her eyes. "Not quite. I just liked the idea of going to work on that lovely structure and having the water to look at all day."

TJ gave her a consoling squeeze. "It wouldn't work anyway – it wouldn't be so much a pier, more like a bridge. Surely it would reach the opposite bank?"

"Precisely, that's what I said!"

"Well it was only a Wibni dream!"

"A what?"

"Wibni – Wouldn't It Be Nice If!"

They laughed. "I bet that's a Granniferism!"

Jennifer smiled. "Uh huh."

Eventually the adventurous day reached its conclusion, the friends all said their goodbyes and Jennifer packed up and made her way to bed. She lay for a while revelling in the fun she'd had.

"It's been a lovely day Grannifer. TJ said he'd enjoyed looking after the girls... and they all behaved... even Pickle!" She yawned. "Yes my darling – a – beautiful – day – all – round." She closed her eyes and was asleep.

The next morning, passing through the kitchen, Jennifer flicked the switch on the kettle. She unlocked the back door and shivered as she opened it. She pulled her dressing gown tighter around herself. "Brrr, that's a bit nippy. Good job we had our day trip yesterday!"

She opened the sty door wide and encouraged the pigs to come out as she made a hasty return to the house. "Mm, coffee first before I do anything, I think."

With the radio on and her hands warmed by the hot mug, she felt relaxed and comfortable. She gathered the girls' food together and started to prepare it. Before venturing back into the chilly garden, again she slipped her jacket on over her dressing gown. "Good job no one can see me!"

With the baby bath full of chopped fruit and veg propped in her left arm and the pig nuts in the rattle bucket held in her right hand, she hurried along the garden. "Here piggy pig pigs. Come on g..."

She stopped, not only mid-sentence, but rooted to the spot. "What on earth ..."

Across the garden there was the skeletal shape of a summer house. She wandered over and clutched the wooden frame work.

"Oh my!" She bit her lip as her eyes glazed over. She swallowed hard as she ran her hand over the structure. She was suddenly jolted back to the reason she was in the garden when the set down rattle bucket knocked the back of her legs.

The girls had helped themselves to the contents and in their excited gusto had rolled it along the ground. Smiling at their antics, Jennifer scattered the remaining food. Collecting the bucket, she made her way back to the kitchen. Before she went in she stood and looked again at the new Willow Bank name plate.

Rummaging through her wardrobe and drawers, Jennifer tried to decide what to wear. "I must have something cosy amongst this lot – at least until the day warms up a bit... I wonder if this will do?"

She pulled out a fleecy shirt and pondered. "No, not cuddly enough." She returned it and tutted. She sighed with an air of frustration. "Oh, there must be something here!"

She sat on the bed. As she did so, she remembered the divan drawer which had been designated as 'snuggly' things. Among the neatly organised collection of woollen socks, gloves, hats and scarves alongside a fluffy jacket and several cardigans and jumpers, she spotted just the thing. With a musical tone she voiced her delight. "Ah ha – perfect! Thank you Grannifer – just what I need for a chilly day."

She pulled out the black and purple jumper that Grannifer had knitted her and cuddled it lovingly. "I remember when you gave me this and I said it looked too big... and you said it was supposed to be like that, and you called it a 'sloppy Joe'! I'll enjoy wearing it and it'll be just like you're here giving me one of your wonderful hugs!"

Back in the kitchen, Jennifer made some breakfast and fed the birds before cleaning the sty and topping up the trough with fresh water. Every so often she stopped and looked at the summer house frame. She smiled happily.

With the garden jobs sorted and the house quickly tidied, Jennifer brushed her hair, popped a few dog treats into her jeans pocket and locked the door. She made her way to the bottom of the garden looking again at the summer house framework.

"I won't be long, girls." She smiled to herself at the thought of the pigs understanding her. She closed the gate and wandered along the tow path.

Although the sun was warming the day, it was still a little chilly. There was a delicious crispness to the air which made her remember childhood days spent with Grannifer and Grandpa. Still in her pyjamas she would don her wellies, grab a basket and go to their chicken run to collect eggs. She was always allowed to choose which she wanted for her breakfast and Grannifer would write her name on them before they were boiled. She thought to herself how no eggs before or since were

159

even half as nice.

Lost in her thoughts and captivated by the serenity of her surroundings, Jennifer was surprised how quickly she had walked to her destination. As the now familiar shape of 'Kingfisher' came into view, a satisfied smile played on her lips. Stepping from the tow-path on to the gangplank she called out, "Hello, anyone aboard?"

She heard Soaki bark. The door opened and TJ emerged. "Ahoy there Captain… or should I call you Mr Builder?"

They smiled at each other. Jennifer bent down to stroke Soaki who had run out to greet her.

"Morning Jenny – you spotted our woodwork then. What do you think of it?"

"It's wonderful. Why didn't you mention it last night?"

"Thought you'd like a surprise when you got up!"

They hugged. "Well, it was definitely that. I thought I was seeing things!"

They all went inside and TJ put the kettle on. They chatted over coffee with Soaki enjoying the treats that Jennifer had brought for her.

"I arranged with Grandad to meet later at yours – Joshua's sending more wood around lunchtime."

"Oh my, you have got it organised haven't you?"

"No point hanging about. Start a job and get it done!"

Jennifer rolled her eyes. "You are so like Jim – that sounded just like him!"

Holding hands, the couple walked back to 'Willow Bank' with Soaki running excitedly ahead of them, then back again in an attempt to hurry them along. In the garden TJ went to the summer house and pushed it. "Still standing then," he grinned cheekily. "Is there no limit to this man's talent?"

Jennifer shook her head. "No, I don't think there is."

TJ grimaced slightly. "I was joking!"

They went inside and Jennifer watched with curiosity as TJ disappeared into her broom cupboard. "What are you doing in there?"

He emerged triumphant with a sturdy canvas holdall on his shoulder. "We put our tools in here so you wouldn't know what we'd been doing while you were out yesterday." He grinned at their sneaky ploy. "Oh, and did you know you've got some type of door in the floor in there? Look, I'll show you."

They went back into the cupboard. Moving things about TJ pointed. "See? Grandad reckons if we can get it open it might lead to a cellar or something."

160

"Ooh, how exciting. Can we try now?"

"Hold your horses missie. We think it's been stuck or nailed down, but let's do one project at a time eh? In case you'd forgotten, we've got a little something in the garden to sort out first!"

She dropped her head and put her bottom lip upwards in a kind of sheepish apologetic expression. Her large blue eyes gazed up at him. "Sorreee!" Then she broke into a broad smile, "...but wouldn't it be wonderful if there is something?"

They chatted animatedly as to the possibilities of what might lay hidden below. Suddenly Soaki went to the hallway door wagging her tail. "What is it girl? You heard something?"

Jennifer opened the front door to Joshua's delivery men. "Morning Miss. We've got your wood."

"Oh yes, good morning. I'll get my boyfriend – he'll show you where to put it. Would you like a coffee or tea?"

While Jennifer organised the drinks, TJ helped unload the lorry.

As they sat with their drinks, Jennifer proudly showed the picture of the summer house. "Very nice – it'll look great when it's finished." They studied the drawing with admiration. As they said goodbye to the men, Jennifer waved excitedly as the familiar 2CV came along the lane towards her.

"Cassie – you'll never guess. Come and see what they did while we were out."

The two friends hugged. "Actually, I know already. Paul told me on the way home, and I got a detailed account from this bloke I picked up on route to here!"

Cassie nodded to the passenger seat. Jennifer looked bemused. "Ah Jim!"

He climbed out of the car smiling. "What do ya think then Jenny lass – surprised?"

"You bet. Honestly – you fellas are so sneaky!"

"Yeah, but we're lovely with it."

Before long the garden was a hive of activity, with everyone joining in with measuring, sawing and hammering the wood into position. Even Soaki and the pigs attempted to move planks around in an attempt to get involved and 'help' the proceedings.

Jennifer and Cassie left the men to it for a while and went indoors to prepare a meal for later. "If we put a casserole and jacket potatoes in, they can cook slowly while we're working."

Cassie rubbed her tummy. "Mm, one of my favourite dinners!"

As they put the casserole and potatoes into the oven, Jennifer shook her head. "What's up mate? Looks OK to me."

"No, there's still space in there. Grannifer would never leave space if she could make use with something else. I know; I'll make a rice pudding for afters!"

Cassie smiled. "She was a very 'eco-friendly' lady wasn't she?"

"Oh gosh yes; she wouldn't waste anything – I reckon she'd have bottled fresh air if she thought it wasn't being used at the time."

They had just finished clearing up and had made drinks when the phone rang. "Do you want to call the guys in while I answer this?"

Cassie called Jim and TJ and Jennifer went to the hallway to see who was ringing. She returned to the kitchen where Cassie, Jim and TJ were sitting at the table.

"It's Joshua; he asked for Mr Barton. Doesn't mind which of you."

"You get it lad – you're nearest."

TJ tutted. "Plus you don't want to let your tea get cold!"

Jim gave a chuckle. "Ee lad, you're so cynical."

Taking a quick gulp of his drink TJ went to the phone. "Hi Joshua, TJ here." He laughed – "Yeah that's right – the young good looking one!"

Overhearing the comment, Jim feigned a slightly hurt but surprised expression. "Bloomin' cheek!"

The girls laughed. TJ continued. "Oh that's great; thanks a lot, so when… oh I see… er…can you hold on for a minute? Cheers, I won't be long."

He rested the handset on the shelf and went to the kitchen. "He's finished making up the door, but can't get a delivery for this week – any chance you could collect it in your car Cassie?"

She looked doubtful. "I know I cart a load of stuff in the old girl but will a door fit?"

"Yeah, should do – it's a stable door so it's in two halves. What do you think?"

She nodded. "Yep – I'll finish my cuppa then nip down there."

Smiling gratefully, TJ returned to the phone. "All sorted Joshua. Someone will be there in about twenty minutes."

"Can I come with you?" asked Jennifer. "I fell in love with the place when we went before and I'd like to see it again."

Cassie smiled at Jennifer. "It might be a good idea – since I've no idea where it is!"

Jennifer rolled her eyes. "Oh gosh yes – I'd forgotten you weren't with us."

As they drove along, Jennifer described the boatyard to Cassie. "This

Joshua chap sounds like a real character."

"Oh, he is: he's a real sweetie, and he's got a lovely old dog. They suit each other well! It's just up here – next left."

Cassie indicated. "Ah, Chandlers Lane – do you know, I've driven past this hundreds of times and never knew where it led to."

"Well, you're just about to find out!"

They parked the car and got out. "Ah-ha. This is the dog I was telling you about."

The dog greeted them. Jennifer started to stroke him but he ran a few steps towards the building. He stopped, looked back to the girls then ran a bit more. Then he ran back to them.

"He's weird."

Jennifer shook her head. "No, he wants us to follow him. I think there's something wrong."

They ran to the building, calling out as they did so. "Joshua, Joshua, are you there?"

They stopped momentarily. "Where'd the dog go?"

"Listen – what's that noise?"

They followed the sound of canine whimpering and a human voice – faint but obviously in pain. "Argh – help me, ow!"

They found the elderly man crumpled on the floor with a large shelf unit on top of him. Items that had obviously been on the shelf were strewn around the room.

"Oh my God, Joshua! It's all right my love. We're here now. Stay still and we'll get you out."

Jennifer started to clear a space so that they could get to Joshua whilst Cassie used her phone to get help. "Yes, hello? An ambulance, please, at…"

Cassie stood at the far end of Chandlers Lane waiting for the ambulance, glancing back occasionally with a concerned expression towards the boat house. Meanwhile Jennifer had made Joshua as comfortable as possible without moving him. Rigger was lying close to his master, nuzzling Joshua's hand reassuringly.

When the ambulance arrived, it made its way swiftly down the lane. Cassie, who was still waiting at the far end waved frantically. As they got near enough she changed her wave to an exaggerated beckoning, and with the vehicle in pursuit, she ran quickly to the entrance of the building. The medics on board quickly joined Cassie who led them to where Jennifer, Joshua and Rigger were waiting. Being made aware of the situation, the crew professionally took charge.

As they checked the elderly gentleman they made friendly

conversation – even the occasional joke. They assessed that their patient didn't seem to have any bones broken, but wanted to take him to hospital for a more detailed check.

Joshua groaned, "Oh do I have to – I hate hospitals."

Jennifer tapped his hand playfully. "Josh you stubborn old thing – you do as you're told. We just want to make sure that you are properly OK." She smiled reassuringly.

With their patient safely on board the ambulance, Cassie, Jennifer and Rigger followed in the 'old girl' to the hospital. When they arrived, the diagnosis was that as they had originally thought, no breakages, but the doctors wanted to keep Joshua in for observation.

He groaned again, "I can't, what about my dog?"

Jennifer reassured him. "No problem darling, I'll take him home with me."

With Joshua a bit more settled, the girls made their way back home, Jennifer comforting Rigger as they went.

Over the next couple of days the group of friends visited and made phone calls to the hospital. The staff were happy for Joshua to go home, but only if there was someone there to look after their patient. This was a problem because Joshua lived alone apart from Rigger, and this was the main reason holding back his mental recovery, with the stress of missing his canine friend. Jim had a possible solution if Joshua agreed. Getting back to Rigger was Joshua's priority, but he realised closing the boat building business would have to happen sooner than he'd intended.

This distressed him with the thought of his beloved boathouse being knocked down and the desirable riverside property redeveloped.

Chapter 10

The next morning Jennifer walked Rigger into the village. She was deep in thought and almost bumped into Cassie outside the tearoom. They hugged. "How are you?"

"Fine, thanks. You? Have you managed to find anywhere new for your studio?"

Cassie laughed. "No. Haven't had time to look. Did you think I'd been skiving off summer house duty then?"

"No, of course not. I just wondered."

Cassie gave a sidewards glance at her friend. "Oh oh – I know that look. You're cooking an idea in that crazy head of yours."

"No, I'm not... well not really... well... maybe a teeny weeny smidge of a possibility..."

Cassie shook her head and gave a rueful smile.

Back at the house, Jennifer walked through the kitchen with a far-away look on her face. With a soft tone to her voice she spoke to her friend. "Cassie - could you make drinks for everyone please... I'll... er, I'll be back in a while."

As she left through the back door TJ looked concerned and they watched as she walked to the bottom gate. "Is she all right?"

Cassie nodded silently. "She's fine, just got something in her head that she wants to think about. I reckon it's a biggish thing – I saw her pick up at least ten stones!" She put the kettle on and got four mugs out.

Sitting on the river bank, Jennifer threw a stone into the water – she watched the ever increasing circle of ripples. Slowly she repeated the process. After several stones she sighed deeply. "Oh Grannifer, am I mad even to be thinking of this as a possibility? I wish you were here to advise me."

She pitched the eighth stone. Pursing her lips in a determined way, she stood up and went to the gate. She replaced the remaining stones on the wall. "I'll save you for another time."

TJ met her halfway up the garden. He slipped his arm around her waist and spoke gently. "You all right?" She smiled and nodded.

In the kitchen Cassie placed a freshly made coffee in Jennifer's hand. "So, how many did it take – and have you sussed out whatever it was?"

Jennifer gave a half smile. "Eight... and yes, I think so."

Jim looked confused. "Timothy – have you got any idea what they are talking about? It sounds like English, but I can't understand 'em."

TJ shook his head and the girls laughed. "Let me drink this, then I'll explain. But I need a pen and paper."

The friends looked on with interest as she began to write. "Cassie, Laura, Jennifer and TJ?"

"So, what do these people all have in common?"

Cassie answered first. "They're all friends!"

"Yes... and?"

"I don't know why I've got a question mark – but the others are all female! I can promise you all, I'm definitely a fella!"

Jennifer laughed. "I know darling; no that's not it. What else?"

"We all live in Miraford."

"Yes, but there's other things."

Jim shook his head. "Dunno lass."

TJ agreed. "You've got me Jen."

"Oh, come on mate; what are you getting at?"

"OK, there are two possible connections – but definitely one! First of all we all have craft or design abilities, and at least we three ladies are looking for somewhere to work from. That's why you have the question mark darling. I wasn't sure if you wanted to set up a business with your art!"

"OK, so we've established the similarities. So what?"

Jennifer made a rough sketch. "So, what's this?"

"Looks like the boatyard."

"Oh good; you recognised my scribble."

Looking a bit more serious, she said "Now we know it's unlikely poor old Josh will be able to get back there any time soon, so it's possible he'll be looking to sell it sooner than he'd planned, yes?"

They all nodded sadly. "But what has that got to do with us?"

"The layout of the building."

"How do you mean Jen?"

With a glint in her eyes and excitement in her voice, Jennifer explained. "Think of the layout of the place – long and thin with several rooms all down one side, each accessed from a wide corridor on the river bank side."

"Yes, so?"

"Think of those rooms as individual units. Cassie needs a studio, Laura needs an outlet for her fabrics and haberdashery, and I need somewhere to base my interior design office and maybe some sort of restoration workshop, and I think you could really make something good with your artistic talents darling. I just wondered if we might turn it into a sort of craft centre. We might even get Helen to sort out an extension of the tearoom and supply some drinks and stuff in a little café."

"My word – no wonder you took eight stones to think out that lot! But why would anyone come to an old boatyard to look for crafts?"

Jennifer smiled. "I've got an idea for that too." She took her sketch and made a few alterations. "We could make it look like something else. Look, what does that remind you of?"

Cassie took the drawing. "Oh my goodness – it's a pier!"

Jennifer beamed. "It's just a shame we couldn't swivel it 45 degrees out over the water!" She giggled at the thought.

Then looking at each of her friends individually, she tried to ascertain their reactions. "So… what do you think?"

TJ answered first. "Well, personally I think you're just a little bit crazy – but having said that, I rather like the idea."

Cassie nodded. "Mm, me too."

Jim smiled. "Me three!" They all laughed. He continued, "Could I be part of this venture? I enjoy my carpentry y'know."

Jennifer promptly added 'Jim' to her original list of names. They continued to discuss the various possibilities of Jennifer's idea.

TJ bought them back down to earth. "This does all depend on what Josh has in mind of course, and in the meanwhile – we still have a summer house to finish!" He rubbed his hands together, then stood up. "If we all get stuck in I reckon we could get the main structure finished today. Then it's just varnishing and the interior and it'll be done."

Jennifer smiled broadly. "Really, I never imagined it would be that quick!"

"Ah well, when the Barton boys gets stuck in we don't hang about. Isn't that right Grandad?"

Jim stood up. "Aye, that's right lad."

They marched comically into the garden singing 'Hi ho, hi ho, it's off to work we go'. The girls laughed then followed the men out, quickly followed by Soaki and Rigger who had been lazily curled up at the feet of their human companions.

The intrepid little team continued with their project, chatting all the while about their possible ideas they could put into action – should the boatyard craft centre become a reality.

With the doors now in position, the summer house seemed just about finished. "Just the glass for the windows needed now and it's all done – yes?"

Jennifer looked at her boyfriend. He shook his head. "No, not quite darling, well not if you only want candle or battery power out here."

She looked quizzical. "Sorry; are you planning to electrify it?"

TJ laughed. "Well not all of it, but a power point and some lights might be useful."

Jim appeared with some spades. "C'mon then troops – let's get digging."

Cassie reluctantly took a spade. "What has gardening got to do with getting power supplied may I ask?"

Jim and TJ, almost as one voice answered her. "To bury the cable!" They chuckled at their unison. "Oh hang on a mo Grandad – Jenny; have you got some flour?"

"Er, yes… why?"

He smiled. "Just an idea – trust me."

They went to the kitchen and he told her to walk 'casually' back to the summer house. Unsure what the flour had to do with it, Jennifer did as he'd instructed. TJ followed her, scattering a trail of flour where she had walked. "There you go; that's what's called a 'desire line'. Not too regimental and a nice natural pathway. If we lay the cable under it, we'll know where to find it if ever we need to in the future."

"Brilliant, plus we won't accidentally cut into it."

Jim chipped in. "You'd have a job lass. It'll be quite deep and tough reinforced cable at that."

Cassie smiled. "So that's something else we've learned today!"

After only a short time of digging, Jennifer suddenly cried out "Stop!"

They all looked at her with concern. "What's up Jen?"

"The girls – if we leave a thumping great trench across the garden, they might fall in and hurt themselves!"

"I don't think they'd get hurt, but I see your point."

They downed tools and debated what to do. Jim was the first to come up with a solution. "How about we put the benches over the bit we've already dug? That should hold 'em 'til we get the cable."

With the temporary barricade in position, everyone piled indoors for a tea break. They'd only just settled down when the hall phone rang.

Jennifer returned after a few minutes. "That was the hospital – apparently the doctors have done their rounds and reckon Joshua can leave tomorrow as long as he has someone to be with him and he promises to take it easy. They think it will be good for him to be back with Rigger – he's stressing about him. So, if it's still OK with you Jim…"

Jim smiled broadly. "Aye lass – that's fine. S'pose I'd better make a move back home and get the place ready for my guest."

"I'll give you a lift when you want to go Jim."

"Oh that's right nice of you lass – thank you."

When Cassie and Jim left, Jennifer and TJ set about organising what was needed to get power into the summer house. Soaki and Rigger found it most entertaining to see the humans on 'all fours' as they followed the meandering flour trail with a tape measure. Jennifer made notes as TJ called out the fixtures and fittings needed.

Pickle was also intrigued as to what was going on, and at one point, she got so close to TJ that she knocked him off balance and he fell head first between the barricades into the trench. He emerged with dirt all over his hands and face, yelling at the bemused pig who obviously didn't understand why anyone one would be upset with her over something which she spent her life doing! Jennifer laughed as she helped him up.

"Hmm – think it's funny do you?"

He chased her around the garden. She squealed playfully as she ran. "No, TJ… I'm sorry!"

He caught her and rubbed his grubby hands on her face. Then, as he cupped her cheeks gently, he looked into her eyes and drank in her beauty, even with a dirty complexion. He kissed her.

Lost in their embrace, they were unaware that Cassie had returned. "Ahem, no wonder I couldn't get an answer at the door!"

They looked towards her. "What on earth have you been up to? Joining the pigs munching roots?"

They laughed as they explained. "Talking of the girls – I'd better do their tea time grub."

They all went indoors. Cassie tutted as she got a closer look. "You two go and get cleaned up and I'll start chopping their food."

When they returned to the kitchen Cassie had made coffees and was in the garden calling the girls. "Here piggy pig pigs!" She returned with a satisfied smile on her face. "I love doing that!"

"Yes, it still amuses me the way they come trotting along." Then Jennifer looked downcast. "Trouble is, they've nearly finished their gardening. Mel will take them back soon."

"Oh Jen, I'm sorry."

Jennifer gave a resigned smile to her friend, shrugging her shoulders and sniffed. "I knew it was going to happen – just didn't think I'd get so attached to them."

TJ slipped his arm around her and gave her a comforting hug. She nestled her head against him. "Mel warned me – I should never have given them names!" She gave a sniff.

Cassie looked at her friend sympathetically. "Come on mate – don't be sad; you've still got them for a while yet."

Jennifer gave a deep sigh and attempted a smile. TJ took the initiative to change the subject. "So, we need to find somewhere to get these bits for the garden hut. Not much use making a list if we don't use it."

"There's a good store in Lamton, but they might be closed by the time we get there. Best give them a call and check."

A phone call confirmed Cassie's concerns. TJ returned from the hallway. "They were just about to shut, but they've got everything we need so we can get them tomorrow."

"Well, if I pick you up early we can go and collect everything."

"Are you sure Cassie? I'm quite happy to go on the bus."

"No, you're fine – it sounds like you'll have a lot to carry, so it'll be easier to let the old girl do the carting."

TJ smiled. "Thanks love."

"I hadn't realised how late it was getting. Any ideas what you'd like for dinner?"

"I've got a fancy for a curry – how about you ladies?"

Both the girls smiled, nodded their heads and rubbed their tummies.

"OK, curry it is! Do you think Jim will want to join us? I wonder how he's getting on with his preparations."

"Do you want to call him and find out, darling?"

"Cheers Jenny; yes I will." TJ went again to the hall phone.

Various arrangements were made and a couple of hours later Jennifer, TJ, Cassie, Paul and Jim were all tucking in to their meal, with Soaki and Rigger happily munching from their bowls.

The following morning it was not the usual warm sunshine which woke Jennifer, but a cold wet nose nuzzling her cheek. She opened her eyes and found a canine face looking expectantly at her. "Oh, good morning Rigger – what is it boy?" She stroked his head.

After a few minutes, she got up and, slipping on her dressing gown, went downstairs. Letting Rigger into the garden, she said good morning to the pigs, then went back to the kitchen to begin the familiar routine of their breakfasts.

As she scattered the girls' food around, Rigger ran past her, barking. She looked at the bottom gate where TJ and Soaki had arrived. "Hello, you're bright and early!"

"Morning Jenny. Soaki insisted we came at this time so she could make the most of Rigger before he goes off to Grandad's."

Jennifer tutted and rolled her eyes. "Yeah right. Anyway they can still see each other even when he's back with Joshua. I think he knows something is happening today. He came and woke me up this morning!"

As she spoke, she noticed a wry smile on TJ's mouth. "What's up?"

"Oh nothing – I just wondered if that is the latest fashion. Is it a sort of 'countryside layered look' with a hint of nightwear'?"

"Huh?" She looked down at her clothes. She'd forgotten that she still had her pyjamas, dressing gown, a coat and her wellies on. "Oh my… sorry, I must look a right mess!"

"No, it's er… very fetching."

They both laughed. "Tell you what, just for being cheeky – you can finish feeding the girls then start some breakfast for us. Meanwhile, I'm going to get dressed."

She handed him the rattle bucket. TJ stood to attention then saluted. "Yes sir!" They kissed and Jennifer went indoors.

They had just finished their meal when they heard the familiar 'beep beep'.

"Oh good; Cassie's here." Jennifer opened the door and greeted her friend. "Hiya Cassie; how's things?"

Closing the gate, she joined Jennifer. "Morning. I'm fine – you?"

"Yeah, good thanks. TJ's inside."

As they entered the kitchen TJ gave them each a mug of coffee. "Ooh, you're a mind reader – thanks."

They sat and chatted. "I popped in on Jim on the way here. He's ready and waiting for Joshua to arrive. He seemed really excited."

"Well, they've known each other for a long time – lots of reminiscing to get through."

"Did Grandad know what time Josh would be there?"

"Mm, yes, around two thirty apparently."

"Right… so if I walk Rigger down at about three, that will give him a bit of time to get settled in. It'll be good medicine for him. This old fella is as important to him as breathing." Jennifer tickled Rigger's ears who had his head resting on her knee.

They finished their drinks and Cassie and TJ went to get the electrical bits from town. Jennifer decided to stay with the animals. "I might even do a bit more digging… if the fancy takes me."

"Well, you'll have to get a move on – we won't be long."

||Cassie was right and they were back within the hour. Walking through the kitchen, they deposited their purchases on the table. TJ joked with his girlfriend. "So, Jenny – finished the digging?" He smiled.

"Not quite, but I've done about half of it."

He gave her a cuddle. "Oh, you are funny!"

Cassie came in from the garden. "Er, TJ… she's not joking…"

He looked stunned. "Not really?"

Jennifer nodded. In the garden they regarded her work. "You're amazing!"

Jennifer smiled. "Can't take all the credit – the girls had done a brilliant job and the soil is really loose – at least away from where we started. I reckon we must have compounded it doing work on the summer house."

With his arm around her waist he kissed her cheek. "Well, that's as may be – I still think you've done a great job. I'll finish off while you have a rest."

"Better still," Cassie joined in, "I'll help with some digging. Jen can make a cuppa – then we can all join together and finish it off. We could have this done by half twelve."

TJ shook his head and tutted. "I've never known lasses like you two before."

Jennifer and Cassie raised their eyebrows in disbelief. "I beg your pardon?"

"No – it was meant as a compliment – not sexist! What I mean is you're both really sweet and feminine but you don't mind getting stuck in and doing the hard work too… it's great. I just haven't ever met anyone like you before."

The girls giggled. "Yeah, we're like buses…"

"Nothing for ages…"

"Then two come along at once!" They all laughed.

***

Meanwhile, in his cottage, Jim was busy chatting to the district nurse. She'd popped in to make sure everything was ready for Joshua to stay. "So, you're happy with this arrangement Mr Barton?"

"Please, call me Jim – everyone does." She smiled and nodded.

"And yes, I'm really happy – looking forward to it in fact."

"That's good. It is a little unusual, but Mr Sanders is missing his dog terribly and the doctor thinks it will aid his recovery…"

"Yes, that's what we were told."

"Oh yes, of course. That's why you offered to help. Well, Mr… um, Jim, I think that's all for now. I'll come back to settle him in and make sure he knows he's got to take things easy."

Jim smiled. "We'll do our best, but if I know old Josh, that'll be easier said than done." He gave a little chuckle and they shook hands.

"Thank you Jim – but it is important. We don't want him back in hospital, do we?"

Jim agreed. They said goodbye and she left.

At Willow Bank House, Jennifer, Cassie and TJ were finishing a lunch of soup and sandwiches. Soaki and Rigger were busy cleaning their bowls. TJ rubbed his tummy. "Mm – that was lovely." Cassie agreed.

Jennifer raised her eyebrows. "Well, it wasn't very exotic…"

"Sometimes, the simplest of food can be fit for a king if it tastes good darling – and that WAS scrummy!"

She smiled at her fella. "Thank you." She glanced at the clock. "We've got an hour before I need to take Rigger to Josh. Have we got time to put that cable in?"

"Coo, don't you ever stop?"

"Well… yes… but unless you want to stand guard over the trench, we still have the girls to consider."

TJ slapped his hands on his knees. "Quite right m'lady – come on then team."

They trundled into the garden and set to work. They were soon into their familiar organised mode of grafting together. Suddenly Jennifer started laughing. "Have you noticed the animals?"

Cassie and TJ looked up. For all the world, it looked as though the dogs and all four of the pigs were an audience, sitting in a semi-circle watching the humans putting on a show.

Regaining their composure, the trio gave a united flamboyant and very exaggerated bow. Then, still giggling, they resumed the work they'd been doing, TJ laying the electric cable and a telephone extension wire, and the girls scattering a layer of sand. Then they filled in with the previously dug out soil.

"We ought to do this for a living – we make a good team."

As he shovelled, TJ responded. "Good idea Jenny. So where do you keep your magic crowbar?"

173

"Eh?"

"Well you'll need something to prise this in to all the other projects you've got planned!"

Cassie interrupted. "Nah – didn't you know mate – when we all go home, Professor J R Cade is in her laboratory inventing the thirty hour day and eight day week!"

Jennifer tutted and rolled her eyes. "OK, point taken."

Meanwhile, at his cottage, the nurse had rejoined Jim. He made them both a cup of tea while they waited for Joshua to arrive. "Won't be long now, lass."

"You're looking forward to this, aren't you Jim?"

"Aye, that I am. Just hope the old boy feels the same. I know it's not his own home, but I'll do my best to make him feel welcome." He gave a slight shrug of his shoulders and a cautious smile.

She laid a comforting hand gently on his forearm and gave an understanding smile. "I'm sure everything will be fine, but I'll be popping in every day to check how he's doing so you can share any worries with me. You're not on your own with this, Jim." He nodded appreciatively.

Jim's hall clock struck the half hour and at the same time a car pulled up outside. "How's that for timing?"

"Yes, our volunteer drivers are very good. Come on then; let's go and welcome in your new house guest."

They went up the garden path. As the driver got out, he called to Joshua. "Hold on Mr Sanders; I'll be a moment and I'll... Mr Sanders – please wait."

Joshua was already getting himself out of the vehicle and heading towards the gate. "Hallo Jimmy. How are you lad?"

Jim smiled broadly. "I'm fine Josh – and you?"

"Glad to be out in the real world... where's Rigger... is he here?"

"He'll be arriving soon; our Jenny will bring him in a bit."

Listening to their conversation, the nurse interrupted. "Come along now Mr Sanders – let's get you indoors and settled."

She went to take his arm. "No need lass – I'm all right on my own. Just lead me to a decent cup of tea and I'll be fine."

The driver joined them carrying his bags. "He's been like this since I collected him – won't let me do anything for him."

Sitting in the comfy lounge, they sipped at their drinks that Jim had brought in. Placing her mug on the table, the nurse spoke to Joshua. "Mr Sanders... I'm extremely happy with your... to be honest, most remarkable recovery, but we do require you to take things easy for...

174

well at least a couple of days."

"But I feel fine lass..."

"Yes, I know, but if you rush into things too quickly, well you could end up back in hospital."

He gave a resigned look of acceptance. "Nay, I'm not wanting that!"

"Didn't seem that bad when we visited you, Josh."

"No lad, nothing wrong with the place – and the staff were really good. It's just me – I can't stand being shut in and not able to see m'dog – can't be doing with that."

"So, we're agreed that you'll slow down and rest for a while. Yes?" He nodded. "Good, I'll be checking in on you to see how you're doing."

She stood up to leave, as did the hospital driver. "Thanks for the cuppa Mr Bart... sorry Jim. Much appreciated."

They all shook hands. "You take care now Mr Sanders. Best of health to you."

"Thanks for the lift. I hope I wasn't too much trouble."

They laughed. After shutting the front door, Jim returned to his friend. "Just you and me now Josh... how are you really?"

Josh gave an upward glance from his bowed head. "Yeah, I'm fine." He pursed his lips and sighed, "Maybe a bit more tired than I let on, but I'm fine, Jimmy. Don't you go worrying about me."

"Why don't you get forty winks before your lad turns up? I'll wake you when they get here."

Josh nodded and closed his eyes.

Turning left at the top of the lane, Jennifer and TJ walked through the pretty village towards Jim's cottage. The dogs trotted along happily, slightly ahead of the young couple. "I'll miss having Rigger around."

"I'm sure Josh would let you walk him."

Mm, yeah, but I was just thinking... I might get one of my own."

He smiled. "I'll keep my ears open."

After a short while he started to chuckle. "What you laughing at?"

TJ gave a cheeky snigger. "I was just thinking; you could advertise... 'Wanted... canine companion required for somewhat weird and somewhat crazy owner. Applicants must be prepared for said owner to change character at the drop of a hat and share same with a group of pigs – almost as manic as aforementioned owner'."

She tapped him playfully on his shoulder. "Oh thanks a bunch!"

He smiled. "Er, I hadn't actually finished the ad... 'Successful applicant will be rewarded with regular food and drink, cuddles and treats a plenty, and enough love to reach to the moon and back.'"

They stopped walking and Jennifer gave him a huge cuddle. "Thank you; that was lovely." They kissed.

They held hands and continued their journey. As they wandered past the attractive cottages to Jim's, TJ noticed a wistful smile on his girlfriend's lips and a faraway look in her stunning blue eyes. He called gently. "Hello... earth to Jenny... are you receiving me?"

She blinked and looked more focused. "Sorry?"

"You looked like you were a million miles away."

She smiled broadly. "Mm yeah. I was just remembering an early morning walk Grannifer and I took – seems like a lifetime ago when I first saw these gardens. It was only a few months really, but..." She gave a sigh. "So much has happened."

He knew this was a precious moment for her and slipped his arm around her shoulder. She nestled her head into his comforting cuddle.

As they neared Jim's cottage, Rigger pulled on his lead and his tail wagged energetically. "Well I'm blessed. Look at that... he must know that Josh is nearby!"

At Jim's gate, Rigger pawed at it and yelped excitedly. "You know he's there, don't you fella?"

They went up the path to the door, Rigger eagerly leading the way. An elated Josh let them in and an emotional reunion ensued. Eventually things calmed down and they all sat down, with Rigger so close to his master he was almost in the chair with him.

"So, how are you feeling Josh?"

"Oh, all the better for having my boy with me again!" He looked at Jennifer and spoke emotionally. "Thank you for looking after him lass. I'm so grateful."

She smiled. "Oh, you're welcome; it was a pleasure!"

Jim came in with another tray of drinks. Conversation flowed easily among the four and the dogs enjoyed the gentle yet consistent attention which they received throughout.

After about an hour, Jennifer and TJ made a start to leave. "Would you like us to pop in for a few days and take Rigger for a walk, just until you're a bit stronger?"

"That would be right nice – if you don't mind."

"I'd enjoy it. We'll start in the morning when I come down for the market, OK?"

"Aye lass, that'd be grand."

They said their goodbyes and Jennifer, TJ and Soaki made their way home.

Back in the cottage the two elderly friends chatted. They reminisced over old times and how much things had changed from when they were lads. "Youngsters these days don't appreciate how good our old ways were…"

"Aye, a lot are all for these 'ere modern ways, but young Jenny is different to most of 'em… she's really fond of older stuff." Jim half smiled as he continued. "I mean, she took to me eh?"

They both chuckled. "Yes, she's a nice lass, and your Timothy. Ah, p'raps they're not so bad after all!"

Joshua sat back in his chair. "Trouble is, I reckon I'm jealous – wish I was their age again. I don't like this getting old thing."

Jim looked at his friend's sad expression. "C'mon mate, age is just a number. You an' me – we're still young in our hearts aren't we?" He gave an encouraging smile.

Joshua nodded in agreement. "Yeah, I know you're right. It's just this stupid fall has made me feel low and the end of me old boatyard – I've had a couple of offers already."

"Really? That was quick."

"Prime location see… they want to knock it all down and build them there fancy luxury flats." His eyes glazed and he swallowed hard, as though gulping away his emotions.

"What you need is someone who likes the building as much as you do, so they won't go bashing it about."

Joshua sighed heavily. "In an ideal world – but you tell me where I could find 'em!"

Jim beamed. "I reckon you need to 'ave a word with our Jenny. She loved the place the moment she clapped eyes on it… and she's got an idea what to do with it, and it don't involve no bulldozers!"

Joshua raised his eyebrows. "I knew I liked that young lady – we'll see what she's got in mind… put the kettle on young Jimmy; we need a mug of tea to celebrate!"

Jim gave a thumbs up and went to the kitchen.

*** *** ***

Jennifer was greeted the following day by a bright crisp morning. "Hum, another cold one. Oh well, to be expected I s'pose; it is autumn after all."

She said hello to the pigs and went indoors to prepare their breakfast. TJ knocked on the door. "Morning darling – cor, it's parky out there!" He kissed her, then went into the kitchen to put the kettle on.

As Jennifer stroked Soaki, she smiled at TJ's comfortable domesticity. "I thought it felt like a porridge morning – are you any good at making porridge?"

He smiled. "I make the best porridge outside of Scotland. You finish

177

the girls and your breakfast will be ready to warm your tummy when you get back." He chuckled as he started cooking.

True to his word, as Jennifer returned from the garden he had just placed two mugs of fresh coffee on the table which was already set with cutlery, side plates and jars of honey and marmalade. He ladled the porridge into bowls and placed them on the table with a flourish. He bowed dramatically. "Breakfast is served Madam!"

Jennifer tilted her head and nodded acceptance. "Thank you Jeeves. Pray, would you care to join one for this wondrous feast?"

They laughed. "There's bread in the toaster when you're ready."

"You're so organised with meals..." she complimented.

"Had to be when I worked in the restaurant – guess that training just stuck with me."

"You were right, this is really yummy." She licked her lips.

He smiled. "Thank you... ready for your toast now?"

She nodded. "Mm, yes please."

Soaki joined her master as he walked to the counter and pushed down the lever on the toaster. "What's up girl – finished your biscuits? We're going to go for a walk soon. We're gonna fetch Rigger!"

She wagged her tail excitedly and ran to the door. "In a while girl – we're not ready just yet."

Jennifer pulled a sad face. "Oh poor Soaki – you got her all happy at the thought of going out and now you've sat down again!"

"Yeah I know. Sorry girl; I forgot you understand every word." He patted her and consoled her with another biscuit.

Before long they were actually on their way. Jim opened his door and kissed Jennifer. "Morning Jenny."

He called to TJ who was waiting by the gate with Soaki. "Morning Timothy."

"Hiya Grandad."

Jim went indoors and reappeared quickly with Rigger and handed Jennifer the lead. "There you are lass. Make sure you have time for a cuppa when you get back. Josh is having a lie-in just now, but he wants a bit of a chat with you later." He smiled and she noticed a brighter than usual twinkle in his eye.

"Why? Is everything OK...?"

"You'll find out later. See you when you get back. Bye bye." He grinned and shut the door.

With a quizzical expression Jennifer walked back along the path. As they approached Market Square, Jennifer glanced across the road. "Oh good, it looks as though someone is in my old flat. That's nice; I don't like to think of it sitting there without somebody to look after."

"Don't you mean, to look after 'it'?"

She shook her head. "No. When I was there it was a safe little haven. I grew through my problems and started to be happy again in there… so yes, I think it looked after me."

He smiled at her. "I see what you mean. That's one of the reasons why I love you – you always have a way of looking at things that's a bit weird, but at the same time, totally logical."

He pulled her gently towards him and kissed her. Soaki and Rigger decided to sit down and almost gave the impression that they were thinking "Here they go again with that smooch stuff!"

They soon resumed their walk and the buzz of activity and the brightly coloured stalls drew even closer. Before long the mingling crowds turned into more defined individuals. Jennifer spotted a familiar head of beautiful tousled auburn hair. "Oh look! There's Cassie!"

As they got nearer, Cassie happened to turn around. She spotted them approaching and gave her familiar broad smile as she waved enthusiastically. When they met up, they all hugged affectionately.

As they walked around the stalls, Jennifer told her friend about Jim's comment when they'd collected Rigger. "Ooh, what do you think that's all about?"

"Dunno mate, but I can't wait to find out. Oh look, there's Laura."

When they reached the fabric stall they explained Jennifer's idea. "Of course, there's no guarantee we'll be able to get the boatyard, but if not we could find somewhere else for a Craft Centre… what do you think? Would you be interested?"

"Er, I need to give this a lot of consideration…" Laura put a finger to her lips and looked skywards. "I've thought long and hard and… yes, of course, I'm up for it. Sounds brilliant!"

They all laughed and chatted happily. "It seems that Josh wants to talk to me about something, so if I get the chance, I'll attempt to ask him about the building. I'll let you know how I get on."

They continued to wander around the market. When they'd finished, they popped in to the Miraford Arms for a quick drink before walking back to Jim's cottage.

Sitting at their usual table, TJ looked at Jennifer with a slight air of concern. He took her hand. "You all right, love?"

She gave a not very convincing smile and nodded.

"You're not. What's up?"

She sighed "Oh, I don't know. What could Josh want to talk to me about? What if it's something bad?"

179

TJ smiled. "It won't be. There's nothing bad that it could be... anyway, Grandad was smiling when he passed on the message, wasn't he?"

"Yeah, I s'pose." She relaxed and sipped her drink.

Cassie rejoined them. "I've arranged with Angela to collect our shopping from here. I'll get the old girl, collect the bags then pick you up from Jim's."

Jennifer looked confused. "We're OK to walk mate."

"Are you kidding? More like swim home – look outside!"

They looked to the window. "Good grief, where did that lot come from?"

Outside, the sudden heavy downpour and the accompanying dark skies gave the illusion that it was much later in the day than just a little after one o'clock.

"Shall we grab something for lunch while we wait for the rain to ease off?"

TJ nodded. "I'm game – what about you Jen; what d'ya fancy?"

She furrowed her brow. "I don't know that I'm particularly hungry."

TJ tutted. "Will you get your mind off Josh!"

She smiled at him. "Sorry, yeah, you're right. Perhaps something to munch will take my mind off it."

Cassie went to the bar to order the food.

Jennifer snuggled up against TJ. "You really do read me like an open book, don't you?"

He gave her a gentle, yet comfortingly strong cuddle. "Yeah, I think so... but with your imagination I do sometimes wonder if I'm completely up to speed with what's happening in that beautiful head of yours." He kissed her forehead.

She smiled and snuggled even closer. It rained hard for nearly an hour – and then, almost as suddenly as it had started, the sky cleared and the deluge stopped.

"Gosh, that was a belter! Do you know what that reminded me of?"

Cassie spoke simultaneously with her friend. "The day we met!"

"Cor, that feels like a lifetime ago!"

"Anyway, before it maybe starts again, I'm going to fetch the car. Do you want a lift, or shall I get you from Jim's?"

"I think if we give the pooches a last bit of a walk, they'd appreciate it, so we'll see you at the cottage."

As they approached the gate, Jennifer gave a look to TJ which was half cautious, half hopeful. "Oh well; moment of truth. At least we'll find out if it's good or bad!"

He smiled encouragingly. "I'm sure it'll be fine."

As Jim opened the door they noticed newspapers on the floor and a pile of towels on the chair. "I anticipated you might all be a bit soggy – come on in, the fire's going well and the kettle's on."

While the dogs were being rubbed dry, Jim hung Jennifer's and TJ's socks on the fire mantle. "Looks like we're ready early for Santa." He chuckled.

Soon they were all sitting with mugs in hand in the cosy room. Joshua gave Jennifer a stern look. "What's this I hear that you want to knock down my boatyard?"

She looked mortified. "I don't! I can't think of anything worse – Jim, what have you been saying?"

Suddenly the men all burst out laughing. "Nay lass – I was larking about. Jimmy said you had a good idea for the old place."

Jennifer exhaled deeply. "You rotten lot. Josh, I thought you were serious!"

He smiled apologetically. "Sorry lass, so come on then – fill me in. If I let you get your hands on my place, what would you do with it?"

Now encouraged by his interested words, Jennifer sparked up with her usual enthusiasm. With her concerns relinquished and replaced with relief, she was soon back to her usual exuberant self. Joshua seemed genuinely interested in her idea for the boatyard, and even interacted with suggestions of things which had not yet been considered.

Suddenly Jennifer stopped talking. She stared hard at the elderly gentleman before her.

"Josh – I thought I was just explaining a possible idea to you, but... well, you... I mean you're almost sounding like you're agreeing with it!"

He smiled, and with a twinkle in his eyes, gave a nod. "Jenny lass, I've been in business since I was a young man. Trial and error along the way, but my instinct for the better ideas has done me OK. My passion for me boats and good friends to encourage me, them an' honest hard work... well, I see that with you and 'part from it being a good idea, you don't wanna knock the old place down!"

"Really?"

"Yes lass – really."

She smiled broadly. "Oh you lovely man, I could kiss you!"

"Well, don't let me stop you!" He chuckled.

Jennifer leapt up and flung her arms around him, planting a big kiss on his cheek. "Ah, thank you Josh – we'll work really hard to make it a success."

Jim interrupted. "I think this is a good time to open a bottle of brandy that I've been keeping for a special occasion. Timothy, can you get some glasses please?"

Jim poured their drinks and TJ handed them around. The excitement of the afternoon was rekindled when Cassie arrived. Jennifer opened the door for her friend and quickly blurted out the news whilst they stood in the hallway. There were squeals of delight.

In the sitting room the men laughed. "I think we can assume that our Cassie is as chuffed as Jenny."

Joshua agreed with Jim. "Aye, reckon so. I'll have to push nursie to let me get up and about a bit quick!"

TJ interjected. "Hold on there, Josh. Jenny may be all fired up about this project, but there's no way she'll be rushing into anything before you are properly fit and well, trust me. Her priority will be your health first – project second!"

Jim nodded. "The lad's right mate. Take your time and do what the nurse says!"

At this moment the girls came into the room. Jennifer looked concerned. "What's that? Has something happened? Josh – do you need the nurse?"

"Calm down lass – I'm fine." He tutted and rolled his eyes. Speaking directly to Jim and TJ, Josh said, "Point proven. I get what you are saying!"

Jennifer looked questioningly at TJ.

"Tell you later…" He gave a reassuring smile.

Cassie noticed that Joshua was starting to look really tired. She caught her friend's attention. With no more than an eye movement in his direction, Jennifer picked up the non-verbal suggestion that it was perhaps time for them to leave. Jennifer stood up and felt the socks hanging on the mantelpiece. "Well these feel dry enough now – if you two gentleman will excuse us, we need to make a move."

They all said their goodbyes and promised to return tomorrow to take Rigger for his walk.

As they turned into the lane leading to Willow Bank, realisation hit Jennifer. "Oh crikey – my garden's gonna be a mud bath! I knew I should have organised a path to the front door. I don't mind wet shoes, but we're going to get absolutely filthy."

Cassie smiled knowingly. "I've already thought of that – I've got my wellies and I've borrowed Mum and Dad's for you two. Hope the sizes are OK. Sorry Soaki; couldn't find any to fit you!"

As though she understood, their canine friend lowered her head. TJ gave her a cuddle. "Don't worry – I'll carry you over the nasty old mud!"

Turning to her master, she gave a kiss by the way of a grateful lick on his cheek. They all laughed. "So when exactly did you teach her everything in the dictionary? She definitely understands more than just the odd word."

TJ nodded. "Yeah, I know – she's a clever old thing." He kissed the top of her head lovingly.

There was a lot of giggling as the three friends gingerly picked their way to the house, slipping and sliding as they went. TJ carried Soaki whilst the girls took the bags of shopping. Once they were indoors, Jennifer vowed to make a path a priority on her 'to do' list.

There had been no sign of the pigs in the front garden. "I'm just going to make sure the girls are OK." She went to the back door. "I bet they've been having a whale of a time – one enormous mud bath!" They all laughed.

Before she went through the door, TJ stopped her. "Hang on Jen; I'll go and check them. It'll be a bit precarious out there and I don't want you slipping over."

She smiled and thanked him. "Why don't we go together? We can hold each other up."

"OK, if you insist." He knew the obstinacy of his girlfriend's nature.

"Mm, I can see Pinky, but where are the others?"

"Let's check the sty."

They carefully made their way to the small stone outhouse. "There you are love; they're in here."

Jennifer shook her head. "Uh uh. Only two – where's Pickle?"

TJ scratched his head in bewilderment. "Well, she couldn't get out. Where the heck is she?"

Jennifer tugged at his sleeve and nodded to the opposite side of the garden. "TJ, the bottom half of the summer house door is open!"

They looked with resignation at each other. With a sigh, Jennifer gave a shrug of her shoulders. "Come on – let's go and check."

TJ thought for a moment. "Hang on a sec…" He disappeared into the outhouse where the bedding straw was kept and rejoined Jennifer holding a large bundle in his arms.

"What on earth have you got that for?"

He gave a knowing smile. "Hopefully it gets us across the garden without slipping over. Hold on to my jumper and follow me."

She did as he'd suggested and they steadily made their way back to the house. "If we go on the concrete edging which surrounds the house

183

to the far corner, it'll be nearer to the summer house – so less mud to excavate."

"But why bring the straw?"

Jennifer's question was soon answered. TJ threw handfuls ahead of them, in effect creating a kind of straw path."

"Oh clever boy!"

"Yeah, I can't disagree!"

"Ah, and so modest too!"

They chuckled. "Mind you, it's still slippery, so mind how you go."

Cautiously they picked their way to their destination. As she peered in through the window, Jennifer's imagining proved to be reality. "Oh Pickle! TJ, look at all the mess. It looks like she rolled in the mud outside and rubbed against all the walls to get it off again."

"Perhaps that's her way of decorating – she was only trying to help you!"

Jennifer looked at TJ with disbelief. "How can you be so calm and… and…well… make jokes? Look… just look at what she's done. All your hard work and she's made it filthy!"

He hugged her. "Calm down darling; it's only mud. We'll clean it up and it'll be all nice again." He kissed her on the cheek. "Come on, let's get her out and go back to the house."

Looking into his comforting eyes, she smiled weakly. "Sorry!"

With Pickle ushered into the garden, they secured the door and made their way back along the makeshift path.

Cassie had been keeping an eye on the escapades in the garden at regular intervals and was ready and waiting with mugs of coffee as her friends returned. She handed them their drinks.

"Ah cheers; you're a mind reader!"

Cassie smiled. "Well I reckoned you'd need one… I've prepared the girls' dinner and er – hope you don't mind mate – I found your camera and took a few shots. Couldn't resist. You both looked so funny out there slipping and slithering about!"

Jennifer thanked Cassie for doing the pigs' food. "I bet while you were snapping the pictures you were really hoping we'd end up face down in the mud!"

Cassie feigned a hurt expression. "As if I'd wish that. Would have made a good shot though!" They all laughed.

As they chatted, TJ said that the straw path had worked well enough as a temporary measure, so to make safer access to and from the front door, he'd do the same out there. He'd just about finished when Paul arrived at the gate. "Hallo hallo – what's going on here then?"

"Oh hiya Paul – anti-slipping device. Take it careful though; it's like a bloomin' ice rink!"

They picked their way back to the house and Cassie's eyes lit up when she saw her fella. "Hello fiancé, how are you?"

"Hiya darling." They kissed. As they hugged, Cassie excitedly outlined the day's events to him.

"Hang on love, slow down! You don't make sense when you talk so fast! Oh, hi Jennifer."

"Hello love." She'd just come into the sitting room with a tray of drinks. Now, with everyone settled in the cosy room, they explained the day properly to Paul.

"Wow – so your dream looks like becoming a reality!"

"Quite possibly. I think we need to give Josh some breathing space for a while though. He seems really up for it, but he looked exhausted today."

Cassie and TJ agreed. "Yeah and that was just roughly outlining the project. He needs time to build his strength up."

Chapter 11

Over the next few days Jennifer concentrated on mostly indoor things. She decided that amongst other things, it was maybe a good idea to prepare the second spare room ready for decorating. With the window in there facing the front of the house, it wouldn't get the early sun, so she decided that the colour scheme should be warm cream with some pink tones. "I'll check my colour charts for ideas," she mused.

There were of course the daily walks with Rigger. Without staying too long, she got updated as to Joshua's progress when collecting and returning his friendly old dog.

"Nurse reckons if he carries on like he is – should be all right to go back home within a week," Jim informed her.

Jennifer noticed a hint of sadness through the smile on his mouth. He sighed. "I've gotten used to the ol' boy's company."

She gave him a hug. "Well, he can always come back for visits and he won't be far away… and I've got loads of ideas of things to keep you busy if you start to get bored." She chuckled.

Jim tutted and rolled his eyes. "I bet you have lass – I bet you have!" He smiled more positively.

***

Keeping herself busy, Jennifer found the days passed by quickly. Luckily the downpour on Saturday had been a one-off and although the autumn weather was quite chilly in the mornings and at night time, it was fairly mild during the afternoons. This was useful as the garden at Willow Bank House dried out well enough so that the clean-up operation in the summer house could be tackled. Jennifer found it necessary to shoo Pickle away on several occasions as the inquisitive, and now not so little pig, would come to see what was happening. Jennifer assumed that her most mischievous porker regarded this as a personal playhouse.

Indoors, the bedroom was coming together nicely and was ready for the actual decorating. Jennifer was pleased and very impressed with the condition of the walls and ceilings. She decided to carpet this room to emphasise the cosy feel she was aiming for. As she busied herself clearing and sweeping, she sang happily to the radio. She was surprised by a harmonising voice from the doorway. Turning around, she smiled broadly at TJ who was standing there with two mugs in his hands.

"I did call you but you were so involved up here, you obviously didn't hear me."

She took her drink and gave him a kiss. "Ah, thanks love – just what I needed!"

They sat on the floor whilst they drank their coffees, Jennifer describing some of the ideas she had for the room. As they chatted, the conversation eventually came round to the Craft Centre idea. "Do you think we'll actually get to use the boatyard?"

TJ pursed his lips and raised his eyebrows. "Well, Josh seemed pretty interested when you were explaining what you wanted to do."

Jennifer gave a hopeful smile back. "Yeah he did, didn't he? Oh darling, wouldn't it just be wonderful if it actually happens." She drained her mug. "By the way, where's Soaki?"

"She's keeping guard downstairs, and with that in mind... you really ought to lock the door if you're up here. If I can walk in without you knowing, so could some stranger."

Jennifer looked suitably told off. TJ put his arm around her. "I'm not nagging, I just care about you." He kissed her and smiled lovingly. "Of course, we could always arrange your own canine warning system – you did say you were thinking of getting a dog."

She smiled. "Yes you're right, and I should do it soon. It will help me when Mel has the girls back. It'll be awful to see them go."

TJ stood up. "Well, let's go and see what the little madams are up to while they're still here."

He took her hand and they went downstairs. As they entered the kitchen the familiar greeting from Soaki was as exuberant as ever. Jennifer stroked and cuddled her with replicated enthusiasm. She was, and would be forever grateful to this wonderful four legged friend for bringing such happiness into her life. On many occasions she had been moved by the obvious and genuinely deep care that TJ gave. Yes, he was an all-round 'nice guy', but there was more... he made her feel safe. He was sensitive to her feelings and when she felt vulnerable he acknowledged the moment, but skilfully defused it. She smiled and thought "I'm such a lucky girl."

TJ came in from the garden. "Oi! – come on slacker; no time for day dreaming. My team is missing a Jenny. We're playing football and the pigs are winning two goals to one!"

Jennifer shook her head and laughed. She joined him and the animals. As they all ran around after the ball, the sound of Cassie's car beeping made Jennifer stop. "Good grief, it must be five o'clock already."

Cassie and Paul came down the side garden. "Hiya."

"Hi, you're just in time – we need more players."

They joined the game of football. "Who's winning?"

"Not sure; I lost count a while back. I think it's about five all!"

As they laughed at the idea of a football match against a team of pigs having equal scores, they were interrupted by the phone ringing. Still giggling to herself, Jennifer picked up the receiver.

"Hello… Oh hi Jim – you all right…? Good, what can I do for you darling…? Uh huh… Yes of course, I look forward to it… See you then… Yep, and love to you and Josh too… byeee."

She hung up and ran excitedly to her friends. "Guys, come in. I've got some news!"

Everyone piled in to the house. "What's all the hullabaloo – why the panic?"

"No panic, just brilliant news. Jim just called, Josh is feeling much better and… he wants to talk seriously about the Craft Centre."

There was a united cheer with beaming smiles from everyone.

Jennifer continued. "Apparently, the nurse has said Josh can go out for a while if he keeps wrapped up nice and warm. He's chosen to go to the pub and said for us to join him for a pint and a chin wag."

"Good old Josh; he knows how to pick a business meeting venue!"

Another cheer rang out. "When's this taking place?"

"Tomorrow lunchtime – can you all make it?"

They nodded enthusiastically. "Brilliant – s'pose we should get our ideas down on paper."

She skipped out of the room to fetch pens and her writing pad. TJ smiled. "Honestly, that girl of mine – I've never known anyone go through so many extremes of emotions almost in the blink of an eye."

Cassie patted his hand. "Well, at least with our Jen around, life is never boring!"

As she burst back in to the room, Cassie, Paul and TJ all looked at her with bemused smiles on their faces. She looked quizzical. "What?"

TJ laughed and patted the seat beside him encouraging Jennifer to sit down. "Come on my little 'whirling dervish' – let's get this project down on paper."

She almost sat down, but jumped up quickly. "Oh my goodness, I haven't fed the girls!"

TJ gave a groan and pretended to tear his hair and slumped forward cradling his head on the table. Cassie and Paul both laughed.

Again, unaware of the joke, Jennifer was mystified. "What is the matter with you all?"

For some reason this made them laugh even more. Their unaccountable giggling was contagious and very soon even Jennifer had joined in, even though she didn't know why. For some reason 'silly mode' had totally overtaken all four of them and every attempt to be serious was futile. They decided to get out their dinner in the hope that food might have a calming effect.

Amazingly, by the end of the evening they had put together a very professional looking business plan, complete with detailed diagrams of layout and even an 'artist's impression' of the end result. "Well guys, I think we're there. All we need is Joshua's blessing and it's full steam ahead!"

***

As they approached the door of the Miraford Arms, Jennifer looked anxiously at TJ. He gave an encouraging smile, squeezed her hand and kissed her cheek. They went in. At the far end of the bar they noticed Jim and Joshua just finishing a game of darts. Jim waved. Moments after, Cassie and Paul came in and joined their friends. "You OK mate?"

Jennifer nodded. "I think so, but I've got butterflies in my tummy."

Cassie gave her a hug. They took up their usual seats at the table by the window. Jim called, "Jenny lass – could you help me get some drinks?"

TJ stood up. "I'll get 'em Grandad."

"No lad. If you could help Josh to his seat please."

TJ realised that Jim specifically wanted Jenny.

She joined him at the bar. "Everything all right, Jim?"

He nodded. "I just wanted a word." He took her to a quieter area. "I know Josh can come across as a happy go lucky fella – but he's a shrewd business man. He hasn't run that boatyard for sixty years by being a fool. I just wanted to warn you that for a while, he'll go very quiet and serious. Don't panic or get worried love… it's just his way."

"Well, we'll know soon enough. Come on, we'd better get these 'ere drinks."

As they approached the table, TJ had a slightly concerned look. He mouthed "You OK?"

Jennifer, with a soft smile, replied silently "Yeah."

Taking her seat she turned to Joshua. "So, how are you feeling? Enjoying being out at last?"

He smiled broadly. "Aye I am. Jimmy's cottage is real nice, but I was yearning to be out an' about. Not used to being stuck inside. So Jenny – where's this 'ere project you promised to show me?"

"Ah, right – we've put it all in here."

She handed him a file. Placing it on the table, he took his reading glasses from his pocket. Putting them on, he slowly hooked the arms over his ears. With his spectacles in place he suddenly looked very studious. His whole demeanour changed as he quietly read through each page. There was no indication from his sober expression what his opinion of the Craft Centre might be. For nearly an hour he studied the words and designs.

When refill drinks were brought he acknowledged thanks with a nod, but never uttered a word. Jennifer bit her lip. She snuggled against TJ and whispered in his ear. "Oh, this is doing my head in. Do you think he likes it?"

TJ returned the whisper. "Darling, I haven't got the foggiest idea!"

Similar frustration was shared with Cassie and Paul as they exchanged silent expressions and shoulder shrugs.

It seemed like an eternity, but eventually Joshua closed the file and removed his specs, his expression still very non-committal. He took Jennifer's hand in his and smiled. "Don't look so worried dear. I think it's a wonderful idea and I look forward to helping you getting it up and running."

Everyone cheered. Their relief exploded into a bombardment of conversations which seemed to completely drown out all other noises within the pub. Although he was really enjoying his first social outing since his accident, it was obvious that the day was taking its toll on Joshua.

"You're looking very tired, love. When you want to go back to the cottage I'll give you a lift... don't worry, I've been on soft drinks!" Cassie chuckled.

"Aye, that would be right nice of you. Thank you lass."

"I'll walk Rigger back for you, Josh."

He smiled at Jennifer. "Thank you Jenny. We'll get the kettle on. I know you'll want a coffee!"

Jennifer gave a smile and patted his hand. "Oh, you've found out – I didn't think anyone knew!" Everyone jeered and laughed.

As promised, when Jennifer, TJ and Soaki arrived with Rigger their coffees were ready and waiting. They all chatted while they drank. Although Josh was recovering well, Jennifer said she would continue walking Rigger until Josh was fit enough to take him himself. They said their goodbyes and made their way home.

Jennifer was grateful for the gentle stroll. The day had been not physically taxing, but emotionally exhausting. As they walked towards the outskirts of the village, Jennifer felt tired but content. They held hands but didn't talk much for a while. TJ looked at her. "Penny for your thoughts?"

She smiled wistfully and sighed. "I was just remembering the first time I walked past these gardens. Grannifer and I had an early morning walk and that completely changed my life. It was only a few months ago but… well, it feels like a lifetime!"

He looked at her lovingly. "I think I know what you mean. Somehow time plays tricks on us."

She gave him a questioning look. "Huh?"

"Well – take us for instance. We've only been together for a short while, but I feel like I've known you forever."

She smiled. "Yeah, good isn't it?"

He kissed her. "Yes, very."

When they got back to Willow Bank House, Jennifer went with Soaki to the kitchen and put fresh water in her bowl, leaving TJ to shut the door. As he did so he noticed a light flashing on the hall phone. "You've got a message on your landline, darling."

"Can you listen to it while I check the girls, please?"

TJ joined her moments later in the garden. "It was Mel, asking you to give him a call when you get in."

"Oh no. I bet he wants the girls back."

A mixture of concern and sadness etched on her face. "Don't get upset. Give him a ring and see what he wants."

She swallowed hard and nodded. "Fingers crossed it won't be horrible."

She went indoors and dialled the number. "Hello Mel – it's Jennifer."

"Ah, hello Jenny; how are you?"

"Er, OK, but a bit worried…"

"Why?"

"Well I'm thinking you probably want the girls back."

"Well, probably soon – how are they doing with the gardening?"

She responded sadly. "Really well – actually they've just about cleared it all."

"That's great. I've got a plan for 'em and they're about the right age now."

She sniffed. "I know."

"Are you all right Jenny? It sounds like you're crying."

"Sorry, I just hate the thought that… oh you told me not to get too attached to them."

"Calm down love. My plans aren't what you're thinking. They're going to be gilts."

"Sorry – they'll be what?"

"Gilts – I'm going to use them for breeding!"

Jennifer started laughing through her tears. He chuckled alongside her. "Thought that'd put a smile on your face! I'll call you tomorrow to sort out picking 'em up – probably next week, OK?"

"Yeah, OK. Chat tomorrow then – byeee."

She put down the handset. Sighing deeply, she wiped her eyes and went back to TJ. He noted that she'd been crying and stretched out his arms ready to give a comforting cuddle. "Oh, I'm sorry love."

"No, it's OK." She took his hug anyway. "They're not for cooking… they're going to be mothers!"

They both laughed with relief. "You do mean all of them? Even Pickle?"

"Yes, even my naughty girl!"

TJ rolled his eyes. "Oh crikey, just imagine a whole litter like her."

Jennifer smiled affectionately. "Yeah, they'll be wonderful – just like their mum!"

As the evening progressed, they shared the various jobs needed to settle the pigs for the night and then organised their own evening meal. It amazed Jennifer how well they worked together. Everything gelled so naturally and, without spoken words, they automatically knew what they and each other were doing. Even Soaki was aware of whether to be near them or keep out of the way, especially when hot pans were in use! They made a good team.

It wasn't too late when TJ and Soaki made their way back to the house boat.

As she made her way to bed she took a moment to enjoy the view from her window. She was glad of the cosy warmth of the house. Outside it was a cold crisp night with barely a cloud to be seen. The moon was only a slim crescent. As she gazed at the inky black sky, she smiled at the beauty of the endless stars which decorated the night like a canopy of sequins.

"Ah my darling Grannifer – what a perfect vision to finish the day with. It's been a roller-coaster of emotions hasn't it sweetheart? But, we've come through it OK, haven't we! Well, time to hit the hay." She yawned. "Cor – I haven't felt this tired in a long time! Night night my darling... love you."

***

The next few days seemed to fly by with Jennifer hardly able to define one from the other. Mel had rung her and arranged to collect the girls on Monday afternoon. There were the usual daily walks with Rigger and the visit to the market on Saturday. This meant passing on the news to her vegetable stall holder that she would no longer be needing the extra bits put by for her. She also gave the good news to Laura about the Craft Centre project.

On Sunday, Cassie and Paul joined Jennifer, TJ and Soaki for a farewell get together for the pigs. They organised as many various games as possible to make it a fun day instead of a sad one. They played football (of course), but the relay race was somewhat difficult to complete when the pigs seemed determined not to keep to the designated lanes.

Cassie and Jennifer, who easily won, called "Which pig is which!" This involved wearing a blindfold!

The boys' team insisted that the girls had an unfair advantage because the pigs grunted their names to them whilst being stroked.

***

All too soon it was Monday morning. Sitting on the edge of her bed, Jennifer sighed heavily. "Oh well, just a few more hours before my girls have to go... better help them pack!" She half smiled at the thought of the four of them climbing into a taxi, each with a suitcase.

In the kitchen she prepared their breakfast for the last time. A tear rolled down her cheek. Taking a deep breath she took the food into the garden. "Here piggy pig pigs... come on beautiful mums-to-be." She smiled as they came running towards her. "Oh my darlings – I am so going to miss you."

After sorting the girls, she fed the birds. Back indoors she filled the kettle. Just as it came to the boil there was a tap on the door. It was TJ and Soaki. "Morning Jenny – you OK?"

They hugged. "Yeah, I suppose. It's just going to be so weird not having them here."

She made the drinks. "I know love, but at least you know you've helped them to be happy and healthy. Just what they need for

193

motherhood."

She smiled. "Yes I know… perhaps I should start knitting little piggy blankets!"

They laughed and he took her hand. "Anyway me darlin'… there'll be plenty to keep you busy, at least a little something called a boatyard to convert. And the garden… and decorating the house… and we've still got that door in the broom cupboard to investigate."

She rolled her eyes. "OK, OK – I get the idea. So we've got a few things that need doing!"

TJ chuckled. "A 'few' things… you make it sound like buying the ingredients for a tea party!"

Jennifer raised her eyebrows and began to speak. "That's a good…"

"No!"

"What?"

"Whatever idea you're conjuring up as a reason for a party."

She frowned and pouted. "But I like parties."

He gave her a soft smile. "I know you do darling, but maybe not just yet, eh?"

They pottered around in the house and garden for the next few hours. Then the sound of a vehicle made Jennifer stiffen – she had a melancholy expression. "Oh dear; Mel's here."

They went to the front gate to meet him. "Hi Jen, TJ – how are you both?" He bent down and stroked Soaki. "Hello girl – and how are you?"

"Hello Mel. Do you want a cuppa before you take the girls away?"

He smiled. "I was hoping you'd say that – but are you not coming to see them settle in at my place?"

Jennifer lit up like a beacon. "Oh really? Can we?"

"Course you can. I assumed you'd want to."

While she made the drinks, TJ and Mel walked around the garden. They joined Jennifer in the kitchen. "You've done a good job with 'em Jenny. They look really healthy."

TJ chuckled. "She spoils them!"

"No I don't – they've worked hard for their treats."

"Oi, children, children, no need to squabble!" They laughed.

"Come on then – let's get these ladies loaded into the truck."

Jennifer had saved four extra especially nice apples to help entice them aboard, not that this was too much of a problem with Mel's expertise.

"Mm, you've done this before!"

He laughed. "Yes, once or twice."

194

They drove through the village, then took the right turn at the fork in the road. "I've never been this way before. Is your farm far?"

"No, not too much further; couple of minutes and we'll be there."

He turned into a driveway and drove to the rear of an attractive whitewashed house. They parked with the back of the truck by a gate which led to a small paddock.

"Could you two open the gates for me please, then I'll back in."

Jennifer and TJ jumped out of the cab with Soaki close behind. Jennifer stood by the perimeter fence watching apprehensively as Pickle and Primrose ran out, closely followed by Perky, and then Pinky. There was a bitter-sweet smile on her lips. She was sad, yet pleased that her girls seemed to be enjoying their new surroundings. They ran around investigating and munching. She put her hand to her mouth. She blew a kiss and almost silently whispered "Bye bye my darlings."

She felt a small hand nestle in hers. She looked down to her right. The hand belonged to a young girl – Jennifer thought about five or six. She had dark brown hair with eyes that were almost the same colour as the ringlets which tumbled around her shoulders.

They smiled at each other. "Hello, who are you? My name is Jennifer."

"I'm Amelia May – but everyone calls me Ami."

"I know a wonderful lady who had Amelia as her middle name."

"That's nice – would you like to see my chickens?"

Jennifer nodded. "Yes please."

Ami led Jennifer and Mel and TJ followed.

"Has your Jenny got magic powers?" asked Mel.

"Eh, how do you mean?"

"Our Ami is normally really really shy – takes forever to talk to anyone, let alone a stranger."

TJ shrugged. "Dunno mate; she's just a wonderful lady, but I don't think I'll ever stop being surprised by her."

In the chicken run, Jennifer and Ami scattered food for the hens. "When we finish here, I'll show you the puppies – I've got a cat and seven goldfish too."

Ami, still holding Jennifer's hand, led her into the house. Hardly stopping, she spoke to a pleasant looking lady who was standing at the kitchen table making bread. "Mummy, this is my new friend – she's been looking after our pigs and I'm showing her my pets."

The lady, with a surprised expression at her daughter's enthusiasm, smiled. "Hello, you must be Jenny. Mel's told me all about you – I'm Nancy."

"Hello; nice to meet you."

Ami pulled her hand. "Come on – they're in here."

Ami led the way across the hall and into a brightly decorated playroom. On top of a three-drawer chest of drawers was an aquarium. "These are my fishes."

Jennifer bent down to look. The little girl left her momentarily. She returned quickly cradling a tabby cat which flopped lazily in her arms. "This is Tabitha."

Jennifer tickled its chin. At the base of a large open dolls' house was a big soft cushion. Ami placed Tabitha on it and went back to Jennifer. "The puppies are with Mummy – you come an' see."

Again, the dainty little hand pulled Jennifer along. By the time they reached the kitchen, Mel and TJ had joined Nancy. The three looked with bemused amusement as Jennifer passed by. She had an expression that indicated that she had no control over the tiny whirlwind who had no intention of stopping until she had completed her mission to introduce her 'new friend' to all the animals.

Eventually, they halted in a scullery type room. Ami pointed proudly to a very large dog basket where on top of the padded bedding were three sleeping puppies. Ami put her finger to her lips. "Shh, they're sleeping 'cos dey eat dinner."

Jennifer nodded and smiled. Mel's voice called them. Ami rushed to the kitchen. "Daddy, shhh, dogs sleeping."

She suddenly seemed to notice TJ and snuggled close to her mum. Jennifer had joined them. "Ami, have you met Soaki? Look, she's down here on the floor." Ami shook her head. "Do you want to stroke her?"

The little girl looked unsure. She glanced suspiciously at TJ. "Oh, you haven't met 'my' friend yet have you? This is TJ – he's like a daddy to Soaki – do you want to come with me and say hello?"

Jennifer offered her hand. Cautiously Ami came to Jennifer who motioned to TJ to bend down. He knelt on the floor. Now at almost the same height, Ami gave a coy smile and with her fingers only, she gave a shy little wave. He mimicked her and in a gentle voice only just beyond a whisper, he spoke. "This is my dog. Her name is Soaki."

Stepping nearer, she gently stroked Soaki's head. She smiled happily at TJ. "Nice doggie."

Mel made drinks, then while the grown-ups chatted, Ami went back to her playroom. It turned out that the puppies were the last three of a litter of six. One was waiting for new owners to return from holiday, Ami had chosen one to keep and the third dog was in need of a home.

"Do you know of anyone who's looking for one?"

Jennifer and TJ laughed. "Well, actually…"

Mel tutted and rolled his eyes. "You? Why didn't you say?"

"I didn't know you had any… I mean… well, you do pigs!"

Nancy laughed. "You're joking. You've seen our Ami – she might normally be shy of humans, but she'd have a whole zoo given half the chance!"

"Yes, I must admit she's brilliant with them despite her age."

They continued chatting. "So how old are these pups?"

"Three and a half months. All weaned and jabbed, and just about house-trained."

"Already? Gosh, that's good!"

"Believe it or not, that's mainly down to Ami. She says to 'em "No! Poo, wee in garden!" They all chuckled.

Ami returned and Nancy cuddled the little girl. "Are the puppies awake yet darling?"

"I'll see."

She investigated and returning, she nodded happily. "Jenny would like to see the one that still needs a home – could you bring him through, please?"

Ami skipped to the basket. As carefully as she'd been with her cat, she carried the podgy little puppy to the kitchen. She placed it lovingly into Jennifer's arms. As she held him he stretched his head up and started licking her neck.

Ami giggled and pointed. "He washing you!"

As they continued chatting, Nancy tutted "Why on earth are we sitting on these benches when we have comfy chairs in the other room?"

They went through to the lounge where there were pretty cottage style chairs and settees. Each had plump soft cushions that complemented the colours in the dainty floral fabric of the suite. As they got seated Jennifer, still cuddling the puppy, smiled. "This is lovely – who's the décor inspiration?"

Mel answered. "That's my Nancy – I can't take any of the credit I'm afraid."

His wife looked slightly embarrassed. "You have other talents my darling!"

TJ noticed a guitar and bongos in the corner next to a piano. "Would those talents include being a musician?" He nodded towards the instruments.

"Er, yeah. I play the ones you can pick up; the piano is Nancy's baby."

Jennifer was intrigued. "It seems wherever I am, I'm surrounded by people who can play. Even my darling Grandpa could get a lovely tune out of his old banjo."

As she spoke, the puppy started licking her and wagging his tail enthusiastically. "Oh yes! What's all this in aid of?"

TJ commented "He seemed to react when you said 'Banjo'!"

The puppy jumped from Jennifer on to TJ's lap still wagging his tail excitedly.

"Oh yes! What's all this about?"

They laughed. "Well Jenny lass – if you want the little fella, I think he's chosen himself a name!"

She smiled at Mel. "I reckon you could be right there."

There was no question that there was a mutual attraction between Jennifer and the friendly little puppy. "I had no idea that when I returned sixteen trotters to you, I'd be going home with four fluffy paws! I'm not at all prepared for a baby dog – anything at the house is for our grown up girl when she comes to visit." She stroked Soaki affectionately.

"We'll keep little 'un here for as long as you need to get prepared – just have him when you're ready."

Jennifer smiled gratefully at Nancy. "Oh thank you. That would be very helpful."

It was a while later. Jennifer gave a little jump. "Crikey – look at the time. I've got to get back and feed the gir..." Her words trailed away. "Oh dear. Old habits die hard!" They all laughed.

They stayed for a little longer then said their goodbyes to Nancy and Ami. There was of course also a cuddle for the puppy. "Bye bye little one – we'll come back soon to take you to your new home." He wagged his tail.

Jennifer gave a final fond wave to the girls. She smiled, happy that they were settled and looking content. She climbed back into the truck with TJ and Soaki.

Back at 'Willow Bank', TJ helped to load the pigs' trough for Mel to take back. Jennifer gave him a couple of carrier bags.

"This is the last of their veggies and pig nuts, and some of the milk that they like – yuck!" She wrinkled her nose.

He chuckled as he took them. "Thanks love; I'll get Ami to give it to 'em in the morning. She'll enjoy that!"

They waved him goodbye as he drove up the lane. TJ slipped his arm around her waist. "Come on missus – let's get that kettle on and I don't know about you, but I'm rather hungry."

"Cor, me too. No wonder; we didn't have lunch did we? I can't remember. Oh what the heck – let's munch something anyway."

Within twenty minutes their usual teamwork had fallen into place and they were seated at the table with drinks and plates adorned with omelette, salad and fresh bread (courtesy of Nancy). Soaki was fed and watered too.

"Gosh, we did that quick enough!"

"Yeah, I think it's a record even for us."

They laughed. "I tell you what: I'm going to get Nancy to teach me how to make this – it's scrummy!"

After their meal they sat in the living room relaxing. "We need to get stuck in and do your garden before any weeds decide to take up residence. Be a shame to let the girls' hard work go to waste."

"Yeah, you're right. Any idea what I'll need to get?"

"Well, you said you want mainly lawn with paths and flower beds, so what sort of paths to start with?"

Jennifer put a finger to her mouth as she thought. "I'd like stepping stones to the summer house and up to the front door... and I think gravel from the kitchen to the bottom gate."

"Sounds OK, so we'll need to membrane under the gravel to stop weeds growing through, and sand and cement for the stepping stones. It's the wrong time of the year really to lay a seed lawn, but being a walled garden might help. It'll cost a fortune to turf it."

She smiled at him. "OK then, I'll get ordering stuff first thing tomorrow."

He smiled back. "You do realise this is going to be hard work, don't you darling?"

"Yes I know – but it'll be worth it."

The phone rang. "Hello... Oh hi Cassie... No not busy... Great see you both in a mo... Yep, OK. byeee!"

She returned to TJ. "Cassie and Paul are on their way. She said to get the kettle on!"

Hearing the car pull up, Jennifer ran out to greet their friends. Cassie was surprised that her friend seemed so cheerful. "Hiya mate. You all right?"

"Yes I'm fine... you'll never guess what happened today!"

They went indoors and Jennifer explained about going to see the pigs back and meeting Mel's family and all about the puppy. "It's been great."

While the girls chatted, TJ and Paul were busy working out the amount of things needed for the garden. "Er – TJ, you've forgotten something."

TJ looked quizzically at Paul. "Have I? I thought I'd listed everything."

"You'll need boards to keep that gravel in place."

"Oh yes, you're right mate. Cheers."

Throughout the evening they made arrangements for the following day. Jennifer would order what she could on the phone, then go to Jim's cottage and collect Rigger for his walk, then Cassie would meet her there about midday.

Jennifer couldn't believe that so much had been packed into her days as she lay in her bed and recalled everything. "I don't know Grannifer – each day feels more like a week with the amount of stuff that gets crammed in – and tomorrow is looking to be just as manic." She yawned. "Ooh – sleep time me thinks. Night night darling; sweet dreams. Love you." She kissed the air and smiled happily. The bed covers seemed to cuddle her as she drifted off to sleep.

***

As she woke the following morning, Jennifer felt a little melancholy, as her beloved pigs were no longer waiting to greet her when she called them for breakfast. She lay thinking for a while.

As she snuggled back under the covers she tried hard to encourage herself to get up. She put her thoughts on hold. "What's that noise?"

She lifted her head off the pillow and listened. Yes, there it was again. "What on earth is that?" She sat up then went cautiously to the window. As she peered out, she shook her head and chuckled to herself. "Oh, what's he like?"

TJ was busy with a spade digging the trench ready for the gravel path. She tapped the glass to get his attention. As he looked at her she waved. He did likewise and gave one of his beaming smiles.

Grabbing her dressing gown she hurried downstairs. She opened the back door. Soaki ran to her, wagging her tail enthusiastically. "Good morning sweetheart." She bent down and stroked and kissed the friendly dog.

TJ joined them. "Hiya Jenny. You all right darling?"

"Good morning Mr Up-At-The-Crack-Of-Dawn!"

They kissed. "Why so early, darling?"

TJ shrugged. "Thought you'd appreciate a busy garden – first day without the girls and all that."

She smiled and cuddled him. "Thank you – you know me too well!"

"Anyway, it needs doing so Soaki and I thought we'd come and make a start, didn't we girl?"

He rubbed her ears vigorously. It seemed that she smiled with the affectionate attention from her master. Jennifer laughed as she watched them interacting. She filled the kettle. "Have you had breakfast yet?"

He shook his head. "No m'dear. We thought we'd share with you."

She smiled. "OK, what would sir like?"

He picked up a bag and placed it on the table. "We brought it with us – a full English! You get dressed and I'll cook."

"Sounds like I get the best out of this deal… sure you don't want me to help?"

TJ put a pretend stern expression on and pointed towards the hall door. "Go!"

"OK, OK – I'm going!" She giggled as she ran through the kitchen.

She was almost ready and had just finished brushing her hair. Suddenly there was a loud banging noise from downstairs. She rushed to the landing and peered down the stair well. "What on earth is that racket?"

TJ was in the hall with a saucepan and wooden spoon. "Excuse me – this is my breakfast gong! Your meal madam, is now served."

She laughed and skipped downstairs. With a tea towel draped on his arm, TJ escorted Jennifer to the table.

As they tucked in to the scrumptious food, Jennifer spoke in almost a serious tone. "This is really lovely darling, but… why?"

"Why not?"

"All the treats and well… everything."

He sighed. "I wanted to make you start your day happy. I knew you'd be missing the girls and there's loads to be done and well… if the day starts well, hopefully it will be good all through, and apart from that, I love you, and I don't want you to be sad."

Her eyes glistened as she listened to his stumbling speech. She swallowed then lent forward and kissed him gently. "Thank you." They smiled and nestled their heads together.

When they'd cleared the table, Jennifer set about making phone calls to various tradesmen to organise the things to be delivered for the garden.

"Right, that's done. Now I need to get to Jim's and walk Rigger. Are you coming with me, love?"

"I thought I'd stay here and crack on with the path… unless you particularly need me with you."

"Not if that's what you want to do, but I'm going with Cassie after to get the bits for Banjo. Anything you want in Lamton?"

He shook his head. "No thanks… but if you're that far, perhaps pop in to Johnston's and see if they've got boards for the path edge."

She smiled and mock saluted. "Will do, captain!"

Cassie arrived at the cottage just as Jennifer was closing the gate, having dropped Rigger back. Beep! Beep! Jennifer looked towards the bright 2CV and smiled. She waved to her friend. She climbed in and they hugged.

"Hiya mate; that was good timing!"

"But of course... didn't you know I'm telepathetic?" They laughed. "Oh crikey. I always get that word wrong!"

They chatted ten to the dozen as always and before they'd realised, they were in Lamton. Cassie parked the car.

"The pet shop is just around the corner or the department store have a selection."

Jennifer clapped her hands excitedly. "Ooh – choices!"

Cassie rolled her eyes. "Come on you nutter – we'll try the little shop first."

They opened the door - 'ka-ding'. The bell announced their arrival. "Good morning, ladies."

They returned the greeting to the assistant. As they wandered around, Jennifer looked to her friend. "Now don't let me buy too much, OK?"

Cassie raised her eyebrows and gave a resigned shake of her head. "I'll try – but short of tying you down, I don't think... oh oh... where's she gone?"

She rounded a corner to find Jennifer enthusiastically selecting toys from a display. "Oh mate, look at these; they're so sweet!"

It wasn't long before she was having to ask Cassie to reach things from a display unit for her, as her own arms were so full of things. "Why didn't you get a basket, mate?"

Jennifer looked sheepish. "Er, well, I, um – I didn't think I needed one."

Cassie smiled. "Yeah right. Your name IS Jennifer Cade, isn't it?"

"Yes, of course."

"Well this is what Jennifer Cade does!"

"Oh yes, I see what you mean."

They giggled and went to the counter. "Oh my – a new litter?" The assistant smiled.

"No, just one puppy – I'm getting him in a day or so."

"Just the one? Wow, he'll be spoilt for choice as to what to play with."

As they loaded the car, Jennifer passed yet another bag of bits to Cassie. "I didn't go overboard did I... I mean I did get a toy and bone for Soaki too?"

"And that accounts for at least half a carrier bag!"

They got into the car. "So, off to the reclamation yard, yes?"

"Mm, yes please."

Being regular visitors they were greeted warmly by the staff. They were shown some floorboards that seemed perfect for the path edges. Jennifer paid and made delivery arrangements.

Back in the car they chatted. "Did you see they had that old turnstile thing that you liked?"

"Yeah... I've bought it!"

Cassie braked and stared dumbfounded at her friend. "Jenny, what the... why on earth... I mean..."

"I've had an idea for it... trust me, it's a good-un." She smiled contentedly as they continued their journey.

As they neared the village, Cassie checked with Jennifer as to where else they needed to go. "I know we've to pop in to Honey Bee Farm, but I've forgotten – is there anywhere else?"

"No darling, I think that's it. But if you fancy lunch, it'll be my treat... as a little thank you for all this driving and stuff." She smiled.

"Well now you mention it, I am a bit peckish. I just need to drop in to the studio for a minute."

Jennifer beamed. "Oh goody – I love your studio. It's been ages since I've been there."

As they stepped in through the door, Jennifer drank in the atmosphere. She closed her eyes. "Ah, this is so unique – I don't know anywhere else that is even close to how it looks, feels, smells... I just adore it."

"Well, if we get our Craft Centre up and running, you can enjoy it every day!"

"I can't wait! But one correction there though mate – it's not if, but when."

"Sorry boss!"

Cassie went to a large cupboard. "Actually Jen – shall we have a coffee here and buy something to munch back at yours?"

"Yes, I like that idea and I've left TJ far too long already. What's that you've got there?"

"This is why we're here – I found them while I was having a sort out. They're moulds for making stepping stones. Thought you might be interested in popping a DIY one in amongst your bought ones."

Jennifer looked through the selection. "These are great – wow look, leaves and stars, and oh Cassie you're such a treasure."

As she put the coffee down she grinned. "I thought you'd like 'em"

Eventually they arrived at the farm. "Gosh, I can't believe it's only one o'clock; we've done so much."

"Yeah, it feels like we've been out all day."

They collected bags of grass seed and a few plants which took Jennifer's fancy. "I want to give one of these to TJ – he was such a darling this morning."

Cassie nodded. "Is that the lot then?"

"Yep – oh no, not quite... what about lunch?"

"They've got some nice cheeses. How about a ploughman's?"

"Brilliant. Quick and easy and no cooking!"

With a selection of cheese and home grown salad, they approached the counter. Cassie looked with a quizzical expression at a jar of honey almost hidden behind the plants.

"Er, it's just a little extra thing for my fella."

Cassie shook her head and tutted. "Jen – you don't have to keep buying us all presents all the time."

"I know – but I'm grateful and it's my way of showing it and saying 'thank you'."

"But you don't have to. We do things to help you because we want to – and because we love you!"

They hugged. "I know – but thanks for saying so."

Chapter 12

As they arrived back at Willow Bank House, Jennifer stared open mouthed. "Bloomin' heck – that was quick. Look mate, there's stuff in the garden been delivered already!"

They started emptying the car. TJ appeared and helped them. "Crikey, have you left anything in the shops for anyone else?"

"Oh don't you start – I've already had Cassie telling me off."

He gave her a sympathetic smile. "Never mind darling – come on, I put the kettle on when I heard you pull up. Let's get you a cuppa and you can show me what you've brought."

With the kitchen table almost completely covered with shopping bags they took their drinks into the garden where the girls admired the newly finished path that TJ had dug out. Jennifer spoke to Cassie in a hushed voice just loud enough that TJ would be able to hear. "He's worked so hard – I don't want to tell him it's not where I wanted it!"

TJ looked shocked. "You what?"

She laughed. "Nah nah – got you back for criticising my shopping!"

"Oh you rotter; I thought you were serious!"

They all laughed. "No honestly darling, it's a wonderful job. Ooh, that reminds me – pressie time." She ran indoors.

Returning moments later with a broad grin on her face she gave her gifts: the plant and honey to TJ, Soaki's bone and toy and another one of the plants to Cassie.

"Jen – I wasn't expecting this!"

"But you do like it? I hope it's the one you were looking at."

"Cor, you don't miss a trick do you? Thank you mate, it's perfect."

TJ kissed her. "Thank you Jenny, but you didn't …"

She put a finger to his lips. "I wanted to. Anyway, I like giving pressies."

Later, as they prepared the ploughman's there was a knock at the door.

"Afternoon Miss Cade. We've got your order from Johnston's."

"Crikey – I thought you were coming tomorrow!"

"Oh sorry; is it inconvenient?"

"No, not at all. Was it one cup with two sugars and one without?"

The men chuckled. "That's very kind, and what a memory!"

The other two were watching through the kitchen window. "Oh, hold on to your hat TJ. You won't believe what she bought from them!"

"Wooden boards, I know."

"Yes, but there's something else too."

"Oh dear, I dread to think. What is it? A life size model giraffe or something?"

"No. She might be a bit batty, but why would she buy a giraffe?"

He sighed heavily. "Why does Jenny buy half the stuff she does?"

As the men unloaded the boards, Jennifer came in and made the drinks.

As the group sat chatting with their drinks, TJ looked at the turnstile and then at Jennifer. He shook his head with a distinct air of exasperation. "Jen darling, I know you like unusual things, but…" He gazed again at her purchase. "I mean…"

He puffed his cheeks and blew gently through pursed lips. "Why? Please, please tell me what you can possibly want with that rusty heap of metal."

She gave a bemused half smile. "It's a turnstile."

"Yeeesss… and?"

"For the entrance."

"To what?"

She tutted and rolled her eyes. "To our pier! It'll be a lovely fun start to our Craft Centre… if people enjoy them like I do. If they don't, they can walk around it! But we'll encourage 'em to use it 'cos the money used to activate it will go to charity." She nodded triumphantly and sat back on her seat.

TJ smiled. "You're not just a pretty face are you?"

Cassie and the delivery men all joined in with agreeable comments.

"Cor, sorry mate, I thought you'd properly lost it – but that's brilliant. Er, just one thing – does it still work?"

Jennifer shrugged. "Dunno – but I'm sure we'll get it up and running." She smiled confidently and they all chuckled.

Throughout the afternoon the little band of friends got stuck in with their latest project of constructing the gravel path. TJ continued digging whilst Jennifer and Cassie had a competition to see who could paint the most boards with wood primer. Soaki munched happily on her bone but occasionally stopped and took her new toy to the humans, forcing them to take a break from their work by throwing the toy in a game of 'fetch'.

By the time Paul arrived, it was early evening. With an extra pair of hands, they soon had the membrane lining laid and the board edging in place. The guys ferried wheelbarrow loads of gravel, while the girls raked it level.

Jennifer stood upright and with her hands supporting the small of her back, she gave a stretch. She puffed her cheeks and blew air through pursed lips. "I think we've all done enough for one day. Time to have a sit down before we fall down."

Cassie laid on the ground. "Too late mate. I'm done!"

Jennifer laughed as she took her friend's hands and pulled her up. They called Paul and TJ, then went indoors. Once inside, the four friends made their way to the living room, closely followed by Soaki. They each collapsed thankfully into their favourite seats. "Phew, that's better!"

Jennifer closed her eyes and luxuriated in the snuggly comfort of her cushion-adorned sofa. A relaxed smile crept across her lips.

"So, who's going to put the kettle on?"

The girls and Paul groaned in response to TJ. "Oh – I made the last lot!"

"No you didn't. I think you'll find I did – you did the round before that!"

They bickered comically for a while. Eventually TJ slid from his chair and crawled on his hands and knees towards the door. "OK OK, enough already... I'll make the drinks!"

The others cheered. Feeling somewhat guilty, Jennifer followed and helped with the refreshments. "S'pose we ought to do some food... not that any of us is up to doing a big meal. What's quick and easy that will fill us up?"

TJ thought for a moment. "Buck Rarebit! Good old cheese on toast with a poached egg on top!"

"Ooh yes. I haven't had that for ages. Let's see if the guys are OK with it."

Their meal was simple but tasty and very much enjoyed by everyone, especially when finished off with fresh strawberries and ice cream topped with chocolate sprinkles for desert.

Cassie sat back and rubbed her tummy. "Oh – that was scrummy!" Paul agreed, "Absolutely – compliments to the chefs!"

Jennifer put on a posh voice. "Corfee en the lounge, I think!" They smiled and went to the other room.

***

As she looked from her bedroom window the following morning, Jennifer was amazed at just how much of the gravel path they had actually done yesterday. "Wow, another five more loads should do it. What do you think Grannifer – do you reckon I could finish it before the guys get here?"

She smiled to herself as she went downstairs. Her feathered friends were ready and waiting around the garden for their breakfast. As she put the food on the bird table she heard the gate opening.

"Morning Jen – you're up early." She smiled as TJ and Soaki came up the garden.

"Hiya – you can talk! What time did you two get up?"

They hugged and kissed each other. "I was going to try and finish the path."

TJ grinned. "Snap – Soaki and I thought the same!"

"Mm, great minds think alike eh? Oh well, two heads are better than one."

Soaki barked. "Oh sorry darling, three heads…" She ruffled the ears of their canine companion. "You're too clever by half, missie!"

Within the hour the couple had finished the path and were sitting down to eat their breakfast. They pottered around for a while then took a leisurely walk into the village to collect Rigger.

"Feels like ages since I've seen Grandad and Josh," mused TJ.

"Well, not much longer. Look – they're up the road walking towards us!"

"Oh yeah… you don't think they've forgotten you'd be turning up for dog walking duty?"

"Shouldn't think so. We'll find out in a minute."

They waved at the two elderly gentlemen who responded likewise. "Good morning my darlings – where are you off to?"

"Hello lass. Hi Timothy – we thought we'd come and meet you."

"So you feeling better then Josh?"

"That I am lad, thank you. Almost back to normal."

"That's good. Grandad has obviously been looking after you OK."

TJ gave Jim's shoulder an affectionate squeeze. Jim looked almost embarrassed – "No more than any friend would do."

208

They walked together towards the village. It was just after midday. "Fancy a pint and a spot of lunch?"

"As long as we share a plate – I couldn't tackle a whole Miraford Arms meal just yet!"

Josh laughed. "Fair enough lass; share-ums it is."

As the four friends sat chatting, Rigger and Soaki settled together under the table.

"I've been talking with my chaps at the boatyard and we can let you start converting it next week if you like."

Jennifer beamed. "Oh Joshua, that's wonderful!" Jennifer hugged TJ excitedly.

"We'll have to finish your garden a bit smartish – this Craft Centre is gonna take up most of our time y'know!"

"Coo yes – yes, you're right there."

Jim chipped in. "Well I can lend a hand… now my patient is just about mended! What needs doing?"

Jennifer groaned slightly. "Er, well… a lot of raking then hours of scattering grass seed around."

Jim smiled. "Well the raking might take a while, but I've got an old gadget in my loft that'll help sow the seed and scatter."

Jennifer raised her eyebrows. "I'm intrigued – tell us more."

He chuckled. "I'll show you when we get back. All I'll say for now is it's called a Fiddle!"

Having enjoyed their lunch break, they left the cosy pub and visited some of the shops to get some bits and pieces. On the walk back to the cottage, Jennifer tried hard to get information out of Jim. "So – this twiddle or dibble thing – how old is it?"

Jim chuckled. "Ooh – fiddle then. How old is it?" He thought for a moment. "Well, it were a bit ancient when I bought it and that was a good twenty or thirty years ago."

She raised her eyebrows. "Coo – so how did you say it worked?"

"I didn't."

Her face crumpled. "Oh Jim… darling… give us a clue!"

"Ha, you'll have to be patient and wait 'til we get home."

"You are sooo mean."

Jim smiled. Jennifer gave an exaggerated pout and Joshua and TJ both laughed. They carried on walking, Jennifer cheekily accusing Jim of dawdling. Suddenly he stopped. "Sorry; I'll have to go back. I forgot I was going to get some tartan paint."

"Jim, is it important? I'll get it for you tomorrow."

The men all laughed.

"What?"

TJ cuddled her. "Jenny darling – there's no such thing!" She threw her arms up with exasperation. "I give up!" They arrived at the cottage. "Put the kettle on Jenny lass – Timothy, can you help me get the fiddle… before she explodes!"

"Right ho Grandad."

As they all sat in the comfortable sitting room, they sipped at the drinks that Jennifer had made. Jim cradled his mug with both hands. Taking a mouthful, he smacked his lips in an exaggerated manner. "Mm – you make a good cuppa Jenny lass."

Frustrated with waiting, she replied curtly. "Thank you."

He smiled to himself and sipped again. Jennifer heaved a sigh. TJ nudged Jim with his elbow. "Grandad!"

"Yes Timothy." He looked quizzical. "What?"

Joshua chuckled. "C'mon Jimmy – you've teased the lass enough now!"

Jim laughed. "I'm sorry love – just bit of a laugh ya know! Here, this is what you've been waiting for."

He felt on the floor beside his end of the settee and handed the object to Jennifer. "It's a box with straps."

"And?"

"Well, it's got a stick too… how on earth does this sow seed?"

"I'll show you. Give it 'ere." He put the straps over his shoulders, box suspended by his chest. "Seed goes in't box and you stroke the stick to and fro like you're playing a violin or a…?"

"A fiddle!" She smiled realising where the name came in. "But how does it…?"

"Ah well, the stick is attached to a cord which is joined to a sort of wheel in't box – wheel goes back an' forth flinging the seed out of here." He indicated. "All you got to do is walk and pretend you're playing an instrument!" He smiled and splayed his hands palms uppermost. "And that is how a fiddle works."

Throughout the afternoon they made arrangements for the following day when Jim would come to Willow Bank to help in the garden.

Jennifer and TJ discussed the day as they and Soaki walked home. "Jim was really teasing me about the fiddle."

"Yep, that's Grandad to a tee. He always used to wind up my Nan! I remember once he said he thought he'd found a bomb in his veggie garden."

"No! Really?"

"No, he'd buried an old saucepan in the ground with a bit of it

210

exposed. There was a bit of writing visible – two letters: B and O."

Jennifer was intrigued. "So what happened?"

TJ chuckled. "Well, he went to Nan all serious like and made her creep very gently to have a look… then he carefully brushed away a bit more soil to reveal more writing."

"And…?"

"Another O and an exclamation mark! Nan was furious 'til she saw the funny side." He smiled. "She couldn't stay mad at him for long."

Back at the house, Jennifer set about making a drink whilst TJ got the garden tools ready to start preparing the lawn. While the kettle boiled, Jennifer made a quick call to Mel.

"Hello… Oh hi… Is that Nancy…? Jennifer here… Yeah I'm fine thanks and you…? Oh good… I thought I'd give you a ring to see about picking up little Banjo."

They chatted for a while and organised relocating the puppy into his new home at Willow Bank House. Ending the call with a cheery 'byeee', she replaced the handset, then skipped happily back to the kitchen.

TJ had finished the coffees. "What are you grinning at?"

Jennifer flung her arms around his neck. "I'm getting Banjo tomorrow!"

He smiled broadly as they cuddled, sharing her joy. "That's great Jen. Hear that Soaki? Another friend to play with!" Soaki wagged her tail.

Jennifer eventually calmed down enough to drink her coffee. "You realise that although it's the wrong time of year to sow a lawn, little Banjo will be running all over it too."

She smiled and nodded. "Yeah, but it's a huge garden and he's only a little puppy – how much damage can one set of little paws do?"

TJ raised his eyebrows. "Anyway sitting here isn't getting the ground ready – c'mon missus, grab a rake!"

They went outside. "So where shall we start?"

TJ grinned. "Let's each have a two foot wide strip, start near the house and head to the bottom wall. Bet I can finish mine before you!"

"You think so, do you?" She rolled up her sleeves. "On your marks… get set… go!"

By making it a race it didn't seem like hard work. If anything, the difficulty of the race was more apparent due to their laughing. Before long they had finished the first length. "I think that was a tie! Ready for the next bit?"

Jennifer puffed her cheeks. "Can we have a breather first?"

"OK – five minutes."

"Ooh sir, you are so generous!"

He chuckled. "Nah, come on wimp!"

She slapped his arm playfully. "Meanie!"

They walked back towards the top of the garden. By the time they'd finished their next run it was quite obvious they'd both had enough for one day. "Whew, I'm done in!"

"Coo, me too, and it's starting to get dark. Time to sort out dinner, eh?"

TJ nodded and they linked arms as they returned to the house.

They relaxed through the evening but it was still a very tired Jennifer who plodded up the stairs to bed that night. She had her usual ponder at the window. A smile crept across her mouth.

"It's getting there Grannifer. I know it's hard work but you never shied away from it – so nor will I. Thank you for being such an inspiration… big day tomorrow. Banjo will be joining our family!" She giggled. "I'm to bed now. Night night darling – love you." She kissed the air.

***

Just after six thirty the next morning, an excited Jennifer woke to a pleasantly sunny day.

With her morning coffee in hand she scattered food on the bird table. "There you are my darlings – early breakfast." She returned to the kitchen and had some toast.

Within an hour she was outside doing more raking at a much more leisurely pace than the previous evening. Immersed in her garden, she didn't hear Jim and Cassie arrive.

"I thought you wanted help… seems to me you're doin' all right on your own."

She turned to face Jim as she heard his cheeky voice. They hugged. "Oh, I haven't done all this… TJ and I started last night."

Cassie had been looking at the river and was on her way back up the gravel path. "He's a glutton for punishment… I've just seen him and Soaki on the tow-path."

"Better get the kettle on then lass – we Bartons always work better after a cuppa to kick start us."

Jennifer rolled her eyes and tutted midst a knowing grin.

"Morning Timothy – just in time for a brew!"

"Ah, just the ticket! How are you Grandad?"

They joined the girls indoors. Having supped their drinks, the quartet of humans and Soaki returned to the garden. As always, the fun-filled competitive nature was key to the plan on how the raking would be dealt with. The girls would work together, racing against Jim and TJ.

They worked hard for a couple of hours and made good progress. By lunchtime they were ready to sow the grass seed. Jim demonstrated how to use the 'fiddle', then passed it on to an excited Jennifer to have a go. She walked up and down the length of the garden giggling as she went. Meanwhile Cassie was preparing the mixture to make stepping stones in the moulds. TJ was busy in the kitchen making sandwiches.

This little hive of industry was accompanied by the radio, and as they sang along to the songs, another sound joined in. Parp! Parp! Parp!

Jennifer squealed with delight. "Yeh hey! Mel's arrived..."

She ran to the front gate. Mel was opening the door of his Jeep and undoing Ami's seatbelt. Nancy climbed down from the other side and placed the lively four legged, tail-wagging bundle into Jennifer's arms. She hugged and kissed him enthusiastically. "Ooh hello Banjo. Welcome to your new home!"

They all said hello properly and went to the house. Ami had instinctively taken Jennifer's hand again. Jennifer smiled. Soaki came to inspect their visitors, wagging her tail in recognition. With Banjo now on the ground, the two dogs ran off to investigate the grounds.

Soaki realised that her companion was little more than a baby and with her being about two years old... well possibly, she was very nearly a grown up! Therefore it was her duty to take on the status of matriarch and she took charge of the youngster and showed him the more interesting areas of the garden.

This done, they ran through the kitchen door and proceeded to scamper all around the house. Eventually they returned to the kitchen and lapped with gusto at their freshly filled water bowls.

The humans were also enjoying drinks and laughed heartily at the canine antics. Suddenly, TJ left the others and went to the kitchen. He returned with plates laden with sandwiches. "I forgot about these... I was making 'em before all the excitement. Tuck in everyone!"

After they'd eaten, Jennifer showed Nancy around the house and they discussed various decorating ideas. Meanwhile, the men continued gardening and Cassie had acquired a little helper in the shape of Ami who was totally immersed in the creation of stepping stones. Nancy watched her daughter from an upstairs window. "I can't believe how comfortable she is with you guys. Usually she is so shy."

Jennifer smiled, "She probably recognises that we're just kids who pretend to be grown-ups." They both laughed.

All too soon the afternoon had turned into early evening and Ami and her parents said their goodbyes. Banjo had found his new toys and was busy sharing them with Soaki. Although it had been a day filled with new experiences for little Banjo, Jennifer wanted him to get started into the routine of a steady walk in the quiet of the evening to calm down before bed time. He'd done more than his fair share of running around, so he didn't require exercise, so just a slow wander up the lane and back was sufficient.

On their return, Jennifer spent a while cuddling and gently stroking him before placing him in his bed. She kissed his head softly. "Night night little one. Sleep well."

As she lay in her own bed, she listened to see if any noise was coming from downstairs. All seemed well so she snuggled down and was soon asleep herself.

***

When she woke the following morning, she noticed that her bedroom door was open wider than she had left it. Drawing back the covers she sat on the edge of the bed. She giggled as Banjo nuzzled and licked her toes – good morning little man! She bent down and stroked his ears.

They went downstairs, Jennifer looking for any signs of 'accidents'. "Can't see any puppy puddles."

She opened the door and Banjo ran out to have a wee. "Young Ami has sure done a good job training you. Come on boy, let's get some breakfast."

Having tidied the kitchen and washed and dressed, Jennifer took the lead from the door handle it had been hanging on. "Fancy a walk, Banjo?" His ears pricked up and his tail wagged enthusiastically. "Ah – you know that word then!"

They made their way to the bottom gate. As they walked along the tow-path, Banjo sniffed and investigated his new surroundings. Soon they reached 'Kingfisher'. "Permission to come aboard?"

The door opened and Soaki ran out to great them, closely followed by TJ, his face adorned with a beaming smile.

"Good morning Jenny – you're out bright and early darling! How's the little fella?"

They kissed. "He's fine. Seems to have settled really well."

They chatted whilst TJ made coffees. They spent a leisurely couple of hours on the boat. Eventually Banjo became restless and they decided to stroll back to Willow Bank.

As they walked, occasional gusts in the otherwise gentle breeze caused flurries of leaves to cascade from their branches. Typical of any youngster, the puppy played and chased the airborne fluttering toys –

this was his first autumn, and it was most enjoyable! Jennifer and TJ laughed at his antics as they wandered hand in hand.

Back at the house and now off his lead, Banjo ran excitedly around the garden. With the dogs enjoying each other's company, Jennifer and TJ took the opportunity to finish doing odd jobs around the house and garden. Most of the hard work had been tackled, so their projects were very much just pottering in a relaxed calm manner. They set some of the remaining stepping stones in place and did decorating in the spare bedroom and the summer house. Even when they were sitting down for coffee breaks, they tweaked Jennifer's lists of things needed for converting the boatyard.

"Next week will be a bit different to today."

TJ smiled. "You can say that again darling – I reckon we'll need a holiday to recover before we open up for business."

She gave him a cuddle. "Then why don't we?"

"I'm game – where shall we go?"

"Anywhere you like – if we think of some possibilities, write them on bits of paper then put them in your hat and draw one out."

He frowned. "How dare you madam, assuming to use my hat as a tombola drum." He feigned looking hurt.

Jennifer stroked his head. "Ah, never mind, we'll use one of mine!"

They laughed and kissed. As they cuddled, they started to ponder some locations for a breakaway. Banjo came to them and pawed Jennifer's knee. "What's up little man? Feeling left out?" She tickled his ears. He stayed momentarily then went to the door. "I think he wants to go out."

She got up from the settee and went through to the kitchen. Before she got to the back door she noticed that Banjo had pulled his lead down, and with it in his mouth, was handing it to her. She laughed. Peering around the living room door she grinned. "He said that Soaki's told him about the Miraford Arms and he wants to go and check it out... fancy a pint?" She giggled.

TJ gave an exaggerated sigh. "Well, if that's what the little fella wants – I suppose I can force myself."

The chilled evening air and the quiet of the comparatively empty village street was in stark contrast to the warmth and cheery conversation as they opened the door to the pub. Soaki and Banjo enjoyed the attention they both received and little-un instigated lots of 'aahs' from everyone.

Eventually Jennifer and TJ reached the bar and ordered drinks. As they looked for seats, Jennifer spotted a familiar flash of deep auburn hair cascading across the neck and shoulders of its owner. Cassie nodded her recognition to TJ.

"I'll get a couple more drinks."

"Good idea. I'll take the dogs over."

As they reached the table, Soaki nuzzled Cassie's elbow. "What the…? Oh hello Soaki." She turned around. "Hiya mate – gonna join us?"

TJ arrived with a tray of drinks. Paul grinned. "Ah, good man – I was just about to get refills."

"Well I won't deny you the pleasure – you can get the next round!" They all laughed.

In their usual inimitable way, the four friends were soon chatting away ten to the dozen, catching up on all they'd been doing. "Well, considering we didn't rush at anything, TJ and I got loads done. We even painted up the old turnstile… it looks just like new."

They carried on chatting through the evening and by closing time it was agreed that all four of them would go on the holiday once the boatyard had been converted and refurbished.

Getting ready to leave, Jennifer peered under the table and smiled. She beckoned Cassie to come and see and her friend joined her. As she viewed what Jennifer was pointing at, she too smiled broadly. "Ah, that's so cute"

Soaki and Banjo were curled up together fast asleep.

"Well, it has been a long day for my little fella, but I'm surprised at Soaki. He's obviously worn her out." They gently woke their pets and made their way home.

Jennifer recollected the day to Grannifer as she snuggled beneath her bedclothes. "I can't believe this is only Banjo's second night – it feels like I've had him for ages." She yawned. "So another day over – night nightie darling. Love you." Her eyes closed and in no time she was asleep.

***

Jennifer's life was, it seemed, constantly busy… but beautiful. The days rolled effortlessly into one another. When she was able to take time to relax, even for a short while, she would indulge herself by reading Grannifer's book. It kept the memories of her formative years fresh in her mind and made her smile. She also took as many photos of Banjo as she could. As with her 'girls', who grew from small piglets into young ladies, she wanted a pictorial record of him growing from a puppy into adulthood.

Before she knew it, Saturday had arrived, and this of course meant the weekly market. Banjo was beside himself with the hustle and bustle, the noises and smells which were previously unknown to him. He enjoyed the prolonged tickling of ears he received at the fabric stall, whilst Jennifer and Laura talked at length about arrangements for next week.

He was also taken to Meadows Tea Room to meet Helen. It had been quite a while since Jennifer and Helen had spent any time together, so in between customers they enjoyed catching up over a coffee. Banjo was very well behaved and lay obediently under the table. Half an hour and most of a second cuppa later, they were joined by Cassie.

"Just finished work, mate?"

"Yeah, I've been organising the studio a bit, ready for the move. I can't believe it's really happening."

Jennifer agreed. "I know… it's really exciting, but a bit scary too."

Cassie nodded. "I know what you mean."

Helen had disappeared to serve a customer and returned with a drink for her daughter.

"Oh thanks Mum – just what I need."

They continued chatting happily for a while and then the girls decided to have a last wander through the market before making their way back to Willow Bank. They gave fond kisses to Helen as they said goodbye.

Introducing Banjo to their stall holder friends made progress through the market quite time consuming. As they left the hustle and bustle behind them and laden with a multitude of bags, a wave of tiredness seemed to wash over them.

"I'll go and fetch the old girl and drive us to your place – don't think I'm up to walking. If you wait here, I'll be back in a mo."

"Actually mate, I was going to pop in to see Jim and Joshua, so do you want to meet up there?"

"Yep, sounds good to me… I can say a quick hello to the guys too. It's been a while since I saw Josh. I won't be long."

The two friends walked off in opposite directions. Approaching the cottage, Jennifer noticed the two elderly gentleman in the garden. Jim was kneeling down weeding and Joshua was pruning the rose bushes.

"He's got you working then Josh. I'll warn you now – he can be a right old slave driver!"

The two men looked up and laughed. "Oh hello lass; nice to see you… oh yes, and who's the little pooch then?"

She smiled. "Ah, I'd forgotten you haven't met yet. Josh, this is Banjo – Banjo, this is my friend Joshua… Give a paw!"

Josh grinned as the little pup sat down then lifted his front paw. Joshua took his paw. "Well, how do you do young man?"

They all chuckled. Rigger came to investigate the new friend. The two dogs sniffed at each other with tails wagging happily.

As they stood in the garden, Cassie arrived. "Hello lass – nice to see you."

Jim offered tea but the girls politely declined, explaining that they had not long been downing mugs full with Helen.

"Fair enough. But you won't mind if I make a brew for Josh and me. Come in in for a while anyway."

They stayed for half an hour or so discussing arrangements for next week. Eventually it was time for the girls to make a move. They said their goodbyes and, securing Banjo in the car, drove back to Willow Bank House. They were excited about the forthcoming weekend and talked endlessly about their plans. Laden with their numerous bags of shopping, they went indoors.

"I'll just give TJ a quick ring to let him know we're back."

Cassie acknowledged her friend. "OK mate, I'll start putting this lot away."

Soon the girls were busy emptying bags. They'd just cleared the table when TJ and Soaki arrived. Amid hugs and kisses they chatted about their day's events. TJ said he'd been working on something – but it was a secret at the moment. Jennifer sidled up to him with a coy smile. "But you can tell mee…"

He kissed the end of her nose then shook his head. "Uh uh, sorry babe… especially not you."

She pouted and frowned. "Oh please…"

"Nope, you'll have to wait… it won't be a surprise if I tell you. So where's this coffee you promised?"

Jennifer tutted and stomped petulantly to the kettle, sneakily smiling at the thought of whatever it was.

Throughout the evening she tried several different ploys to eke out even a hint of what the secret surprise might be, but TJ remained astute and no matter how subtle and cunning her investigations, he concealed his project completely.

The following day, Jennifer proclaimed, was to be a 'lazy day' – well, as lazy as possible. She started making breakfast for Banjo, the birds and herself. Then she prepared vegetables and a joint ready for dinner. She'd invited TJ, Cassie and Paul, Helen and Don and Jim and Joshua around for a traditional 'Sunday roast'. "It's been a while since I've had a few friends together for a proper home-made meal."

It wasn't until she was preparing the huge amount of vegetables required, that Jennifer realised that her lunch for a 'few friends', had actually turned out to be rather a substantial dinner party. "Oh well Grannifer, 'in for a penny in for a pound', as you would say. And there's not one of them that I wouldn't want to be here."

She smiled at the thought that she would soon be surrounded by such beautiful people – each of them a dear and treasured friend. Taking the vegetable peelings down to the compost corner at the bottom of the garden, she reminisced that, not so long ago, these would have been happily munched by the girls. "Must give Mel a ring to see how they're doing."

She returned to the house kicking a ball for Banjo as she did so. The puppy scampered excitedly after it, bringing it back to Jennifer to repeat the game. "Last one boy – then I must get changed and ready for our guests."

It wasn't long before Jennifer was back in the kitchen. She checked that the contents of the oven were OK, and set to getting the vegetables started. As she was giving the cutlery a polish with a tea towel, she smiled. "I know they're clean, but you always taught me presentation is important, so sparkly knives and forks should be on the menu… so darling, are these shiny enough?" She held a few aloft for Grannifer's inspection.

She was distracted from her moment of indulgence with Grannifer by Banjo's whining at the back door. Seconds later there was a knock and TJ and Soaki came in.

"Hiya Jenny. We're here!"

They greeted each other with a kiss while the dogs also nuzzled each other affectionately. His eyes twinkled as he smiled. "You look nice."

She play-acted astonishment. "What, this 'old' thing? I only ever wear it when I cook a dinner." She held her apron as if about to curtsy.

They laughed. "No, I meant your dress and hair and stuff…" He rolled his eyes.

"I know what you meant, and thank you." She kissed his cheek.

In their usual teamwork fashion they laid out the table. As they finished, TJ stood back with his hands on his hips and studied their work. He cocked his head from one side to another. "Mm, not bad… but it's missing something."

Jennifer stared at the table. "No, I don't think so."

He slipped out of the back door. Before Jennifer had time to ask where he was going, he was back. "I think these will do the trick." He held out a pretty bunch of flowers. "With my love."

"Oh TJ, they're beautiful. Thank you." She smiled with delight and kissed him.

With the floral display in position, the setting was indeed quite lovely.

Before long there was a knock on the door. "Hello Jim, hi Josh. Come in. You're the first to arrive." She kissed them both and greeted Rigger with a cuddle.

Standing in the hallway, Jim produced his hand from behind his back. "For you lass."

"Oh my, thank you. This is my second bunch today. Aren't I a lucky girl?"

They all joined TJ who was preparing drinks.

Another knock had Jennifer scuttling to the door. "Hiya – come in."

It was Cassie and Paul. With more hugs and kisses Jennifer welcomed the couple in. Cassie was as exuberant as ever, and with a flurry of conversation explained a dozen or more things to her friend. "So that's kind of my day. Mum and Dad should be here soon. Oh, I suddenly realised that we forgot yesterday to get flowers for the table, so I brought you these."

By now they were in the kitchen and the display on the table, and those brought by Jim and Josh, were greeting her with colourful blooms. The two girls looked at each other. Huge beaming smiles lit up their faces and they burst out laughing.

"Thank you darling. I had forgotten to get any. I'm lucky to have such lovely friends who treat me with such beautiful gifts."

It was about ten minutes later when Helen and Don arrived. Cassie was nearest the door and let her parents in. Helen was mystified as to why her daughter started to giggle. Jennifer also stifled a grin as she welcomed them.

"Oh thank you… they're beautiful… I'll pop them in some water and arrange them later."

With her guests all chatting happily together, Jennifer checked that everything was cooking properly. TJ dealt with drinks and the dogs, who had already been fed and watered and were now settled.

With an 'over the top' voice, Jennifer announced "If you would like to take your seats ladies and gentleman, dinner is served!"

Everyone cheered. As they sat together in the cosy, country style kitchen, the conversation flowed easily – as did the laughter. Jennifer smiled as she took in the scene. A room filled with some of the dearest friends she had ever known, and with the gifts they had each brought, her kitchen had the appearance somewhat akin to a florist's!

As the meal neared its conclusion, Jim tapped his wine glass with a spoon. Hearing the noise, everyone fell silent and looked at him.

"Aye, right. Now I've got your attention and we still have liquid to be supped... I would ask y'all to raise your glasses and thank our lovely lass for a cracking lunch and a right enjoyable afternoon. To Jenny!"

They all repeated his toast and applauded her. Jennifer smiled bashfully. "Oh thank you. I hope you've all enjoyed it as much as I have."

They had coffees and continued chatting and laughing. It was mid-evening when Jim and Josh said they were going to make a move back to the cottage. Helen said they too needed to go home and Don offered the two elderly friends a lift. Rigger stretched and joined his master. They all said their goodbyes and arranged to meet up at the boatyard in the morning.

Back indoors, the remaining four friends continued their usual jovial banter. They cleared the table, washed up, dried things and put it all away. Their natural teamwork had kicked in without any of them realising.

Jennifer looked around the neat and tidied kitchen. "Oh my goodness – I hardly noticed that we had done that – thank you guys." She gave a bemused grin.

Paul shook his head. "Nuffin' to do wiv' us lady – must of bin the fairies!"

TJ agreed. "Yeah and look... they've even made coffee!"

As they sat in the living room with their cuppas, they mulled over the day and also where they should start with the boatyard conversion. As always, when they were involved in deep discussions, the hours just flew by. Realising how late it was, Cassie and Paul decide to make their way home. "I'll pick you up in the morning. Make sure you are in 'work' mode – we've got lots to do!" They hugged and said goodnight.

Although the dogs had spent time playing in the garden during the evening, Jennifer and TJ took Soaki and Banjo for a walk before they too parted.

"See you in a little while!"

Jennifer smiled as he kissed her. "Yeah, when I've got some beauty sleep."

He put a finger to her lips and shook his head. "Don't say that. You couldn't be more beautiful if you slept for a hundred years."

They gazed into each other's eyes and smiled. They kissed again before TJ and Soaki walked back along the tow path towards 'Kingfisher'.

Jennifer settled Banjo and made her way to bed. She recalled the day as she said goodnight to Grannifer. Blowing a kiss, she closed her eyes and very soon was sound asleep.

Chapter 13

The following day, Jennifer and Banjo were up early and playing in the garden. It was a cold crisp morning, the sky was pale blue and the sun gave a gentle, almost watery light. Midway through chasing his ball, Banjo ran along the side of the house to the front garden. He had heard the engine of Cassie's 2CV and as she pulled up, the familiar 'beep beep' announced to Jennifer her arrival.

Jennifer went through the kitchen, then greeted her friend at the front door.

"Morning – kettle's on!"

They beamed excited smiles at each other and hugged. "Ooh, I can't believe we're actually going to start the Centre today!"

"Yeah, I know… I keep thinking that I'll suddenly wake up." They chatted excitedly as they made coffee.

Amid their excitement, it was a little while before they noticed Banjo with his nose pressed hard to the floor at the back door. His bottom was in the air and his tail wagged enthusiastically. Jennifer smiled. "I think maybe TJ and Soaki have arrived."

She opened the door and in a trice the young canine had whizzed past her to greet their visitors. As the humans hugged each other, the dogs ran playfully in the garden.

With a bit more chatter and yet another round of coffees, TJ slapped his hands on his knees then stood up and, with an attitude not unlike his grandfather's, rubbed his hands together. "OK troops – let's get this show on the road!"

They all bundled excitedly into the car. Soaki and Banjo sat in the back with TJ and were being very well behaved. The human passengers however, were not being so controlled and with a mixture of nerves and anticipation laughed and sang all the way to the boatyard.

The grass-edged tarmac of Chandlers Lane merged into a grand parking area. There was an almost welcoming soft crunchy noise as the 'old girl's' tyres trundled to a halt, her bonnet facing the river just a couple of yards in front.

Everyone tumbled out of the car and started towards the long wooden structure that was the boatyard workshops. Jennifer stopped for a moment and felt in her bag. Locating her camera, she took a few shots. "This is definitely one project I want a 'before', 'during', and 'after' record of!"

Cassie, TJ and even the dogs posed exaggeratedly by the entrance. Jennifer snapped again then joined them. Still feeling like a visitor, Jennifer knocked on the large door. She waited a moment then tried the handle. It was locked, but at the same time she was doing all this, Cassie joined her. "I've just had a call from Jim. He said they're on their way and Josh says to let ourselves in. Apparently the key is under the windowsill."

Jennifer looked dumbfounded. "What is it with old fellas round here? Do they all put door keys under windowsills?" She shook her head incredulously and they laughed.

TJ joined the hunt (there were several windows). Even Soaki and Banjo seemed interested in the humans investigating around the building.

"Wa-hay! Found it!" Cassie shouted excitedly.

They all congregated at the entrance. "Here you are mate – you do the honours." She offered the key to Jennifer.

"No, you found it – you do it, and after all, this is a joint venture."

Cassie smiled. "Ooh thank you mate."

They opened the doors wide and before she had a chance to step inside, TJ scooped Jennifer up in his arms. She squealed with surprise. "What the heck are you doing?"

"It's good luck to carry you over the threshold!"

As he placed her back down, she kissed him. "Thank you. I think you made that up, but it was very nice!"

Cassie coughed an interruption. "Er, when you two have quite finished. Have you noticed how huge this place is now it's empty?"

They stood and looked around them. "Oh crikey – it is, isn't it? You don't think we've taken on too much do you?"

Noticing a blanket of doubt enveloping the two girls, TJ stood between them and put his arms around their shoulders. With a comforting squeeze he kissed each of them on the cheek. "Come on guys, this is what we've been itching for... our dream. A mad little idea that's been growing and growing. You're not going to tell me that my two feisty females are turning into a pair of wimps, are you?"

They looked at him, then each other. Determination grew on their faces. "Who are you calling wimps? It was just a..."

"An insey-kinsey moment of feeling a bit... er..."

"Small."

They smiled at each other and nodded in satisfied agreement at finishing each other's comments. With renewed vigour they walked around inspecting the interior, their voices and footsteps echoing.

With the mini blip in confidence now just a fading memory, the excited trio were busy making suggested layouts for various units. So much so, that they didn't notice the arrival of Josh and Jim. They were first aware when Rigger trotted in.

"Oh, hello boy!" Jennifer patted his back. "Hiya Jim – morning Josh. How are you both?" They all hugged.

Within half an hour their numbers had increased even more when Laura turned up. She had two muscly men with her. The first, although twice her size, had similar features to Laura.

"This is my brother Danny, and his best mate Grin. They've come to help us with setting up. They're very good at woodwork!"

Everyone said hello and Jim's eyes lit up with two fellow carpenters on board. "Welcome to you young 'uns. You be just what we're needing!" He shook their hands and was soon in deep conversation exchanging experiences.

Knowing the appearance of the Craft Centre was to replicate a seaside pier, Joshua had left some of the 'bits' from his boat-building business which could be used by Jennifer and her friends. There was a large selection of beautiful planks of wood, masts and brass fittings.

The team were soon deciding what was needed amid their familiar laughing and joking and were soon busy creating shelves, cupboards and counters.

When they all stopped for a well-earned break and some lunch, Joshua took Jennifer to one side.

"I know you liked my little office when you first came here."

She remembered the day with a smile. "Oh yes, it was beautiful."

"Well," he continued. "I'd like you to have it – I'll take a couple of bits home, and if you don't mind me popping in for the occasional visit..."

She stared open mouthed. "Oh Joshua... are you sure? Your beautiful things... I don't know what to say." She hugged him tightly.

"Nay lass, it's no problem. I knows ye'll look after 'em."

They chuckled. Joshua stood up from his chair. "Well lass, much as we both enjoy being in 'your' office..." Jennifer giggled. He continued "I think we'd better find the others and see if they've left us any lunch."

They left the room and walked the length of the building to where Cassie and Laura were chatting over mugs of drink and plates of sandwiches. "Oh, the wanderers return. We wondered where you'd got to."

"Let me make a cuppa and I'll tell you... where are the guys?"

"Oh, they're outside. TJ wanted to pick their brains about something out there."

Jennifer gave Joshua his tea then spoke directly to Laura. "If it's not a silly question, where did Grin get his name?"

Laura smiled. "Well... his actual name is Peregrin – he hates it and doesn't much care for Perry either, and because he's always been the joker, even in school, he just got called Grin by his mates and it stuck." They all laughed.

Moments later Grin came in. "Er, excuse me. Mr Joshua?"

Josh looked at him a little surprised and with half a smile on his mouth. "Yes lad. What can I do for you?"

Grin moved closer. "All this wood you've got... it's all rather nice, and we wondered if you had any that's, er, well a bit rough and ready like? More sort of tatty floor boards... if you know what I mean?"

Josh laughed. "Nay lad; mine's all proper boat building good stuff. Why, what ye needing it for?"

"The outside pier walkway."

Jennifer joined in. "You need a trip to the reclamation yard – I'd put money on them being able to help."

By this time Jim, TJ and Danny had joined them. "Of course, why didn't I think of that – the love of my life's favourite shopping centre!"

Jennifer pulled a sarcastic expression at TJ. "No darling. It's a good idea."

He hugged her approvingly. She smiled at him with just a hint of a gloat. "I'll give them a call in the morning."

"We could pop down there now if you like."

Jennifer responded to Cassie's offer. "Oh crikey yes. For some reason I thought it was much later than it is." She gave a childlike shrug of her shoulders.

When they finished their lunch break, Cassie, Jennifer and TJ got in to the 2CV and headed towards the reclamation yard. Banjo went with them. He enjoyed the trips out in the funny car that always seemed to make the humans sing when they got inside it. He couldn't believe his nose when they got out: so many new smells and piles of objects to investigate.

Jennifer held tightly onto his lead. "No you don't young man. If you get loose in this lot, I'll never find you!"

They made their way to an assistant who instinctively made a fuss of the friendly pup. "Wooden planks you say? Not too posh!" He chuckled, "I think we might just be able to help you out... and save us a bit of work as well as it happens!"

The three friends looked at each other somewhat confused. He indicated for them to follow him. As they peered in to the back of a lorry, Fred (the assistant) spoke. "This lot any good for you? Only just picked it up... not even had time to unload!"

The girls looked to TJ. "Well?"

He smiled. "Just the job – how lucky is that?"

With her most appealing smile that said 'pretty please', Jennifer asked the price. She and Banjo walked with Fred to the office while Cassie and TJ waited outside.

TJ wondered "Did you hear what they cost?"

Cassie shook her head. "No, but she'll have got a good deal... she always does."

Getting back in the car they waved goodbye and started back towards Chandlers Lane. "So, what's the damage?"

Jennifer looked quizzically at TJ. "Sorry?"

"The boards! How much did they cost, and what do we owe you?"

"No, that's OK – I'll get them."

"Nah, come on babe, we'll chip in. How much were they?"

She gave him a secretive smile. "Guess?"

"Er – two fifty – three hundred?"

She shook her hair. "Nope."

"More?"

She grinned and shook her head again.

"Less? You're joking... how much?"

"One hundred and seventy five pounds and a chocolate cake. Oh, and a cuppa when they deliver!"

Cassie laughed. "I told you she'd get a good deal!"

Also laughing, TJ leant across to his girlfriend. "Honestly Jen... I don't know how you do it." He kissed her.

As they pulled up, Jim came to meet them. "How'd you get on? You weren't long."

He chuckled when they told him. "That's my gal. So when's the bargain load arrivin'?"

"Er, in about an hour."

"Oh right. We'd better sort out where to store it."

"And get the mugs ready!"

They went indoors and told the others. Grin smiled broadly. "You don't hang about, do you?"

Cassie replied. "When our Jenny gets her mind set on something, she's like a tornado!"

There was unanimous agreement to this comment from everyone who knew Jennifer well. She looked coyly embarrassed. "OK, OK! Not that you lot sit about doing nothing."

Jim pitched in. "Talking of which… we've still got lots to do. Come on team – noses to the grindstones!"

Everyone got back to their jobs. They did manage to persuade Joshua to go down to the office for an afternoon nap. "You're looking a bit done in darling – I promise to wake you in a bit with a nice mug of tea."

He smiled at Jennifer. "Thank you lass." He walked along the building with Rigger by his side.

When they heard the Johnstone's van arrive, Soaki and Banjo ran around excitedly letting everyone know that new visitors were outside. As they all exchanged greetings, Jim inspected the boards. "Aye, these will be just right."

Everyone joined in and helped to unload. "Right, now for that cuppa I promised you!"

Jennifer brushed off her hands as she went indoors to put the kettle on. The driver and his mate followed in with everyone else. They were intrigued with the project taking place and admired the work already done. They all chatted happily whilst they drank.

At last, the driver remarked "Right, we'd better get back to the yard. We'll no doubt see you again soon."

Jennifer smiled and nodded. "I wouldn't be a bit surprised!" They said their goodbyes.

A little later, Jim walked past Cassie, Jennifer and Laura who were talking in hushed voices. "Oh yes, and what are you three cooking up?"

Laura beckoned him to join them. "Shh, we don't want Joshua to hear."

"Actually Jim – you might be able to help. We know it's soon, but not the actual date."

He looked quizzical. "What?"

"Oh, Joshua's birthday. We want to do something special."

"Well, it's the last day of this month… but he's not really a big party person."

The girls looked a little disheartened. Then a smile crept across Jennifer's face. "I think I've got just the thing!"

They all looked at her. She continued "What does Josh like that has been the main thing in his life?"

As one, they all said "Boats!"

"Right, so we give him a little party, but on a river boat trip!"

"Oh yes… that would be ideal."

As they were in deep discussion as to what needed to be arranged, Jim cleared his throat with an exaggerated cough. "Hello there Josh – awake already?"

The girls quickly changed the subject and Jennifer put the kettle on. "Tea won't be long darling – sorry, I forgot the time. Did you have a nice snooze?"

"Aye lass, thank you. Amazin' what forty winks can do to get ye goin' again." He chuckled.

The friends worked on for another hour or so, then realising it had started to get dark, decided to make a move home.

"Well, we've made an 'eck of a start – who's up for a quick visit to the pub?"

There was unanimous agreement to TJ's suggestion. Laura, Danny and Grin went in their car, Cassie gave a lift to Joshua and Jim, and TJ and Jennifer said they'd walk with the three dogs to give them a proper bit of exercise.

"See you soon guys – we'll have your drinks waiting!" Cassie gave a cheery 'beep beep' on the car's horn and trundled off the gravel and back down Chandlers Lane.

It was a pleasant walk back into Miraford village. "I love this time of the day: there's that kind of… well, in-between light that's almost luminous… know what I mean?"

TJ nodded. "Yeah. It's got a hint of mystery about it."

They held hands and chatted as they walked along. The peace and calm of the village's near empty street was in stark contrast to the buzz within the Miraford Arms as they opened the door.

They greeted friends as they walked through the bar towards their usual table where the group of 'workers' were already seated. Rigger went eagerly to Joshua who rubbed his faithful friend's head affectionately. As promised, drinks were ready and waiting, including bowls of water for the dogs.

Jennifer and TJ sat thankfully on the comfy seats. "Ooh, that's better. It's not 'til you stop that you realize how exhausted you are."

Everyone agreed with Jennifer, then laughed as she pretended to flop like a rag doll! She smiled and straightened herself. Now upright, she held her drink aloft. "I propose a toast to us all for an excellent first day's work... good effort guys. Cheers to 'Team Boatyard'!"

They all chorused her last words and drank to the toast. TJ continued. "Can I add a huge thanks to Danny and Grin – we may have only had you for today, but you've been a massive help."

Grin smiled broadly. "Actually we'd rather like to come again... if you'd like us to."

Everyone cheered. Danny looked at his friend. "I think that's a 'yes', mate!"

The cosy atmosphere of their local was just what everyone needed after their busy day with all of them relaxing amid their chat and laughter. Another round of drinks was bought.

When Jennifer finished her glassful, she stood up and said goodbye to everyone. Cassie looked surprised. "Oh, you off already mate? S'pose you need an early night. It has been bit of a long day."

Jennifer gave a smile and shook her head. "No such luxury I'm afraid darling – I've got that cake to make for the Johnstone guys."

"No way – you're telling me after the day we've had, you're going home to start

baking?"

"Uh huh... a deal is a deal... and I promised."

Cassie rolled her eyes. "Well, at least let me give you a lift."

TJ made to leave with the girls, but Jennifer said there was no need. "Why don't you stay with the guys for a while... you can make sure that Josh and your grandad get home safely. There's no knowing what these oldies might get up to when they've had a few!" She smiled cheekily at Jim.

"I heard that missie!"

Joshua supped his drink. "Aye, so did I!"

They all chuckled. TJ kissed her. "Well, if you're sure." He sat back with Laura and the men.

Back at Willow Bank House, Jennifer put the kettle on for a coffee, then got Grannifer's book to find the recipe for the cake. As she gathered the ingredients together, Jennifer noticed a quizzical look on Cassie's face. "What's up?"

Cassie tilted her head slightly. "How come you have this reputation with your family for not being able to cook… apart from flapjacks?"

Jennifer smiled. "Because I couldn't!"

"But everything I've tasted that you've made has been lovely."

"Thank you; you're very kind to say so." She looked pensive. "When I was in London I didn't have Grannifer guiding me – but she wrote her book so well… it's kind of like her standing beside me. She's showing me what to do as though she's telling me step by step."

"And Grannifer was a good cook…?"

"Oh yes, the best!"

They continued chatting whilst Jennifer combined the mixture for a Madeira cake with cocoa powder and chocolate chips. "I'm going to split it then sandwich it together again with chocolate spread, then dust the top with more cocoa… if that isn't chocolatey enough for them I don't know what would be."

When it was ready, Jennifer put most of the mixture into a large round baking tin and then spooned the remainder into a small loaf tin.

"Why are you making two?"

Jennifer smiled and raised her eyebrows. "Don't you want to see what it tastes like before we inflict it on the Johnstone boys?"

Cassie beamed. "Oh yes. Goody gum drops!" They laughed and licked their lips in anticipation.

While the cakes cooked, the girls looked through local directories for river boat trips. "Look, there's a place in Lamton."

"Great, I'll ring them in the morning."

"Better still, we'll drop the cake into the reclamation yard then drive on to town and see them in person. They might even have boats handy to look at."

"Brilliant! Hopefully by lunchtime, we'll have it all booked and sorted." They gave each other 'thumbs up' signs.

As the cakes cooked, their aroma wafted through the house and very soon it was time to take the smaller one out of the oven. "Ooh, that looks yummy. How soon can we try it?"

Jennifer rolled her eyes. "Cor, you're worse than a kid. Give it time to cool down first!"

Cassie pretended to sulk. They were laughing when they were surprised to hear a knock at the door. "Gosh – a bit late for visitors."

Jennifer and Banjo went to the hallway. Looking through a side window she saw the familiar outline of TJ. She let him in. Soaki ran past them and she and Banjo nuzzled each other.

Stepping into the hallway, TJ sniffed. "Ooh, that smells goood!"

"We've made a tester as well as the main cake – so you can see if it

231

tastes OK too!"

He smiled. "Excellent… lead me to the trial munching area." They joined Cassie in the kitchen.

They were surprised to see her waving a magazine over the cake. She looked a little guilty. "I'm trying to help it cool down."

Jennifer shook her head in despair. "Let's make a cuppa then it should be ready." She gave a resigned chuckle at her friend's impatience.

It wasn't long before the three of them were picking up even the smallest crumbs from their plates. "Cor mate, that was yummy!"

"Absolutely Jen – we ought to sell it in the pier's café."

"Maybe just one day a week – we won't get any work done if Grannifer's cakes are always on the menu… we'll just sit around eating all day!"

They finished their drinks in the living room, listening to music and chatting. When everyone had gone home, Jennifer realised how tired she was. She settled Banjo down for the night and went to bed.

"Cor, what a day this has been Grannifer. Your recipe was just the ticket; thank you darling." She smiled and blew a kiss as she said goodnight to her precious lady.

***

Jennifer woke the following morning to overcast skies and slight drizzle. "Oh bother – I was hoping it would be nice for our trip to Lamton."

She went downstairs and greeted Banjo. "Hello boy, sleep well?"

She ruffled his neck as she unlocked the back door. "It's a bit muggy out there." She opened the door for him to go in the garden.

The kettle was soon boiling and the radio playing songs which Jennifer sang along to. There was a news report followed by the weather… "The dull start to the day will brighten by midday, although occasional showers should be expected in the South East. Elsewhere should remain fine."

She smiled. "Ah brilliant… hopefully we won't get soggy."

Banjo came in and shook. "Unlike you mister! Come here little man and I'll dry you." She took his towel and rubbed him. She made coffee and put fresh water down for Banjo.

After the usual routine of breakfast and getting dressed, Jennifer sorted a container to transport the cake in. She'd just finished when she heard the old girl's hooter. Beep! Beep! Banjo ran to the front door in anticipation of Cassie's arrival.

Cassie looked skywards with a slightly despondent expression.

Jennifer hugged her friend. "Don't look so glum mate – the man on the radio told me it's going to brighten up soon."

Later, as they pulled away from the reclamation yard, Cassie chuckled. "Well, I don't know about your man on the radio, but you certainly brightened the Johnstone guys up… did you see their faces when they saw the cake?" They both laughed.

As predicted, the weather did change and by the time the girls arrived at the River Boat Trips booking office it was quite dry. Banjo investigated the new surroundings with interest. As they opened the door, a friendly gentle bell was activated – Ka-ding!

They walked in and went to the counter. A young woman came through from an adjoining room. "Good afternoon. How may I help you?"

"Oh, hello… we'd like to book one of your boats please."

"OK, er, we have seats available on the four o'clock trip, but otherwise it would have to be tomorrow, I'm afraid."

Jennifer laughed. "No, you misunderstood me. We were hoping to hire a whole boat. It's a birthday surprise for a friend. Is that possible?"

"Oh I'm sorry. Yes, of course. Just let me get my book and we'll sort some details." She smiled and went back into the other room.

She returned with a large album and a smaller book labelled on the front 'Booking Forms'. "We have three boats. Would you like to look through here and select which one you'd like?"

She handed over the album that had lots of photographs in it. "Can I get you a coffee while you browse?"

"That would be lovely. Thank you very much."

As they sipped their drinks, Jennifer went through the paperwork with the young lady and Cassie browsed through the pictures. Suddenly her eyes widened. "Er Jen… can I interrupt you for a mo?"

"What is it, darling?"

"Have a look at this." She pointed at one of the photos.

Jennifer scrutinised where her friend indicated. "What a coincidence!"

She spoke to the assistant. "This plaque at the stern… what is it?"

"That's the name of the boat builder."

Cassie and Jennifer stared at each other. "You don't think…?"

"It couldn't be… could it?"

There, on the brass plate was engraved 'Joshua Sanders'.

"Oh my giddy aunt!"

The assistant looked quizzical. "Is there something wrong?"

The girls laughed. "Oh gosh no, far from it! This is going to be the

233

icing on the cake. Our friend who we're doing the surprise trip for...
well, he built this boat!!"

"Not just that one then. All our fleet came from the same place."

They finished the booking and made their way home. They were so
excited, they hardly noticed the journey.

TJ and Soaki arrived at Willow Bank soon after the girls. Jennifer
was so excited as she babbled out the story to him, that she didn't notice
the large bag he was carrying.

When she calmed down, he kissed her cheek. "Now, sit down – I
have something for you."

"Ooh, what is it?"

"Well, do you recall I said I was working on a surprise? Here it is."

He smiled at his girlfriend's impish giggle. "Can I open it now?"

"Only if you want to know what it is!"

She smiled coyly. Taking the bag, she kissed him. "Thank you!"

With anticipation, Jennifer pulled at the ribbon which was tied on the
bag handles to keep it closed. She peered inside. There were two
wrapped parcels. One was like a picture - thin, flat and about eighteen
inches wide and thirty inches long. The other was a box shape, similar to
a tin of biscuits in size. This was the one she opened first.

There was a box and inside this was a drawstring bag. "It's very
heavy and lumpy. What on earth...?"

"Open it and see!" He smiled as she did so.

"They're old pennies!"

"Uh huh, for your turnstile! We've all been hunting for them and I
noticed in your book that Grannifer had a tip to clean them by soaking
them in cola. So all nice and sparkly and fresh."

"Oh wow, thank you."

"You not going to open the other one?"

"Of course... I was just enjoying the coins." She carefully removed
the paper and gasped. "Oh darling, it's wonderful!"

They hugged affectionately. What she had unwrapped was a board,
decorated around the edges with dainty 'canal boat style' flowers. There
were words written in complementary lettering.

'Welcome to the Jenny R Cade Penny Arcade. We're supplying these
old pennies, all pre nineteen seventy-one. Please use them for the
turnstile. (It's just a bit of fun!) We don't charge for entry; it's all
completely free. But any gift you'd like to leave will go to charity.
Thank you.'

Jennifer eventually let go of TJ. "This really is terrific darling, but
one turnstile hardly constitutes a 'Penny Arcade'."

He smiled cheekily. "Ah, you noticed… we've actually got something else to show you."

Cassie joined them. "Have you told her yet?"

"Er, not quite…"

Jennifer looked from one to the other. "What is going on?"

"We've got things to pick up from Johnston's when we've sorted the pier."

"What is it? Oh please tell me!"

TJ teased her. "Let's have some lunch first."

She gave a frustrated growl. "Timothy James! You are the biggest meanie!"

He laughed. "OK, a coffee, and then we'll tell you."

With their mugs filled and more of the cake, TJ and Cassie explained that they'd managed through the reclamation yard to get some old fairground games. "They're the 'amusement only' type so we didn't need a licence."

A broad smile stretched across Jennifer's mouth. "Gosh, what fun – that'll keep the kids happy whilst the parents look around the Centre!"

Still munching, Cassie wiped her lips. She swallowed. "Mm, I forgot to mention – have you noticed your garden recently?"

"No, what? Is something wrong?"

Cassie shook her head. "No, but your dirt isn't brown any more… it's got a greenish tint to it."

"You're joking." Jennifer ran to the door. "Yippee, the grass has started to grow! Gosh, this is one of the best days ever!" She cuddled Banjo and Soaki who had come to see what all the excitement was about.

When Jennifer had calmed down, the three friends sat fairly quietly in the living room. They discussed various things which they needed to do: obviously more work on the boatyard conversion. ""We'll need a van to get the heavy stuff there… my kiln weighs loads and there's the turnstile which is mega heavy."

"And the games machines!"

Jennifer crooked her finger and rested it on her lip. "I wonder if we could hire Barry for a day."

TJ nodded sagely. "Mm, good idea sweetheart, but I think his vehicle might be more useful."

She tapped his arm playfully and tutted. Cassie stifled a giggle as she imagined them piling everything on Barry's back.

"We need the fascia sign – have we settled on 'Riverside Pier Craft Centre'?"

The girls nodded. "Yeah, I think so."

"Mm, I like that."

"OK, that's sorted then. I know Laura, Josh and Grandad like it."

"So now we need to let people know about Josh's boat trip party."

"Yeah, but it's got to stay a secret from him. I've asked Jim to try and find out some of the old darling's friends. Oh crikey, I feel another cake in the pipeline!"

"And drink, and nibbles."

Jennifer beamed. "Ooh, I love parties!"

"We know!"

***

For the next few days everyone worked like beavers with various tasks. Grin and Danny managed to join in as much as they were able, and in what seemed no time at all, the men had built an authentic looking board-walk along the outside of the building. It was raised off the ground with the underside edge boarded up. This was then painted in such a way as to give the illusion of looking at water beneath the pier.

"It's called a 'trompe l'oeil' - literally a trick of the eye."

Jennifer looked at the stunning creation with awe, cuddling TJ. "You really are a brilliant artist, darling."

He looked somewhat bashful. "Thank you, but I did have help you know."

Grin had overheard. "Yeah, he told us what and where to fill in… it was like painting by numbers!"

"Well, however it was done, it's amazing and I need to get my camera."

During the daytime everyone concentrated on the Craft Centre, but evenings tended to be party orientated. Laura sorted brightly coloured fabric and joined Cassie and Jennifer at Willow Bank House for sewing sessions to make huge lengths of bunting to decorate the boat for Joshua's birthday.

It had been a hectic, yet very productive week, but as she snuggled into bed on Friday night, Jennifer gave a happy, somewhat relieved sigh. "Whew Grannifer. I'm glad it's the weekend. A couple of days to chill out before we get stuck in again on Monday." She kissed the air as she said "Night night darling." Smiling, she got cosy and was soon asleep.

***

As she and Banjo wandered through the market the following morning, Jennifer was surprised to see Laura. "Morning – you're a glutton for punishment. I thought you'd be having a day off after the week we've had."

Laura smiled as she shrugged her shoulders. "I couldn't get anyone to cover for me, but never mind, I enjoy it here, and I've only got the pitch for a few more weeks… so, make the most of it eh?"

"Well, it won't be long before we get the Centre open so that'll be easier." They gave excited giggles at the thought.

As they continued chatting, Danny turned up. "Hiya sis. I've got a spare hour. Do you want a break?"

Laura gave a welcome smile. "Oh you angel. Yes please; that'd be great."

They hugged and she took off her money belt and passed it to her brother. Jennifer took charge. "Right missie – let me treat you to lunch. Tea Rooms or the pub? Your choice."

Laura gave a thoughtful expression with a finger at her cheek. "Well, I've still got the afternoon to work, so perhaps Helen's would be the more sensible option."

They laughed and walked to the top end of the market and into the Tea Rooms. They were greeted, cheerily as always, by Helen. "Hello girls, what a lovely surprise. How are you?"

"Good thanks, and you?"

"Yes, I'm fine."

They ordered food and drinks. "Actually Helen, can I pick your brains for a moment?"

Helen gave a knowing smile. "This will be about Joshua's birthday, I bet!"

Jennifer rolled her eyes. "You know me too well darling!"

As she brought their lunch she had an extra drink for herself. They exchanged various ideas for the surprise boat party. Helen stopped mid-gulp. "Ooh, did Cassie tell you, I'm getting all the locals to sign a card for him? I reckon I've already got nearly half the village."

"Wow, that's brilliant. What a super idea."

Sitting with her back to the door, Helen was unaware of Cassie's entrance. She crept quietly towards her mum with her finger to her lips indicating to Jennifer and Laura not to acknowledge her. She grabbed Helen's shoulders and planted a kiss on the surprised woman's cheek.

"What's all this? I've been slaving away in a hot studio while you lot are lazing around drinking tea!" She pulled out a chair and sat down.

"It's coffee actually!"

"Ooh, I stand corrected!"

They all laughed. Helen got some more drinks as they chatted a while longer. "Well, I s'pose I need to get back to my stall – Danny only had an hour to spare. Thanks for lunch Jen; that was lovely."

"You're welcome darling, but hold on a tick; we'll walk back with you."

All the girls and Banjo bade Helen goodbye and walked back through the market. Cassie and Jennifer pondered over the last few stalls then, with Banjo leading the way, made their way back to Willow Bank.

Cassie started chuckling. "I thought Banjo was going to give me away when I sneaked up on Mum... did you notice his tail waggling?"

Jennifer nodded. "Oh yes!"

While they were putting the shopping away, Cassie got a call on her mobile. "Hello darling... yes I'm fine... oh, at Jen's... uh ha...OK... I'll see you tomorrow then... yeah, love you too... byeee."

She looked puzzled. Jennifer queried "What's up mate?"

"I'm not sure... are our fellas cooking up anything we don't know about?"

"Not to my knowledge, why?"

"They're having a 'boys' night' apparently and he said they'll see us tomorrow."

Jennifer looked thoughtful. "Well, we could do the female equivalent – I've got a bottle or two of wine, some good music to check out and a comfy spare bed."

"Oh, I like the sound of that, and I get to sleep in that beautiful room!"

It was a long time since they'd spent what they called 'nothing time' together. They did as much or as little as they wanted, hardly even thinking about the finishing touches to the Craft Centre, but enjoyed chatting about Josh's party. "I do hope he enjoys it."

"I don't think that there's any doubt that he will, as long as we can keep the secret. It'll be wonderful!"

***

The afternoon had soon melted into evening. The two friends took Banjo for his last walk of the day and they all settled in for a cosy pleasant night.

Although Banjo spent most of the time snuggled at Jennifer's feet, he didn't mind the endless chatter with occasional outbursts of laughter. Before they knew it, their 'girly night' had turned into Sunday morning.

"Oh crikey mate – look at the time!"

Jennifer made sure that Cassie had everything she needed and they wished each other goodnight before snuggling into their beds.

***

It was half past ten when Jennifer tapped on Cassie's bedroom door. She went in and placed a mug on the bedside cabinet. She smiled at the

238

lumpy covers and the delicate flower pattern on the pillow case almost obliterated by the cascade of fiery auburn locks of her friend's hair.

She called gently "Cassie – you awake?"

"Mm, er yes I think so. What's the time?"

Jennifer replied and Cassie's face suddenly appeared from beneath the covers. "You're joking! I'm never later up than nine. Tell you what though, I could stay in here for hours and hours; it is so comfy."

"Glad to hear it. There's a drink there for you. Shall I start breakfast or do you want to sleep a bit longer?"

Now fully awake, Cassie said she'd get up. She slipped a dressing gown on and went downstairs.

When Jennifer suggested that she might want to put her shoes on, Cassie looked confused. "Er… if you want me to, but why?"

"More comfy underfoot. I thought we'd have a 'breaknic'!"

"Sorry, a what? I don't speak Russian!"

Jennifer laughed. "I'm not talking Russian… I thought we could have a Breakfast Picnic… a 'breaknic'! Come on, I've got everything in the hamper."

Cassie raised her eyebrows. "Just one thing Jen… we're still in our dressing gowns!"

"Doesn't matter; we're only going to the bottom of the garden to sit on the riverbank. Come on, it'll get cold!"

Taking a handle each of the small suitcase-style basket, plus a couple of rugs, they walked along the path giggling. Once settled on the grassy bank, they began their 'breaknic'. Tin foiled packages revealed hot egg and bacon toasted sandwiches; lidded containers had slices of fresh fruit and a flask kept them topped up with piping hot coffee.

Banjo lay happily alongside, munching on his treats. "If you didn't know we were so close to the village, you'd almost imagine that we were in the middle of nowhere."

Jennifer agreed with her friend. "Yeah, good innit!"

When they had finished eating, Jennifer shared the last of the coffee in the flask. She handed Cassie's mug to her. She thanked her friend and took a sip.

Drawing her knees up to her chest, Cassie wrapped an arm around her legs, and with her other hand which held the mug, she took another sip. She had a wistful expression and was staring, unblinkingly at the water.

Jennifer broke the silence. "Penny for them? Or do you want some pebbles?"

"Mm, sorry?"

"You were miles away – what's up?"

"Oh, I don't know... I was just wondering about Paul. He seemed... well, secretive."

"I'm sure it's nothing, but if you're concerned, we'll ask him."

"No, it's OK – he'd think I was neurotic, or crazy or something."

Jennifer smiled. "Crazy? You... no way!"

They both laughed. "Come on, let's go in and get a fresh cuppa; that last drop wasn't very hot." They collected everything together and with Banjo leading the way, went indoors.

It was some hours later. The girls were pottering in the garden, intermittently throwing toys or kicking a ball for Banjo. Suddenly, the young dog bounded towards the riverside gate. He yapped a few times with his tail wagging energetically.

"What's up boy?" Jennifer went to join him. Holding his collar they went through to the tow-path. Smiling, she let him go and waved. Banjo scampered along to meet Soaki, who in turn was running to join her friend. Paul and TJ were following close behind. The two couples hugged and kissed.

TJ took Jennifer to one side. He whispered "Is Cassie all right? She looks... well, a bit saddish."

"Yeah, she's OK; just a touch perplexed 'cos Paul was a bit, well, secretive last night."

TJ laughed. "No secret, babe!"

They joined their friends. "You're freaking your fiancée out mate! Tell her what we were doing yesterday," TJ demanded.

Paul took Cassie's hands. "I've been learning, and thanks to this chap here... I would like to invite you to dinner tomorrow night. It will be three courses and I will be your chef."

Cassie looked stunned. "But darling, you can't cook! I've never even known you to do toast without burning it!"

"Precisely why I asked TJ to teach me. So, if you and your delightful friend would like to join us aboard the 'Kingfisher Restaurant' at about seven thirty, I will attempt to impress."

Cassie's expression changed from total disbelief to a quizzical uncertainty, then slowly, a broad grin came upon her face. She laughed and hugged him affectionately. "Paul darling, thank you. That sounds lovely." She kissed him and they snuggled into each other's arms.

Jennifer smiled. "So what is this gastronomic delight going to consist of?"

Paul tapped the side of his nose. "Ah. Now, that is a secret!" He and TJ gave each other knowing nods.

The rest of the afternoon flew by, and as the evening drew in, it turned decidedly chilly. They laughed and groaned through a game of Monopoly. Jennifer made use of her time 'In Jail' and served up hot buttered crumpets.

It was to be a busy day tomorrow for TJ and the girls at the boatyard, and Paul was to have the use of Kingfisher so that he could prepare the evening's sustenance. Therefore it was not late when the friends bade each other goodnight.

Chapter 14

Amid the hustle and bustle of the work being done at the boathouse the following day, the girls had the extra anticipation of the evening meal on their minds. "He really can't cook, you know."

"Well, that's as maybe, but TJ can, and if he's taught Paul what to do... well, it should be OK."

"Yeah, I s'pose. I think he'll have shown him something simple, but added little tips to make it look good."

Jennifer nodded in agreement with her friend. "So, what do you think he might do?"

Cassie put a finger thoughtfully to her lips, forgetting she was holding a paintbrush and added a large splodge of blue to her cheek. She didn't seem to notice and carried on with the conversation. "I think starters could be grapefruit, but made pretty with a cherry, and maybe mint leaves for decoration."

"Yes, that could work. And for the main... well, what could be easier than a casserole? Cooked slowly with all the meat, veg and seasoning, that's really yummy!"

"Ooh, and pudding might be bananas and ice cream – that would be nice."

"Ah yes, and sprinkled with flaked almonds."

They licked their lips at the thought.

TJ joined them. "Hi guys... new make-up Cassie?"

She looked confused. "Huh? I'm not wearing any today except a bit of lippy."

Jennifer laughed. "He's talking about the paint which you've decorated yourself with! Don't worry, it will wash off."

Cassie tutted. "Cor, you could have told me!"

Jim walked up. "'Ere lass, you're s'posed to put that on the post y'know – not yourself." He chuckled.

"Oh, for goodness sake… who's next with the wisecracks?"

Joshua approached, his finger pointing. "Did you know…?"

"Yes Josh – it has been pointed out to me. Thank you!"

He looked confused and shrugged his shoulders. "Oh well, anyone want a cuppa?"

Everyone went with Joshua into the building and made themselves comfortable in the café area. Cassie, having looked in the mirror, saw why her friends had been amused at her unintentional decoration, and with it removed, was back to her usual jolly self rather than the slightly disgruntled lady of earlier.

The afternoon passed quickly and as they prepared to go home, they all agreed that the transformation of the Craft Centre would soon be complete.

TJ was bemused by the conversation between the girls about 'grapefruit, casserole and bananas'. He smiled to himself as he sat in the back of the car cuddling Soaki and Banjo, who sat either side of him.

It was about ten past seven when the three friends, now spruced up and looking quite elegant, walked along the tow-path led by their faithful canines.

"Do you think we look the part for this culinary experience?"

TJ looked her up and down. "Jenny darling – you always look beautiful, but I think both of you ladies suit the occasion perfectly."

Both the girls thanked him and giggled with excited anticipation. 'Kingfisher Restaurant' came into view and the dogs ran ahead. Paul emerged and welcomed everyone aboard. He looked quite pleased, but with a hint of nervousness.

With an expression that spoke volumes more than the one word, TJ asked "OK?"

"Think so. I've tried to remember everything you've shown me." He puffed his cheeks and held his hands up with crossed fingers.

Everyone settled down in Kingfisher's cosy lounge whilst Paul organised drinks. Jennifer gazed through the window at the serene river and the far bank. The early evening activities of the waterside residents had calmed to a minimum, as most of the creatures had settled for the night. Gentle light from the boat and so too the moon, gave pleasant reflections, fragmented by the flow of the river.

Paul emerged from the adjoining dining room. He looked a little apprehensive. "Er, if you would like to come through... dinner is served."

The girls smiled excitedly at each other. They sat at the attractively laid out table and admired how nice it looked. Then Cassie said in a whispered voice to Jennifer "Have you noticed he's got the wrong spoons out for the starter?" Jennifer nodded.

They both looked in amazement. "Your soup ladies – I hope you both like cream of mushroom – and please help yourselves to croutons."

They were equally surprised with the steak and ale pie with steamed vegetables and roast potatoes.

As they eagerly scraped the last spoonfuls of their dessert – meringue nests with fresh fruit and piped whipped cream sprinkled with almond flakes – Jennifer dabbed her mouth with a napkin. "Wow, that was delicious, and the only thing we guessed right was the nut topping! I propose a toast. Well done Paul – a wonderful meal. Thank you."

They clinked glasses, drank the toast then gave a big round of applause. Paul looked slightly bashful but very, very pleased. He gave thanks to his teacher. "To a brilliant master!" They clapped again.

As they chatted over coffee, the girls confessed their images as to what the evening's menu might be.

"But why that?"

"Er, well... we thought it would be nice, but... well, easy!"

Paul and TJ pretended to be hurt. "As if we'd go for the easy option... there had to be some effort for our special ladies!"

Both Cassie and Jennifer smiled coyly at the compliment. It seemed no time at all before it was time to go home. The dogs, who had been very well behaved all night, got excited at the hint of a walk.

The conversation as they wandered back along the tow path revolved mainly around Josh's birthday. "We've only got ten days to prepare everything."

"And keep doing the Centre at the same time."

"Oh gosh, yes we can't let that slip – he'll get superstitious."

The other three laughed. Jennifer queried "What?"

TJ hugged her. "I think you meant 'suspicious' darling. Maybe one glass of wine too many?" She giggled at her mistake.

***

It was just after half past eight the following morning when Cassie wandered into the kitchen, rubbing her eyes and yawning. She was surprised to hear the bright, alert greeting "Morning. Sleep well?"

"Mm? Er, yes, thanks. You?"

"Yeah, like a log... must have been that wine!" Jennifer gave a little

244

giggle.

"Jen mate, what are you doing up so early?" She sat at the table. "And what's all this paperwork? Looks like hours of work here."

"Ah well, I was mulling over what we were saying about Josh's party, so I came down to get it written down so I didn't forget anything."

"So, when did you get up?"

"Um, about half six."

"You must be mad! Oh thanks for letting us stay by the way – I really wasn't up to driving."

They both smiled. "It was a really good night, wasn't it?"

Cassie made a drink and they studied Jennifer's notes.

The two friends continued to chat for a while, then decided to make some breakfast. "S'pose I ought to get our chef from last night up. I thought he'd have been awake by now."

Jennifer nodded in agreement. "Why don't we send someone else to get him? Banjo, here boy... fetch Paul!" She pointed to the hallway.

The exuberant puppy ran excitedly from the kitchen and bounded up the stairs. The girls followed the sound of him running around from one bedroom to another. The gentle padding sound stopped and was quickly followed by a loud yell.

"Whoah! What the heck?"

Downstairs the girls giggled. "I think he found him!"

Soon after, Paul entered the kitchen. "I can think of better ways to be woken than a cold nose and a dog licking my cheek."

They laughed. "Never mind darling. We sent Banjo so that we could be getting on with breakfast."

Paul looked at Cassie as though to say "Yeah – like I believe that!"

When they had finished their meal, Jennifer returned to her paperwork. "I think I'm ready to make a start on these calls – hope everyone is in 'phone answering mode'." She smiled.

"While Jen's doing that, do you fancy a walk luv?"

Cassie nodded. "Mm, yes, that would be nice. Er, shall we take...?" She looked at Banjo.

Jennifer called him. "Do you want a walk, boy? You going with Cassie and Paul?"

He ran excitedly to where his lead was hanging then pulled it with his mouth and gave it to Jennifer.

As she put it on she rubbed his ears then kissed his head. "You be a good boy. I'll see you in a little while!"

When the house was empty, Jennifer set about going through her lists. Totally engrossed in her project, she was surprised to hear voices in the garden and then her friends coming through the back door. "Gosh, you were quick!"

"Er, not really mate – we stayed with TJ for a cuppa then took the dogs for a walk up river for a couple of miles.

Jennifer looked astounded. "How far?"

"Well a mile each way-ish."

"Oh right. I thought that you meant my poor baby had walked nearly five miles, including to and from Kingfisher! Is TJ not with you?"

"Oh yes; he's just looking around the garden – he said to get the kettle on."

At that moment, he came into the room. "Hello Jen – how are you sweetheart?" He kissed her.

"I'm fine thanks; didn't realise how the time had gone though! Did you enjoy the walk?"

They all joined in with the conversation. As the men made drinks, Cassie looked with interest at Jennifer's lists.

"You've made good progress here mate. Looks like there's only a couple more to deal with."

Jennifer nodded. "Yep, just some old workmates to call – if they come I think Josh'll be really surprised. Apparently he's not seen them for several years." She gave a hopeful shrug.

As a matter of interest, TJ picked up the list with the heading 'Boat Party Guests'. After a few minutes he put it in front of his girlfriend. "You've missed a couple of names off there, babe."

She nodded. "Yeah, Josh's old workmates – I'm waiting to confirm."

He shook his head. "No darling – look at your address book under 'C'."

Her brow furrowed. "Who?"

"Your mum and dad, silly!"

"But Josh only met them once…"

"And he really liked them! C'mon Jen, he'd love them to be there." She smiled happily. "OK, I'll ask them." She gave a little giggle.

TJ smiled as he watched the expression of delight on his girlfriend's face. He gave her a hug. "While you are busy with these arrangements I'm going to make a start on the fascia board sign for the Centre. OK if I use the summer house, darling?"

"Yes, that's fine. I'll come and help in a bit."

As always, they all worked hard throughout the day, stopping only briefly mid-afternoon for a lunch break. Otherwise, their labour was almost continuous. Soaki and Banjo made sure that a spontaneous game of football saved the day from being too quiet and studious.

They decided to spend the evening in the pub. As they climbed out of the car, the welcoming glow from the lights in the Miraford Arms encouraged their pace to pick up.

"Don't forget – if Joshua's there, keep shtum about the party." Everyone OK'd the instruction.

There were the usual warm greetings from the familiar faces around the bar. "Evening folks – what can I get you?"

"Hi Angela. The usuals please, and whatever you'd like." She smiled at TJ and thanked him.

They settled at their usual table. "Anyone fancy food?"

Cassie nodded. "Jen, you're a mind reader. I was just going to suggest the same!"

They all checked the menu and the 'specials' board. "I'm going for a jacket."

Paul looked slightly concerned at his fiancée. He began to drape his coat around her shoulders. "Are you all right darling? I didn't realise you felt cold."

She kissed his cheek. "You soppy old sweetheart – I meant potato. I was going to have a jacket potato!"

He tutted and rolled his eyes. "Sorry, I forgot we were eating!" They all laughed.

Taking his hand, Cassie looked at him softly. "Don't apologise darling; that was very thoughtful."

They chose their meals and Jennifer placed the orders. Returning to the table, she had a larger than usual grin on her face. TJ asked "What's put that smile on you? Did you win the Lottery between here and the bar?"

She nudged TJ. "No silly… but good news: Angela said she'd do any food and drinks we want for the boat!"

A while later as Angela walked up with their meals, the four friends broke into a spontaneous round of applause. She smiled appreciatively. "If you could give me a list in the next few days, in case I need to order anything in?"

They enjoyed their meals and continued to relax in the comfort of the cosy pub, the crackle of the log fire, as always, adding to the atmosphere. In the less busy moments, Angela would join them to discuss more arrangements for Joshua's birthday.

All too soon it was time to go home. They said goodnight to Cassie and Paul, then Jennifer, TJ, Soaki and Banjo strolled back through the lamp-lit streets of Miraford.

The next few days were spent busily attending to the Craft Centre throughout the day, and early mornings and evenings concentrating on the party.

Come the weekend, Jennifer and Banjo enjoyed their regular wander around the Saturday market. By now the friendly little dog was well known to the stall holders, and happily allowed them to tickle his ears and stroke him. Soaki had taught him that 'pleasant as this is for us, it is very beneficial to humans and makes them happy too!'

They chatted for a long time with Laura. She was very excited that the Centre would soon be up and running. "It'll be so nice not to have to keep loading and unloading all my stock." She gave a happy smile at the thought.

Laura took a dog biscuit from her pocket. Banjo sat obediently to her instruction, then offered a paw. Meanwhile, Jennifer had taken a shopping list from her bag and crossed out various things. "I seem to have got most things – just some last ingredients for Joshua's cake."

"Do you think we made enough bunting? I can make some more if you like."

Jennifer smiled. "I think we already have plenty... unless you want to go twice round the boat."

Laura shook her head. "Er, I don't think so."

Banjo had finished munching, so he and Jennifer said goodbye and continued with their shopping.

By the time they got home, Jennifer's arms and fingers were aching from the weight of the bags, but she had been kept amused by Banjo who had carried a few items in his mouth. Admittedly they were very light weight, but he'd been happy to help. "This deserves an extra big cuddly fuss and a large marrowbone biscuit." He wagged his tail enthusiastically and disappeared into the garden to enjoy his treat.

Jennifer relaxed for a while with a coffee before putting the shopping away.

To find the recipe she needed, Jennifer leafed through the pages of her beloved book. As she scanned the beautifully written and illustrated sheets, her eyes moistened. Holding the book which Grannifer had so lovingly compiled always bought the precious lady even closer to Jennifer. She drew an emotional breath as she held the ledger tightly to her heart.

As if in a daydream, her mind wandered: she was momentarily lost. She drifted as she remembered the past. Suddenly she was brought back to the present when Banjo pushed through the door to come in for a drink. Jennifer was surprised to see Soaki following close behind. "Hello sweetheart – when did you arrive? And where's your mate?"

She went into the garden but there was no sign of TJ. "Mm, that's weird. The gate's shut, so how did she get in?"

Back in the kitchen Jennifer encouraged Soaki. "Come on girl – where's TJ? Good girl, where's your dad?"

The two dogs ran eagerly to the summer house. She peered through a window. "How long have you been out here?"

He looked up, a broad smile on his face. "Hello Jen." He joined her outside. "I've been here for a few hours babe – I thought I'd do a bit more to the fascia board. It's coming on darling... have you been crying – are you OK?"

As he held her, a concerned persona replaced the happy grin.

She nodded. "I'm fine; just been wandering down memory lane. I'm all right... honest!" She smiled. "Want a cuppa? You must be parched!"

"Cor missus – thought you'd never ask."

Chuckling, they walked arm-in-arm into the house. "Before I get started on this cake, do you fancy some lunch?"

TJ gave a 'yes please' smile and rubbed his tummy. "Sounds good to me... what shall we have?"

"Er, something easy. How about soup and a toastie sandwich?"

"Excellent choice madam. Which bit shall I do?"

"Well... I think if sir could attend to the soup, I shall slave over the toaster."

She put the back of her hand dramatically to her forehead. He smiled now that his Jenny was back in cheerful play-acting mode again.

Just as Jennifer was emptying the plates and soup mugs, the phone rang.

"Could you pop those in the sink please babe?"

He rolled his eyes, turning to the dogs. "She planned that call you know, just so I'd do the washing up!"

He'd just finished when she returned. "Oh you sweetie. I didn't mean for you to clean everything."

He raised his eyebrows. "Good call? I heard you laughing!"

"It was Cassie – she'll be round later when Paul gets back." Jennifer started to put things onto the table.

"Can I help at all?"

She smiled at TJ. "Well, Grannifer taught me to always get out everything you'll need before you start – I didn't once, and found I only had one egg for a recipe that needed five! So if you want to, check her book and make sure I've got it all."

He mock saluted. "Will do, captain!"

Together they carried on with creating the cake, enjoying the fun interaction of the project. "This is going to take a while to bake. Shall we put some potatoes in for dinner?"

"Sounds good to me, but Cassie had jacket spud last night... do you think she'll mind it again so soon?"

"No, but if she does, I can always suss an alternative!"

TJ nodded. "Okey dokey... shall I make some chilli con carne to go with it?"

"Ooh, yes please!"

The afternoon passed quickly, and before they realised, it was nearly six o'clock.

'Beep beep!'

"Ah, they're here. I'd better stick the kettle on."

TJ smiled. "Absolutely – why break the habit of a lifetime?"

"Grrr... cheeky!"

Cassie and Paul came in – hugs and kisses abounded as they all greeted each other.

"Cor, there's some good smells going on in here. What's cooking?"

"Cake, potatoes and chilli."

Paul gave a knowing nod. "Exactly as I would have deduced!"

"Oh yes, professor!" They all laughed.

They took their coffees through to the living room, plus some biscuit treats for the dogs. "So Paul, Cassie said you've been out and about today... anywhere interesting?"

Finishing a gulp of his drink "Actually yes... I met up with a colleague from work, and if you guys fancy it... I've found us a holiday cottage in Wales." He gave a self-satisfied smile. "Oh, but the best bit is... it's free!" All we've got to do is feed his chickens and water some plants. What do you think?"

"I'm game!"

"And me!"

"Sounds good – can we take the dogs?"

"Absolutely! Yeah, I even remembered to check that with him."

They cheered "Look out Wales... here we come!"

They continued chatting, and more often than not, laughing too. Suddenly Jennifer looked with concern at Cassie who was shaking her head and tapping her ear. "You all right mate?"

"NO! I've got this ringing noise."

Jennifer jumped up. "Ooh, the cake... I set my alarm clock for when it was ready!"

She left the room. Cassie rolled her eyes and followed her friend to the kitchen. "Smells good – so what are you treating us to with this one?"

"A boat."

Cassie furrowed her brow. "Mm, boat flavour – that's different."

Jennifer laughed. "I thought you meant what decoration!"

She tested with a warm skewer to see if it was cooked enough. "Lovely – nice and clean. And to answer your question... cherry and almond."

Cassie licked her lips. "Yum yum!"

The men had joined them. "Is it OK?"

"Yep – so far so good."

"So shall we eat now or later?"

"Oh now please. That con carne smells scrummy."

They dished up and tucked in to the meal. Paul licked his lips. "Jen, this is absolutely delicious. Do you think you could teach me how to make it?"

"I could probably try luv, but you'd be better off asking the person who made it." She proffered her hand in her boyfriend's direction.

"TJ? Wow mate, how come you are such a good cook?"

Jennifer answered. "He used to work in a restaurant and picked the chef's brains."

"I did indeed, and I'd be happy to show you."

Cassie grinned. "At this rate I'm going to end up with a cordon bleu husband – just think, I'll never have to cook anything when we're married!"

"Any idea when that might be? And I hope I'm set to be chief bridesmaid!"

Cassie nodded vigorously. "'Course mate, goes without saying – but let's get the hols out of the way first."

Paul joined in. "We've got some saving to do first babe – these things don't come cheap you know."

Jennifer looked at them sympathetically. "I bet we could all help to keep the costs down though. I'm sure we know enough people who can do things without charging the earth."

"Well, it's a thought, but we've still got other stuff to deal with first. Josh's party, holiday and opening the Craft Centre."

TJ smiled. "True, true, but you know our Jenny – if she's not at least planning things at a hundred miles an hour, she just ain't happy."

Jennifer looked slightly embarrassed. Everyone laughed, and Jennifer responded with a light-hearted smile and joined in with her friends' laughter.

Later, with the meal finished and washed up, the four friends all helped to cut the large cake into a boat shape. The offcuts were used to make a 'wheel house' and 'glued' into position with jam.

"If we have a drink and sit down for a while, then I'll get the icing organised."

A couple of hours later, after a lot of giggling, the cake was covered. "I'll let it dry overnight and decorate it tomorrow."

"Which one are you going to call it?"

"Well, he made three – 'Crystal Blue', 'Sapphire Blue' and 'Aqua Blue'."

TJ grinned and nudged Paul. "Who'd have guessed that – triplets?"

"Yeah... and all girls!"

Meanwhile, the girls were studying postcards from the booking office. "Well, 'Crystal' was his first, and I asked if we could have her, so..."

They nodded to each other. "'Crystal' it is then."

"Oh, I do hope he'll like it."

Jennifer noticed that Paul and TJ had picked up the postcards from the table and were muttering to each other in a somewhat conspiratorial fashion.

"What are you two cooking up?"

"Er, just an idea babe. Have you got a knitting needle by any chance?"

She looked confused. "Um... yes... I think there must be some in a bag of needlecraft bits I got from the charity shop... would it be a silly question to ask why?"

"Just an idea, babe."

"Yeah – you said. Hang on. I'll fetch the bag."

Banjo was curious and followed his mistress out of the room. They returned moments later.

They all watched with interest as TJ rifled through the contents of the bag. He counted the needles. "Ah, thirteen – that's lucky!"

"Er darling, how can thirteen be lucky?"

"Well that means there will be at least one odd one."

They paired them up. "OK, we have five pairs and three odds."

"Great! So will you tell me what this is all in aid of?"

"Flag pole!"

"Flag pole to you too! What are you on about?"

TJ smiled. Paul pointed to the stern of the boat on the postcard. "Flag pole, see?"

The girls grinned. "Oh the cake! Ooh, you are clever!"

"Well, we think it's rude to disagree with a lady, so... yeah, we're clever!"

They all laughed. "We'll have to cut it down a bit, but I reckon it will be the biz."

**

With Saturday having been a pleasant, but rather busy day, Jennifer allowed herself to a lie-in on Sunday morning. Not too long, but a snuggly couple of hours.

When she woke up, she lay for a while watching the crystal spectrums reflected on the wall. These were more subtle than during the summer months now that the sunlight was not so bright.

Eventually she got out of bed. Slipping on her dressing gown, she went downstairs. As always, she received a warm 'good morning' welcome from Banjo. She opened the back door to let him out to the garden. There was a cold nip in the air, but the remains of dew made glistening pockets around the areas visible from where she stood. She fed Banjo and the birds, then made herself a drink and some breakfast.

Later, after she'd played in the garden with Banjo, Jennifer got the things together that she needed to decorate the cake. "Well here goes Grannifer; let's see if I can do this justice for the old darling and make it look like a miniature of the real thing."

She crossed her fingers. "OK, brushes, food colouring, a glass of water and paper towels to clean the brushes, postcards to copy… hang on…oh bother, I've lost one!"

She studied the two in her hand. "So what have I done with Sapphire? Oh well, at least I've got Crystal."

She chose the colours to match the photograph on the postcard and started to paint the icing. With the radio playing and a cup of coffee nearby, she was surprised how quickly the white cake transformed into a very credible copy of Joshua's actual cruiser.

Last night, using her expertise with modelling clay, Cassie had made fondant icing seats and benches. Now hardened, Jennifer painted these ready to add to the cake later. Now it was time to make some royal icing to pipe details such as railings and ropes.

"Oh, what's he barking at?"

She went in to the garden. A broad smile crossed her face; it was TJ and Soaki. They greeted each other with hugs and kisses while the dogs chased each other playfully around them.

"Come and see what I've done." Jennifer led him to the cake.

"Wow, that's really looking good babe – who's a clever girl then?"

She smiled. "Thank you – I must admit, I'm rather pleased with it. Should be even better when the piping detail is on."

As they chatted over coffee, Jennifer noticed a large bag. "What have you got in there?"

"Ah – a couple of bits I hope you'll like. I've been busy too!"

He pulled out the knitting needle, now cut to size, then a shaped piece of wood veneer, hand painted, identical to the plaque on the stern of Josh's boats.

"Oh, that is beautiful – how did you get it so perfect?"

"Oh, I borrowed this." He placed the postcard on the table.

"I wondered where that had gone!"

"Oh and I know you've got the cake on top of a board, but I thought we could put it on top of this as well."

She stared in amazement at the large board. It was painted to look like the river, but although the water was cleverly realistic, TJ included cartoon characters, such as a fish and ducks with amusing expressions.

She gave a squeal of delight as she clasped her face in astonishment. "Timothy James, you are incredible!"

"You like it then?"

She planted a massive kiss on his lips. "Yes darling – I like it." They laughed.

They decided to play with the dogs for a while, then have some lunch before continuing with the cake. It was mid afternoon when they began positioning things as alike to the pictures as possible. Icing on the reverse of the plaque acted like glue and it was a perfect addition. "I'll wait 'til I've made a flag before we put the needle in."

They juggled with the tiny seats to get them just right before fixing them down. "This reminds me of playing with my dolls' house when I was little. Er TJ – why's there a bench on top of the wheel house?"

"I thought it could be a lookout post... kind of like the crow's nest on a ship." He smiled.

Jennifer shook her head. "No darling, I don't think so!"

He feigned disappointment and it was repositioned correctly. They double-checked everything then 'glued' them in place. It wasn't long before all the piped detail was finished. They stood with their arms around each other studying the finished project.

"All we've got to do now is put it on your river!"

"Yep – a cuppa first I think."

As the kettle boiled, they heard an engine... 'beep beep'.

"Honestly, that girl's got better coffee antennae than I have!" She giggled and went to the hall to open the door.

Cassie, Paul and Jennifer hugged in the doorway. "Now before you go into the kitchen, I want you to close your eyes." She led them in.

"OK, you can look!"

Paul gasped. "Oh my God – it's TJ!"

Cassie tapped his arm. "Idiot!"

"Jen, that is fabulous."

Paul looked serious. "Absolutely, mate. Very realistic. Well done."

"But look at this... TJ did it... it's brilliant." She showed his painting.

"Oh wow! Josh is going to love it."

As they drank, they chatted, mainly about the party but also the holiday. "So when are you planning to launch this boat on to the river?"

Jennifer looked a little confused. "Paul... you do realise it's a cake – I doubt it would float, apart from anything else!"

"Er Jen, I do know it's a cake... I meant TJ's river picture."

Slightly embarrassed, she giggled. "Of course – I knew that's what you were talking about! Well, now's as good a time as any."

When it was in place Jennifer shook her head. "I forgot about the edge of the cake board. It spoils the effect." She tutted and looked miserable.

Cassie responded. "Fear not dear lady – we'll make splashes!"

She picked up the unused icing and deftly covered the board with drips against the bottom of the boat as if it was agitating the water. "Just one more thing to finish it off – TJ, what's missing?"

He looked carefully. "Got you, Cassie...!"

He used the food colouring. Jennifer and Paul watched the two artists with interest. A few strokes with the paintbrush later and "Hey Presto!"

Jennifer looked in wonder at the fragmented colours on the water. "Of course – reflections!"

Paul cuddled his fiancée and slapped TJ's back. "That's brilliant. So clever, and you made it look so easy."

Jennifer grinned. "It's called 'talent'! Thank you guys; you've definitely put the icing on the cake!" They all laughed.

Chapter 15

As the friends relaxed in the living room they listened to music and chatted. Jennifer was enjoying herself doing some needlework.

"What you making babe?"

"Josh's 'Happy Birthday flag', see?"

She showed him the daintily embroidered piece of fabric.

"Very nice. So is that the last thing for the party?"

"Yep. Just down to keeping it secret from the old darling and hope that the timing all goes to plan on Friday."

Cassie looked at the clock. "Cor, I thought I was hungry – it's gone nine o'clock… anyone fancy a take away?"

Jennifer nodded. "I'm up for it – what with this cake, I'd forgotten all about dinner."

"You girls are very keen on getting takeaways – I'm going to make sure we do more home cooked meals when we're married – it's cheaper y'know."

TJ agreed with Paul. "I was just thinking the same thing." He looked sheepish when the others stared at him. "Er, I mean, er, you'll be wanting to save up for a house and stuff I s'pose."

He gave a weak throat clearing cough. "Um, I'll get the menus." With flushed cheeks he quickly left the room.

"Erm, and I'll put the kettle on. I presume you ladies would like a coffee." Paul followed quickly after TJ.

The girls stared at each other. "What the hell happened there?"

"He wasn't taking about Paul and me was he?"

"You don't think… no, he must have meant it how he said."

Cassie raised her eyebrows. "Yeah, whatever!"

The men returned with the drinks and menus. "Are any of these going to be open on a Sunday?"

"Hope so. They should have days and times by the phone number."

TJ checked. "Looks like The Curry House or Oriental Garden, but they both close at ten, so we'd better order soon – we've got twenty three minutes."

They decided on Chinese and TJ phoned through the order. He returned from the hallway. "That was close. They said a few minutes later and their delivery man would have gone home."

"Right – better get some plates and stuff ready. Anyone want chopsticks, or is it forks and spoons?"

In next to no time it seemed, the food had been delivered and they were eating. Cassie recalled the time she'd fetched the food. "I couldn't believe it. I'd only been gone a short while and madam here, she'd made hats and lanterns and several other things!"

With all the details of her story, everyone agreed that Jennifer could easily have been on the stage.

"I've said it before, haven't I mate? She just slips so easily into different characters."

Jennifer smiled. "I must admit, if there was an Am Dram group nearby, I might be tempted, but I've not heard of one."

"Bet you'll do something one day!"

"Yeah, like I've got nothing else going on in my life!"

The evening continued with them happily enjoying each other's company. By the time Banjo had had his evening walk and Jennifer had said goodnight to everyone, she was extremely tired. But before going up to her bed, she made sure that the cake was well out of harm's way and covered it with a large box.

"I don't think you'll get curious, little man, but just in case..." She patted Banjo and left him a biscuit. "Night night darling – sleep well. I'll see you in the morning. Good boy." She kissed his head and he wagged his tail.

With the house now quiet without those rowdy humans, Banjo soon fell asleep. Upstairs his mistress lay in her bed. "So Grannifer – another day has hurtled to an end and I feel quite shattered." She yawned. "Oh, 'scuse me darling!"

She smiled, knowing that her Grannifer would be happy that she'd remembered her manners. "Did we imagine that bit with TJ? It was a bit weird! Oh well sweetheart, sleepy-byes time. Night night to you and Grandpa. Love you."

She kissed the air as always and snuggled under the bed clothes. Her head nestled into the pillow and the muted sound of the night time riverbank made her smile. Very, very quickly she drifted into sleep.

***

In the morning she went through her usual routine of breakfast for Banjo, the birds and herself, but she couldn't resist lifting the edge of the box to peak at the boat. She smiled. "Though I say it myself, I reckon we've done an OK job there."

Later at the boatyard it was back to the business of conversion and prepping each unit ready to display their goods when the Craft Centre was open. Before Jim and Joshua arrived, Laura and Jennifer were chatting. "I can't wait to see this creation. So you'll bring it here on Thursday night?"

"Uh huh. Jim says he'll make sure they don't come near the place until Friday afternoon. He's going to make some excuse to leave early on Thursday evening."

Laura hunched her shoulders. "I'm getting ever so excited!"

"Oh yes lass. What about?" It was Josh.

"Well, the Centre of course... we'll be opening soon."

Jennifer rolled her eyes and blew a silent breath of air. When out of Joshua's earshot she complimented Laura. "That was very well recovered – so cool and calm."

Laura laughed. "Years of practice when you've got a nosey brother like Danny. If we weren't on the ball he'd have never had a surprise for Christmas or birthdays."

"Well, it came in useful... that was very good."

Cassie joined the girls. "Hiya mate – I was just thinking of coming to find you. Where have you been?"

"Getting that brick outhouse ready for my kiln. Barry's picking it up for me tomorrow."

"Oh you should have said. I'd have helped. Is there anything that I can do?"

"Absolutely, Jenny old girl. If I don't have a coffee soon, I'm likely to keel over."

Laura laughed as Jennifer saluted and marched off comically. In the snack bar area she filled the kettle, and whilst it heated, got mugs out. She went to the walkway outside the door and shouted. "Kettle's on – who wants a drink?"

Within two minutes, the girls, TJ, Danny, Grin, Joshua and Jim were all congregated and finding a seat. Jennifer gave out the mugs and TJ filled bowls with fresh water for the three dogs. Jim offered biscuits from a large tin.

"Oh Jim – posh assorted bickies – you had a windfall, splashing out like this?"

"Nay lass. They had a raffle in the pub and I got third prize! Tuck in everyone."

They all thanked him. "Don't you want to take them home and indulge yourselves?"

"No, we're going to do that with a huge box of chocolates – Josh got the second prize!"

Everyone laughed and raised their mugs.

"Well done the pair of you – cheers!"

When their break was over, everyone got back to their jobs. As always, the day passed quickly. Jennifer and TJ decided to walk back home along the tow-path.

"It's crazy – all this time here and we've always gone back via the village."

"If it's a good walk, we can get to and from the centre more easily. Of course babe, we could always get a little boat and row to work."

Jennifer looked aghast. "You are joking? I've never handled anything outside of a boating pool, and even then I crashed into the side."

He laughed at her. "Well my dear, I think it's about time you learned properly. Anyway, it's a bit daft having a river at the bottom of your garden and not being able to enjoy it fully."

As they walked, following Soaki and Banjo who were running ahead, she pondered. It was a particularly pretty and peaceful waterway. "I see your point, and I... I s'pose it does make sense."

He squeezed her waist. "That's my girl... er, you can swim I presume?"

She glared at him. He kissed her forehead. "If not, I can teach you that as well."

"Yes Timothy, I can swim thank you."

He stifled a giggle at her indignant reaction. He changed the subject, and as they strolled along he pointed out things – varieties of plants and trees, breeds of birds and what creature made a particular noise or splash.

She was very interested and yes, it had to be said, most impressed by his knowledge. "Oh my gosh, here's my gate!" She looked at her watch. "Crikey, that didn't even take forty minutes, and we were only dawdling."

They kissed. "Would you teach me all that stuff, please?"

"Well, since you ask so nicely…" He smiled.

They called the dogs and they all went into the garden. As they walked along the path towards the house, Jennifer rummaged in her bag for the key. She unlocked the door and flicked the light switch. Simultaneously, the light came on and the phone started ringing.

"That's a clever trick babe, but you are very good at multi-tasking!"

She grinned. "Could you make the coffees while I get this please?"

She went to the hallway with Banjo by her side not wanting to miss out on anything.

"Hello… Oh hi Mum… yeah I'm fine thanks. You and Dad?… Ah good… Uh huh… Right… That's brilliant… Yeah, he's fine… Yes and the dogs… Yes we're all really good… Yep, all OK so far… No, you're all right; just have a good journey… Uh huh, just two minutes earlier and I would have missed you!… OK darling… Can't wait to see you both… Yes, I love you too… Night night."

She replaced the receiver and joined TJ. "That was Mum. They're coming down on Wednesday."

He smiled. "Great. It'll be good to see them again – I like your parents."

They chatted happily about Jon and Sally's impending visit as they prepared their evening meal. "They'll be surprised when they see what we've done at the boatyard."

"Gosh yes and I've got step by step photos of our progress!"

TJ looked thoughtful. "I know you've sorted this boat trip."

"Not just me darling – we've all organised it together."

"OK, but I think you've done most, but that apart, have you got him an actual pressie?"

"Not as yet – I couldn't think what to get the old sweetheart."

"Well, why not an album with all your pictures? It'll be nice for him to look back on – especially when he's been so involved with it."

"What a super idea – he'd really like that and I can take loads of his party to add later." She gave a broad and very contented smile.

Soon dinner was ready and TJ dished up while Jennifer organised meals for Soaki and Banjo. She was surprised as she sat at the table that candles had been lit. TJ turned off the main light then put their plates on place mats. Before taking his seat, he kissed her on the cheek. "Bon appétit my Jenny."

"This is lovely – why the candlelight?"

"Well, it could be to save electricity, but it's actually to share a romantic moment with you – it's not often we get time just we two. I thought it would be a nice change."

"And it is darling. Very nice – thank you."

They enjoyed the rest of the evening just relaxing. They cuddled on the settee and listened to their favourite music. They chatted about their pasts as well as forthcoming events. All the while, Soaki and Banjo were snuggled together close to their owners.

The following morning, Jennifer phoned Cassie to see if she needed them to help with the kiln. "No, we're OK for manpower thanks darling – I'll pop round later and let you know how we've got on." They laughed for a while.

When she had finished the call, Jennifer set about preparing the bedroom ready for her parents' visit. TJ and Soaki arrived and enjoyed sharing breakfast before he and Jennifer put the finishing touches to the fascia board sign for the Craft Centre.

They had just completed it and gone from the summer house into the kitchen to make coffee; the kettle had just boiled. 'Beep beep'.

"Bloomin' heck, she's done it again! I swear the girl has some sort of radar for when we've got coffee on the go!"

Jennifer laughed. "Absolutely – Cassie and I are fine-tuned to mugs being filled." She giggled as she went to the door.

She hugged her very happy friend. The beaming smile indicated that all had gone well. "Oh I feel like my new studio is really real now – y'know what I mean?" She looked at her friends who were chuckling. "What?"

"Mate, if you smile any harder, I swear your head will divide in two!"

They all laughed as they revelled in Cassie's excitement. Cassie was still beaming when Paul arrived.

"Darling, if you don't calm down a bit you'll explode. Tell you what will change your mindset away from everything else… I'll thrash you at Monopoly."

She raised her eyebrows at him discernibly. "You reckon?"

"Jenny, his Lordship has challenged us to a game!"

Jennifer had heard Paul and was already setting the pieces out. "Mm, we'll see about that. First one to Go To Jail has to make coffee."

The game was a good distraction for them all, and by the end of the evening they were tired, but relaxed and happy. Although she was excited about her parents' visit, Jennifer was surprised how well she slept that night.

It was a gentle autumnal sun that greeted her the following morning. When she got to the kitchen, she rubbed Banjo's ears enthusiastically.

"Good morning my darling. You're going to meet my Mum and Dad

261

today, and they're going to love you... yes they will." He responded to her excitement and wriggled about and panted.

She had just finished getting dressed and was tidying the kitchen when the phone rang. It was Barry arranging to come at midday to pick up the turnstile. TJ arrived as she finished the call. "Shall we take the fascia board as well?"

"Might as well if he's got room in the van. Oh, and don't forget the amusement machines from Johnston's."

Jennifer shrugged her shoulders and grinned. "Ooh, it's all coming together isn't it?"

He hugged her tightly. "Yes my darling, it definitely is."

True to his word, Barry arrived at Willow Bank House at twelve o'clock.

"Hiya – coffee before or after we load up?"

"Oh, I'm easy; whichever you prefer, Jen."

She smiled. "I'll put the kettle on – you never know, we could end up with a cuppa either side of loading!"

TJ rolled his eyes. "I don't know where she puts it all."

They all went indoors excitedly, accompanied by the dogs. Barry and his mate, Colin, both had tea, whilst Jennifer and TJ stuck with coffee. Colin was very interested in the Craft Centre project and they chatted animatedly about it for quite some time.

"Show him your photos babe." He turned to Colin. "She snaps at anything and everything! These will give you a real idea of what we've done."

Jennifer returned with her pictures.

"Are you a professional photographer then?"

She laughed. "Good grief no – I just enjoy snapping with my camera."

He looked thoughtful. "Would you consider a day's commission? I'll have to ask my fiancée, but we can't really afford an official bloke, and these are really lovely."

She looked quizzical. "Sorry, what do you want snapped?"

"Oh, didn't I say? I was thinking of our wedding."

"Your WEDDING! Crikey, er, I don't think that's a good idea – I mean what if something went wrong? I would never forgive myself if I ruined your special day."

He looked a little sad, but also sympathetic at Jennifer's panic. "It was just an idea. Don't worry. Nice cuppa by the way." He sipped his tea.

Jennifer felt a little guilty at her reaction and humbled by his. She

262

pondered for a moment. "Er, will you all excuse me for a minute? I won't be long."

She exited the kitchen and walked down the path. TJ watched her with Banjo close by, picking a few stones as she went. He smiled.

Colin was concerned. "Did I upset her?"

"No, but you've given her cause for thought. She'll be back soon."

Ten minutes passed and TJ went quietly to the gate and watched Jennifer. Banjo sat beside her as she threw the last stone into the water. "Have you decided yet?"

She turned her head. "Possibly." She stood up and stroked Banjo's neck.

The pair returned to the garden. TJ's arm held her comfortingly as they returned to the kitchen.

"You all right Jenny?"

"Yes thanks Barry. Er, Colin – I'm not saying yes, but perhaps we could talk, maybe sort something out..."

He gave a grateful smile. "Yes, that would be good. Thank you."

Barry stood up. "Right then – let's get this roundabout shifted!"

"It's not a roundabout, it's a turnstile."

"Well, whatever it is, let's get it in the van."

It was heavy and cumbersome, but using his trolley, they soon manoeuvred it to the roadside. Barry opened the van doors. "All we've got to do now is lift it up and in."

Almost as if destiny had arranged it, a car drove along the lane and pulled up alongside. Jennifer squealed with delight.

"Mum – Dad! I didn't think you were arriving 'til this evening!"

They hugged and kissed enthusiastically. Jennifer introduced them to Barry and Colin and started to explain the fact that they had a turnstile by her front gate.

"Tell us later. Can I just ask... is it arriving or leaving? Do I presume an extra pair of hands to load it would be useful?"

It didn't take long to sort with the extra help and very soon they were all indoors.

"Put that kettle on darling and get some plates – we've brought cake!" ordered Sally.

TJ rubbed his tummy. "Is it one of your home-made?"

Sally nodded. "Yes dear, it is."

He licked his lips. "Oh goody gum drops."

She laughed. "You've caught that off our Jennifer. She's said that since she was a little girl."

Jennifer rolled her eyes. "Mu-um!!"

263

As they tucked into the cake, compliments abounded. "This is really delicious, Sally."

"Thank you. It's actually one of Grannifer's recipes."

As they chatted, Jon and Sally patted the dogs. "This little fella is very friendly, isn't he? I see why you couldn't resist him."

"Yeah and he and Soaki get on so well, I think it was just meant to have been."

"Er, Barry, couldn't help noticing those old game machines in your van – are you involved with a fair or something?"

Barry chuckled. "No Jon, it's all to do with these two!" He gestured towards Jennifer and TJ.

"Why am I not surprised?"

"We were just getting it all ready to take to the Centre; just the fascia board to get, then we were going. Will you be OK here for a while; we shouldn't be long."

"Are you kidding? I want to see what you've done with the place! Do you want to come, Sal?"

She raised her eyebrows. "Don't be daft, of course I'm coming – I can't wait! Anyway, you'll need help at the other end to unload." She flexed her muscles and they all laughed.

They piled into the vehicles and drove in convoy through the village. Approaching the far side of Miraford they turned left into Chandlers Lane. The familiar crunch of the gravel gave a welcoming 'you've arrived' noise as they parked. The colourful 2CV was in its usual spot facing the river.

Hearing the arrivals, Cassie came out to meet them. She broke into a run with her arms outstretched as she spotted Jennifer's parents. "Sally – Jon! I thought you were arriving later. How wonderful!"

They hugged enthusiastically. "Hello Cassie, how are you darling? We surprised our dilly daughter too. Well come on… let's see what you've done to this place."

As they toured the building, Jon nodded approvingly and Sally beamed. "This is wonderful – you've all worked so hard and I love that water illusion on the outside."

"That's down to TJ… isn't it great? I'm glad you like it."

"So where are the elder statesmen?"

Cassie smiled. "Went about an hour ago. Jim felt 'unwell', so they went back to the cottage… he'll make a miraculous recovery late tomorrow afternoon!"

Sally looked slightly confused and then realised. "Oh, I see – to keep Joshua out of the way 'til his birthday."

Laura had joined the ladies. Their conversation was interrupted by noise at the main entrance. The men had been getting the things from the van.

"Hang on guys, we'll help out."

"Don't worry – we've done it!"

"Oh... you should have said – we didn't realise you'd started."

Jennifer gave one of her 'innocent little girl' looks as TJ laughed. It wasn't long before the turnstile and amusement machines were in position. TJ's board, describing 'Jenny R Cade Penny Arcade' was attached and then they all went outside to 'help' with the fascia sign.

"I think it's too high."

"No no, the left end is just right, but the other end needs to come up a smidge."

"Shouldn't the whole thing be moved over towards the river?"

"If we do that, there'll be a big gap at the other end of the building."

And so it continued. Danny and Grin climbed down from their ladders and put the board on the floor.

"That was making my arms ache."

"Yes mate. Me too."

The others looked guiltily at the women who were now sitting down either side of the large entrance and massaging their shoulders. "Sorry guys – that was not one of our best planned operations."

TJ put his arm around Jennifer's waist. "What do you reckon darling? After all, the whole venture is your idea."

She pondered. "I think we should do a sketch and make a paper fascia – that will be much easier than our acrobats wobbling about on ladders."

Danny chipped in. "Oh yes please. I like that idea."

They all trooped inside.

"Right, we've got a slope up to the other doors and the whole entrance is the same width as the slope. I say keep it symmetrical. We can find the centre of the entrance, the centre of the board and position it like that. Have a six inch gap above the door frame and that should give a nice border, yes?"

Everyone cheered. "At last, a decision!"

Within an hour it was securely bolted in place and the whole group were sitting in the snack bar area with piping hot drinks.

"Oh my goodness – that's it, isn't it? All we have to do now is get our stock in and we're ready to open." Jennifer exhaled "Wow!"

As they drove home, Jon suddenly pulled up and parked the car. "What's up, Dad?"

"Nothing pet, but have we got anything planned for dinner?"

"No, not really… why?"

He sniffed the air. "It's just that the smell coming from the chippy is rather tempting. Anyone fancy fish and chips?"

Smiles abounded.

"Ooh, yes!"

"Absolutely!"

"Only if I can treat you – what does everyone want?"

They made their decisions, then Jennifer and TJ went to the shop. Sally and Jon waited in the car with the dogs.

While they waited for the food to be cooked they chatted. TJ said "I was talking to Colin earlier when we were all emptying the van. It's really sad. He and Ruby – that's his fiancée – well they both worked at a residential home for the elderly. He did caretaker stuff and Ruby was in the kitchens. They were enjoying their jobs, saving what they could to get married, and lo and behold the place closes down!"

"Oh that's a shame. What are they doing now?"

"Well, he's working with Barry as you know, but Ruby's still looking. Oh, that's our order. Cor, I'm looking forward to this! Anyway, that's why they're doing the wedding as cheap as they can."

They arrived back at the car. Jon sniffed the air. "Mm, that smells yummy. Get your keys ready pet. We'll be home in two ticks."

As he drove, Jon suggested a plan of action. "When we get in, I'll make the drinks. Sal, you and Jenny dish up. TJ – you're dogs' dinners."

"Charming! I thought you liked me Jon and there you are calling me names!"

"No lad. I meant you 'do' the dogs' dinners!"

The others laughed. "He's joking, Dad."

They arrived and piled into the house. Within minutes they were seated at the table. TJ refreshed their glasses, finishing the bottle of wine that they had been drinking.

Sally smiled. "Thank you love. So darlings, what have you got planned for tomorrow?"

Jennifer thought for a moment. "Actually there's not a lot, so whatever you fancy. All we need to do is take the birthday cake to the boatyard so it's ready for Friday."

"Ah yes, the cake… you've told me about it on the phone. When do we get to see it?"

"Well, now if you like. It's over there on the side, underneath that box."

Jon and Sally both stood up, carefully lifting its cover. They gazed in awe. "Oh my goodness – that's amazing!"

"I'll say pet. It'll be a shame to cut it."

"I like the river – your handiwork I believe TJ?"

"Absolutely it is Mum – isn't he clever?"

Jon was studying the 'water' more closely. "Here Sal, have you seen these fish and things? Look at the soppy expressions on them!"

They all laughed as they noticed even more of the fun characters. "Joshua is going to love this."

"I do hope so – we had fun creating it."

It had been a long day. Jennifer noticed Jon trying to disguise a yawn. "If you're tired Dad, your room is ready. Go up to bed whenever you want."

He smiled at his daughter. "You know pet, I might just do that. Would you mind?"

"Don't be daft. I think you are amazing to have lasted this long. We've spent all day doing stuff since you arrived and that's on top of the long drive to get here."

"I reckon you're right, and I want to build up some energy for this party. Er, this boat we're going on… it is safe isn't it?"

Jennifer laughed. "What do you think TJ?"

"Oh I think it might be – she's been swishing through the water for a good many years now and we haven't heard of any mishaps."

Sally stood up and took her husband's arm. "Come on, you land lubber – it will be lovely, and since you've all been talking about bed – I'm feeling rather sleepy myself."

They all kissed goodnight.

When Jennifer herself snuggled into her bed, she realised just how tired she was too. She wished her love to Grannifer as always. She closed her eyes with a smile playing on her mouth. Very, very soon she was asleep.

***

As Jennifer opened the back door the following morning to let Banjo out into the garden, she noticed it had been raining overnight. "Oh, that's a shame – I hope it gets brighter."

She fed the birds whilst she watched her four-legged friend investigating the refreshed smells. She laughed when he sneezed and shook his head after he disturbed a large leaf that dispensed water all over his face. Hearing noises from within the kitchen, she returned inside.

"Morning darling."

"Morning Mum – did you sleep OK?"

267

"Oh yes, like a log. We always do in that bed."

"That's good. Is Dad awake? I'll get a cuppa going anyway." She put the kettle on. "Any ideas what you'd like to do today?"

Sally helped her daughter with the drinks. "I don't think we have anything specific in mind – I wouldn't mind having a look around Lamton sometime. I liked it when we were down before."

"Yeah I do too – it's a large town, but it feels… well, villagey." They acknowledged agreement with nods and smiles.

"Good morning pet. Your Mum said it wouldn't be long before there'd be a cup of tea on the go." He chuckled as he kissed her cheek.

"Hello Dad. Sleep well?"

"Definitely. I said to Sal – we ought to get a bed like that for our home."

They chatted as they drank, dunking the occasional biscuit.

"So, are we going into Lamton then?" asked Jennifer.

Jon and Sally both nodded. "Seems unanimous."

"Good. I've got a couple of calls to make, then I'll make us some breakfast before we go."

Jon shook his head. "No you won't – I'm going to treat us all to M B S E food today!"

Jennifer looked confused. "Pardon?"

"Made By Someone Else!"

"But it won't take a minute to…"

"No pet – you've been working hard with this party, and anyway, I want to treat my two favourite girls." He smiled with satisfaction.

Jennifer hugged and kissed his cheek. "OK, you win, but I must make those phone calls first."

She went to the hall and dialled Jim's number. "Hello darling. Just a quick call to check if you're feeling better… oh that's good… are you able to talk about tomorrow… oh, is he standing right there? I can chat to him myself. Hello Josh, I was just wondering if Jim was any better… Ah, so it's been your turn to look after him." Both callers laughed with each other.

"What's that… you want him better by tomorrow…Why…? Oh, so he can join you in a birthday drink? Wow, is that tomorrow? Gosh that's come round quickly. Well, hopefully we'll try to raise a glass with you. Take care then darling. Love to you both. byeee."

By now Sally was by her daughter's side. "You are naughty – poor old Josh is thinking you forgot his special day."

"Yeah, but tomorrow afternoon, he'll know different, and how much we love him." She grinned excitedly. "Right, one more call, then we can go. Are you both ready?"

Her father responded from the kitchen "All three of us are ready."

With a quizzical expression, she peered around the door. She smiled when she saw TJ. "Hello darling. You're early."

"Morning Jenny. Your Dad asked me to come round last night."

Jon interrupted them. "I didn't want to be outnumbered by females, did I?"

Jennifer rolled her eyes. "Oh, for goodness sake! Ooh, put the kettle on babe while I do this other call."

"Your wish is my command oh beautiful one." He held her shoulders and kissed her. "And calm down!" He smiled as she gave a relaxed sigh.

Minutes later she joined TJ and her parents. She sipped her coffee. "Right, I've spoken with the booking office – everything is OK for the boat and they said if we drop off our bunting and stuff, they'll decorate her for us. Isn't that nice of them?"

Suddenly the back door opened and the dogs ran in. "Hello Soaki – I wondered where you were." Jennifer stroked her and Banjo too. "We'd better dry those paws before we get in the car."

It wasn't long before they were ready to go. They carefully put the cake into the boot, wedging it securely for its journey. Everyone climbed on board and they were on their way.

"Does Helen do breakfast?"

"I think so, Dad. Is that where you want to go?"

"Well, it would be nice to see her… and it is close."

Sally added, "And your dad's hungry!"

Jon parked the car in Market Square and they all climbed out. Sally and Jennifer started looking in shop windows. They were distracted by an exaggerated cough. "Ahem! Hum!"

Looking up they saw Jon rubbing his tummy. They laughed, and linking arms, strode deliberately towards him. TJ watched the family pantomime with amusement.

As they all entered Meadows Tea Room, Helen looked up to acknowledge her new customers. When she saw who it was, she quickly moved from behind the counter and joined them. Hugs and kisses abounded.

"Oh, how wonderful to see you. Are you down for the party?"

Jon held her waist. "Absolutely dear lady, but first of all, please answer me a question."

"Yes, what is it?"

"Dearest Helen. Please tell me… do you serve breakfasts?"

She giggled. "Yes of course – take a seat. I'll get drinks while you look at the menu."

She got their beverages, chatting for a while as they chose their meals.

"Mum, Dad – before we leave, make sure you write in Josh's card. It's a beauty and Helen has got almost the whole village to sign it."

Amid the conversation, Sally noticed a wistful look on her daughter's face. "Are you all right, darling?"

"Mm? Oh yes. I was just remembering a lifetime ago – well that's what it feels like. I used to sit in this chair and stare out at this view. Didn't know anyone. Had no idea where my life was heading but just a matter of months later and... well look how it's all turned around." She gave a gentle smile.

Sally reached across the table and they held hands. The light squeeze of their fingers spoke volumes. Helen arrived with their breakfasts.

"Ooh, they look good!" Jon licked his lips in anticipation.

"Hope you enjoy them – let me know if you need anything else."

After a leisurely hour of eating, more drinks and animated conversation, they said their goodbyes and made their way to the boatyard.

With the cake safely inside, they continued their journey into Lamton. At the booking office, the assistant greeted them with her usual bubbly smile.

"Hello, it's Miss Cade isn't it?" She bent down and stroked Soaki and Banjo.

After a moment of ear tickling, she stood upright again. "Sorry, I can't resist 'em! Now then, you have all your decorations for 'Crystal Blue', yes?"

TJ handed her the box of goodies. "It's good of you to do this for us."

"Ah, not at all – we have all been most excited since we knew who the party was for. The crew can't wait to actually meet Mr Sanders."

They confirmed the final arrangements then continued towards the town. They studied with interest the various window displays and, as they ventured into the occasional shop, they were soon laden with bags.

* * *

It was late afternoon and they made their way back to the car in single file because of the pavement narrowing. They were walking in staggered procession with Jon bringing up the rear.

"Whoa, hang on troops!"

Turning to see why he'd called out, they found him looking intently in the window of an antique come bric-a-brac shop. "Sal, have we got anything for Josh's present yet?"

"Well, kind of. Nothing out of the ordinary, why?"

"Look at that door knocker – I'm not sure, but doesn't it look like the old boy's dog?"

Jennifer was astonished. "Oh my goodness Dad – you're right. It looks just like Rigger!"

TJ smiled. "Could have used him as a model."

Jon and Sally went into the shop and minutes later emerged with another bag to carry.

"Now, let's get home before we buy anything else!"

Back at Willow Bank House they all chipped in with various jobs which needed to be done. Jon made drinks whilst the others put the shopping away. Then later Sally and Jennifer made cakes for the party, leaving the men to deal with dinner.

"It's a good job you've got a big kitchen babe – if we were on Kingfisher we'd be tripping over each other."

Jennifer smiled and nodded. "Yeah, but although she's compact, she's a beautiful vessel."

Sally agreed. "Absolutely, and even though she's a boat, it's almost like you step on board and she gives you a cuddle."

TJ smiled. "Why thank you Sally – that's nice of you to say so."

While everything was cooking, they sat in the living room and wrapped Joshua's presents. Soon the aromas were wafting from the kitchen and filling the house with scrumptious smells.

As they sat in the cosy farmhouse kitchen eating their meal, Jennifer gave a contented smile as she looked at the surrounding surfaces which were filled with an array of cakes. There was a mixture of large and small, all sitting on cooling wire racks. She marvelled at the fact that so much had been accomplished in so short a time.

"Thank you guys. Dad, TJ, the dinner's lovely and Mum – I couldn't have managed all these without your help."

"You are most welcome – anyway, we've enjoyed it."

They managed to decorate and put the cakes into containers ready for tomorrow… well, most of them. Jon and TJ did persuade the ladies that it was their duty to test them. "To make sure they were suitable for such a distinguished gentleman, such as Joshua, to allow his guests to eat."

It was unlike her, but as she lay in her bed, Jennifer just couldn't get to sleep. She tossed and turned, puffed her pillows, tried counting sheep – nothing worked. For an hour she fidgeted.

She decided to go downstairs. Creeping past her parents' room, she forgot the one squeaky floorboard and cringed. "Oh darn!" she whispered. She waited momentarily, as if this would make the noise disappear.

She sat, frustrated, in the living room. Banjo was asleep in his favourite place. "You lucky little man – I wish I was in dreamland."

The door opened. It was Sally. "You all right, darling? I heard you come down."

"Oh, I'm sorry; didn't mean to disturb you."

Sally joined her daughter on the settee. "What's the matter, sweetheart?"

"I can't sleep. Normally, I'm out like a light. I think I've forgotten something for tomorrow, but I cannot think what." She sighed.

"Let's do some hot milk and go through a few ideas." Sally led the way through to the kitchen.

Sitting with their hot mugs, they went through the notepad of 'things to do'.

"What about plates, glasses, cutlery – that sort of thing?"

"All on the boat."

"Serviettes?"

"Angela from the pub."

"A knife to cut the birthday cake?"

"Helen."

"A lighter or matches for his candles?"

"Oh crikey – that's it! You're a genius Mum – I haven't got candles for him to blow out. Oh no – he won't be able to make his birthday wish!"

Sally cuddled her. "Calm down; we'll sort it in the morning … or should I say later on this morning?"

Jennifer looked at the clock. "Oh goodness – we've got to be up in about four hours! Sorry Mum."

"Not a problem. I'll race you back to bed."

"Ha – that's not fair; yours is nearer!"

Sally smiled. "Yeah, by about eight feet!"

They kissed goodnight. "Thanks Mum."

***

This time, as she snuggled down, sleep came easily. With Sally's help to settle her mind, Jennifer managed five or six deep and peaceful hours of sleep. She woke feeling completely relaxed and ready for the day ahead.

Simultaneously, as she let Banjo into the garden, the phone rang.

"Ha-llo…! Ah Cassie, good morning. You OK?"

272

She chatted with her friend awhile, eventually explaining about her initial problem getting to sleep. "So now all I've got to do is get cake candles."

She listened to her friend with an ever expanding smile growing on her mouth. "You're kidding me! That's brilliant... No don't worry about it... Yeah, looking forward to seeing it. OK darling, see you later. byeee."

She almost skipped into the kitchen. Sally had made drinks and was sitting at the table.

"Oh hello Mum. I didn't hear you come down."

They kissed. "So what was all that excitement I could hear?"

Jennifer smiled incredulously. "You'll never guess – Cassie was sorry, she forgot to tell me before, but she's made a keepsake holder for Josh's candle, and has the candle and a lighter!"

"So the sleepless problem wasn't a problem anyway?"

"It would seem not – but thank you for being there for me. I appreciate it."

Sally smiled. "That's all right darling; I'm happy to help. It's my job – I'm a mum!" They both laughed as they hugged.

Jon joined them. "Morning ladies and how are my best girls today?"

"Hello Dad – we're fine."

Cradling his mug, Jon licked his lips. "I fancy a good old bacon sandwich for breakfast – that all right with you two?"

They nodded. "Ooh, yes please."

Jennifer looked at the clock. "TJ and Soaki might be on their way. I'll go to the gate and see."

Banjo joined her as she walked along the path. Once on the towpath, she waved at the figure walking towards them. Banjo ran up to meet TJ and Soaki. An elderly couple walked by her. "Good morning dear."

"Good morning! Enjoy your walk."

As they passed by, Jennifer realised she'd popped her boots on to go outside, but still had her dressing gown on. She quickly went back into the garden. TJ and the dogs followed her.

As they munched on their bacon sarnies, Jennifer giggled. "I forgot I wasn't dressed. No wonder they gave me a weird look."

TJ remarked that it wasn't quite as strange as the outfit she'd worn to feed the pigs a while back.

She rolled her eyes. "Oh gosh yes – I'd forgotten about that."

In their usual good-humoured, yet well organised manner, the two couples got themselves ready for the party. While the dogs played in the garden, Jon and TJ loaded the car. Sally made coffee whilst Jennifer made a phone call.

"Hello Jim. How are you...? Great! Now darling, we're going soon to the boatyard. 'Crystal Blue' is due there at three o'clock, so can you have Josh there for half two...? Uh ha... OK, and you're sure you don't need a lift...? No you don't need to make an excuse. Put him on the phone."

"Hello Joshua! Happy birthday darling. Look I'm sorry about yesterday, forgetting the date and everything... No, I know you're not bothered, but we felt guilty, so we've made a few sandwiches and got a cake and we've just about finished getting the Craft Centre done, so if you come and see the end product, we'll have a little tea party while we're there... Well, if you can, we'll see you later at, err, how about two thirty...? And don't eat any lunch or you won't want your cake!"

Joshua and Jennifer both laughed. "OK sweetheart. See you later – byeee."

She went to the kitchen where the others had been listening. "Well, if I didn't know otherwise – I'd believe you!"

Jennifer grinned. "I just hope he'll like the surprise and forgive me for fibbing."

They finished their drinks and got into the car.

Chapter 16

When they arrived, Cassie was already there. "Hiya. Laura and the guys are inside and Mum called me. Everyone else is ready to get on board – so far so good, eh mate?"

They all went into the building. Paul, Danny, Grin and Laura greeted them. Cassie took her friend to one side.

"What do you think, Jen. Will this do for his candle?"

She placed a delicately crafted miniature dingy into Jennifer's hand. Where the boat's name would be she had, in dainty script, written 'Joshua 90'. At the stern was an elevated lantern containing a colour coordinated tea light.

Open mouthed, Jennifer replied "Oh mate, it's beautiful. You're so clever. He's going to love this."

They positioned it on the 'river' alongside the birthday cake. The time was approaching twenty past two. "I'm going to wander up the lane and meet our elder statesmen."

"Hold on Jen; I'll come with you."

Like two excited schoolgirls, Cassie and Jennifer made their way to Chandlers Lane. As they turned the corner they saw Jim and Joshua a short distance away.

Meeting up, they gave kisses. The girls linked an arm with each of the two men. They chatted merrily, Jennifer keeping a sneaky eye on the time. Joshua was impressed with the newly erected fascia board. As they entered the building, a loud cheer went up, then a round of 'For he's a jolly good fellow.'

Joshua smiled broadly. "Oh thank you everyone. Oh my word – it's

Sally and Jon too. How nice!"

Amid the hugs and handshakes, Jennifer was keeping a check on the time. She caught Cassie's attention and looked at the clock. Cassie nodded and, with Paul and TJ, went to the snack bar area. They lit the candle, then stood in front of the table obscuring the cake.

Meanwhile, Jennifer took Joshua's arm. "Come with me, birthday boy – we've got something to show you."

Everyone followed them. Cassie and the boys stepped aside. Joshua gasped and stared open mouthed at the spectacle in front of him. Everyone sang 'Happy birthday'. Joshua bit his lip.

"Come on then. Blow out your candle and make a wish!"

He did so and they all cheered. Now seated, cards and gifts were given. It was five to three.

"Did you know I built the real thing, lass? Aye, she was the first of three – looking at this 'ere cake, well, for a moment there I thought I 'eard her engine!"

"Cor, it must be a realistic look alike!"

"'Ere lass, I reckon I'm going daft – could've sworn that was the old girl's hooter and bell!"

"Probably some other boat – let's go and see."

She ushered him outside. With Rigger by his side, he stood and stared. He wiped a tear from his eyes. "It's her – it's my Crystal Blue – but how, why, I mean…"

Jennifer held his waist. "Darling Josh – you're a very special gentleman and all your friends wanted to share your special day, so we're going to have a party while we chug along the river! Do you fancy a boat ride for your birthday?"

"Aye lass. Let's get on board!" They hugged tightly.

Those already on the river boat gave a loud cheer as he stepped towards the gangplank. With everyone on board, Crystal Blue gave a cheery hoot and she was on her way.

With background music playing over the tannoy, Joshua made his way around the boat greeting his guests and thanking them for joining him for this wonderful surprise. It seemed that half the village were there – at least the people who were special in Joshua's life.

After about half an hour of 'meeting and greeting', Jennifer suggested that he should perhaps take a seat and rest a while.

"We're on here for a good couple of hours y'know love. Can I get you a drink and something to eat?"

"No thank you lass – but you can sit and tell me how you knew about my old Crystal Blue. How did you find her?"

Jennifer explained, Joshua's smile growing ever wider with the extra knowledge that the fleet of three boats was still going strong.

"I had no idea – and so close too. I must go to Lamton and see 'em all again!" They hugged.

Jim joined them with a drink and food for his friend.

"Mm, that looks good. I'll leave you boys for a mo while I get myself a snack or two."

She left them and went to the lower deck where things were being served. Helen and Angela were helping the regular crew. Helen waved as she spotted her daughter's friend entering.

"Ah Jenny, there you are – can I have a word darling?"

"Yes of course. Is everything OK?"

"Oh yes, it's going well isn't it! I wondered if we have anyone to run the snack bar in the Craft Centre when we open. I know I'm supplying everything, but I can't man it and the tea rooms at the same time."

"I think we'd decided to take it in turns to do an hour here and there when we could. Why?"

Helen ushered an attractive lady towards Jennifer. "Let me introduce Ruby. She's a very competent cook with up to date hygiene certificates and looking for a job. She came to me to do her work experience from school years ago, so well, I kind of got her started in her profession." Helen smiled.

The two young women shook hands. "Hello Jenny. I've heard a lot about you."

"Pleased to meet you Ruby – hang on - are you by any chance engaged to a chap called Colin?"

Ruby smiled cheekily. "Wow, fame at last!" Then more seriously. "Is that a problem?"

"Oh gosh no, he's lovely!"

They chatted for a short while, then Jennifer remembered why she'd come down.

"Look, I'm going to get some of this delicious looking food down to my tummy, but after the trip, come to the Centre. Have a look round and meet the rest of the gang. OK?" She gave an encouraging smile.

Ruby nodded and grinned. "Thank you. I look forward to that."

Jennifer filled a plate with various items from the tables, chatting to Angela as she did so. "Thank you so much for your help. It's very much appreciated."

"Wouldn't have missed it for the world love – our Josh is worth every second."

"Oh absolutely. I'll see you later and thanks again."

Returning to the upper deck, she found her parents who were sitting with TJ and the three dogs. Each canine was behaving well. Rigger and Soaki were lying down and Banjo was sitting, his tail wagging rhythmically as he took in this wonderful new experience. Yes, he'd been on the Kingfisher 'floaty thing', but this one made a chugging noise and moved on the road made of water! He was beside himself with wonder. The humans of the group tucked into the plates of food.

"Mm, these are yummy!"

"Is someone going to organise a 'happy birthday' sing-a-long with everyone on board?"

"Absolutely, and I think we need to charge everyone's glasses for a mass toast too. Mum, Dad – are you OK with the hounds if TJ and I go and get Cassie and Paul to help get drinks?"

"Of course darling. No problem." She thanked them and the couple went to find their friends.

Before long, the refills had been sorted. The captain slowed the engines to a gentle purr and stopped the music.

He spoke into the microphone. "Ladies and gentlemen – boys and girls – and not forgetting our trio of four legged friends." Everyone laughed.

"Can I please have your attention for a minute? Now we all know that we are joined together for this trip to celebrate the 90th birthday of our dear friend Joshua." Everyone cheered.

"But were you aware, dear guests, that without the aforementioned fine gentleman, you would not be riding upon this magnificent vessel? The reason being that many years ago, 'Crystal Blue' and her two sisters in our fleet, 'Sapphire and Aqua' were all built by our prestigious host! A round of applause, please everyone, for Mr Joshua Sanders!"

Cheers and clapping filled the air with many standing in appreciation. Jennifer took the microphone with Cassie, Paul and TJ around her.

"Some of you have known Josh for a long time. Others like myself, have only had that privilege more recently. But all of our lives have been made much richer by being able to include him as one of our precious friends. Please everyone, join in now in your very best voices and sing a special birthday song for our extra special birthday boy, our Joshua!"

Everyone on board, including the crew, sang loudly, finishing with 'For he's a jolly good fellow' and an enormous cheer. Joshua was overwhelmed and amidst his beaming smile, tears glistened down his cheeks.

Eventually, when calm descended again, the captain spoke again.

"Thank you everyone. Now please, if you would all raise your glasses – I give you our host – Joshua!" Everyone repeated the toast.

"And Joshua sir, it would be a real treat for the crew if you would take the helm of your creation and steer Crystal for a while."

Joshua beamed and stood up in a fashion much sprightlier than would be expected of a man many years his junior. Wearing the captain's cap, Josh spent a good ten minutes in charge of the river boat he loved so much. He was a very happy man.

The party continued with much laughter and joy from everyone. Jennifer, with a relieved smile on her lips, sat and relaxed for a while. Several minutes passed. A familiar gentle small hand nestled in hers.

"Hello, my friend Jenny." It was Ami.

"Hello sweetheart – are you enjoying the party?"

"Yes it's lovely. I like boats. My daddy wants to tell you something – come with me!" She smiled. "Don't worry – it's a nice something."

Jennifer was curious. Shrugging her shoulders, she followed her young guide. Nancy watched her daughter protectively as the little girl went about her mission. Ami held Jennifer's fingers tightly as she led her nearly the full length of the boat.

As they approached her father, the determined expression on her face broke into a beaming smile. "I found her, Daddy!" She presented Jennifer as if she were a trophy.

"Well done poppet – you're very clever to see her amongst all these people."

He gave his daughter a big hug and kissed her nose which made the little girl giggle.

"Hello Jenny; take a seat. I have some news for you. Great party, by the way!"

Jennifer settled down and Ami promptly clambered onto her lap.

"It's the pigs."

"Oh, are they all OK? You got rid of them… they are all well, aren't they?"

Mel put a finger to his lips to quieten her. "Calm down Jen, they're fine – more than fine, they're blooming. We have four happy pregnant pigs!"

"Oh golly gosh – my girls are going to be mums! How long before the babies arrive?"

Ami tapped Jennifer's hand. "We call them piglets!"

"Oh yes, I forgot. So when should they arrive… I have no idea how long a pig's pregnancy is."

"It's not necessarily exact – but a rough guide is… do you want to tell Jenny, Ami?"

In a loud clear voice she made her announcement. "Three months – three weeks and three days!"

"Really? Well that's easy to remember. Oh heck, we're going on holiday – when are they due?"

"Ooh, not for another eleven weeks or so yet. Enjoy your holiday. You'll be back in plenty of time to see them arrive."

"Do you know, this has been a wonderful day all through... and we still have the evening to come yet."

Nancy had joined them with a selection of cakes. "Are you pleased, Jenny? Your young girls all grown up, eh?"

Brushing crumbs from her mouth, Jennifer nodded. "Absolutely. Coo, I feel like I'm going to be a grandmother!" They all laughed.

It was about ninety minutes into the journey when the constant, almost gentle drone of Crystal Blue's engine changed to a hearty growl. The boat juddered.

Ami looked concerned. "Don't worry love, we're just slowing down for some reason." Mel comforted the little girl.

"Gosh yes – it's time to go back. That hour and a half went quickly!"

Ami, now calmed, started to giggle. "Look Daddy, we're going backwards!"

Another judder and then the engine groaned again. "Daddy look – we've turned around!"

The familiar drone reinstated – they were on their way home. The merriment continued. Along with the background music there was conversation, lots of laughter and singing. People took photographs and periodically refilled their plates and glasses.

The light started to fade as the evening settled and hundreds of multicoloured light bulbs were switched on. They were strewn the length and breadth of the boat and gave a fairyland type ambience to the party.

From a distance, Jennifer caught Joshua's attention. She did a 'thumbs up' sign and mouthed "OK?" He in turn did a 'double thumbs up' and. nodding, smiled enthusiastically.

Eventually the engines cut out as they moored alongside the landing stage by the Centre. Everyone thanked the crew as they disembarked. Before they returned Crystal to Lamton, Joshua insisted that all the staff must come and see his edible version of their vessel.

Sometime later, Josh was reminded that he had presents to unwrap. "Ee – I'd right forgotten them – it's been such a busy day. I've never known one like it – quite the best I've 'ad in many a long year.

Wonderful!"

With a somewhat bemused expression, he sat surrounded by a sea of brightly coloured parcels of many shapes and sizes. There was also a large pile of cards.

"I don't know where to start – I had no idea I had so many friends!" He chuckled.

"How about taking your cards home and reading through them over a cuppa? I would suggest you look at this one though."

It was the huge card from Helen's Tea Rooms. He was amazed at the contents.

"We think practically everyone in the village has signed it."

He was overwhelmed. His gifts included bottles of his favourite tipple, tins of scrumptious biscuits and chocolates, hand-knitted hats and scarves, books and picture frames, some slippers and a board game plus many more goodies. His eyes opened wide as he undid the tissue paper surrounding Jon and Sally's gift.

"Oh my word – looky 'ere Rigger old boy – it's just like you! How did you know my door knocker had broken? I planned on gettin' a new 'un when I moved back. Thank you… it's just the ticket!"

Jennifer and TJ gave him the photo album. "I've got more still to develop, so you can add them, and when you've done with the cake, you can have a blown up shot of the actual boat with everyone on board to put on TJ's river picture."

"Aye – that'll be just right to go in my bedroom. I don't know how to thank you all. This has been my best birthday ever!" They all hugged.

Reluctantly, he agreed to cut the first slice of his boat cake.

"Don't fret darling; it was made to be eaten – and you'll have a shot of it for your album."

With Josh given the first piece, Cassie, Laura, Sally and Jennifer cut the rest and gave slices to all the guests who were dotted around the building admiring the transformation.

The party was drawing to a close. Families with young children left first, many with their offspring sleepy in their arms. As the guests departed, they bade each other goodnight and with smiles on their faces, all agreed it had been a brilliant party. Hugs and kisses abounded. Many lived within walking distance, others shared taxis and a few non-drinkers gave lifts.

Before long, just a dozen or so remained. As they tidied up, Helen, Dan, Ruby and Colin made teas and coffees for everyone before they locked up and ventured back to their homes. Laura and Sally helped Joshua and Jim to pack all the gifts and cards into boxes. As they all congregated in the snack bar area they chatted happily, recalling various parts of the day.

"Well, we've all enjoyed your birthday! How do you think it turned out Josh? Did you have a good time?"

He sipped from his mug. "It wasn't just good... it were bloody marvellous. Thank you all so much. It's been the best ninetieth birthday I've ever had!"

They all cheered and clapped their approval of the elderly gentleman.

En route they helped Angela to return things she had used from the pub. For all her hard work and contribution to the day, it seemed only polite to stay in her bar for another celebratory drink before continuing on their journeys. Jon insisted on buying the round and complimented everyone on their hard work. He was given a cheer that was more than just a tad alcohol influenced.

Next step was Jim's cottage to deposit the pressies and see the two somewhat tipsy inhabitants safely in.

As the door shut, Jon promptly rattled the letter box. Jim answered with a woozy expression. Jon handed him a dog lead. "Sorry, I forgot I was holding Rigger!"

Eventually Willow Bank House was in sight.

Kicking off their shoes, they collapsed in the comfy chairs. Jennifer expelled an exhausted "Ooh! I can't believe it's still Friday – I feel as though I've been awake for a week. Oh crikey, Friday! That means it's market in the morning."

Everybody groaned.

"Well, if that's on the menu for tomorrow – I'm off to bed. G'night folks; see you all post sleep," yawned Jon.

"Mm, me too my darlings," said Sally.

Sally kissed her daughter and TJ, stroked the dogs and followed Jon up the stairs. Soon after, TJ and Soaki made their way along the garden path. "See you in the morning, darling. Night night Jenny... love you."

He blew yet another kiss as they went through the gate. She pretended to catch it, and smiling, blew a kiss back. She locked the door, settled Banjo and made her way to bed.

As always, she shared her thoughts and reminiscences of the day with Grannifer. "I hope you enjoyed the party with us my darling. Night night precious lady. Love you." She smiled and kissed the air. Then, oh so quickly, she fell asleep.

***

It was no wonder to anyone that they all had a good night's sleep.

What did amaze them was being up, ready and actually walking around the market by ten o'clock. Whichever stall they were at, it was almost guaranteed that within earshot, somebody would be talking about the previous day's big event. Anecdotes were abundant as people relived Joshua's celebration.

Miraford market was always fun, but today had an extra buzz as the friendly little community seemed especially united on the main topic of conversation.

One of Angela's Miraford Arms 'share-um-platters' seemed an appealing choice for brunch. The tea and toast when they got up was a good stopgap, but more sustenance was now required.

"How long can you and Dad stay before you have to go back to London?"

"Well, you're off to Wales soon, so we'll go when you go on your hols."

"Why don't you stay on for a bit? You both know loads of people here – treat this as a holiday yourselves."

Sally looked thoughtful. "Mm, I'll see what your dad thinks."

Jon and TJ returned from the bar and set drinks on the table. "Food's ordered. Be about fifteen minutes."

The men sat down and Sally moved her chair nearer to her husband. With her fingertips she drew softly on the back of his hand. Jennifer watched her mother. Knowing her parents well, she suppressed a smile, covering her mouth with her hand. To get TJ's attention she tapped her toe against his foot then nodded in Jon and Sally's direction.

With a subdued, gentle and slightly questioning tone to her voice, Sally spoke. "Dar-ling?"

He looked at her. "I know that sound – what are you after?"

Mother and daughter both laughed. The holiday was explained. "Funny you should say that 'cos while we were at the bar – TJ offered the same for 'Kingfisher', so looks like you've got a choice... unless you don't want to stay and you're drawn back to the capital."

With their meal finished, TJ got another round of drinks. Returning to the table he told Jon that he'd put their names up for the dartboard. "Fancy joining us, ladies?"

"Er... no, you two enjoy yourselves. We'll sit here and suffer the cosy log fire and a bit of girly chat. But thanks for the offer."

Jennifer treasured the precious moments spent with Sally and Jon. Yes, they were her parents, but they were good friends too. She'd been brought up in a loving and extremely caring family, but was not cosseted, nor wrapped in cotton wool. As parents, they'd obviously protected and nurtured their daughter through her formative years, yet they were canny enough to let her venture into the big wide world without restriction, secure in the knowledge that they trusted her to make sound decisions. If she stumbled on her journey, they were there to help if needed without any acrimonies - "See; we told you it was going to go wrong!"

The love was strong in each of them. They were good companions who enjoyed having fun. It gave Jon and Sally comfort and pleasure that TJ obviously loved their girl very deeply – and he gelled with them all as if part of the family.

However long the time spent in the friendly Miraford Arms, this typical 'country style' pub always guaranteed a pleasant experience. The Cade family and TJ would happily have stayed longer, but made the decision to go home around four o'clock. They said their goodbyes and left.

The contrast was overwhelming. A light drizzle made the road and buildings shiny with the occasional lights reflecting in the wet. A chill was emphasised in a light breeze which had developed.

"Brrr – shall we go back in and sit by that fire again?"

"Oh come on you lightweight – it's bracing!"

"Yeah, if you say so!"

"What are you going to be like when the winter sets in? This is just a bit of autumnal weather."

"I'll hibernate!"

Sally and Jon laughed at the banter between the younger couple. Arriving back at 'Willow Bank House', they set the shopping down and warmed up with a hot drink.

"So, what's got you delving into Grannifer's book Jen?"

"I'm checking her soup recipes. I think it's called for, considering the change in the weather. We were lucky it wasn't like this yesterday."

"You're right there… crikey, was it only yesterday? Feels like longer."

They spent the evening playing their favourite board game. Sally was the ultimate winner having bought anything and everything she could lay her hands on.

"You're just lucky you didn't have to pay maintenance on that lot, Mum, or you would be broke!"

***

Sunday they decided would be a lazy stay-at-home day. And apart from taking Soaki and Banjo for their walks, that was what they did.

"Do you know darling, since we arrived I haven't investigated your

284

garden. I'm going to have a good old nose around."

Jennifer escorted her Mum, paying particular attention to her summer house.

"We've been decorating it when we have had a moment here and there. Look, it's even got a phone socket."

Sally was impressed with the chalet style building.

"I'll show you Pickle's contribution when we go indoors – I've got photos. I'm amazed that the grass seed is growing. I'll get a lawnmower sometime."

"Looks like you need to redo your hanging baskets too – shall we go back to the farm tomorrow and get some plants?"

"If you like – but I was going to wait 'til after the holiday, then I can tend them."

"Ah, but we'll be here… so…"

"Of course. OK then, Honey Bee Farm it is!"

They went indoors. Sally giggled at Pickle's trotter print art. "Well, it's original!"

They enjoyed a traditional Sunday roast with apple crumble and custard for pudding. In his usual flamboyant manner, Jon rubbed his stomach exaggeratedly. "Cor that was yummy… what's for tea?"

"Dad!" They all laughed.

***

They woke on Monday morning to a watery sun, yet still quite pleasant day. The biting wind of Saturday was gone so the chill factor was absent. Arriving at the farm, Jennifer looked with interest at the promotional signs.

As they wandered around the pleasant establishment, Jennifer's eyes grew even wider. TJ spoke knowingly to Jon. "I'm going to get a trolley. Your daughter hasn't been shopping for a few days and I think she's going to make up for it today." Jon smiled at TJ's intuition.

"Oh well done darling. I can't carry any more." She placed trays onto the trolley. "Look, winter flowering pansies and violas. I've picked up these beautiful cyclamens and Mum's got two lots of trailing ivies – they've got the prettiest variegated leaves and… what?" She'd noticed TJ's grin.

"Nothing babe; you carry on!"

Jennifer shrugged and headed off towards the shrubs. "I'd like some evergreen bushes in the garden – ooh look!"

Jennifer's exuberance was infectious and Sally, Jon and TJ were soon pointing out various pots. "These hollies are nice and the conifers' softness is a good contrast to the holly leaves."

"Oh yes, you're right – can you pick out three of each please?"

They continued looking. "Here Jenny – those big plants you just found – have you seen these?"

TJ had found small versions. "Oh, little babies – aren't they sweet?"

"Yes, but they're not babies, they're miniatures – what do you reckon for your baskets?"

She beamed. "Cor yes – I like that idea. Aren't you clever?"

He tried momentarily to take the credit but then pointed out some sample baskets made up as he'd suggested.

"Well, at least you noticed them for me!" She hugged him and kissed his cheek.

"Is that the lot, pet? Your Mum and I are going into the shop to have a look in there."

"Yep – we're right behind you Dad."

Apart from the usual goodies which were so familiar, a new section had been erected.

"Of course – time to plant bulbs. I want lots so I know when it's spring!"

Sally rolled her eyes. "Come on then, oh daughter of mine – let's go choose some spring indicators."

The two women linked arms and strode away together.

As they drove home, Jon quipped that "At least I can see through the car windows this time."

"Mm, yes – well we haven't got all those trees like in the summer."

Even so, when they unloaded, it was very apparent that there was a considerable amount of planting to be done.

"We'll get them all in over the next couple of days."

"Er, I think you've misjudged that babe – we go to Wales on Wednesday."

"Oh crikey, you're right – I thought we had more time."

Sally cuddled her daughter. "Don't worry darling. Dad and I can finish off anything we don't get done before you leave."

There were still a few hours of daylight left before the stillness of the autumnal evening would set in. Sally and TJ made a late lunch of sandwiches and soup, whilst Jennifer and Jon delved into the bulbs, making a plan as to where they would look best in the garden.

"I definitely want early spring flowers around the fruit trees; it always looks nice – especially if the tree has blossom at the same time."

After they'd eaten, they went outside armed with the bulbs and digging tools. A trowel and small fork were ideal for the smaller bulbs – snowdrops, crocuses and suchlike, but they also used another clever device. This, when squeezed, held soil aloft leaving a hole to put the bulb in to, then, with one's grip eased, it released the soil and voilà! - bulb planted. This was perfect for things that needed to be dug in deeper, like the daffodils and tulips.

"If we scatter them then plant 'em where they land, they'll look more natural than putting them in rows." Jennifer gave a satisfied smile as she felt this made her sound as though she knew what she was talking about.

"Are you going to mark where you've put them pet?" said Jon

"Er no, I don't think I will Dad. Then it will be a nice surprise when they pop up."

It was a fulfilling but back aching job. "Ooh, daughter of mine, I love you dearly... but did you have to buy quite so many?" Sally stretched and rubbed her spine.

After cleaning his hands, Jon assisted, massaging his wife where she couldn't reach. He kissed her neck. "There my darling – is that better?"

She smiled responsively. "Yes love. Much better, thank you."

Jennifer was always happy with her parents' open displays of their love for each other.

"Come on then my darling; that's enough for today – time for a cuppa... Oi! Banjo no! We've only just planted them. Don't dig them up again!" She ushered her pet indoors.

TJ laughed. "Ah poor little fella; he probably thinks he's helping."

***

During the evening mother and daughter disappeared upstairs to sort out things for Jennifer to take on holiday. The men and dogs settled in the living room with the television on.

When they had done as much as possible, they came back downstairs chattering as they descended. "I'll find out what they want if you get the mugs ready."

Jennifer entered the living room. "We're making a cuppa – what do you fan...cy?" Her words trailed away and she called to Sally. "Mum – come here a moment."

The two women stood in the doorway staring with amusement at the contents of the room. Jon was laid out on the settee, his tongue lolling from the corner of his mouth and Banjo was sprawled on his lap, paws upright. TJ and Soaki were across the room cuddled together, all snoring in various rhythms and the TV had a documentary on about insomnia and solutions for sleep problems.

"How about we leave the hot drinks for a while and have a glass of wine?"

Sally smiled and nodded in agreement. They went giggling to the kitchen.

It was a good hour later. The kitchen door opened and Jon walked in. "Oh hello; you're down already. That didn't take you long!"

He looked a little mystified when his family began laughing. Shrugging his shoulders he switched on the kettle. "Would you like a cuppa? TJ and I are having coffee."

Back in the living room with their drinks, the men vehemently denied that they had fallen asleep, and if they had cat-napped for a minute or two... they definitely didn't snore!

***

That night, before climbing into her bed, Jennifer stood at her window. The moonlight, though subtle, cast a soft glow across the garden. Outlines were muted and the shadowy shapes held a hint of eeriness about them, but Jennifer liked the variation from her daylight property. She pondered how it might look in the spring and looked forward to more planting tomorrow. She said goodnight as always to her precious Grannifer, then snuggled beneath the bedclothes.

***

Tuesday morning was bright, but with a distinctive nip in the air. Opening the back door, Jennifer gave a shudder as the chill enveloped her. Banjo didn't seem to mind the cold and bounded around the garden with his usual exuberance. Having donned her jacket, his mistress took food out for the birds.

Soon, with a mug of coffee warming her hands, she wandered around surmising the best places for the holly and conifer bushes. Every so often she would throw toys for the playful little dog, laughing at the way he pounced on them before bringing them back for a re-throw.

Placing her half-drunk mug on the table, Jennifer picked up plant pots and positioned them near the perimeter wall. She relocated them a few times until she was happy. "Yep – I think they'll be good like that. What do you think Banjo?"

She ruffled his ears and he wagged his tail enthusiastically. "Come on little man – this coffee needs reheating. Let's go in. I might even find you a biscuit." They ran together back to the kitchen.

"Morning darling." It was Sally. "What is he after?"

Banjo was sitting staring intently at his biscuit tin, his tail swishing across the floor in happy expectation.

"Shake hands."

He placed a paw on Jennifer's hand. "Good boy." She gave him a treat which he took to his bed before munching.

288

Bowls of steaming porridge, each with their preferred toppings, was a Cade family favourite, and with this warming their tummies, they trundled into the great outdoors to sort the rest of the planting. Sally and Jennifer started the hanging baskets, whilst Jon began digging holes for the bushes. He looked up gratefully at the sound of the gate.

"Oh well timed lad – you've arrived just right to help me put these in."

TJ rolled his eyes. "Cor – and there I was thinking you'd have it done by now!" He chuckled.

He kissed Sally and Jennifer then went to help Jon. Soaki and Banjo played together and before they knew it, all of the day's previous purchases were sitting happily in their new earthy beds, ready and waiting to be nurtured and tended by the young woman who, not so very long ago, dreamt of maybe one day having a garden of her own.

Back in the house, Jon rubbed his hands together. "Er – Jenny love – does the pub have a dress code at all?"

"No Dad… why?"

He smiled. "Well, with you lot disappearing for the next fortnight…"

"Ten days actually."

"OK, ten days. Well I wondered if you fancy a bevvy or two before you go… my treat."

"Yeah sure… when?"

"Well… now. If we don't need to 'posh up', we can go just as we are."

"I'm game, but let's walk, then you can have a drink or two."

They did all wash their hands, but within minutes were walking up the lane and heading towards the village centre. As they neared the Miraford Arms, they recognised some figures ahead. TJ whistled. Jim and Joshua turned around.

The friends all greeted each other and went into the pub together. It wasn't long before they commandeered the dart board and a game was quickly under way. The chat and laughter was as always loud and constant.

After a couple of rounds the group increased from six to ten when Cassie and Paul, Helen and Don joined them. It was almost like another party. The ladies sat by the fire discussing events since they were last together.

"Have you packed yet, Cassie? I got most of mine done last night."

"Are you kidding? I've had mine sorted for a week! I'm so excited, I feel like a kid again. It's been ages since I've been on a proper holiday." The girls giggled like children.

Helen and Sally looked at each other and shook their heads. "Oh dear… do you think Wales knows what is going to hit it?"

It was no surprise to anyone that the intended 'quick couple of drinks' had turned into a much longer time spent in the friendly village pub, but realising they'd been there for almost three and a half hours was more than they had expected. There were still things to do at home, so they finished their drinks and said their goodbyes to everyone.

There were calls of 'have a good holiday' and 'send us a postcard' as they left. Banjo and Soaki had picked up on the excitement around them and were more skittish than usual.

Back at 'Willow Bank', Jennifer flitted from room to room checking she hadn't forgotten anything. TJ grabbed hold of her and his strong arms held her firmly but gently. Kissing her cheek he whispered in her ear. "Darling, calm down, we're only going for a week and a half and… if we do forget something – guess what – they actually have shops in Wales."

She smiled. "I know, I'm just all of a flutter because I'm excited."

They kissed again. "But I do need to pack Banjo's things."

TJ shook his head resignedly. "OK, I'll give you that one."

He chuckled as she skipped to the kitchen. Taking a large rucksack from the hook on the broom cupboard door, she proceeded to fill it with towels, food, bowls, toys, a blanket and anything else she thought her beloved pet would require. Watching from the hall doorway TJ, with his arms folded, nodded wisely.

"Mm – now that's what I call a doggie bag!"

***

Despite TJ's calming words earlier that evening, Sally knew that now he had gone back to his boat, her daughter's fertile mind would start worrying again. "So m'darling, before we go to beddy byes, do you want to run through a quick check-list?"

Jennifer nodded eagerly. "Oh yes please, Mum!"

Sally suggested things all the time knowing that they had been packed. As they chatted, Sally was calmly making a milky bedtime drink. She placed the mug in her daughter's hand.

"So everything is sorted. Drink that and you can go and snuggle down and dream of the next ten days with nothing to do but enjoy yourself."

They smiled at each other. "Thanks, Mum."

She did indeed have a good night's sleep and woke the following morning refreshed and bubbling with anticipation. There was no doubt in her mind that this would be a wonderful holiday. Why wouldn't it be?

She would be with three of her favourite people plus two amazing canines. They were about to experience a new country which, ironically, none of them had been to before.

Yes – all of this and more, indicated a fun, new and interesting time for them all. But something was telling her that a big change was imminent – a defining change in her life. It felt exciting.

Sally was in the kitchen. "Morning darling. Sleep well?"

"Yes thanks, you?

"Oh yes, like a log!"

They chatted over coffee. "I'll do some breakfast when Dad wakes up."

"Oh he's already up and gone to help TJ with his bags and things."

"Oh, OK. I'll see if they're in sight, then we can get started."

Returning from the garden with a broad smile, Jennifer began organising the meal. "They're nearly here!"

Sally helped lay the table. "When are you planning to get going?"

"Cassie reckons around mid-day, so we've got a good couple of hours."

The men arrived carrying the luggage between them. TJ had on the hat which Jennifer had bought him.

"Ooh, you look as if you're off on your hols or something!"

He smiled cheekily. "How perceptive of you missie – care to join me?"

"Ooh sir – how kind of you. Don't mind if I do!" They all laughed at their play acting.

At half eleven the phone rang. It was Cassie.

"Er Jen, problem mate – the car's broken down."

"Oh, you're joking!"

"'Fraid so. I'm at the top of your lane. Get the kettle on darling!"

Jennifer returned to the kitchen shaking her head. "Honestly, that girl. I thought she was serious. Stick the kettle on – Cassie and Paul are nearly here."

"Correction babe... they've just arrived!" Jennifer squealed and ran outside.

The two girls, with arms linked, sashayed into the house singing as they went. "We're going on holiday – hip hip hip hooray!" They laughed and danced along the hallway.

"How old are you two? Do you want coffees, or perhaps squash in a lidded beaker?"

Suitably restrained, the two friends stood breathless, but still giggling. "Ooh that was fun! Come on mate, let's empty these mugs and get on the road."

Paul and TJ watched their ladies, bemused. "Do you think they'll be like this all the time? I feel exhausted just watching them."

"Yeah, I know. Shall we book a holiday now to recover from this one?" They shrugged and joined the girls.

Drinks finished, they loaded the car. Hugs and kisses abounded as they said goodbye to Sally and Jon.

"Are you sure you've got the keys, Mum?"

"Yes darling… I don't think I've lost them since you asked me five minutes ago."

Jennifer looked sheepish. Cassie revved the engine. "All aboard that's getting aboard!"

They settled the dogs, then the four friends sat in the car and clicked their seat belts. "Are we ready?"

"Ye –e – ess!"

Cassie released the handbrake. As they moved off, Jennifer called to her waving parents.

"Hope you enjoy yourselves as much as we will – we'll have a lot to tell you when we get back! Love you! byeee!"

About The Author

Patricia Joyce Hughes was born on 25th September, 1952 at Bearsted Maternity Hospital, Hampton Court, the only daughter of Joyce and George Hughes. She spent her childhood years in Shepperton and her mother still lives in the house Trish grew up in.

Trish attended Thamesmead School in Shepperton, a place where she developed her love of the written word and for English poetry and her parents were always enormously proud of all she achieved; Trish was always, 'the apple of their eye'.

Like many youngsters of the time, Trish left school at 15 and went straight into work. First as a shop girl in a hardware store, then in a fabric shop, then as a pump attendant at a nearby garage.

Trish was married at 18 and had her first child, Simon. Things didn't work out as planned, they divorced and Trish eventually remarried and went on to have three more children: Tristan, Heidi and another daughter, Dory, tragically stillborn.

Her life took on a complete change of direction in 1996, when she moved to West Dorset with her husband and Heidi. She and Heidi opened up a gorgeous little gift shop called Zoot Allures in the historic market town of Bridport, which they enjoyed running enormously.

Sadly, her second marriage broke down in 2001 and shortly afterwards, she lost her sight to diabetes. This devastating calamity threw her into complete disarray for a while and she immersed herself into her dark new world with positivity and determination not to let her circumstance beat her. It was at this most challenging point in her life that Trish found tremendous solace in one of her greatest passions: writing.

With no knowledge of braille, or ability to work a computer, Trish had to find a way around the problem and she developed an ingenious method for getting the words down on paper, in spite of the fact that she couldn't actually see a thing. She placed rubber bands over a notepad on a clipboard and used them as line markers, then armed with a simple pen, she sat and wrote to her heart's content.

Trish wrote every single one of the 110,000 words that went to make up Grannifer's Legacy using this method and she completed her gargantuan task in February 2017.

In January 2017, she was diagnosed with terminal breast cancer.

About SWDTN

The South West Dorset Talking Newspaper for the visually impaired is a charity that provides a weekly memory stick of local news, and a magazine for the visually impaired of South West Dorset. We have over 130 listeners who find that they can listen to local news in their own home, and at their own pace. The paper and magazine are all edited, recorded and distributed by our team of over 80 unpaid, dedicated, volunteers, a few of whom have been involved from the very start of the newspaper. We give each listener their own player, and help them to use it if neccessary. This year, 2017, is our 30th anniversary year.

We have many messages and letters from our listeners, who tell us that it helps them to feel part of the daily local life of their community and stops them from feeling isolated, a common feeling amongst visually impaired people. The talking newspaper started from very humble beginnings, indeed in somebody's lounge, and now we are in our second studio based in Weymouth. The volunteers work on a rota basis, and our chair and committee work hard to ensure that this runs smoothly, as we produce a paper every week, except for Christmas. This is quite a large, ongoing task which can only be acheived by the kindness of both our supporters and volunteers.

We rely solely on donations and fundraising and that is why this kind gesture means so much to us. We are very appreciative that somebody who has encountered the difficulties in life that Trish has had to deal with, has had the thoughtfulness to think of our Charity, and the effect that receiving the weekly newspaper has on our listeners. The mayor of Weymouth came to visit recently and referred to the newspaper as 'a window to the world' for visually impaired people, to help them connect with both the outside world and their local community.

We would like to say a big thank you.

About Magic Oxygen

Magic Oxygen Limited is a small, green publishing house based in Lyme Regis, Dorset. It was founded in 2011 by Tracey and Simon West, who share passions for organic, seasonal, locally grown food which they enjoy turning into an adventurous array of vegan delights.

They're also advocates for simple green living, they encourage sustainable behaviours in local and global environments and they share a common love of the written word.

Magic Oxygen is also responsible for creating the greenest writing contest in the world, the only one to plant a tree for every single entry and to build classrooms in impoverished communities too.

This little literary company has published over 30 titles from some outstanding authors over the last few years, including Bridport Prize winning Chris Hill and the much loved children's writer, Sue Hampton who has also branched out into adult fiction.

They've got a pipeline full of new stuff waiting to burst into print, including a love story from Trish Vickers, Ulster based comedy memoir from Wendy Breckon and a children's pirate adventure from Sophia Mosley. There's also a deliciously colourful body of work coming from the Dorset based Italian poet, Monica Ciriani.

Tracey and Simon do their level best to match the strength of the big boys by producing high quality, planet-friendly products in an ever competitive market and thankfully, they are lucky enough to represent some great authors who work hard to promote their writing (an absolute pre-requisite for any ambitious writer).

See MagicOxygen.co.uk/shop for their full range of titles and remember, every single paperback can be ordered from local or national bookshops, and online too.

They actively encourage readers to consider placing orders with small, independent local retailers, which helps keep money in local communities. Magic Oxygen are also very happy to fulfil orders; they might even have a signed edition to hand!

Lightning Source UK Ltd.
Milton Keynes UK
UKOW05f1956170317
296938UK00017B/467/P